Revenge List

POWER

POWER

SINNERS AND SAINTS
BOOK TWO

KATHY LOCKHEART

Editor: Susan Staudinger
Proofreader: Jovana Shirley, Unforeseen Editing, www.unforeseenediting.com

Cover design:
Model cover design: © By Hang Le
Photographer: Michelle Lancaster
Discreet Cover: Wild Love Designs

ISBN:
ebook: 978-1-955017-56-5
Paperback Cover: 978-1-955017-58-9

Published by Rosewood Literary Press

BLURB

I wrote a revenge list about my boss and accidentally handed it to my new CEO. Then I accidentally slept with that billionaire CEO. You'd think things couldn't get any worse, but spoiler alert: they absolutely did.

Let me explain.

That revenge list was supposed to be private—the kind you write after three margaritas and burn in the morning. And that wild weekend with a gorgeous stranger? Definitely wasn't on my to-do list. (Though maybe it should've been, because... wow.)

Watching him stride onto our company stage as the new CEO Monday morning wasn't part of the plan either.

Now I'm trapped in the world's most dangerous forbidden workplace romance, where every heated glance reminds me of what those hands can do. And Jace (Mr. CEO) won't stop until he exposes the truth—unaware that his best friend is the one behind my list, and a man hiding secrets that could bring down an empire.

The question isn't whether this will blow up in our faces.

It's who will lose more when it does.

From International & Amazon Top 25 Bestselling Author Kathy Lockheart, POWER is a forbidden workplace romance featuring a dangerously obsessive, morally gray CEO.

- *Possessive, Protective Hero*
- *One-Night Stand*
- *"Touch Her and Die" Energy*
- *"Who Hurt You?" Vibes*
- *Banter & Spice*
- *Revenge*

Standalone. HEA.

Trigger Warnings: Please visit the author's website for the full list.

AUTHOR'S NOTE

POWER contains content that might be triggering for some readers. For a full list of triggers, please visit my website at Kathy-Lockheart (dot) com.

For my fellow collectors of problematic book boyfriends with deep pockets and deeper issues. May your CEOs be possessive, your workplace romances be wildly inappropriate, and your popcorn never run out.

1

SCARLETT

Do not snap your boss's fingers in half, Scarlett. It would be a seriously bad mark on your résumé and probably give you a rap sheet.

My hands curled into fists at my sides, nails biting into my flesh as I tried to focus on anything but his palm on my thigh. The Chicago skyline stretched beyond his office windows, the city humming with life, yet somehow, I'd never felt more trapped. One wrong move, and two careers would end today: his for harassment, mine for assault.

Make no mistake. He deserved for his to end, but after years of seventy-hour weeks, of missing holidays to handle crises, of turning the North American division's biggest failure into the greatest success, I had fought too long and too hard for him to ruin my career in one meeting.

Actually, let me clarify a couple of things.

First of all, he wasn't my boss. Not technically. He was an executive at this company. One, unfortunately, with immense influence over promotion decisions.

Which brought me to my second point. This wasn't a meeting; it was an interview. The coveted promotion I was up for—vice president of North American operations—was the most pivotal moment in my career, and this wasn't supposed to be how my big moment played out. After six interviews this week (the others had gone brilliantly, thank you very much), I was one step away from getting my first executive role. One step closer to my dream of running this company someday.

The promotion wasn't just another rung on the corporate ladder either. In this company, making it to the executive level was like getting inducted into an exclusive club. Once you were in, doors opened. Opportunities appeared. The kind of opportunities that came with salaries big enough to help someone start a new life. Someone like Mom.

I'd promised her, standing in that tiny apartment, watching her shaking hands, that I could cover her rent for at least a year. That she wouldn't have to worry about money while she rebuilt her life. That she could finally stop looking over her shoulder. I'd sworn it on everything I had because the alternative—her getting kicked out, *him* finding her again—was too unfathomable to even consider.

Right now, I was barely keeping that promise, one missed paycheck away from disaster. This promotion would change everything. Every interview, every late night at the office, every sacrifice had been building to this moment. But if you didn't make it through the evaluation process? The company didn't believe in second chances. If you failed to get the promotion, you'd become a carton of eggs with an expiration date.

But back to the point at hand. Namely, his hand on my goddamned thigh.

Deep breaths, Scarlett. You've handled worse. You've watched worse. You will not let this man reduce you to that frightened twelve-year-old who couldn't stop—

No. Focus. File that trauma away in the mental cabinet labeled Things My Therapist Will Need Extra Sessions For.

I glanced down at his thin fingers giving my thigh a squeeze.

Maybe this is a test, my brain scrambled to rationalize. *You know, like if you want to be an executive, show us that you can handle yourself in the unfathomable position of sexual harassment in the workplace.*

But his thin-lipped smile and wandering fingers suggested this was no HR-approved scenario.

I grabbed his hand, removing it from my leg with what I hoped was just enough force to make my point without landing me an assault charge. Shifting back in my chair, as far as physically possible without being obvious about it, I cleared my throat.

"I see big things in my future here too." I tugged at my knee-length skirt, which suddenly felt about as protective as tissue paper.

Grabby Hands compensated for my retreat by leaning forward, head cocked like a predator sizing up prey. If predators wore appalling cologne and had receding hairlines that fought losing battles with their foreheads, that was. "I've been watching your progress since the moment I got here."

Three months. He'd been here three months. Barely long enough to figure out where the good coffee machine was, and somehow, he thought that gave him the right to—

"You have a certain ..." His eyes had shifted, taking on an unsettling gleam that made my skin crawl. "Spark about you. Something special that sets you apart."

Annnnnd the hand is back. You know what else came with it? Visions of snapping his penis off. Bet he wouldn't do this to women if he was missing his dick.

This time, I clutched his fingers hard enough to hurt him and shoved them off me.

"I appreciate your recognition of my passion, but I believe my work speaks for itself."

I needed to escape this room. Now, without blowing up my career in the process.

He shifted forward, his elbows on his knees, his face wayyyy too close to mine for comfort. The scent of expensive cologne couldn't mask the stench of entitlement.

"A role like this would open the door to a fantastic career trajectory for you." His voice dripped with suggestion.

"I believe my skills and experience make me a very strong candidate for this position, and I'm eager to let my qualifications shine."

"And what do you feel sets you apart from all the other candidates?" His eyes raked over me in a way that made me want to shower for ten years.

"In addition to my experience," I said, enunciating each word like I was explaining things to a particularly dense child, "I've always been commended for being a team player and for making people feel appreciated. And respected."

His lips tightened at that last word.

"In fact," I continued, warming up to my new theme, "one thing I've always admired about this company in my years here"—*Years, you temporary little parasite. Not months, like you*—"is how it promotes people who foster a culture of mutual respect and professionalism. I believe I'd contribute to that positive work environment."

Translation: *I know exactly what you're doing, and I'm documenting every second of it in my head for HR.*

"This position works directly with me," he murmured like that was supposed to be a selling point rather than a warning label. "And I think we'd work very well together."

Over my dead body. Or yours, if you don't back off.

"Do you have any other questions about my—"

He grabbed my knee this time, cutting my thoughts off midstream. How dare he touch me like this? How dare he do this to people, just because he was in a position of power?

"Your track record is impressive," he purred, "but it'll take more than that to reach the next level here."

When his fingers stretched toward my inner thigh, I shot to my feet so fast that my chair threatened to topple over. My throat swelled painfully, eyes stinging with tears I refused to shed. Not here. Not in front of him. I swallowed hard, clearing my throat as memories of other moments when I'd felt this powerless threatened to surface.

"If you have any other questions about my qualifications," I said, ice crystallizing around each word, "you can ask HR."

Instantly, his facial expression changed from pervy to hard angles. Thin lips. Narrowed eyes that shot silent warnings. He sat back in his chair, legs spread wide in an arrogant *you can't touch me, how dare you even hint at alerting HR to me* stance.

Straightening my spine, I added, "Thank you for your time." *You waste of oxygen.*

I made it to the door in ten strides, but when my palm reached the cool silver handle, his voice thundered through the air.

"You leave, your résumé goes to the bottom of the pile."

I spun around, trying to keep my jaw from falling to the ground. He nodded to the chair where he'd been trying to molest me while my thoughts tumbled down the stairs of shock. Was he actually saying what I thought he was? Escalating this from unwanted sexual advances to a downright warning that if I didn't do ... whatever the hell he'd had in mind when I came in here, I'd lose any chance of this promotion that I'd earned?

Of course he wasn't saying it outright; anyone who wanted legal deniability wouldn't be that careless. Technically, all he was saying was that if I left, the interview was over. But his domineering gaze that ordered me back into the groping chair said something very different.

With clenched fists, I locked eyes with him. I considered threatening him that I'd take this to HR, but I didn't want to tip my hand, so I chose a different weapon.

"You ever touch me again," I said, "I'll break your fingers."

With that, I opened the door and stormed out.

Luckily, no one was immediately outside his office to see my expression or the tears I was blinking back, but near my desk was my work bestie, Dakota. She'd stayed late so she could see how my last interview went. The plan had been to go for martinis to celebrate.

One look at my face though, and her smile vanished. "Oh shit."

"Yeah. I think I might have just lost my job."

Dakota grabbed my hand. "Emergency drinks. Let's go."

Little did I know, going to that particular bar was about to catapult me directly into the path of someone who would change everything ...

2

SCARLETT

"I bet he has a microscopic dick," Dakota declared with the kind of venom usually reserved for people who kicked puppies.

"Bold of you to assume there's anything there at all," I muttered. "Maybe he's just a Ken doll down there. All plastic and disappointment."

I waved down the bartender, silently begging for another drink. The first hadn't done nearly enough to dull the edge of this nightmare.

"I'm going to destroy him," I decided.

"I'll help."

"I don't know how, but I will. I just need to ... process this, and I'll come up with something iron-clad."

"There's no way he hasn't done this before. He gives off subtle creep vibes."

"I thought this company had a strong ethical code." I rubbed my temple. Hard. "What if he's just a symptom of what's really going on behind the scenes with the executives? What if I've spent years building my career somewhere that I'd never want to work once I got a peek behind the curtain?"

Losing the promotion was terrible. My job? Even worse. But the thought that executives at this company might have been demanding sexual favors all along? That would mean I'd hitched my wagon to the wrong company from the get-go, and that—that was the kind of realization that made me want to time-travel back several years and slap some sense into my younger self.

"First of all"—Dakota leaned in, her voice dropping to that conspiratorial tone she used when dispensing prime gossip—"I've never once heard of sexual harassment from anyone." That was something at least. She was nothing if not the gossip collector. "And secondly, this guy isn't homegrown; he just joined this company three months ago. Probably has some seedy-ass past where they fired him, and he snuck under our radar like a perverted ninja."

The bar erupted into cheers over some sporting event, the sudden noise making me jump. Just like sudden noises often did. I took another sip of my drink, trying to ignore how my shoulders seemed determined to merge with my ears.

"What company did he come from?" I wondered.

"Sexual Harassers Incorporated, evidently." Dakota's deadpan delivery actually pulled a reluctant snort from me. "Their benefits package probably includes a legal defense fund."

"I can't believe I just lost my job." My throat clenched, a familiar pressure I hadn't felt since those years with *him*. When my father had wielded power like a weapon, making Mom and me shudder with a single footstep.

"You don't know that for sure," Dakota insisted, but her optimism bounced right off my wall of doom.

"I threatened to snap his fingers." I shot her a look. "Pretty sure my belongings will be in a box when I get back to work on Monday. Probably with a security escort waiting to make sure I don't go on a finger-breaking spree."

"He groped you," she countered, and, dammit, I appreciated the steel in her voice. "He'd be a special kind of shortsighted to tell people you threatened to snap his fingers because then they're obviously going to ask why you, their star operations director who's never had a single complaint or bad employee review, suddenly threatened to go all WWE on him."

Her logic should have penetrated my fog of depression, but my brain was too busy playing a greatest hits compilation of all the things I wished I'd said to that pervert. If I was going down, I wished I'd told him off. Big time. A spectacular, verbal fireworks show.

"Do you know how much I've sacrificed for this job?" The words tumbled out, fueled by premium vodka and premium rage. "Happily, mind you. My choice, every step of the way. I've worked seven days a week almost every week for years. Hell, I've worked so many hours, my social life has virtually gone extinct. The last time I had any balance to my life, people still thought Pluto was a planet and Netflix mailed DVDs."

"That's an exaggeration," she chided.

"Maybe. But I haven't gone on a date in so long, the rules of dating have probably completely changed." In fairness, I didn't want to date, but that wasn't the point. The point was, I wouldn't have given myself the time to date even if I wanted to. "And I haven't had sex in so long, I'm probably categorized as some kind of secondary virgin. At this point, I'm pretty sure my lady parts have filed for abandonment. To have it all go up in smoke because some handsy executive couldn't keep his paws to himself? That's some royal-grade bullshit right there."

Hello, anger, my old friend. Pull up a chair, grab a drink.

"Can I ask you something?" Dakota shifted in her seat.

"Since when do you preface a question with that?" I wondered.

"Why does your career mean so much to you?"

"Careers mean a lot to a lot of people."

"Right, but ..." She shrugged. "Even among workaholics, you've been extra about it. It just seems to be like ... *everything* to you. Why?"

"I enjoy it."

She probably saw right past my BS answer. Surely, deep down, she suspected part of the real reason, but to her credit, she must've sensed that now was sooooo not the time to ask me about my deep, dark needs because she nodded and got back to the conversation at hand.

"Maybe you should march back over there, give him a piece of your mind," Dakota suggested, that dangerous glint in her eye that usually preceded spectacularly bad decisions.

"It's eight o'clock on a Friday. Even if he's still there, the office will be dead, and getting sexually assaulted isn't on my bucket list."

"See, this is bull. The fact that you're even worried about how dangerous of a predator he might be? HR needs to know about this yesterday."

She was right. They did. But that would be *Monday Scarlett's* problem. *Tonight Scarlett* just needed to process this tsunami of emotions without drowning in them. I needed to formulate the most professional speech I could give HR, preferably one that didn't include the phrases *dickwad* or *perverted octopus hands.*

Tonight was about finding a way for my brain to stop feeling like a pressure cooker of rage. Rage that had gone from burning-eyes frustrated to *Game of Thrones* season finale in record time. Was this how all women felt in these situations? Or was this reserved for me: a woman who'd fought to build herself from the ashes of pain? A woman who'd sworn she'd never let a man control her again. The fact that it was taking everything I had not to cry? That just pissed me off more. I refused to let that piece of trash break me.

"We could go over there together," Dakota suggested. "Confront him, united front and all that."

"Pass." I took another fortifying sip. "If I saw him right now, I would kick him in the dick, and *aggravated assault against your boss's penis* doesn't look great on a résumé."

"We could call him. Really let him have it."

"Knowing my luck, he'd record it. And then I wouldn't just be out of a job; I'd be unemployable."

"We have to do something," Dakota insisted, drumming her fingers on the bar with increasing intensity.

"I will." I shifted on the barstool, trying to find a position where my spine didn't feel like it was made of glass. "Monday. But right now, I just need to vent until this rage stops feeling like it's going to choke me. I can't face HR if I'm still seeing red."

"We can do better than that," she declared. "It's not fair for you to sit here and feel like crap while that walking HR violation is probably somewhere high-fiving his reflection in the bathroom mirror."

She was right. He didn't deserve this anger.

"You should let a guy take you home tonight and bone his brains out." She waggled her eyebrows.

I gave her my best *are you serious right now* glare. "Yeah, nothing heals the wounds of sexual harassment like having random sex with strangers. Brilliant plan. Got any other gems of wisdom?"

"Sex always makes people feel better."

"Hard pass."

Dakota tapped her chin, and I could practically see the light bulb appear over her head. Never a good sign.

"Okay, if going off on Douchenozzle and picking up men are out, then let's do something about that rage."

"I'm not picking a bar fight, if that's what you're suggesting."

"Writing helps with anger, but we're going to make this one fun." She waved at the bartender, who was too busy flirting with some college kids to notice.

"*Fun* anger? What the heck does that even mean?"

"Okay, you know all those things that float through your mind for a hot second when you're upset with someone, but you would never actually do? Like when someone cuts you off in traffic, and you think, *God, I'd love to shove an ice pick through their skull*?"

"Remind me to never ever cut you off in traffic," I muttered into my glass.

"We'll make a list of imaginary ways we'd get revenge if we could. Pure fantasy, totally therapeutic."

"Get him fired," I offered.

She cocked her head. "That's boring. Think more fun like …" Her eyes lit up with unholy glee. "Undoing the seams of his pants so they split open in the middle of a board meeting. While he's presenting to the CEO."

I couldn't help the smirk that crept onto my face. That would be pretty satisfying, watching Mr. Grabby Hands try to maintain his dignity with his tighty-whities on display.

"Excuse me!" Dakota called to the bartender, finally catching his attention. "Can we get a few napkins?"

She produced a pen from her purse. By the way, Dakota's purse was like a doomsday prepper's bunker: prepared for everything from nuclear winter to impromptu revenge plotting, though, ironically, not a single scrap of paper today. With a small sigh, she unfolded one of the napkins.

"What are you doing?"

At the top she wrote in bold capitals: REVENGE LIST.

"Writing this down. It'll be fun."

"So you say."

She pinned me with a glare. "Come on. We can't just sit here and sulk. It's not good for you, and more importantly, it's boring."

Fair point. I was sulking harder than a teenager who just got their phone confiscated. Even worse, I had zero desire to pull myself out of it. I wanted to skydive into the sky of suckiness and let it plummet me and my bad mood all the way to earth until … splat.

"I bet he's not even giving this a second thought," I grumbled.

"He's probably smirking in his evil lair right now, twirling his metaphorical mustache and practicing his villainous laugh in front of a mirror."

"The complete and utter asshat," I agreed, mentally adding

him to my collection of *People Who Deserve Painful Paper Cuts Between Their Fingers for All Eternity*.

"He's not going to let this ruin his weekend," she pointed out, hitting me right in the pride.

I gripped my glass tighter, the condensation cool against my palm. The woman had an annoying habit of making sense tonight, making me realize I did not, in fact, want to wallow. I refused to let him ruin my entire weekend. He didn't deserve that kind of power.

"Fine," I said, draining my glass with the determination of someone about to make questionable life choices. "But if we're doing this, I'm going to need another drink. Something that makes terrible ideas sound intoxicating and comes with a side dish of poor judgment."

"That's the spirit!" Dakota coaxed. "It'll make you feel better. Trust me."

Dakota was the best work friend anyone could hope for, giving up her Friday night to listen to me grumble about some guy being the world's biggest dick. The least I could do was try to pull myself out of this mood. For her sake.

So, fine. A game.

What could possibly go wrong?

"Laxatives in his coffee," I offered. "Extra strength."

She wrote it down, adding, "Right before the board meeting with our mystery buyer."

Mystery buyer. Because, apparently, work wasn't stressful enough with handsy executives. Management decided to spice things up by a) selling the business (cue collective panic attacks and stress-eating the entire vending machine inventory), and b) keeping the new owner's identity locked down tighter than the Pentagon's new weapons technology. Even Dakota, with her black belt in corporate gossip, couldn't crack this one. When Dakota couldn't get intel, it meant someone had basically buried it in the Mariana Trench.

And now, I wondered if the sale would add an extra level of complication to this whole thing.

"Ooh, shove an ice pick into his balls," she proclaimed with disturbing enthusiasm.

My smile dropped. "That's ... surprisingly violent. Remind me to check your basement for missing persons before I accept any more dinner invitations."

"We'll never actually do it." She waved her hand dismissively before jotting it down. "And don't criticize my fantasy revenge ideas. This is a judgment-free zone of petty vengeance."

Okay ... fair enough. Mental note: file Dakota's fantasies under *Yikes* and maybe suggest therapy.

"Glue his desk drawers shut," I suggested. "With industrial-strength adhesive."

She smiled, adding it to the list.

"Replace his hand sanitizer with superglue," she suggested.

"What about signing him up for every embarrassing email newsletter in existence?"

"Erectile dysfunction support groups." Dakota nodded solemnly.

"Adult bed-wetting solutions."

"DIY hemorrhoid treatments."

"Farm animal breeding techniques," I countered.

Dakota almost spat out her drink. "That got weird fast."

"So did his hand on my leg, but here we are." I shrugged, surprising myself with a genuine laugh.

Then she wrote another one of hers, each suggestion getting progressively more creative and, at times, concerning.

Still, I added another, letting myself get caught up in the ridiculousness of it all.

"See?" she said, surveying our masterpiece. "This is so much better than sulking. And don't worry; nobody will ever see this."

Famous last words. Because "nobody" was about to walk through those doors and see our revenge list in all its glory. And that nobody? Was the worst person, out of eight billion people on planet Earth, to see this list ...

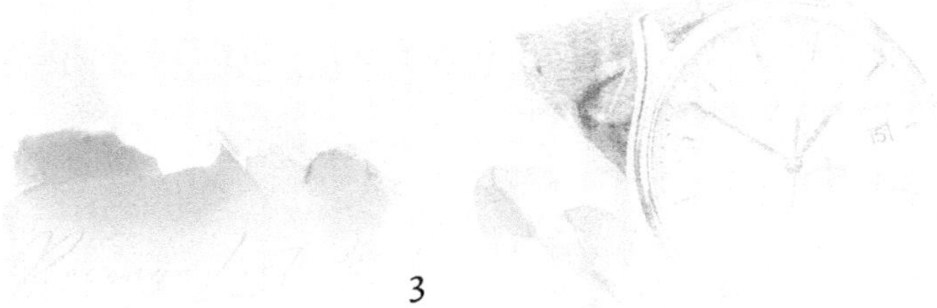

3

JACE

"You're telling me there's absolutely nothing we can do?" I kept my voice low, but the edge in it could've cut glass. The August heat pressed against my skin as I paced outside a Chicago bar, my running shoes hitting concrete that was still radiating the day's warmth. My workout hadn't done a damn thing to burn off this tension.

"Not until Monday," Finn said, maddeningly calm.

"Monday is the announcement."

"I'm aware."

I clenched my phone harder than iPhone standards would advise and glared into the night. Skyscrapers stood with a plethora of lights still on, all of them having teams of people working until whatever hour they demanded, while here I was, cut off at the knees. And it wasn't like it was the middle of the night. Hell, the sun had *just* set. It was eight o'clock on a Friday. No way I'd tread water for two entire days.

"Have them fire up my jet." I turned to the direction of the hotel I was staying at during this deal.

One might argue staying at a hotel saved me commute time, and it did. But the honest answer was that when I was in the final weekend of a merger, I always chose a hotel right next to the building for last-minute issues. Last-minute fire? I walk over.

"He's at his daughter's wedding."

"If he didn't want to be interrupted, he should have dotted his i's and crossed his t's before he left."

"Jace." Finn's voice took on that particular tone he used when he thought I was about to do something monumentally impatient. "It's *one* page he failed to sign. Page sixty-seven of ninety-nine."

"Might as well be all of them. The purchase isn't legal without all pages signed. And frankly, I'm surprised I have to tell you to get worried here. With all the complications going on, this is the last thing we can afford."

"The purchase will go through."

"You're presuming he did this by accident."

"Ziegler has every reason to sell. If he doesn't, he's so far underwater financially, he'll need gills to breathe."

I pinched the bridge of my nose. "Yeah, well, *hostile takeover* doesn't have the word *hostile* in it for decoration." A blast of cold air hit me as someone opened a bar door, carrying the scent of beer and the buzz of Friday night freedom. "This is the most important acquisition Lockwood Holdings has ever pursued."

Lockwood Holdings was a well-run and highly regarded private equity firm that purchased, renovated, and either sold or held the previously struggling businesses. With a fresh surge of cash and operational expertise, we turned the companies around and not only gained a hefty profit doing so, but also saved the jobs of people who would otherwise have been unemployed.

But our business wasn't without problems. Acquiring companies in massive debt or operational chaos came with, well, problems. There was no such thing as an easy acquisition, and we'd had a string of bad luck recently that left my board of directors worried. Losing this deal, or delaying it, could jeopardize the board's confidence in me. Freaking ironic. The board *I* established, for the sake of expanding equity partnerships to bring in more cash, might have the power to decide I wasn't fit for this job.

"My father's best friend started that company before Ziegler bought it," I added, the words tasting bitter. "My father would roll over in his grave if he knew it was about to go under."

"Jace." Finn's sigh crackled through the phone. "It's done. The deal is solid. This is a technicality. Monday, you'll have the metaphorical keys. Until then, find a way to ... take the edge off."

"I want to see the paperwork again."

"You've memorized it. Hell, you probably recite it in your sleep."

"Why can't he sign remotely?"

"Because he won't sign anything without his lawyer present, and his lawyer is out of state for the weekend, probably thanking God he's not dealing with you right now."

"So, we just sit here with our dicks on the table," I snapped.

"Why don't you leave town for the weekend? Fly to a sandy white beach and sip a cold beer, or go snorkeling, or—I don't know—build a snowman in Antarctica for all I care, just get off the grid before you do something unwise, like crash a wedding."

"You're making me sound like a loose cannon." A siren wailed in the distance, and I had to raise my voice. "Need I remind you whose name is on this company? I didn't build it by being reckless."

"*Reckless* isn't the word. You're wound tighter than a virgin at prom, and you need to stay away from temptation. Why don't you take a mini vacation?"

"I'm not leaving the city."

"If you stay here, you might do something impulsive. Like fire up the jet in the middle of the night and crash his daughter's wedding weekend."

"That's not reckless; it's business."

"You do that, then we *do* have a big problem. Ziegler's been acting in good faith, but if you interfere with his only daughter's dream wedding, his mood will sour, and he might invite one of the other private equity firms who he kicked out of the bidding process back in."

"I wouldn't crash the goddamned wedding. Showing up to his hotel or rented house with one sheet of paper that he failed to sign isn't—"

"Do you want this purchase to go through or not?" Finn interrupted, his tone curt. He was one of the few people who could get away with talking to me like this.

"How the hell will I get through the entire weekend without working?" I demanded.

"Just ... find a way to blow off steam until Monday."

"I don't blow off steam."

"I know. Go find some steam. Blow. See you Monday."

Two days. Bloody hell, how would I endure two entire days of a ticking clock?

I ended the call, glaring at the city skyline like it had personally offended me. Two days. Over forty-eight hours of watching the clock and hoping Ziegler didn't get cold feet or another offer.

I swiped open the group text with the men I considered my brothers: Blake, Axel, and Ryker. Knox was one, too, but he was in prison, not available by phone. Maybe the rest of us could meet at the mansion we'd dubbed the Sinners and Saints Club for an impromptu game of poker.

SINNERS AND SAINTS GROUP CHAT

Me: Anyone up for a game of poker? My brain's about to crawl out of my skull.

Axel: Did I just have a stroke? Did Jace Lockwood, corporate overlord who schedules bathroom breaks, just suggest spontaneous human interaction?

Blake: Check his location. Someone's stolen his phone.

Ryker: Or his identity. Quick, Jace, what did you say when Axel lost five grand to Blake last poker night?

*Me: *middle finger emoji**

Axel: It's him. Unfortunately.

Me: The board meeting today nearly ended with me committing multiple homicides. Need a distraction before I make national news.

Blake: Sorry, man. Elbow deep in engagement ring shopping.

Me: You're what now?

Blake: Repeat that to Tessa, and I'll personally replace your car's custom leather interior with a bed of surgical needles while you sleep.

Ryker: Wait, you're seriously proposing? To my sister?

Blake: No, I just spend my rare free time jewelry shopping for fun. Yes, to your sister.

Ryker: And this is how you're telling me?????

Blake: I told you at poker night.

Ryker: I thought you were JOKING. You've been dating for five seconds.

Blake: We're in love. And we've known each other for years. Stop being so dramatic.

Axel: Marriage? Voluntarily? Did we not vaccinate against this?

Blake: Unlike you, some of us aspire to relationships that last longer than a carton of milk.

*Axel: *coffin emoji* *headstone emoji* Here lies Blake's freedom, dignity, and the last known evidence of his spine.*

Ryker: Fine. I guess if I had to pick one person to protect my sister for the rest of her life, you're ... marginally acceptable.

Blake: Your flattery is making me tear up.

Ryker: Though, as her brother, I'm legally obligated to threaten your life at least once before the wedding.

Me: Can we get back to MY question? Can you guys meet?

Ryker: Buried in case files. Starting your own law firm has its downsides. Like explaining to a prospective client that stabbing your neighbor with a fondue fork over a property line dispute isn't self-defense.

Axel: Currently entertaining a woman who thinks NFTs are designer handbags. But she has 3 million Instagram followers, so ...

Me: Your dating algorithm remains catastrophically broken.

Me: I need to blow off steam before I commit a felony involving my board of directors.

Axel: Says the workaholic who hasn't seen sunlight since flip phones were still cool. When's the last time you did anything fun that didn't involve a spreadsheet?

Ryker: Why don't you grab a drink somewhere?

Me: I don't do bars alone.

Axel: Then enjoy your breakdown.

Me: Fine. If I end up on TMZ, I'm blaming all of you.

Axel: That's the spirit! And if you see any models there, tell them you're my much less attractive and far less successful friend.

Me: I'm worth more than the GDP of several countries.

*Axel: Yes, but can you touch your toes? No? Sad. *flexing emoji**

Ryker: I'm muting this before I throw my phone into traffic.

Axel: Finally. Now go drink something that costs more than my first apartment and stop bothering us with your human emotions. It's unsettling.

I shoved the phone into my pocket and ran a hand over my face.

Option 1: I could go home, stay at my penthouse. No. Even outside of this bigger paperwork issue, there could still be other last-minute fires that popped up, and I needed to be close in case they did. I'd seen too many deals fall apart over a weekend. If I was at my penthouse, I'd be at least twenty minutes away from fixing whatever went wrong. Besides, if I went home, I'd spend the entire weekend staring at my phone.

Plus, going home felt like giving up, and I didn't do that.

The bar's sign flickered again. Maybe the alcohol would give me some ideas about how to survive the weekend without completely losing my mind.

When I yanked the door open and stormed inside, the

universe crashed my perfectly molded distraction into my chest. And then a tangle of limbs and blonde hair yelped and fell to the ground.

4

SCARLETT

A smirk played on my lips as the knot in my shoulders finally began to loosen. Who knew revenge fantasies could be better than therapy? The vodka probably helped, too, but mostly, I had to credit Dakota's twisted genius.

"Told you this would be fun." Dakota's eyes sparkled. "I'm heading to the ladies' room. Order me another drink, okay?"

I nodded, watching her weave through the Friday night crowd. For someone who'd drawn the short straw in the family lottery, I'd somehow hit the jackpot in the work bestie department. Leave it to Dakota to transform my murderous rage into actual laughter in under an hour, with nothing but a pen and questionable suggestions.

Once she disappeared around the corner, I couldn't help but admire our masterpiece scrawled in black ink:

REVENGE LIST

- Slip industrial-strength laxatives into his morning coffee right before a board meeting. (Bonus: schedule said meeting in the furthest conference room from any bathroom.)
- Shove an ice pick into his balls.

- Glue his office chair wheels in place.
- Put his car up for sale on Craigslist: Luxury vehicle, priced to sell, owner must flee country immediately.
- Program his phone to autocorrect his name to Asswipe.
- Undo the seams of his pants so they split open during his next presentation.
- Send him anonymous glitter bomb packages.
- Sign him up for embarrassing newsletters including: erectile dysfunction support groups, adult bed-wetting solutions, DIY hemorrhoid treatments, farm animal breeding techniques.
- Hide sardines in his office vents.
- Set his email signature to Best Wishes, Your Friendly Neighborhood Pervert.
- Replace his desktop background with a looping GIF of him picking his nose.
- Superglue his desk drawers shut.
- Change his phone's language settings to Medieval Latin.
- Replace his hand sanitizer with superglue.
- Reschedule all his calendar meetings to 3 a.m.
- Change ringtone to Britney Spears song.

I smiled, running a hand through my hair as I scanned the bar, and promptly choked on my drink. There, perched at the far end like karma's favorite vulture, sat Jessica from HR. The new hire who didn't know me from Eve, hadn't been involved in any of today's disaster, and yet still managed to make my stomach drop through the floor.

Because what if he'd already gotten to her? Spun some story about the operations director who threatened him for no reason? And now here I was, coauthoring what basically amounted to a criminal manifesto on cocktail napkins. Nothing said *stable professional* quite like the words *ice pick* and *balls* scrawled in loopy handwriting. This wasn't just a bad look; this was career death, wrapped in bar napkins. One glimpse of this list would validate every lie he could possibly tell about me. Worse, she might tell other people. Namely, other HR people with influence over my career, both inside and out, via word of mouth.

And it wasn't like I could explain this away: *Oh, this violent revenge fantasy? Just a little therapeutic exercise after your executive tried to cop a feel.* Yeah, that would go over great. My credibility would be shot, and I certainly couldn't afford to give him a leg up on the whole he said/she said situation.

Just my luck. Jessica's attention did a sweep of the place, landing on me. It was only by the grace of the universe that someone was saying hi to her; otherwise, she might already be on her way over here.

I need to get rid of this. Now.

Dakota had taken her bottomless-pit purse to the restroom, and my own purse, with its temperamental clasp that had been giving me grief all week, felt untrustworthy. With my luck, the napkin would fall out at Jessica's feet the moment she came over to say hello.

Grabbing the napkin, I spun off my barstool and made a mad dash to the trash can, keeping my eyes on Jessica during my frantic (while trying to *not* appear frantic) speed walk. Which, as it turned out, wasn't the safest idea. With my gaze fixed to the side, I slammed into what had to be an escaped Greek statue and discovered that Newton's laws of motion were alive and well as I bounced backward onto my ass with a yelp.

Two shoes appeared before me. More specifically, gray athletic shoes of the handsome variety, which led to a pair of black athletic pants that looked soft enough to make cashmere jealous, wrapped around legs that had to be sculpted by Michelangelo himself. And because my brain was clearly still scrambled from the fall, I had the completely inappropriate urge to reach out and press a finger to those shins. Just to make sure they were real. For research purposes.

But those legs? They were just the opening act. His black athletic shirt might as well have been painted on, displaying a set of abs that looked like they moonlighted as a washboard. My gaze wandered higher (hello, research mode) to find his chest and shoulders waging an epic battle for Most Likely to Make a Girl Forget Her Own Name. Spoiler alert: they were both losing to his face.

Eyes brighter than any sparkling emerald I'd ever seen stared back at me. Even from all the way down here—and the guy was tall, let me tell you—I could see various shades of forest green blending into sea foam, with flecks of gold that seemed to dance in the bar's light. His hypnotic eyes were set in a chiseled face that would make artists weep as they sculpted his refined jaw, broad cheekbones, and supple lips that could command an entire army of women to obey his every command.

He was, to put it mildly, striking.

I'd never had an instant flutter in my chest by merely locking eyes with another human being, and the involuntary response both thrilled and unnerved me. Evidently, I wasn't prepared for the impact of encountering such a magnificently beautiful guy because I just sat there. On the ground. Making no effort to be a human and get myself up.

The man's eyes remained fixed on me as he extended his hand. "Are you okay?"

Holy smokes. His voice was like ear sex, penetrating my brain with a low rumble of pleasure.

"I fell down." *Interesting.* Evidently, the ear sex killed my IQ. And for the record, I didn't fall down, exactly. I'd bounced off his granite body.

Those godlike lips of his curled up slightly on one side, a faint line appearing between his perfectly shaped dark eyebrows that matched his hair.

He finds me amusing. And he's looking at me like the rest of the bar vanished from existence.

My cheeks incinerated, and my brain ordered me to climb out

of the hormone-induced coma and rejoin the land of the mentally functioning.

Why, exactly, was I still lying on this nasty-ass ground, with his hand still stretched out, waiting to help me up like I was frozen? While I'd never had a guy have this effect on me, I was a grown woman with an MBA, for Criminy's sake, not some middle-school girl meeting her boy-band crush for the first time.

Get a grip. Get up.

When I accepted his hand, a flash of heat shot up my arm, down my chest, and right to my stomach. I froze again—because I hadn't done that a sufficiently awkward amount of times yet—and held his stare, wondering ... *Did he feel that too?* I didn't know if I was seeing what I wanted to see, but his lips *did* fall open slightly, and his eyes snapped to our enclosed palms.

How could one small moment feel like everything, shattering my existence into white noise, until the only thing that existed was his hand in mine, his eyes sweeping back to my face? An impressively seductive silence stretched between us until he cleared his throat, and with one graceful pull, he tugged me to my feet.

Stop staring at him. Say something. Walk away. What is wrong with you?

"I'm sorry," I managed. "I wasn't looking where I was going."

Now that I was standing, I could appreciate how much more gorgeous he was up close and how heat radiated off his body.

As a new couple entered the bar, a gust of warm air swept through the door and past us, accomplishing two things: First, it made his hair move so delicately, I wanted to run my fingers through it. Second, and more importantly, it drew our attention to the napkin, which had previously been lying unsuspiciously on the ground.

Floating through the air for a second, it, horrifyingly, drew the attention of Ear Sex's eyes. I swear, the particles of time slowed around me as he reached his unfairly gorgeous hand down and picked it up before I could stop him.

Based on the way his arm was originally swooping in my direction, only to freeze, he hadn't intended on reading it, but I guess when the words REVENGE LIST caught someone's eye, their natural curiosity took over. Even Greek gods, apparently.

He froze for a moment, drew the napkin a little closer, and while my body and brain decided to become useless bystanders, his eyes roamed over our list of ideas. Those perfect lips of his twitched once, twice, and then ...

Oh God.

His emerald eyes lifted to meet mine, dancing with something that looked dangerously like amusement.

Plot twist: My Friday night was about to go from bad to catastrophically entertaining. And this was just the beginning ...

5

JACE

A vision of perfection lay before me, her lean body a masterpiece, wrapped in a gray pencil skirt and crisp white blouse. As she propped herself up on her elbows, the fabric strained tantalizingly across her breasts, and a single button clung for dear life, threatening to break.

A cascade of shiny blonde waves with a hint of strawberry framed her face, catching the light like champagne bubbles. But it was her green eyes that truly ensnared me, those deep pools of stunning mystery that locked on to mine with an intensity that stole my breath. She was a siren's call made flesh, and I was helplessly, hopelessly drawn to her.

As the bar around us ceased to exist, I extended my hand, eager to feel her supple skin against my own.

"Are you okay?" I asked.

Her beautiful lips—lips I could imagine kissing me all over my body—parted slightly.

"I fell down."

Her voice hit me like aged whiskey: smooth, intoxicating, and guaranteed to make me do something impulsive. A blush crept across her cheeks, and I found myself wondering how far down that blush went.

When her hand slipped into mine, every cell in my body snapped to attention. The gentleman in me wanted to buy her a drink, learn her story. The devil on my shoulder had other ideas, involving that bar top and significantly less clothing. Both sides agreed on one thing: I needed more of her.

"I'm sorry," she murmured. "I wasn't looking where I was going."

Neither was I, and now I can't look anywhere else.

I didn't date women for good reason. The moment they discovered my last name, dollar signs would appear over their eyes. Us four Lockwood brothers were wealthy through inheritance before we started our ventures, and while many people didn't know my face, my name echoed through Chicago like a drumbeat. I'd lost count of how many times I'd watched genuine smiles turn predatory the moment women connected the dots. It was always the same dance: their laugh would get a little louder, their touch a little longer, their eyes a little sharper. And then I never knew if they were interested in me or my prestige.

In fairness, I probably hadn't met the right women. Plenty of women, I would argue, didn't care about things like wealth, but that wasn't the point. The point was, I'd given up on dating, but now, that rule seemed as absurd as it was impossible. Instantly, I wanted to know everything about this woman. Her name. Her story. The taste of her lips. The sound of her in bed when I—

A gust of air blew the tendrils of her hair slightly, sending a piece of paper dancing between us that she'd been holding when we crashed into each other. I picked it up because, apparently, I was now the kind of man who chased windblown trash just because it belonged to her.

But what I read made my insides flutter with amusement:

REVENGE LIST

Well, well. Maybe she wasn't the angel she appeared to be. And maybe, just maybe, that made her even more irresistible.

6

JACE

When I glanced up, I found myself staring into a pair of wide, panic-stricken eyes. The woman's cheeks were flushed so scarlet, you'd think she was coming down with a life-threatening fever.

"Put laxatives in his coffee?" I read aloud, cocking an eyebrow and fighting to keep a straight face. "Remind me never to accept a drink from you."

She thrust out a delicate hand, chin tilted defiantly despite her obvious mortification. "That's private. Can I have it back, please?"

I couldn't help but grin, holding the napkin just out of her reach. "Who's the unlucky guy?"

She lunged for the napkin, but I was faster. And taller and not at all ready to let this go because this was one of the most amusing things I'd come across in, well, ever.

"It's just a joke," she insisted, her voice pitched higher than before, her gaze darting between me and something behind me.

"Shove ice picks into his balls," I read dramatically, watching her wince. "Damn. What'd this guy do? Kick a kitten?"

"It was just a ... creative writing exercise," she mumbled.

"Are you an author?"

"Of that napkin, yes. Now give it back," she retorted, a spark of sass breaking through her embarrassment.

Her eyes darted behind me again. Was the target of her wrath here? That could get interesting.

"You shouldn't glue his office chair wheels," I advised. "Unscrew them instead. When he sits down, he'll go flying. Much more satisfying."

Her mouth twitched. "Are you ... critiquing my revenge fantasies?"

"Someone has to maintain quality standards in the vengeance industry."

She stared at me, mouth slightly agape. Then—God help me—she smiled. The kind of smile that could power Chicago for a week. But she dropped it immediately, as if reminding herself there was nothing funny about this situation at all.

I disagree.

"I've never seen someone use a pen like a weapon of mass destruction," I said, finally extending the napkin. As she reached for it, I couldn't help but notice her elegant hands with fierce red nails that suggested she wasn't always the type to plot revenge on bar napkins, but rather, the feminine, alluring type. The moment her fingers brushed mine, something like fire crackled through my veins. "It's a work of art. You should frame it."

"Right," she said, tucking a strand of hair behind her ear. Watching her bite her lower lip was doing dangerous things to my self-control. "Well, uh, thank you. I promise I'm not actually a violent person."

I couldn't help but lean closer, drawn in by her nervous energy and that hint of vanilla perfume.

"You know, most people just fantasize about getting revenge. But you? You've got style. Terrifying, possibly criminal style, but style nonetheless." I winked, enjoying the way a fresh pool of crimson burst beneath her cheeks.

Behind us, someone cleared their throat loudly. Right. We were still blocking the entrance. The Friday night crowd was building, and judging by the grumbling, they weren't thrilled about our impromptu conversation near the doorway.

"Right, well, uh, nice meeting you," she stammered, fidgeting with the napkin.

"Jace," I said, extending my hand.

"Scarlett."

What a gorgeous name for a stunning woman.

Her hand fit into mine like it was made to be there. I reluctantly let go, already missing the warmth of her fingers against mine.

Focus, Lockwood.

"Scarlett, I'd like to buy you a drink," I announced.

With her eyebrows shooting up, she looked surprised. And based on the softening of her lips, amused.

"You said that as a statement."

"Too bold?"

She smirked, and her tone was a shade of feisty I wanted to hear more of. "The fact that you said that as a statement tells me a lot about you."

A couple squeezed past us, muttering under their breath. She shifted closer to make room, and suddenly, the air between us felt charged.

"Oh?" I challenged, trying not to get caught staring at her mouth, but my God, look at those lips.

"Most men I've met would have framed the invitation as a question," she continued.

"I'm not like most men. What kind of drink do you like?"

"But you said it as a fact," she pressed, studying me with those sharp eyes. "Which tells me you're used to getting what you want."

I leaned in. "And right now, what I want is to buy you a drink." *So I can learn everything about you.*

"Actually," she amended, "I'd argue most men, after seeing that list, would be running by now."

"Most men are boring."

"How do you know I'm not some psycho, making that list about things I want to do to my ex?"

I leaned in, closer still. "My intuition says whoever made it onto that list deserved every word."

"Your intuition could be terrible."

"My intuition is currently telling me you're stalling because you find me intriguing."

She bit her lip, fighting a smile. "Your intuition is awfully full of itself."

"My intuition would also like to point out that we're still blocking the door, and"—I nodded at the growing crowd trying to squeeze past us—"we can find a quiet corner, where you can tell me all about this list of yours."

"And if I'm actually dangerous?"

I grinned. "Then this is going to be the most interesting drink I've ever bought."

Her soft chuckle was worth every second of waiting. "You're either very brave or very foolish."

"I prefer optimistically reckless. Now, about that drink ..."

Her eyes traveled to a woman emerging from the restroom, and when they met mine again, I could see something processing in her facial expression. Pretty sure she was debating taking me up on my offer, but after a few seconds, she flashed a smile that looked disappointed.

"Sorry. I'm here with a friend. It was ... nice meeting you, Jace."

After clearing her throat, she graced me with one final look before ambling away. My feet stayed frozen in place, my eyes glued to her delicate frame as she tore up the napkin and tossed its confetti-like pieces into the trash like evidence from a crime scene.

Which was when it struck me: For the first time in an eternity, work wasn't consuming my thoughts. My mind wasn't racing through acquisition strategies or market projections. It was entirely captivated by her. The smart play, the Lockwood business instinct that rarely steered me wrong, would be to let her walk away. My life was already overflowing with complications, deadlines, and responsibilities. Adding a beautiful, intriguing stranger with a flair for creative revenge to that mix was the definition of a poor risk assessment.

But as I watched her weave through the crowd, something inside me shifted. Call it insanity, call it a desperate measure to avoid sabotaging this work deal by chasing this distraction, call it the worst decision of my life, but I knew with absolute certainty that if I let her walk away without finding a way to see her again, I'd regret it.

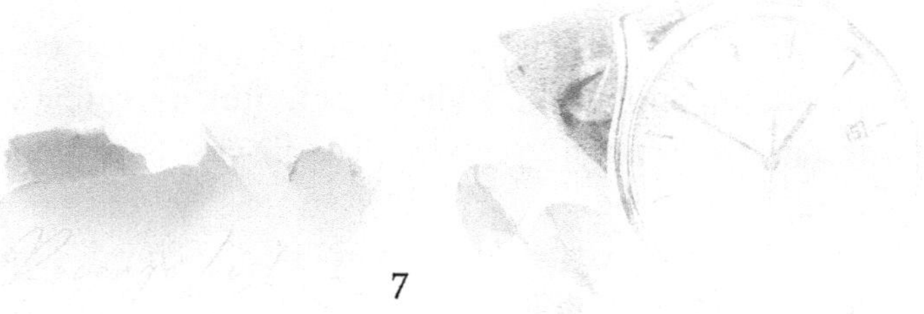

7

SCARLETT

"Holy smokes," Dakota said, watching Jace amble to the end of the bar and toss his two fingers in the air to signal the bartender, the movement making his shirt pull across his broad shoulders. "Who's the sex on stilts?"

"We should leave," I announced.

"What?" She balked. "Why?"

"Because Sex on Stilts just read our secret revenge list, and I don't care to be in the same room as someone who has evidence of my newfound evilness." I tried to shrink behind my glass, which was particularly difficult, given that I could feel his gaze burning into me from across the room.

"You're not evil."

The hottest guy in human history thinks I'm evil. And I was being evil. Maybe I had a good reason to, but fantasizing over hurting someone? What lows had I sunk to, and why, why, why did Ear Sex/Sex on Stilts have to see it?

"And that little interaction you just had didn't look like a guy repulsed by you." Dakota's eyebrows performed an elaborate dance of suggestion. "In fact ..."

The bartender appeared in front of him with a fresh drink. Something amber in a glass with ice cubes, and then, to my horror, Jace pointed in our direction. My pulse quickened as Sex on Stilts smiled (dear God, that smile) and pushed his credit card across the bar.

"He's buying you a drink," Dakota announced with unholy elation.

"How do you know it's for me?"

"Because he hasn't taken his eyes off you since I exited the bathroom. Trust me, I've been watching."

Sure enough, the bartender approached us with two fresh drinks. "Compliments of the gentleman at the end of the bar."

She gave me some sort of victorious smirk. I knew that smirk all too well; it was the one that appeared right before Dakota started plotting, and Dakota was nothing if not the queen of fun. It was one of the things I envied about her; she never took herself too seriously while I, on the other hand, liked to plan life out in multistep road maps.

"See? I told you! He bought you a drink, and he's totally staring at you. Go over there," she pressed.

"Did you not hear the part where he read the list?" I repeated. "You know, the one that included things like *shoving an ice pick into someone's balls*? Of course he's staring at me. He probably thinks I'm a freak."

"If he does, a freak is what he wants, based on the way he's smoldering at you. You should go over there and talk to him."

"That's not going to happen."

"Why? Based on your body language, you totally looked into him," she challenged.

"I'm not into him."

As if to call my bluff, he rolled up his sleeves, revealing tanned forearms. Damn it.

"Liar." Her voice dropped into her *I know you better than you know yourself* tone. "You know, it's okay to have fun sometimes, Scar."

"I have fun," I retorted.

"When's the last time you did something impulsive?"

"Saturday. I bought that new purse. Didn't even do any research ahead of time or anything."

She rolled her eyes. "Go have that drink with him."

"I'm not interested in getting into a relationship." My fingers tightened around my glass as memories of my last relationship surfaced. "In case you forgot, I tried having a boyfriend once. Reluctantly and against every screaming instinct I had." When you grew up with a father like mine, you didn't exactly have optimistic expectations of the male species. "And the only thing that got me was a thorough reminder of why I should've trusted my gut. Three months of manipulation and control later, I swore boyfriends off. Forever." Who needed that? Certainly not me and certainly not now, with my career hanging by a thread.

"So, you want to be celibate for the rest of your life?" Dakota leaned in closer, her voice dropping to a conspiratorial whisper. "Never want to feel a man's kiss again? Never want to feel his hands on your body? Or feel the heat of him on top of you?"

Heat flooded my cheeks. "Why did you have to put it that way?" My vibrator was probably threatening a strike from overuse, and sure, it did the job, but not like a man could. My inner thighs quivered to bring home the point.

She chuckled. "You don't have to marry the guy. Just have a drink with him and see where it goes. If he's interested in relationships, then you just be honest, but, Scar, for God's sake, you think some hot guy *wouldn't* be okay with a casual night?"

"You're talking like we'd have sex."

"I'm just ... covering all the possible bases."

"Sure you are."

And now she'd put those naughty bases all up in my head. *I wonder what he looks like without a shirt.*

"Look, you were just saying how you've given everything to your career," she pushed. "You haven't had a date in forever. Now's your chance. Let loose. Because come Monday morning, you'll turn into a pumpkin with a bucket of stressful career problems."

"Thanks for the reminder."

"I'm just saying, let your hair down."

I eyed him in all his glory, trying to hold on to my thread of resistance. I didn't normally throw caution to the wind, but, hell, he wasn't just wind. He was a tornado, ripping all my logic and reasons up from the floor. It was like some kind of polar vortex or something.

A group of women in cocktail dresses sashayed past him, their heads turning in perfect synchronization to eye our mysterious stranger. One of them, a leggy blonde, actually stopped walking.

"You need to take him up on his offer before it's too late," Dakota warned, nodding toward the blonde, who was now "accidentally" dropping her clutch near his seat. "Look at this place. Every single woman here is eyeing him like he's the answer to all their prayers. Right now, he only has eyes for you, but if you don't make a move soon, someone else might win his attention. Or he might leave, and you'll never see him again."

Why did that thought make my ribs tighten?

I swirled the drink he'd bought me, watching the ice cubes clink against the glass. Anything to avoid looking directly at him, though I could feel the weight of his gaze. In my peripheral vision, I could see the blonde was now perched on the barstool next to him, but I noticed his body was still angled in our direction.

"I have more important things to focus on right now," I decided. "Namely, salvaging my promotion and my career."

"Which you can do starting Monday morning. For the weekend? You deserve to let loose and forget about all this bullshit." She paused, watching as the blonde tried, and failed, to capture his attention. "Look, here's all you need to know: He's hot. He's into you. He bought you a drink. You need something to take your mind off your career crisis." She spread her hands wide. "Do you not see how perfect this is? Plus, I know you. You're not trying to convince *me* that spending time with him is a bad idea. You're trying to convince yourself."

Fine, I was totally imagining things I shouldn't be imagining shortly after meeting him. Dare I say, I was intrigued by the idea. But this wasn't me. I was in control. Thoughtful before my moves. And, hello, I had a no-men rule.

"I think we should finish this drink and go," I decided, even as my traitor heart skipped when I caught him checking me out again in the mirror behind the bar.

"Not happening." To my horror, Dakota stopped trying to convince me and started heading right for our witness.

"Dakota! What the hell are you doing?"

She turned around, holding still for a second as she explained, "If you go home tonight, you're going to spin yourself into an anxiety attack over all this. You need to take your mind off it."

"I did. I am." My panicked eyes darted to Sex on Stilts who, yep, was most definitely looking straight at me now. More accurately, his gaze was darting between me and the woman I was whisper-yelling at. The blonde beside him was mid-story, but he wasn't even pretending to listen.

But did Dakota listen to me to stop? No. No, she did not.

She stormed right over to him.

8

SCARLETT

I had to launch myself off my barstool to chase her down as she closed the distance between her and Jace, my heels clicking against the hardwood floor in rapid succession. The warm glow of bulbs cast dramatic shadows across the exposed brick walls, making everything feel more intense than it already was. But I was too late.

Dakota leaned her back against the bar next to him like she'd known him a thousand years, the epitome of casual confidence I'd always envied.

"Hi. I'm Dakota."

Jace's eyes—they'd been different with me. Warm, curious, like liquid amber in the bar's dim lighting. But with Dakota, they were guarded. Understandably so. She wasn't what I'd call good with boundaries. It was another of the things I adored about her, but right now?

Right now, I hated it.

"Dakota!" I scolded.

Jace's eyes swept to me, and as they locked on mine for, like, ten heart-stopping beats, they softened, his mouth relaxing from its firm-ass line to a ghost of a smile. The kind of smile that made the crystal glasses behind the bar seem dull in comparison. I hated that his almost smile had this effect on me. That it made me feel special—because in my opinion, Dakota was far more gorgeous than I was. The girl always got all the looks when we were out together. And of more importance, his smoldering intensity had this magnetism that drew me to him like a current I couldn't stop.

I wondered who he was or if he realized that every single woman in this bar—and I mean, every freaking one—was *still* staring at him with pure longing and desire. The rock music floating through the speakers couldn't mask the collective sighs of them hoping Dakota and I would "bomb" and they'd get their chance with him.

"This is my friend Scarlett, whom I think you met," Dakota continued while Jace continued staring so intensely, I wasn't even sure he was listening to her. His focus was a tangible thing, like a spotlight. "She's had a terrible day and needs some cheering up."

Her ridiculously embarrassing words were the only thing that had the power to snap my focus away from Jace.

"Dakota, so help me."

"You look familiar," Jace said to her, a deep crease appearing between his brows. His eyes narrowed as he studied her face, and he tilted his head, like someone trying to place a half-forgotten nightmare. "I never forget a face. Where do I know you from?"

God, even the crease was sexy. I wanted to lick it.

She didn't take the time to explain her familiarity was probably because she was a huge influencer on social media and that she got recognized from time to time. I mean, I was assuming that's why he recognized her.

Because what else could it be?

Instead of addressing his question, she wiggled her eyebrows at him and said, "You look like a big boy, capable of lots of cheering."

Dear God, please open the ground beneath me and just ... let me free-fall to the core of the earth.

"Enough." I literally yanked her by the arm away from the damn bar.

She half smirked, half looked annoyed that I'd cut her off short.

"I'm sorry about my friend. She was born without social skills."

I dragged Dakota back to our barstools.

"I'm going to suffocate you," I whisper-yelled. I loved her, I did, but, "We aren't in middle school. I don't need you sneaking notes to a guy I like!"

"So, you *do* like him." She arched a knowing brow at me.

My attraction (okay, fine, G-force pull) to him wasn't the point. The point was, "That was embarrassing as hell. Honestly, it's a good thing I'm not interested in dating anyone right now because if I was, you'd have just ruined it with the first guy in an eternity I'd actually want to!"

Damn her for that knowing look.

"He probably wasn't even listening to what I was saying," Dakota claimed. "He was too busy staring at you with *let's get it on* music playing in his head." My *former* best work friend glanced over her shoulder before returning her face to me, smirking victoriously. "He won't stop looking at you."

"Yeah, that's what happens when you make a *scene*. We've become the car accident in the bar."

"Puh-lease. He's eye-fucking you from across the room."

Desire heated in my lower belly at the mere thought. *Great. Even my freaking hormones are betraying me now.* I clenched my fists at my sides, willing my body to *heel*.

"Where are you going?" I balked with eyes so wide, my forehead ate my eyelids as she tossed her purse string over her shoulder.

"I want details Monday."

Oh, hell no. "If you're leaving, I'm leaving."

"I have an appointment," she claimed. "Forgot to mention it."

"You drove me to work this morning. You said nothing about an appointment, and it's Friday *night*."

"Like I said, slipped my mind."

"Don't you dare leave me."

"He's waiting to talk to you," she pointed out.

"He could be a serial killer."

"That can be one of your opening questions," she suggested. When I cocked my head in my not-amused tilt, she countered with, "Statistically, he's more likely to be a guy that's good in bed."

"This so isn't like you," I countered.

"You need cheering up. He looks like a body full of cheer." Another wiggle of her eyebrows. "I want details Monday. Byyyyeee."

"Dakota!"

Goddammit. She was out the door before I could stop her, leaving me alone with my thoughts. I knew she was trying to "help" in her own way, but she knew me better than this. She knew I didn't have casual sex, even though I wasn't morally opposed to it, and she should know that flirting or having sex with some stranger was the last thing I'd do to make myself feel better.

It angered me that she left me here, having to find my own ride. If she couldn't drive me today, fine, but now I had to rely on a rideshare, which, in downtown Chicago on a Friday night, usually came with a freaking seven-year wait.

Punching in the order—and firing off a *get your ass back here* text to Dakota that I knew she'd never answer—I plopped down on the barstool in defeat.

"This is from the gentleman at the end of the bar." The bartender appeared, motioning to Jace.

In addition to a fresh drink I'd be having (mental note: Jace took the time to order the drink I wanted, not just a drink. *Girlies, allow swooning to commence*), the bartender set down a napkin with neat penmanship on it that read:

You look like you don't want company, thus the note versus an in-person invasion. But I have one question: What made your day so terrible?

I didn't look to my left, but I could feel Jace there, his presence as tangible as the air in a gathering storm. For the life of me, I couldn't fathom why he was this intrigued.

It must be the Revenge List. I guess it's not every day you meet a woman who's written a fantasy of felonies and misdemeanors on a napkin.

"Can I have a pen and a napkin, please?" I asked the bartender.

To his credit, the guy, who sported tattoos all over his hands, smiled like he thought this was adorable (it wasn't; it was just a method of communicating with someone who didn't deserve to be ghosted) and handed me a stack of napkins.

A stack.

Didn't need it; this was a one-napkin text exchange.

Me: Thank you for the drink. Sorry my friend invaded your night.

I handed it to the bartender, who acted like my little mail pigeon and delivered it, back a minute later with another napkin.

Jace: The invasion was welcome. You still haven't answered me. Why was your day so bad?

I took a sip of my drink, looking at his penmanship. Jeez, even the guy's handwriting was sexy, a delicate blend of curved letters and easy-to-read font. The guy could moonlight as a calligrapher.

The appropriate thing to do, if I was serious about being left alone, would be to end all communications right now. No more napkin exchanges.

I pushed the note aside and stared defiantly in front of me, but of course, my damn eyes wandered. They claimed it was just curiosity, but it took eight milliseconds to find his gaze locked directly on mine. Heat exploded in my cheeks, and my eyes were unable to break from his, like they'd been locked with a dead bolt while the rest of the bar—muted conversations and cackles of laughter, clanking of glasses, and the smell of beer—faded around us.

In that instant, I wanted to throw caution to the wind and join him.

But my stress relief was more of the *go home and organize my closet* variety. Besides, Prince Charming himself couldn't kiss the disaster spell of my life away, so I shot back one final conversation-ending message.

Me: I'm not in the mood to talk. I'm sorry. P.S. Everyone has bad days.

Another returned. This time, the bartender wasn't smiling though. Not that I could blame him. We were being high maintenance and a little selfish, making him pass notes.

Jace: But I'm interested in yours.

I stole a quick glance at Jace. He was leaning on his elbow, seemingly casual, but his eyes were fixed on me.

Me: Don't be. It's not interesting, I assure you.

As I passed this note, I bit my lower lip when another returned, surprised the prospect of opening up didn't come with irritation. But rather ... was that intrigue? Especially because I'd seen Jace slip the bartender a cash incentive to keep this up.

Jace: I presume this has to do with the guy whose balls you want to shove an ice pick into?

The bartender retrieved my next message.

Me: My friend helped with the FICTIONAL revenge ideas. I'm more of the glitter bomb fantasy kind of girl.

Jace: Glitter is brilliant; the guy would find it in nooks and crannies for years. The herpes of craft supplies, if you will.

When a laugh escaped before I could catch it, Jace's lips quirked up, clearly pleased with himself for breaking through my armor.

Sipping my drink, glancing at the time on my phone approximately every twenty seconds, I resisted the urge to look over at Jace.

Until another napkin appeared.

Jace: Hair remover mixed in shampoo.

I reread the sentence as if it would help it make sense. But it didn't. I glanced over at him (finding him looking at me expectantly, by the way), and I bet my expression was something along the lines of *what the school of assclowns did this mean?* With a devilish smirk, he motioned toward the bartender with the grace of an angel, and another napkin appeared before me.

Jace: You tore up your revenge list. I'm starting a new one.

I couldn't believe after everything I had been through tonight, my lips curled up into a smile. But I guess the simple gesture put me at ease a little, for three reasons.

First of all, I had lost my *former* (let me repeat, former) friend in Operation Don't Panic Over Losing My Job. Having him step into her place as my cheer-up squad was nice. Second of all, I assumed this guy would think I was a nutcase or something, but here he was, playfully joining my distraction party, making me feel like I wasn't the worst human in the world for making such an immature list. And third of all, his playful banter in beautiful penmanship unwound some of the tension coiled around my ribs.

Evidently, Sex Ears wasn't just a big bucket of eye candy. Clearly, he had a charming and fun personality to go along with it.

God help the other women in this bar when they discovered that.

Feeling the smile reach my eyes, I made an adjustment to his napkin and sent it back.

Hair (I crossed out remover) DYE mixed in shampoo. HOT PINK. With glitter for extra spite.

Jace's eyebrows shot up as he read it. He swiped his lower lip with his thumb, visibly suppressing a laugh, then met my gaze with a mischievous glint. His pen hovered over the napkin for a moment before he scribbled something down and sent it back.

Jace: Unscrew all his doorknobs and handles 99% of the way. Each time he uses one, it'll pop off. Bonus points if you film it security-camera style.

I couldn't help but chuckle, shaking my head in amusement. Jace's grin widened at my reaction.

Me: Set his computer language to Mandarin. Then his phone to Korean. Then his tablet to Russian. Watch him try to Google translate his way out.

Jace read it, and his shoulders shook. He glanced up, giving me an impressed nod before hunching over to write his next idea.

Jace: Put a bumper sticker on his car that reads: Ask me about my llama collection.

This time, I had to cover my mouth to stifle a laugh. Jace noticed and winked while I took a sip of my drink to compose myself before writing again.

Me: Rearrange the keys on his keyboard.

Jace's eyes lit up at this one.

Jace: Replace family photos with pictures of Nicolas Cage. But, like, really subtle Photoshop. Just enough to make him question his sanity.

I nearly choked on my drink, coughing and laughing at the same time. A satisfied smirk played on his lips.

Me: Hide alarm clocks set to go off at random times throughout his office.

This time, Jace's shoulders shook harder, and when he looked at me again, there was a new warmth in his eyes. He twirled his pen between his fingers before writing his next idea.

Jace: Put a For Sale sign on his car in the parking lot with a really low price AND his phone number on it.

A deep chuckle escaped my throat. Jace's smile seemed to warm at the sight of it, watching me with growing interest, which, of course, made a blush creep up my neck.

I penned my next suggestion.

Me: Replace his office chair with a child-sized one.

As Jace read this last one, he didn't even try to contain his laughter. The rich sound filled the bar, drawing curious glances from other patrons. But I didn't care. In that moment, it felt like we were the only two people in the room.

Jace locked eyes with me, tilting his head as if I were a mystery that he wanted to unravel.

Remind me: Why was I holding back from Jace again? He was freaking hot as hell, funny, charming, and now, the thought of *not* talking to him (without a napkin) left me with anxiety. Did I *want* to let Grabby Hands ruin my mood for the entire night? Did I want to give him that kind of power?

I had forty-five minutes to kill until my ride got here. Would it be so terrible to talk to Jace to pass that time? Maybe Dakota was right; maybe spending time with him would be fun.

I was about to get the courage to walk on down there, but suddenly, some bombshell in a tight red dress made her move. She'd been on the sidelines, biding her time, gaining courage perhaps, but now, she was standing next to Jace, smiling, twirling her hair, and leaning at the perfect angle to flaunt her cleavage in his face. Why was I glaring at her with this flash of ... was that irritation? And why was I this relieved that Jace was not the type of guy who looked at her chest, even once? If anything, he shifted his body away from her, giving a polite smile that didn't reach his eyes.

I watched him wait for her to get distracted by ordering some complicated martini before turning his body and jotting something on a napkin.

Jace: Save me. Offering generous reward. No questions asked.

My mouth curled up.

Me: She's pretty. And she'd be in a better mood than I am. You should talk to her. I bet she's very passionate about llama collections.

His gaze snapped to mine with playful indignation as the woman graduated to touching his arm, her purple nails stark against his skin. Only the bartender giving her extra olives distracted her so Jace could fire off another note.

Jace: I'm sure she's lovely, but there's only one woman I want to speak to. The one with the surprisingly devious mind and excellent taste in revenge tactics. Can I please join you?

Through the windows, Chicago's lights twinkled like they

were in on the moment. I took one last look at his neat handwriting, my heart doing a little dance in my chest.

Me: Yes.

9

JACE

For a moment, elation coursed through me before reality slapped me across the face. What kind of man was I acting like?

My "relationships"—if you could call them that—had always been casual for a reason. Casual meant no messy emotions, no complications. It meant having short, monogamous arrangements where I never thought about the women when they weren't warming my bed. I definitely never sat there, analyzing their body language, or felt my chest constrict at the thought that they might walk out of a bar and disappear from my life forever.

This laser focus on a woman, this hunger that rivaled a starving man's desperation, wasn't me. Hell, I prided myself on control, on keeping emotions at arm's length. But here I was, completely unsettled by a woman I'd known for all of twenty minutes. Who felt a pull like this so quickly?

This had to be about distraction. It was the only logical explanation, and I was nothing if not logical.

The timing fit perfectly. I'd been told to find a distraction for the weekend, and then she literally fell at my feet. My mind must have latched on to her and her mysterious revenge fantasy as an escape from my professional hell. Something to stop me from doing anything rash, like taking that flight. That had to be it.

Right?

But if this was just about distraction, why was I suddenly consumed with knowing who had hurt her badly enough to warrant that revenge list? My fingers twitched at my side, itching to pull that information from her like I pulled confessions from lying business partners.

A relationship wasn't in the cards, but perhaps I could help navigate whatever storm was raging in her life. Not that she seemed incapable. Something in those sharp eyes told me she could handle herself just fine, but for reasons I couldn't explain, a protective instinct kicked in.

Who are you, Scarlett? And who the hell hurt you enough to make you write that list?

The real question was: Why did I care so much about either answer? And why did I just vow to find the answers to all of the above?

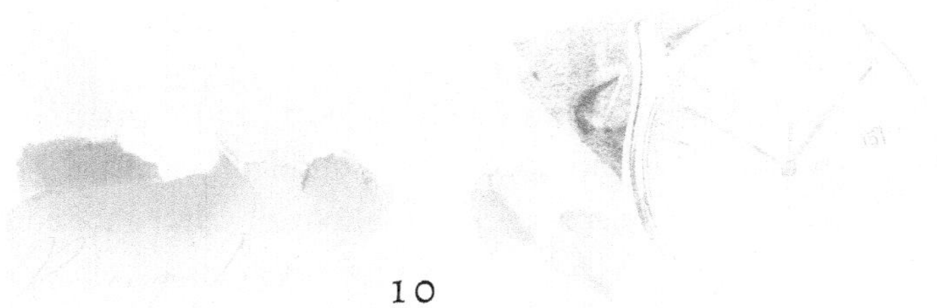

10

SCARLETT

“I owe you one.” Jace materialized at my side, his presence sending a ripple of awareness through the crowded bar.

One stare into his breathless eyes, and my witty retort lodged in my throat. As captivating as it had been to see him before, seeing him now, when I wasn’t freaking out over him reading my revenge list or trying to stop my best friend’s mortification attack, I finally allowed myself to surrender to the depths of his gaze. Those emerald orbs, flecked with amber, held an undercurrent of something mysterious. The authority that radiated from him should have been intimidating, but something in the way the corner of his mouth lifted made my pulse react.

The fact that he’d shown me a lighter side only deepened my intrigue of him because his sharp, dominating features suggested he didn’t do it often.

“You don’t strike me as the type of guy who needs rescuing,” I challenged.

One. Two. Three seconds passed before Jace chose his response to my playful accusation, angling the right side of his mouth up. My inner thighs heated at the sight, evidently waiting for him to tell them what to do.

Traitor thighs.

"And what type of guy do I seem like to you, Scarlett?"

My God. My name had never sounded as sensual as it did rolling off his lips, an effortless symphony of velvet and seduction. There was a challenge to it even as he leaned his left elbow on the bar next to me, waiting patiently for my response.

My brain cells attempted to unionize and take me down though, so it took several seconds before I replied, "The kind of guy who has a good sense of humor, but doesn't normally let people see it."

Hallelujah! My vocabulary and ability to string words into coherent sentences have returned.

As he scrutinized my features, wandering vision and all that, I couldn't tell if I'd offended or impressed him.

"Observant, aren't you?" he cooed.

Impressed, I guess.

"She's pretty." I cocked an eyebrow, gesturing toward Red Dress with my drink. Better to acknowledge the elephant in the room—or rather, the gorgeous woman who'd been flirting with him earlier.

"Didn't notice."

Something in his tone sounded absolutely sincere. Or maybe I was just hearing what I wanted to hear. Either way, it was mean to feel flattered that he sat with his back to the woman, who was now pouting, by the way.

Jace claimed the barstool next to me, angling his entire body in my direction like I was north to his compass.

"She was probably nervous talking to someone who looks like you," I managed, wiping a droplet with a fresh napkin.

The right side of his mouth lifted in that criminally unfair half smile, one perfect eyebrow arching upward.

"Someone who looks like me?" Each word dripped with amusement, like he was savoring my verbal stumble.

"In case you haven't noticed, almost every woman's been staring at you since you walked in." *Including me. Especially me.*

Despite the ridiculous attraction, I found my muscles relaxing into a more comfortable posture.

"Every guy in this place has been looking at *you*," Jace countered, his eyes roaming my face like an artist memorizing every curve, every shadow so he could draw it later from memory.

"That's not—" I cleared my throat, scrambling for solid ground. Preferably ground that didn't sound self-deprecating, insisting no one would be staring at me. Instead, I opted to change the subject. "I'm sorry my friend bothered you earlier."

"I'm not. Gave me another excuse to talk to you."

Another. That one word floated through my chest like a joyful hummingbird.

"Tell me about this revenge list." The edges of his words sharpened.

Poor hummingbird. I could hear its little heart attack in my chest as it dropped from disappointment.

I could feel my face fall, too, as I muttered, "If that's why you want to talk to me, you should go back to the girl in the red dress before it's too late." I tore my focus away from his dangerously handsome face and stared at my glass.

"This revenge list thing lands next to a nerve, doesn't it?" He studied me—way too perceptively.

Many nerves. And you know what? That made me even angrier. Why would I care if his *only* interest in me was that ridiculous list?

Ego. That was the only explanation. It would be nice if he was interested in *me*, not just my randomly weird behavior.

"I'm sorry," I deflated, smoothing my napkin. "I assure you I'm not normally this rude, and for the record, I've never made a list like that before."

"So, whatever this guy did to you must be really bad." It wasn't a question. His eyes had turned calculating, like he was piecing together a puzzle I hadn't meant to hand him.

"I'm not talking about the list." *Or about how your concern is doing dangerous things to my heart rate.*

"May I ask one question about it?" *May.* Who even used proper grammar while flirting? This man was doing unfair things to my inner language nerd. "Should I be worried this is some violent ex that'll come in here and hurt you?"

Stand down, hormones; he's just checking on my safety. Don't get all bent out of shape at the fierce protection pulsing through his stare.

"No," I assured him. "I'm not in any danger." *Except of losing my job. And maybe my sanity if he keeps looking at me like that.* "I don't want to talk about the list *or* work."

Jace raised his dark eyebrows. "I take it, the guy is a douchebag from work?"

I cocked my head, scolding him with my glower. Evidently, he didn't find that intimidating; he found it adorable, based on the way his eyes roamed over my face and his lips slanted up.

"No discussion of the list or work," he conceded, his voice smooth as hell. "I can handle that, but I do have a request."

"And what's that?"

"Tell me everything about yourself," Jace said.

"Everything's a long list," I retorted.

"I have all night."

The promise in those words made my pulse skip. The bar buzzed with energy around us, but he seemed perfectly content here, alone with me. Still ...

"Are you meeting someone?" I wondered aloud.

Jace's lips pressed against his glass as he took a long, casual drink. Seriously, even watching him take a sip of his drink was borderline pornographic with how sensual it was, his lips softly pressed against the glass, his forearms on full display.

Oh, and let's talk about those forearms. Long lines. Tattoos sprawled across his skin, which stretched tightly over lean muscles, yet his hands remained unmarked. Long, elegant fingers that drew my gaze. I couldn't help but wonder how those bare, stunning fingers would feel, gliding over my skin.

"No. Just came in for a drink," he answered.

"Stressful day of work?"

"You said you didn't want to talk about work." His eyes glistened with amusement.

"*My* work," I clarified. "We can talk about yours."

"I'd rather not." Something dark flickered across his expression, gone before I could analyze it.

"Want to make a list of your own?" I offered playfully.

"Other people's incompetence is infuriating to deal with." The way he said it, resigned yet authoritative, made me even more curious about what he did. Sales maybe? You had to be good with people to exude this much natural charm. "Enough about me." His tone bordered on playful again, this time with a sexual undercurrent. "I want to hear everything about you."

I checked the rideshare app. "I have thirty minutes until my ride shows up."

"That's all you'll give me?"

"You want more?"

"I was hoping for all night."

My cheeks incinerated. Did he seriously just say that?

"That's rather forward of you." Delightfully so actually. Dampening-of-my-panties so. "We just met."

"Indecision is one of the leading causes of failure," Jace said. "When you see something you want, you need to make a choice and go for it."

"Am I something you want?"

"Without question."

"You know nothing about me." I forced myself to sound reasonable. "I could be a stalker. Or someone who collects dead animal skulls."

Jace's lips curved as his gaze traveled over me slowly. My body responded, unleashing a tidal wave of warmth that rippled over my skin and pooled between my legs.

"I know you came to a bar to blow off steam with your friend after what, apparently, was a terrible day, most likely terrible at work," Jace mused. "Based on the fact you made a revenge list after said day, I'm guessing something big went down. Some asshole did something completely out of line, maybe even hurt you, and I'm banking on that asshole being someone you're forced to work with every day."

Holy observant, Batman.

I was frozen in his storm as he continued, "Based on the fact your friend is the one that came over to me and tried to hook us up, you're not the type of woman that goes to bars and hits on men. At least not often. The way you carry yourself with a sophisticated elegance tells me you're intelligent and care about your career. Most women who are half as stunning as you have body language that says they know every eye in the room is on them, but not you. You stare forward, looking at your drink, or during the best moments of the night, look over at me. All of it with the body language that you're not acutely aware that you're the most gorgeous woman in this bar. By far."

Good Lord. Who actually talked like that? And why was it working so spectacularly well?

"How am I doing?" Jace asked.

I shrugged, resisting the urge to push back on the claim I was the most gorgeous woman here. Something made me want to match his confidence.

"Not bad," I answered.

"I want to know more though."

"Such as?"

"Do you live in Chicago, or are you visiting?"

"Full-time occupant," I answered. "You?"

"I live near Chicago, but not close enough to commute home when work is heating up here. Staying in a hotel at the moment."

Hotel. With a bed. Stop imagining him lying on it naked, Scarlett.

"I should have asked this sooner," he said, his tone shifting to something more serious. "Do you have a boyfriend?"

"No."

"Good."

"That would have been a deal-breaker?"

"Never been one to cheat."

That one moral line drew me in even more. In the times I'd been hit on by men, if they asked about my dating life, none of them had ever made it clear cheating was off-limits.

"Have dinner with me."

Jeez, this man is nothing if not aggressive with what he wants. And I'm all for it, my hormones squealed, *especially if what he wants is me.*

"Again with the statements rather than questions." I smirked.

"*Will* you have dinner with me?" he revised.

"I don't know if that's such a great idea," I allowed.

Although, suddenly, once again, I couldn't remember why. And once again, a twinge of panic seized my stomach at the thought of him walking away and never talking to him again.

Worse, after all his persistent attempts to spend time with me —each one that met with my rejection—Jace finally seemed to accept the message. He took a sip of his drink, his expression shifting from hopeful to resigned. He sighed, his voice dropping an octave when he spoke again, the flirtatious tone replaced with unmistakable disappointment.

"May I have your phone?" Jace held his palm out.

Eyeing him curiously, I handed it to him and watched as he put his contact information in and handed it back.

"I hope you'll call, Scarlett."

What was I doing? I didn't want to let him go! Was I this much of a prude? Was Dakota right? Was I too stuck in my own thoughts to let loose and have fun?

Regret washed through me as he rose, and even though I had his number, there was something magical about tonight that might never be repeated again. He could leave, these feelings could cool, and I'd always wonder what would have happened if I'd just ... stayed.

Before I could think of what I'd say or do to unravel the worst decision I'd made since arriving at the bar, I rose to my feet too.

Only ... my high heel caught on the barstool's base.

Gravity betrayed me for the second time tonight. The second time in front of Jace, thank you very much, only this time, he caught me. Easily. Effortlessly. His strong hands held my forearms, steadying me, and as my attention drifted up his stomach, his chest, the beautiful base of his throat, and to his jaw, I found his smirk was back. The one that suggested he found my tumble utterly and devastatingly adorable.

"Are you clumsy, Scarlett?"

His fingers trailed up my cheek, tucking a strand of hair behind my ear, but he didn't stop there. His touch ghosted down my jaw, leaving a trail of heat in its wake while his focus drifted to my lips.

My heart beat its chant of yes-yes-yes as he stilled for several seconds, unable to look away, unable to step away, unable to release his fingers from my jaw. Instead, he glided his finger beneath my chin, and still staring at my mouth, he tilted my face up.

My body stretched higher, willing his mouth to come faster, but I swore to criminy, time decided to go all slow motion on me as those full, sexy lips inched agonizingly closer until finally, gloriously, they pressed to mine.

Heat exploded from my lips and traveled down my throat, my stomach, and shot right between my thighs. I'd never had this reaction to anyone kissing me before. Never. It was soft but charged with so much chemistry as his tongue trailed a line along my lower lip. When he slid his tongue past my lips, I actually let out a groan.

In public.

Dear God, this man could kiss.

I could kiss like this all night, all day, all year. His tongue was gentle yet dominant, his grip on my face growing firmer as he stepped closer and opened his mouth wider. Surrendering to his vortex, I reached my hand up and trailed my fingers through his silky hair. I wanted him to set me on the bar and bury himself in me. I wanted him to rip my clothes off and spread this magic across my body, my breasts, and my sex. I wanted to look him in the eyes as he buried himself in me.

"Please." His voice was rough with need. "Don't leave."

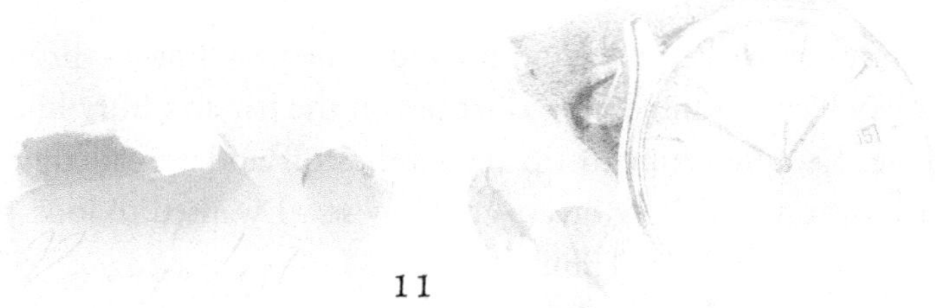

11

SCARLETT

The kiss evolved into something I'd never experienced before, with an electric current of need that only increased in strength the longer our mouths moved together.

And I certainly never experienced what came next. When our kiss deepened into an almost frenzy, rather than having my rideshare take me home, Jace and I got a taxi to his hotel. There, the kiss continued, only broken up when we needed to watch where we were walking. It was only when I was standing in front of his now-open hotel door that I wondered what the hell I was doing.

At the risk of coming off like a prude, I had never done this before. Don't get me wrong. I wasn't opposed to a one-night stand, nor having the gumption to sleep with a guy shortly after you just met him. If anything, I envied the women who were so free and confident in themselves that they would make those types of decisions, but for a brief moment, a small part of me wondered if I was being reckless.

Dangerous even. I didn't know this man, and I'd let him lure me to his hotel room.

Yet my instincts told me he wouldn't hurt me. We were in a public hotel, with shared walls, a phone, and plenty of places to run. My protective nature ceased and desisted, paving the way for the biggest question on my mind: Why was I doing this?

My life was a series of multistep plans strung together and organized around a goal. Hell, if I did relationships (which, again, I did not), I'd probably create a PowerPoint presentation and some sort of scoring list for men. And sadly, the only ones I'd ever be open to dating would be the kind you'd never marry. I wanted nothing to do with powerful men, thanks to my past, so that probably left the weak and unmotivated. That was a huge cup of *no thanks*, but I digressed.

All these years of carefully, strategically, exhaustingly working up the corporate ladder and going without much of a personal life. I was the girl who, when walking on a path, kept my eyes on the end of the sidewalk, on the destination for which each step was meticulously designed. I didn't just fail to smell the flowers; many times, I didn't even notice them along the way. Telling myself I could have fun tomorrow. I could watch that movie that had been on my list forever, make a sizable dent in my TBR, ride my horse daily rather than just on weekends, and do all the other things I had been sacrificing *tomorrow*. That today was about discipline and working toward my goal. Responsible, careful, and preplanned.

And for what? I'd missed all those flowers to find the end of the path, the career I'd sacrificed for, to be a mirage. A jackal in a suit who sabotaged what I'd been working toward.

Now, with Jace waiting for me with an open door, he beckoned me from my comfortable, predictable life into the unknown. Which made me realize something else: I had never embraced the simple act of being desired. This thing with Jace was me trust-falling into the opposite of everything I'd been. Led by desire and fun only. And you know what? I needed this. Like a cleanse of some sort. Uninhibited, don't think too much about this, just have fun, and have (hopefully) mind-blowing sex. Then, Monday morning, I'd go back to work and move forward in a constructive, thoughtful manner.

Tonight, I couldn't control if I'd be able to salvage the promotion that consumed my life to earn, nor could I control what HR did to Grabby Hands once I reported him. But I could control my reaction to flowers. And Jace was a stunning bouquet of my favorites.

All I needed to do was step inside his garden.

12

SCARLETT

"I'm going to ravage you." Jace pressed me against the inside of his hotel room door, his warmth radiating through my clothes.

A quick glance past his shoulder—and trust me, it was lightning fast with his mouth blazing a path down my jaw—revealed this wasn't so much a hotel room as it was a luxury suite, bathed in amber lighting that made everything feel dreamlike.

And, oh my God, the possibilities. With so many surfaces besides just a boring old bed. Which was perfect. The only place I'd ever had sex before was in a bed. Traditional, missionary, and if I was really doing this, if I was really pushing myself to get the hell out of my head and have some fun, then why not act out a fantasy or two with this sexy stranger?

And what a stranger he was. I loved that he was so tall, he had to duck his head just to kiss me, loved how his muscles rippled beneath that black shirt with every movement, building the anticipation of seeing what lay underneath. When his hand gripped my outer thigh, teasing the hem of my skirt higher with torturous slowness, his impressive erection pressed against me, making my breath catch.

The thought of him inside me sent heat pooling between my legs. Maybe I hadn't been with a man in forever, but that didn't mean I didn't want it. Heaven, did I want it? Going without a man's hands on my body, his tongue working magic while his eyes locked with mine, feeling him fill me until I cried out in bliss ... apparently, all those desires hadn't just been simmering on the back burner of my mind. They'd been smoldering, waiting for the match that would ignite them into an inferno.

"How do you like it, Scarlett?" Jace's lips traced down my collarbone as my skirt inched higher.

It struck me, in the best possible way, that he'd taken a moment to consider my needs. Not just his. The other men I'd been with had never done that. If Jace was even half as talented as his kisses in the sex department, the man needed no instruction, but my word, him asking me?

Okay, panties are officially ruined.

As a bonus, his consideration emboldened me to answer.

"I want you to taste me until I shatter," I breathed.

He groaned, the sound vibrating against my skin.

"And then I want you to bury yourself in me until I shatter again. Hard."

Jace's lips found my neck, his tongue trailing fire up my skin as his hand slipped beneath my shirt to cup my breast.

"I'm going to make you scream, Scarlett." His mouth captured mine again, hungry and demanding, his tongue sliding between my lips as he tugged my bra down and rolled my nipple between his fingers.

Yes. Hell yes.

I threaded my fingers through his hair, rolling my hips against his impressive length as I tugged at his shirt until he broke our kiss long enough to pull it over his head.

Sweet baby hippos. I'd known he was built, but this was straight out of a fantasy. Intricate tattoos embraced his torso, following the contours of his muscles like they were designed to enhance every ridge, every plane. Broad shoulders tapered down to a set of abs that had me contemplating a career change to professional body-licker. And since when was a belly button sexy? *Because hot damn.*

While I was busy drooling over his physique, Jace made quick work of my buttons, his lips trailing down my neck and across my collarbone until my shirt fluttered to the floor. He reached behind me to unfasten my bra, and when my breasts sprang free, his kisses blazed a path down my chest until he drew my nipple into his mouth.

I arched into him with a gasp as he swirled his tongue over the sensitive peak, his hands already working at my skirt's zipper. I kicked off my heels, standing before him in nothing but a scrap of lace that barely qualified as underwear. As he lavished attention on my breasts, jolts of electricity shot straight to my core, which was pulsing with need.

Reading my body like a master, Jace slid his fingers beneath the lace and groaned.

"You're soaked for me," he purred. "Good girl."

Oh. That was new. I would've thought, given my control issues with men, that being called *good girl* would've sent me running. But nope. In this context, with this man who'd taken the time to ask what I wanted rather than just imposing his will? It lit me up like a roman candle. Whether it was the moment, the man, or the way he balanced dominance with consideration, I got wetter from those two words.

And I got even wetter as Jace knelt before me, his eyes locked on mine as he slowly, torturously peeled my panties down my legs, drawing out the anticipation until I stood completely bare before him.

When he finally looked at my sex and traced a finger through my folds, I was practically dripping.

"Look how you glisten for me," he murmured, sliding a finger inside.

The throbbing between my thighs intensified to its own desperate heartbeat, so primed that I might shatter from this touch alone.

Grasping my calf with his free hand, Jace draped my leg over his shoulder and then ...

Holy mother of—

His tongue swept across my folds.

My head thunked back against the door, and when he circled my sensitive bundle of nerves, I nearly combusted on the spot.

Keep it together, Scarlett. Let it build.

Though maybe being the fastest orgasm in history wouldn't be the worst record to hold ...

"You taste like heaven, *Trouble.*"

Through the haze of pleasure, I registered the nickname. "Trouble?"

He gave me two slow, deliberate licks before explaining. "That list is trouble," he said, his breath teasing my sensitive flesh. "And you. You're definitely trouble for me."

His tone suggested I was a temptation he couldn't resist, a crack in his normally impenetrable armor.

File that under *Things That Shouldn't Be Hot But Absolutely Are.*

Jace's tongue glided up my folds once more before he sealed his lips around that desperate bud, swirling and flicking with devastating precision. The pressure and heat of his mouth sent shock waves through my body, each movement of his tongue a deliberate stroke against my most sensitive skin.

Trembling, I grabbed the back of his head and watched him work, my fingers tangling in his thick, dark hair. Here was a man, the most devastatingly handsome guy I'd ever seen, on his knees with my leg draped over his shoulder, his face buried between my thighs. His powerful shoulders flexed with each movement, the muscles in his back rippling beneath tanned skin and tattoos. The contrast of his masculine strength against his submissive position —servicing me, worshipping me—was intoxicating.

The sight alone almost made me come undone. Every sensory detail bombarded me with each swirl of his tongue, and the slight stubble of his jaw scraped against my inner thigh, leaving a delicious burn in its wake. His fingers pressed into my skin so tightly, they left white impressions that bloomed pink when he adjusted his grip. Those large hands that could easily overpower me instead anchored me in place for his mouth's heaven.

I couldn't tear my gaze away from the erotic sight. The length of his tongue circling, flattening, then pointing with meticulous attention. His lips puckering as he sucked that sensitive bud into his mouth with a groan that vibrated through my core. The sound was primal, hungry, like I was the most delicious thing he'd ever tasted and he couldn't get enough.

His hair bobbed slightly as he worked his mouth up and down, side to side, around and around while my thighs began to tremble around him. My skin flushed hot, then cold, perspiration beading across my collarbone and between my breasts. I could hear my own breathing turn ragged, punctuated by soft moans that grew more desperate with each passing second.

To my side, there was a full-length mirror that reflected us in the sexiest image. My naked form pressed against the door, head thrown back, one leg hooked over his broad shoulder. His hands gripping my thighs, spreading me open. My glistening folds with his tongue between them, his jaw working as he devoured me. The image was raw, carnal, and utterly mesmerizing.

My climax began to build with embarrassing speed from the dual assault of sensation and vision. Heat coiled tight in my belly, my legs quivering as tension built to an almost-unbearable peak. Usually, I squeezed my eyes shut during release, but something made me look down at this gorgeous man. Shirtless. His tattooed skin gleamed in the amber light as those green eyes—now darkened with desire to a deep forest hue—held mine captive.

He watched my face intently, studying every micro expression, seemingly memorizing how I looked on the edge of ecstasy. The intimacy of that eye contact pushed me over. I shattered completely, crying out his name as waves of pleasure crashed through me, my body arching and convulsing against the door. And through it all, Jace maintained his relentless rhythm, his tongue and lips working in perfect coordination to draw out every last tremor, every aftershock, until I went limp against the door, utterly spent and gasping for breath.

Rising to his feet, he wiped his mouth with his thumb, then sucked it clean with a wicked glint in his eyes as he removed his pants, revealing black boxer briefs bulging with desire.

"You taste divine, Trouble. Now get on the bed so I can take you."

I shook my head, still catching my breath, shocked I was bold enough to say this.

"Not the bed."

The bed was boring, and although I doubted Jace would make it boring, I wanted different tonight, and shockingly, felt comfortable enough to ask for it.

He arched a playful eyebrow. "Pick the place, Trouble, but choose quickly."

My core clenched at his words. Options, options ...

There was a massive glass table that looked sturdy enough to hold us, a plush couch, several chairs, even a mini bar. But the enormous mirror ...

Oh, yes.

It had me moving closer to it, to the couch. Jace groaned when he realized my intention was to watch us. After he removed his boxer briefs—and, holy hell, let me tell you the size of him made my heart squeeze in a small panic—he disappeared into the bedroom and returned with a condom, which he rolled onto his impressive length.

"Bend over."

I chose the side of the couch that would give us the best view in the mirror, spreading my thighs and leaning forward to grip the armrest. A flutter of nervousness hit me as I glanced back.

"I don't know if you'll fit," I admitted.

"Don't worry, Trouble." He lined himself up, the nickname sending a fresh wave of heat through me. "I'll go slow at first. But trust me ..." With one hand gripping my hip and the other guiding himself, he breached my entrance. A bite of discomfort made me instinctively tense. "Relax," he murmured, rubbing soothing circles on my lower back. "I've got you."

I focused on melting into his touch as he pressed forward, inch by delicious inch, stretching and filling me until I felt impossibly full. When he was finally buried all the way inside of me, we both groaned.

"I knew you could take me," he purred, his voice rough with need.

He held still, letting my body adjust, waiting for the slight burn to fade into pleasure. Yet another thing no other man had bothered with. When he finally pulled back and eased forward again, the sensation elicited a moan from deep in my throat.

"Look at us," he commanded.

I lifted my gaze to the mirror, and holy hell. The sight of him behind me, all rippling muscle and intensity with his jaw clenched as he gripped my hips, was almost enough to send me over the edge again. He looked barely contained, like a predator fighting his instincts, waiting for permission to devour his prey. In the sexiest, best possible way.

The fact that he waited, that he cared about my pleasure as much as his own, made me trust him even more. So, when the last trace of discomfort melted into pure need, I pushed back against him.

"Please ..."

Jace's control snapped. He pulled almost completely out, then filled me so wonderfully, I cried out as he found his rhythm. I had never been ravaged like this before, and instantly, I could feel a wave of pleasure building inside of me.

"You're so gorgeous, Trouble. Dripping for me."

I'd never been this wet, this desperate. There was something about Jace, like he was designed in a lab specifically to activate every nerve ending in my body. It was probably just because he was a stranger, right? It made me more uninhibited because I'd never see him again.

Whatever the reason, I lost myself in the sensation of him driving into me, in every bruising grip and sharp smack against my flesh. I watched his reflection, mesmerized by the way his muscles flexed, by the tightening of his stubbled jaw that betrayed his own approaching release. But what drove me wild was how he watched my face in the mirror, waiting for my pleasure before claiming his own.

I shifted my hips slightly, changing the angle to watch him sliding in and out of me, and the new position had him hitting a spot that made my vision blur. I crashed over the edge, so hard that my entire body trembled, so hard that I was no longer grounded on this earth but taken to a completely different plane.

With a roar, Jace's rhythm turned erratic. He slammed into me one final time and stilled, his chest heaving against my back.

"Holy shit," he breathed, pressing his lips to my shoulder blade. "I've never had anything like that."

Well, that was flattering to hear. Incredibly flattering actually, and I wanted more of him, more of this. We stayed connected, both sticky with sweat and struggling to catch our breath.

"You are going to be trouble for me, aren't you?" The wonder in his voice made my heart skip.

"Was this what I've been missing all these years?" The words slipped out before I could catch them.

"Missing?"

"I haven't done this in forever."

"No?"

"No," I admitted. "And never like this."

"Sounds like you had some serious pent-up sexual tension."

"Apparently." I laughed as he pressed another kiss between my shoulder blades.

"Shower?" he offered.

"Please."

"Scar?"

"Yeah?"

"After the shower, I'm going to fuck you again."

Well then, maybe trouble is exactly what I need.

13

JACE

"So, tell me about the guy." I traced my fingers along her spine, admiring how her blonde hair spilled across my chest like liquid gold.

"The guy?" Scarlett lifted her head, one eyebrow arched. The sheets were tangled around us, evidence of our latest round of passion. The city lights filtering through the windows cast a gentle glow across her skin.

"Revenge list guy."

"Pass." She dropped her head back to my chest, but I caught the tension in her shoulders.

"Oh, come on," I coaxed, threading my fingers through her hair. "The curiosity is killing me."

She chuckled, but remained silent, her fingers drawing lazy patterns across my tattoos.

"It might feel good to get it off your chest," I suggested. "And you'll never see me again, so what does it matter if you tell me?"

"That's fair." She seemed to consider this for a moment, then propped herself up on her elbow, her hair cascading over one shoulder. Her eyes met mine, and something in them made my chest tighten. "So, I'm in my boss's office, right? And he literally puts his hand on my thigh."

"He what?" I shifted up, the muscles in my jaw clenching.

"I know, right?" Her laugh was bitter. "I can't believe stuff like this still happens. At first, I tried to handle it with professionalism, but he just got more aggressive."

Anger began to simmer in my veins at the thought of someone touching her like that. Witty, funny, charming Scarlett. Scarlett, who made me laugh for the first time in forever and who my instincts said didn't have a mean bone in her body. Scarlett, who had kept my mind off work and had given me the best sex of my life. Who had been ravenous in bed, then sweet when she'd washed my back in the shower. The thought of someone violating her ...

My hands fisted in the sheets.

"When I finally got up to leave," she continued, her voice tight, "he threatened to hurt my career if I didn't come back and sit down."

"Fucking hell."

"I know."

"So, what did you do?"

A dangerous smile played at her lips. "I told him if he ever touched me again, I'd break his fingers. Then I went to the bar and made a revenge list about him."

"Jesus. You need to report him."

Her eyes flashed, and she pulled away slightly.

"What?" I asked, though I already knew I'd stepped in it.

"Respectfully," she bit out, "I'm perfectly capable of handling the situation myself. I didn't confide in you to get your advice. I told you because you were curious, and, yeah, maybe it would feel good to get it off my chest. But I don't need to be told what I should do. I'm very aware of that."

"Yikes." I trailed my fingers through her hair. "I really hit a nerve, didn't I?"

Her features softened into something like regret. "I'm sorry," she said, dropping back onto the pillow. "Hairpin trigger. I don't like men trying to control me."

Men trying to control me. I filed that phrase into my mind, wanting to dissect it and uncover its source, but resisting the urge. The last thing I needed to do was hit another nerve. I was having far too much fun with her to send her running for the hills.

I brushed a strand of hair from her face.

"In my line of work, people come to me with problems every moment of every day, and it's my job to give them solutions. Knee-jerk reaction. Please disregard and accept my apology."

Relief softened her expression. Her fingers found their way back to my chest, tracing the lines of my tattoos.

"So, what are you going to do?" I asked carefully.

"I'm going to report his ass." After a moment, her voice softened into something that bordered on despair. "He'll probably just say it was consensual."

"Does your office have a no-fraternization policy?" I shifted to look at her, CEO instincts kicking in despite myself.

"Yeah. Why?"

"There's a reason many companies strictly ban relationships between employees and enforce it," I explained, careful to keep my tone neutral. "Fraternization causes too many problems."

She stiffened slightly. "This wasn't a relationship. It was harassment."

"Exactly my point." I caught her gaze. "That policy will work against him and in your favor. He can't use breaking one rule as an alibi for breaking another. The moment he claims it was consensual, he's admitting to violating company policy. Either way, he's screwed."

A slow smile spread across her face, and something in my chest tightened at the sight.

"Okay, that's actually a really good point."

"Thanks. I have them from time to time."

But after a minute or two, her smile faded, and she sighed. "But he might claim I'm the one that came onto him. He's the superior, so he might claim I was doing it to get something."

I raised an eyebrow, but before I could offer any thoughts, Scarlett was already thinking out loud.

"If he does that, I'll ask HR why I, an employee with a spotless record, would suddenly do something so out of character and appalling. I've worked there for years and should have significant credibility."

"Good." My voice dropped lower, more intimate. "And for what it's worth, I believe you."

Something shifted in her eyes: relief, gratitude, and a flicker of something warmer. She reached up to cup my face.

I leaned down to kiss her, and within moments, the kiss deepened, sparked into a flame. We tumbled to the floor in a tangle of sheets and limbs, and I lost myself in her all over again.

An hour later, she stood up and got dressed, pulling her purse strap over her shoulder.

"Stay," I said, my voice low and urgent. "For the weekend."

She'd done an excellent job of keeping my mind off work. Off everything except her, in fact. My fingers ghosted over her arm.

She turned to face me, her expression caught between amusement and wariness.

"I don't do relationships," she stated flatly.

"Who said anything about a relationship?" I countered, stepping closer until her lingering perfume wrapped around me like silk.

Her eyes narrowed. "Staying implies it's more than what it is. This is fun—that's it."

There was a firmness in her voice, confidence in her posture. Scarlett was a woman who knew what she wanted and was beautifully emboldened enough to say it. There was something about her assertiveness that made me respect her all the more for it.

I held up my hands in mock surrender. "No relationships. I promise I won't fall in love. It's only two days."

"Fall in love?" She arched an eyebrow, that delicious smirk playing on her lips. "Now you're being dramatic."

I grinned, thoroughly enjoying our verbal sparring. "It's two days. After how much fun we had, do you really want it to end?"

"Fun," she echoed with a mischievous tilt of her brow. "Is that what you call this?"

"Sex is fun." Mind-blowing, earth-shattering fun.

Her laugh was pure melody, but when it faded, I saw the truth in her eyes: she didn't want this to end any more than I did. Maybe this was the best sex of her life too. The thought sent a thrill through me.

"Come on," I coaxed playfully. "Midnight on Sunday, you can turn into a pumpkin. I'll even arrange a carriage ride home."

My own personal Cinderella.

She wavered, fingers toying with her purse strap. I seized the moment, closing the distance between us to graze her jawline with my knuckles, thrilled when her mouth parted, her chest rising and falling faster than it had been a moment ago. Sensing she needed a nudge, I moved my hand to the fabric of her pencil skirt.

She didn't stop me.

Nor did she stop me when I lifted the hem of it slightly, grazing her bare skin with my fingertips. Instead, she locked her gaze with mine, as if challenging me to continue. Daring me even.

I didn't know what game we were playing, but I wanted to win if she was the prize. So, I slid my hand higher, tracing the inside of her thigh.

"I promise to give you the best two days of your life," I murmured, finding that sweet, slick heat I craved. That I needed to bury myself in, to feast on until she screamed my name.

Her gasp was victory itself. I couldn't hold back my smirk as I circled that sensitive spot, daring her to stop me.

"Stay." This time, it was a command, firm and resolute.

And this time, she dropped the purse to the floor. Surrendering to me.

I told myself I wanted her to stay because she was gorgeous, because this was the best sex I'd ever had. Who wouldn't want more of that drug before it was gone? That was what I told myself because it wasn't possible to fall for a woman this quickly. That didn't happen in the real world, let alone in mine ...

"We need rules," she said.

I smiled and pushed two fingers inside of her.

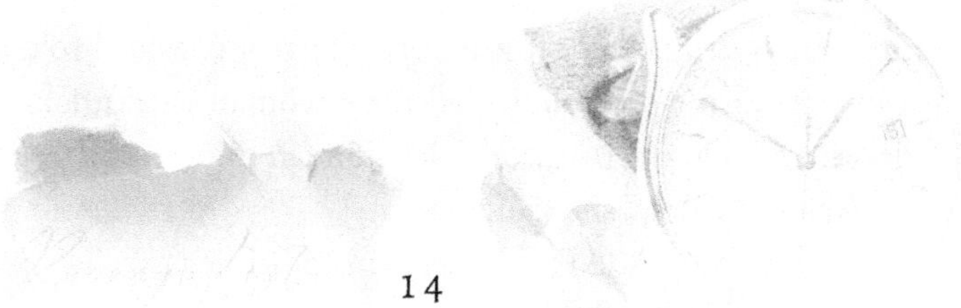

14

SCARLETT

"So, these rules," Jace said, trailing his fingers through my hair as I lay on his chest, our skin still sticky from what had to be record-breaking sex. "What are they?"

"Well," I mused, fighting the urge to purr like a cat under his touch, "this'll be two days of fun, no strings attached. Right?"

Because why not? I'd decided. Sex with Jace hadn't just been the best in my life; it made every other experience seem like an instructional manual by comparison. Besides, I had no plans this weekend. And this was far better than laundry, let me tell you.

"Mmhmm," he answered.

"So, rule number one: After Sunday night, we never talk again."

"Ouch. Is my company that abysmal?" His fingers never stopped their hypnotic movement across my scalp.

"I want to be crystal clear about expectations." I forced myself to focus. "This weekend isn't going to turn into anything. I don't do relationships, and even if I did, now isn't the time. My career needs my full attention. There's stuff going on that I need to handle, so I can't afford any distractions right now."

Jace's eyebrows rose, his lips curling into that dangerous half smile. “That’s some impressively firm honesty. And clear goal setting. So, this is a non-relationship agreement then?”

“Exactly.”

“You don’t do relationships. Can I ask why?”

“No.”

“If we’re never going to see each other again, what does it matter if you tell me your secrets?” His voice held a challenge.

I considered his argument, which was sound.

“Maybe,” I conceded. “But there’s a limit to what I’ll share.”

“And what’s the limit?”

“I don’t know. We’ll figure it out as we go, I guess.”

He kissed the top of my head, and I definitely didn’t melt.

“Okay.”

“Rule number two—”

“How many rules will there be?”

“I’ll figure it out as I go.”

His chest vibrated with a laugh that made my toes curl. “Of course you will.”

“We don’t just have sex.”

“Your Honor, I object to rule number two.”

“Very funny. I mean it. We need nourishment.”

His lips found my jaw. “Certainly. We can order room service.”

“I was thinking more like going out. We have twelve hours ahead of us today alone. We can’t spend all twelve having sex.”

“I respectfully disagree.”

“We can do other things for fun. Plus, I need to go home for clothes.”

“I can buy you a new outfit.”

“What, are you rich?” The words slipped out before I could stop them.

He tensed underneath me, his fingers freezing in my hair. Shit. I’d clearly hit a nerve. Now that I thought about it, the signs were everywhere: the luxury hotel suite, the casual offer to buy clothes. Whatever he did for work, he was successful enough to stay downtown instead of commuting to the suburbs. But why was money such a sore spot? Most men would flaunt their wealth.

"I just mean buying clothes instead of picking them up seems excessive," I backpedaled, but his silence spoke volumes. I propped myself up to look at him. "You know, one of the beauties of this being no strings attached is that I don't have to overanalyze everything I say. I clearly hit a nerve, but I have no idea why."

His muscles softened slightly.

"Want to tell me why money is such a touchy subject?" I challenged.

"Want to tell me why you don't do relationships, Trouble?"

"Nope." I popped the *P* with extra emphasis. "What I do want is breakfast. And since you're weird about money, I'll buy."

He smirked, and I couldn't help noticing how his abs clenched as he shifted.

Poor guy. Maybe he was one of those men who wanted to appear wealthy, but was actually buried in debt up to his eyeballs and couldn't afford anything beyond the appearance of riches. In other words, he was actually broke. That had to be why he was so sensitive to the money question.

"What if we did tell each other everything?" he mused, propping himself on his side. "It could be interesting, sharing things with someone we'll never see again. This no-strings situation might bring out honesty we wouldn't share with anyone else."

I cocked my head. "Why do I get the feeling you have an agenda behind that statement?" That damn smirk again. "Look, we can decide what we share as we go, but here's the new rule number one, which bumps all others down the list. Don't fall for me, and I won't fall for you. Got it?"

"That's an incredibly important boundary of yours."

"Iron-clad. Do you agree to the terms or not?"

"You're an excellent negotiator, Scarlett—"

"No last names."

Though that was silly, wasn't it? My last name wasn't what I was trying to protect. It was my feelings. And my spectacularly messy life.

"Now, come on." I hopped up, trying not to feel smug about how his eyes tracked my naked form. "Breakfast. On me. Then we're going on an errand."

"An errand?" He groaned, running a hand through his already-mussed hair. "This is supposed to be a fun weekend."

"It's a fun errand."

"Those two words don't belong in the same sentence."

"Okay, think of it more like a field trip. We'll have an hour drive to get there."

"An *hour*?" The look of horror on his face was almost comical.

"It's a beautiful day," I said, snapping open the curtains and gesturing at the cloudless sky. "We could use some fresh air."

He studied me for a long moment before sighing. "Fine. But we're taking my bike."

I blinked. "You have a motorcycle?"

"You find that strange?" There was that amused half smile again.

"You don't look like the motorcycle type." *You look like the* luxury car with a driver *type. But maybe your car got repossessed, and you bought a motorcycle in its place.*

"Helps clear my head." He crossed the room to me, planting a kiss on my temple that I absolutely refused to swoon over. "Besides, like you said, it's a beautiful day for a drive. And I get to feel your arms around my waist the whole time."

Something warm fluttered in my chest. *Dangerous territory, Scarlett.*

"I'm wearing heels and a skirt," I reminded him. "A *pencil* skirt. I'd have to hitch it up high as hell to fit on the bike, so I'd probably flash the entire city."

His mouth kicked up. "I'll give you a pair of sweatpants to wear." *Wouldn't fit, I'm sure.* "We can stop by your place to change."

Well, I mean ... I guess that worked. "Okay ..."

"So, where are we going?"

I grinned, already picturing his reaction. "That's for me to know and you to find out."

His eyes narrowed. "You're enjoying this."

"Immensely." I started gathering my clothes.

He caught my wrist as I passed, pulling me in for a kiss that made me second-guess ever leaving this hotel room. "But be warned, I have ways of making you talk."

"Is that a threat or a promise?" I started backing away playfully.

"Both."

Don't fall for him, don't fall for him, don't fall for him ...

"You can take me on your mysterious errand," he said. "But before we leave, I want one more thing ..."

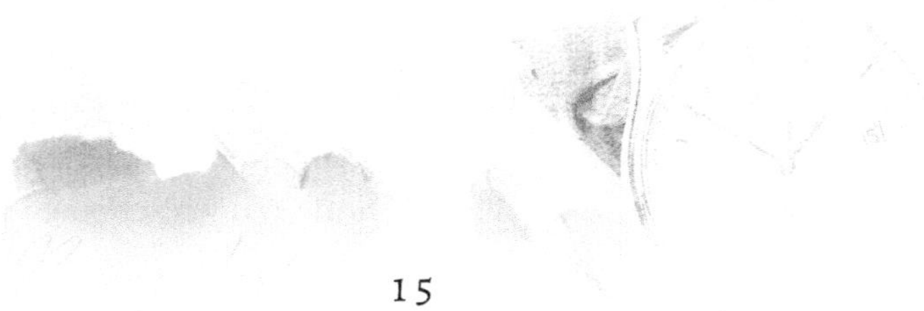

15

SCARLETT

Jace slid a silky tie from where it had been thrown over the chair. A tie, I noted. So, he was definitely a professional of some kind who wore a suit. When he approached me with that tie, I knew what he wanted, and instantly, my mouth went dry.

I took a step back.

He froze.

It was strange, to have this visceral of a reaction to something so playful. I mean, earlier, I'd done things with Jace that gave him control, let him take me in a way I'd never been taken before, and through it all, he'd been more thoughtful of my wants and feelings than any guy I'd been with. And yet, even with him, this was next-level trust ...

"I won't be tied up." The words came out more panicked than I wanted them to, but I would never surrender to a man like that. Never.

Jace went still, cocking his head. "I was going to suggest blindfolding you. You know, for fun." His voice was gentle, but something in his expression shifted as he watched me.

I took another step back, shaking my head. "No."

"I'm not into BDSM," he assured. "I don't normally do this."

Yeah, don't care.

"Well, being helpless and at the mercy of a man isn't my thing."

He didn't look offended. If anything, the slight arching of his brows suggested curiosity, like he'd noticed my reaction and knew it meant something deep.

"Okay," he said simply and turned to toss the tie back onto the chair.

But mid-turn, he froze. The muscles in his back tensed, and when he pivoted back to face me, his eyes studied me. With a calculated movement that spoke of confidence no man should rightfully possess, he raised the tie to his own eyes and secured it with a knot behind his head.

"What are you doing?" I wondered aloud.

He finished securing it and stood there, hands at his sides, palms out. "You don't want to give control to me," he realized aloud. "So, how about I give it to you?"

Somehow, he had the confidence to take a couple steps forward, guided by memory or maybe the sliver of light at the bottom of the blindfold. His hand found my hip, his touch sure despite his covered eyes.

A small gasp escaped me, half shocked, half aroused. No man I had ever been with was secure enough in himself to surrender like this.

"Why do I get the feeling that you never give up control?" I pressed.

"I don't."

"Then why are you giving it to me?"

"You need to be the one in control right now. I don't need to understand why to respect that. I just need to know it matters to you, and I want you to feel safe this weekend. I want to feel you let go, and if you holding all the cards is what you need to make it happen, so be it."

And that ... that turned me on like nothing else ever had before. Instantly, I was pulsing between my thighs, imagining him in whatever position I wanted him.

I glanced around the room, tempted to put him on the bed, but deciding that was too predictable and safe, too much like the normal me. Instead, I guided him by the hand and drew him into the dining room area, where I moved the bowl of fruit off the elongated table.

"Stand with your back against the table and hold on to it with both hands. Don't let go."

He didn't ask why; he simply complied, so I rewarded him by dropping to my knees.

"I've never gone down on a guy before," I said, easing his boxer briefs off.

"Never?" He smiled.

"Nope."

I didn't explain that pleasuring a guy had always felt a little too much like control. But now?

Now, this didn't feel like a battle for power. If it did, he'd just waved the white flag and given it all to me. Which meant I could just ... experience anything I wanted without the baggage of my ghosts.

I might have control issues, but I also had fantasies. Plenty of them.

"I've always wanted to try to deep-throat," I admitted, grasping the base of his shaft and watching his reaction.

He clutched the table harder, groaning.

Groaning that grew louder the moment I licked his crown, swirling the head. Jace was more well-endowed than any guy I'd been with (not that there were many), so I wasn't sure I could get him all the way in. But I'd try.

I swirled the tip several more times, coating him in my saliva before drawing my tongue down his shaft. Slowly, smiling when he'd twitch or let out a grunt of pleasure. Repeating the move up and down a few more times, I finally wrapped my lips around him and took him into my mouth.

One inch. Then two.

"Damn, that feels good," Jace said, his thigh muscles clenching as I drew him further into my mouth.

I got only halfway down his shaft before it hit the gag reflex, and I had to bring him back out.

Undeterred, I soaked him in my saliva and gripped his base, pulling him in again. This time, I went a little farther before I gagged, and the next time, a little farther still. I liked him filling my mouth. I liked the smooth, silky skin of his perfect length, and I liked training my throat to relax with each motion.

Jace was being a very good boy, holding still.

"You want to grab my head right now, don't you?" I smirked, licking his base.

"I want to fist your hair and claim your mouth," he admitted. But he didn't move.

"And yet you're not moving your hands." I kissed his crown.

"You told me not to."

"Good boy," I said, shocked at my brazenness.

I'd never given thought to the praise kink. Let alone the reverse one, but heaven help me, did that turn me on. And he was a good boy. He deserved to be rewarded.

I opened my mouth, relaxed my jaw, and sank my mouth all the way down his shaft.

"Damn, Trouble ..." he roared, throwing his head back as I started to move at the base of him. Keeping most all of him in my mouth while rocking up and down.

A fresh need pulsed between my thighs, wanting him inside of me, making me scream his name, but this wasn't something I could stop easily.

I liked this.

Jace, whoever he was, might normally be in control, but right now, I had all the power, moving up and down on his length. I could make him come. I could leave him hanging. I could do anything I wanted, and that made me wetter than hell.

I sucked and licked and moved, taking him into the back of my throat.

The sounds he made—raw, unfiltered groans that echoed through the room—stirred something unexpected inside me. This wasn't just about control anymore. Something shifted as I watched his chest rise and fall with each labored breath, as I felt his thighs tense beneath my fingers. For the first time in my life, I wanted to please a man. And I genuinely wanted to see him come undone.

My whole life, sex had always been transactional. A means to an end, a way to scratch an itch without letting anyone too close. Even with that one boyfriend I'd experimented having. But with Jace blindfolded and vulnerable before me, I found myself caring about his pleasure in a way that terrified and thrilled me simultaneously.

I wanted to be the reason Jace trembled. I wanted to be the one he remembered when all this was over. The thought made my movements more deliberate, more passionate. This wasn't just sex anymore; it was ... connection.

"If you don't want me to come in your mouth, you need to stop," he warned.

Hmmm. This wasn't my original intention, but a new idea took shape.

I took him all the way inside. His lips curled, his teeth clenched, and the veins in his neck throbbed as I sucked and moved, until finally, he started trembling.

"Scarlett!" he roared.

I could feel his release in the warmth of my throat, the trembling of his body, and I could hear it in the shudder of his breaths. I rode each tremble until it was over, licking up and down his shaft until every last drop was gone.

"Damn," Jace sighed, running a hand through his hair. "That was incredible."

"Lie on the table."

Jace felt the furniture. "It's made of glass. If we lie on it, it might break."

True. The safe, reliable, predictable thing to do was to avoid something that could literally kill us if it broke.

This was when I knew I'd gone slightly off the deep end. Willingly. Thrillingly.

"Lie down," I repeated.

Jace hesitated for only a moment, then did as he was told. He was tall, but thankfully, the table was long. Hopefully, that gave it more stability, but still. When I climbed onto it after discarding my undergarments, I watched for any hint that it might fail and we'd free-fall into shards of vein-slicing glass.

Straddling him, I looked down at the masterful body beneath me. Muscles chiseled from granite, tattoos wrapped around the skin like a pulsing work of art, and that jaw—holy hell, that jaw—that, suddenly, I wanted to feel beneath me.

I inched up, reveling in the smile Jace gave when he must've sensed what I was doing.

Positioning my knees on either side of his head, I lowered my sex to his mouth.

"Lick me," I demanded.

Groaning, Jace flattened his tongue and drew a long, slow glide up my glistening folds. Look at him. Wearing a tie as a blindfold and pleasuring me as I watched him. I didn't have to feel self-conscious of anything: not the look on my face or whether my stomach creased in an unflattering way. All I had to focus on was his masterful mouth devouring me.

He swirled his tongue around my sensitive bud and lifted his head off the table slightly so he could suck it.

"Oh ..." I moaned, cradling the back of his head, pressing his mouth harder against me.

While he licked, I ground on his face up and down, back and forth, circling his mouth. Not that he needed the help. Jace literally worked my body blind, but he hit all the right spots, inciting a fresh orgasm that began to build in my lower stomach.

"I like sitting on your mouth," I whispered. "But in a minute, I'm going to ride you until you scream my name."

He groaned, the vibration against my skin making the orgasm

inch closer, and then he thrust his tongue inside of me. I quivered, gasping at the sensation as he moved it several times before returning to the apex of my sex.

Throwing my head back, I caught a glimpse of us in the mirror again. More specifically, at Jace's body beneath me, my legs spread wide over his face while he feasted on me.

"Just like that," I said breathlessly, tangling my fingers in his hair. "Don't stop."

He didn't stop. He circled and circled until finally, the orgasm crashed around me. Around his mouth. Around his face.

And I cried out his name. "Jace!"

Holding my thighs, he kept me there until the last ripple broke free.

When it was over, he smiled.

"Get a condom, Trouble."

A condom. Right. Glad he remembered because, dear Lord, I wouldn't have. When I tell you I ran to his nightstand, I actually ran, ripped open that package, and rolled that protection on fast. Back on the table, I lined him up at my entrance.

And sank down.

Jace's fingers pressed into my thighs so hard, it might bruise, but I took all of him in. And then I began to rock.

The table threatened us, swaying slightly, so I eased my movements, pulling up and pressing down rather than slamming, all while rocking back and forth. At the same time, Jace filled me, stretched me, and hit every bundle of nerves both inside and out in the most unimaginably delicious way. I was having the absolute best sex of my life with this man, and I never wanted it to end. He made me feel so ... at ease. Comfortable. Sexy. Protected ...

"You feel so damn good," Jace said.

"What would you do to me?" I wondered aloud, rocking and feeling a fresh climax growing in my pulsing sex. "If I was blindfolded, what would you do to me?"

I placed his hands on my breasts, welcoming the squeeze.

"First, I'd lay you on the bed." Jace pulled my nipples between his thumb and finger, pinching them with a bite. "I'd glide an ice cube all over your skin and lick up the droplets of water. The ice cube would glide over your folds, and I'd taste that, too, before I'd pleasure you with my tongue."

Oh my ...

"If you let me," he continued, "I'd straddle your face and claim your mouth. Deep and hard."

My movements intensified, my sex warming impossibly hotter with each of his words.

"Then I'd flip you over and take you from behind. I'd hold your head to the mattress and pin your arm behind your back until you screamed through your orgasm."

"Jace!" I moaned, my body coiling tight as his words painted vivid pictures in my mind.

"That's it, baby."

The orgasm hit like a tidal wave: powerful, overwhelming, all-consuming. My legs trembled so violently, I could barely move, my inner walls clenching around him in rhythmic pulses. Sensing my complete surrender, Jace took over, his hips rising to meet mine, driving deeper with each thrust.

"I'm close," he growled, his breathing ragged beneath the blindfold.

I circled my hips, the movement sending fresh sparks of pleasure through my already-sensitive body. His fingers dug into my thighs as he thrust upward one final time. I felt him pulsing inside me as I clenched around him again, our releases perfectly synchronized, like we'd been lovers for years instead of hours. The intensity left us both gasping, sweat-slicked bodies pressed together, hearts racing.

For several long moments, we remained frozen in that position, neither willing to break the spell. His chest rose and fell, our breathing gradually slowing. The blindfold had slipped slightly, revealing just a sliver of his piercing eyes.

I could stay here all day, I realized. In this room, on this table, with this man I barely knew but whose body was starting to feel like home.

"Shit," he breathed, finally breaking the silence.

Indeed.

"Baby, you can blindfold me anytime."

I smiled, tracing a finger down his chest. "Good, but for right now, we'd better get to that errand I talked about."

"Your secret errand?" he asked, raising an eyebrow as he removed the blindfold.

"A little excursion. And something tells me you're going to be very out of your element with what I'm about to do."

Still smiling, Jace helped me off the table, and after I got cleaned up and dressed, he got himself ready and grabbed something from the hall closet.

Dear everything holy. Jace was wearing a fitted, long-sleeved black shirt that showcased his muscles, black pants, and sported a motorcycle helmet, tucked under his muscular arm. The type of helmet with a polished green face shield and sleek black exterior that would turn him into one of those thirst traps I was guilty of watching online, where all you saw was the muscular, godlike body, face masked so the man could be whoever you wanted him to be.

In my wildest fantasies—and, God, I'd had many about a bike-riding hottie—I imagined the guy beneath the mask would be a sex lord who knew my body better than I knew myself. I swallowed, trying to play the role of unaffected human. Based on the heat boiling my cheeks, I was failing miserably. Based on the slant to Jace's lips, he knew it too.

"You look like you're dressed for the city," I said. "Hope you're ready for some country."

His brow furrowed in confusion. "Where exactly are we going?"

I grinned, feeling the power shift. Now it was my turn to keep him guessing.

"Let's just say, those fancy shoes are about to get very, very dirty."

16

JACE

Waiting for Scarlett to perform her finishing touches of getting ready, I opened my phone and typed a message directly to Axel.

Me: Need your expertise. Time-sensitive.

Axel: My specific areas of expertise include tequila brands, luxury watches, and making women forget their own names. Which one do you need?

Me: The last one. Sort of.

*Axel: *skull emoji* HOLD UP. Is Jace "I'll Die Alone with My Stock Portfolio" Lockwood asking ME for advice about WOMEN? Dude, I'm totally screenshotting this.*

*Me: *middle finger emoji* I'm exploring a no-strings arrangement and have a question.*

Axel: I don't know whether to be flattered or check if the world is ending. The mighty Jace Lockwood, taking romantic advice from the guy you called, and I quote, "emotionally stunted with the commitment capacity of a goldfish."

Me: Have you ever ... had trouble walking away from someone?

*Axel: Oh, yeah. This one woman could bend her legs behind her head. Like a human pretzel. *pretzel emoji* Still dream about that flexibility.*

Me: Not what I meant. Ever develop actual feelings?

*Axel: *barfing emoji* Not once. That's your first mistake. Catching feelings is like catching an STD. Preventable if you're careful.*

Me: Your analogies remain disturbing as ever.

Axel: Wait. WAIT. You're actually INTO someone? The same guy who told me relationships are "inefficient business mergers with excessive emotional overhead"?

Me: I don't want these ... complications.

*Axel: Damn. All these years, I thought your emotional suppression meant your hardware was defective. *laugh out loud emoji**

Me: At least I don't need a spreadsheet to keep track of my "dates" like some people.

Axel: That spreadsheet is a work of art. Color-coded and everything.

Me: You're useless.

Axel: Yet you still ask my advice. Look, just because I don't do feelings doesn't mean I can't spot them from a mile away. And you, my friend, are in deep shit.

Me: Thanks for that stellar observation. Really helpful.

Axel: What can I say? I'm a giver.

Me: This conversation has been about as useful as a screen door on a submarine.

Axel: But seriously ... tread carefully with feelings. They have a way of ...

Axel: ... [typing message]

Axel. Never mind. Just avoid them.

I stared at my phone, wondering what he had been about to text.

But right now, it didn't matter. What mattered was that I was no closer to understanding or preventing this swelling desire to see Scarlett past this one weekend. And what, if anything, I was going to do about it ...

17

SCARLETT

"I've never brought anyone here before," I admitted, the words catching me by surprise, even as they left my mouth.

After grabbing breakfast, then a change of clothes from my place, we'd driven on his motorcycle all the way here. Holy hell, was that sexy, with my arms wrapped around his waist, fingers spread against his tight abs beneath the soft cotton of his shirt. He'd insisted I wear his only helmet, and as the wind wrapped around us like a promise of adventure, I couldn't help but admire how his biceps flexed as he handled the bike. Now, we were here, in the pasture, where I stood, stroking Buttercup's velvet nose while she nickered softly against my palm.

She was perfection, wrapped in a bow. A giant tawny goddess of unconditional love.

"Never?" Jace's voice held genuine curiosity, none of the mockery I'd expected.

"Never." I breathed in the sweet scent of hay. "It's kind of my safe space. When I come here, everything else just ... falls away. It's just me and my horse, feeling her love and giving it right back. Fresh air and freedom."

"Why did you bring *me* today?"

That was a seriously good question. The kind that made my stomach do a little cartwheel. I ran my fingers through Buttercup's coarse mane, buying time.

"I guess there's something liberating about knowing I'll never see you again. No pressure to turn this into something it isn't, you know?"

The logic had sounded good in my head, but as soon as I spoke the words out loud, an unexpected pain hit my chest. Why did the thought of never seeing Jace again feel less like relief and more like ... grief?

Must be the mind-blowing sex. And the no-strings-attached fun. That has to be what this is.

And that flicker of a grimace on his face—that had to be something I was imagining.

"So, this is your errand," he said after clearing whatever he'd considered saying from his throat.

"Every Saturday. Sundays, too, if I can. I want to come more often. To give her treats and take her out on the trails but ..." But I'd been working so many hours that Buttercup had often paid the price of getting less attention.

"She's beautiful," he said, reaching out slowly to let Buttercup sniff his hand.

"Wow, she normally doesn't like men."

"Is that so?"

"I rescued her," I explained. "Her last owner was a man who abused her." Lord, how many nights I'd cried, realizing what she'd been through. The only thing that comforted me was knowing I would never ever let anyone hurt her again. I'd sell all my possessions and live in a shoebox if that was what it took to maintain the expense of her. "She's everything to me." My voice wavered slightly.

Jace's eyes found mine, sharp and perceptive. A warm breeze ruffled his dark hair, carrying the scent of wildflowers and sun-warmed grass.

"Something's bothering you," he said softly.

Again, not a question. *This guy with his statements.*

I let out a deep breath, watching a pair of sparrows dart across the field.

"I could tell you, but you'd probably think it's silly. Especially with what other people are going through, not to mention what's going on in the world right now."

"Scarlett." The way he said my name made me look at him again. His emerald eyes caught the sunlight, making them even more mesmerizing against his dark stubble and sharp jawline. "Nothing you could say would sound silly to me."

That ache in my chest grew. Something I tried to swallow down.

"Horses are social creatures," I explained, watching Buttercup's ears prick forward at the sound of my voice. "The whole time we've been at this stable, Buttercup has had a best friend. Her friend moved last month to a stable not too far from here. It's like the Rolls-Royce of horse stables. Bigger pastures, more staff so the horses get more attention, more time outdoors rather than being trapped in their stalls, better riding trails, better views, better care."

"And you want to move Buttercup?" His voice was gentle, understanding.

This time, the pain swelling in my throat had nothing to do with thoughts of Jace and everything to do with guilt.

"I want to give her more than I can." Just like my mom. "That other stable is really expensive. More than I can afford." Yet another reason I'd so badly wanted that promotion: it would have given me the means to pay for that other place. "But every time I'm here, I feel like I'm letting her down. I can feel her sadness, missing her friend, you know?" My fingers traced the blaze down her face. "Like, I can imagine how it would feel to have your best friend taken away and not understand why or where they went. And as if that's not bad enough, now, without her bestie by her side, there's another horse that's kind of bullying her."

It struck me how parallel our existences were right now. Every day, Buttercup would wake up and worry about that bully horse, worry whether she would get bitten or kicked or chased from her favorite patch of pasture. And come Monday morning, I'd be worried about the same thing with Grabby Hands. He infected my space just like the bully horse infected Buttercup's. The only difference was that in my life, I had the ability to do something about it. I could go to HR, find some kind of recourse, but Buttercup ... she was just an innocent victim, vulnerable to my ability to protect her.

I didn't realize my eyes were watering until a tear escaped, trailing down my cheek. Jace stepped forward, his thumb gentle as he wiped it away.

"She has you," he cooed. "The amount of love you have for her is something she can feel. Hell, even I can feel it, and I've never had a horse. Had a hamster but ..." He grinned, breaking the tension. "That thing escaped its cage. We eventually found him with an Oreo in his mouth, but my mom never let me have a pet again."

Despite myself, I smiled.

"Someday, Buttercup," I whispered, pressing my forehead against hers. "Someday, I'll earn enough to move you to the better stable and reunite you with your best friend."

It was hard to let go of the emotion of that conversation, but I didn't come here to feel sad. I'd come here to give Buttercup attention and love, to give her the fresh air and exercise.

"So," I said, "I thought we could go for a ride?"

Jace's face fell. His attention snapped to Buttercup, then back at me, all traces of Brooding Sex Lord gone, replaced with horror.

"Both of us?"

"Of course." I bit back a laugh. "It wouldn't be much fun, leaving you here with the manure pile while I take her for her weekend trail ride."

"I'm fine waiting." He took a deliberate step backward. "I'll just ..." He glanced around desperately. "I'll commune with nature. Count hay bales. Contemplate the meaning of life."

I cocked my head, trying not to smirk. "You ride a motorcycle at eighty miles an hour, but you're afraid to get on a horse?"

"I'm not afraid," he claimed. "I just haven't done it before. Plus, I *control* the motorcycle. This"—he gestured at Buttercup, who chose that exact moment to snort loudly—"giant animal has a mind of its own. It could chuck us off, stomp on our face, and be back at the barn before we even bled out. Probably stopping for an apple on the way."

Smirking, I was already moving, gathering the equipment we'd need.

"I'm not getting on a thousand-pound animal with a possible attitude problem."

Buttercup huffed, as if she understood the insult.

"Buttercup is a perfect lady. She's thirteen hundred pounds of pure sweetness."

"That's ... not helping your case."

"And for the record, you'll be riding Turtle." I motioned to the beauty in the stall next to us.

Jace eyed the horse up and down, as if to assess its trustworthiness.

I tossed him a set of riding gloves. "You'll be fine. It'll be nice to get some fresh air. Besides ..." I arched a brow and deliberately let my gaze drift down his body. "I know a beautiful pasture where we could stop. Very private. No one around for miles."

"Are you bribing me with sex?"

"Is it working?"

The hint of orgasms was the only thing that made Jace pause. He eyed the horse warily, then the gloves in his hands, and finally me.

"Fine. But if I die, I'm coming back to haunt you, Trouble."

"Deal." I grinned. "And I promise to say nice things at your funeral."

After packing a blanket and snacks the barn manager let us have, we set out on a ride through the trails. With every rhythmic hoofbeat, every breath of wind through my hair, every whiff of lilacs and warmth of sun on my face, I found myself looking over at him.

Sometimes, I caught myself swooning. He looked like he belonged on the cover of a romance novel, with his fitted shirt pulling against the broad planes of his chest and those powerful shoulders on full display as he handled the reins. The midday light caught his dark hair, highlighting traces of gold I hadn't noticed before, and his strong thighs gripped his horse's gait. Sinfully attractive didn't begin to cover it. Women everywhere would swoon if they had the view I had right now.

But other times, I found myself smirking. Jace wasn't what I'd call a natural. He'd try to guide the horse forward, and she'd step to the right. I heard him cursing on more than one occasion, and even his horse seemed annoyed by his presence. I swear, horses sensed people who didn't know what the hell they were doing. To his credit though, he didn't complain. Not once.

But most of the time, I found myself staring at him with something dangerous blooming in my heart: longing. I'd never brought anyone out here before, but now that I had, it struck me how much his presence heightened this experience rather than detracting from it.

"Can I ask you a question?" Jace's voice broke through my thoughts as we got off our horses at the bluff over Lake Michigan. The water was a deep blue, crashing against the rocky shore beneath us, stretching out until it touched the horizon like it was reaching for its dreams. "What is it about horses that you love?"

"Everything," I said, the word carrying more weight than I intended.

"Name the biggest reason." His voice held genuine curiosity, not the casual interest people feigned when they were just waiting for their turn to speak.

I stood beside Buttercup, my fingers finding that sweet spot beneath her mane that always made her lean into my touch. The familiar warmth of her pressed against my palm centered me.

"Horses don't hurt you the way that people do. And they see right through you, you know? No games, no hidden agendas. When a horse trusts you, it's because you've earned it, not because you manipulated them into it." I scratched her side, finding comfort in the familiar motion. "Humans can use love as a weapon, but animals never do. They're pure. All they want is your heart, and they give theirs right back. No scorekeeping. No power plays. Just ..." I swallowed hard. "Just love. Feed them, shelter them, show them kindness, and they're yours forever. They don't wake up one day and decide to use that love against you."

Wow. I don't think I've ever said that out loud before.

Jace was quiet for a long moment. When I finally gathered the courage to look at him, I found his eyes not on the breathtaking vista, but fixed entirely on me. There was something in his gaze—not pity, which I would have hated, but a clear, unwavering understanding that made my chest tighten.

He stepped closer, close enough that I could smell the subtle notes of his cologne mingling with leather and pine. His voice, when it came, was low and intimate, meant only for me. "She's not just your horse," he realized, reaching out to brush his fingertips against Buttercup's neck, inches from my own hand. "She's your safe harbor. She's the only one you allow to love you back, isn't she?"

Something fluttered in my stomach. With anyone else, I'd be guarded about revealing anything personal. I'd be worried they could take this information and use it against me, use it to control me someday. But knowing that I would never see Jace again, it crumbled all those pretenses and worries and just let me be ... me.

"Someone hurt you," Jace continued, his eyes never leaving mine. "And whatever they did went deeper than whatever sparked that revenge list."

His perception sliced through my shields like they were nothing but morning mist. But instead of feeling exposed, I felt ... seen. Truly seen, maybe for the first time.

But I wasn't going to talk about that. Not ever. It was in the past, where it belonged.

"Come on." I cleared my throat and grabbed the contents for the picnic I'd assembled from the barn, setting it up in the gorgeous meadow. You know, the one I'd mentioned when I'd hinted at romantic things ...

18

SCARLETT

The picnic I'd procured from the barn manager in advance was perfect in its simplicity: fresh bread, cheese, and fruit, all spread out on the worn plaid wool blanket. Everything about the day felt beautiful: the sweeping view, the golden sunlight, the easy way conversation flowed between us.

With the horses secured nearby, contentedly grazing in the shade, we gravitated toward each other. The first brush of Jace's lips against mine sent a buzz of electricity over me.

Oh. My. God. Had kissing him always felt like this? No. This ... this was not the same as before.

Everything felt different right now, which both thrilled and terrified me. I knew it wasn't just my imagination or the scenic backdrop doing the heavy lifting either. Because something had shifted for Jace too. I could feel it in the way his movements had slowed, become more deliberate. The tender press of his lips as he traced my collarbone, the intensity in those emerald eyes as he carefully undressed me. But mostly, it was the way he looked at me.

This was more than just desire. As he trailed kisses down my stomach, his gaze never leaving mine, it felt like he wasn't just looking at me like a lover. It was like he was looking at my soul.

Danger, Scarlett. Danger, danger, danger.

My brain flashed warning signals, but my body had already surrendered the controls.

There were other tells something had changed. Like how, with every inch of my skin exposed to the unforgiving light, I should have wanted to hide. Instead, I found myself completely at ease, running my fingers through his dark hair as his mouth worked up and down my glistening folds. I arched my back as he spread my thighs even wider, claiming everything I offered.

"God, you taste incredible," he murmured against me.

I let myself sink into the moment, overwhelmed by the symphony of sensations. The whisper of the breeze across my heated skin, the rustle of leaves overhead, the distant rhythm of waves against the shore below us. Nature's melody mixing with our mutual, erotic moans.

Because that was the other difference. Before had been raw fantasy. This was pure romance.

Romance that could be felt in the tender way Jace's fingers slipped inside me, his eyes studying my face before his mouth returned to its sweet torture. It was in how he watched me over the curve of my breasts as I kneaded them, pleasure coiling tighter in my core. It was in the gentle but firm grip on my thigh as he held me to him.

"Jace!" I cried out, my back arching off the blanket.

"Let go for me, Scarlett."

And I did. Spectacularly. Like *seeing stars and possibly blacking out* spectacularly.

After, he crawled up my body with a trail of kisses that set my skin aflame, lavishing attention on my breasts before claiming my mouth. Slow. Deep. His fingers tangled in my hair as he pressed against me until I was aching for him.

"I want you," I breathed against his lips.

"You have me, Trouble," he replied, the words carrying a different meaning that I wasn't sure I wanted to acknowledge.

A flash of fear sparked through me that it wasn't just sex I wanted, but I pushed it aside, mesmerized by the sight of him kneeling between my thighs, his muscles flexing as he rolled on the condom he'd thankfully brought.

As he positioned himself at my entrance, he opened his mouth to say something, then quickly shut it, choosing to swallow whatever he was about to confess and opted instead to kiss me as he breached my entrance. Leaning forward, he swallowed my gasp, my moan, as he gradually filled me, stretching me in the most delicious way.

And when he started to move, finding his rhythm, it was unlike anything we'd shared before.

Tender yet consuming. His kisses along my jaw and throat felt like worship, like he wanted to memorize every moment, every sensation.

This is too much. Too good. Too ... everything.

With him buried inside me, his hips rocking against that sensitive bundle of nerves on the outside of my body, his massive girth hit the sensitive peak inside me, making another orgasm build fast.

"You're so beautiful," Jace murmured, his voice rough with emotion. "Everything about you is beautiful, Scarlett."

I wanted to deflect his profession with something snarky, but the words died in my throat. Just before I came apart, Jace captured my gaze with his. Eyes locked, watching, memorizing as I trembled beneath him, and with one final thrust, he followed me over the edge.

His forehead dropped to mine, our breaths mingling as we both tried to recover from whatever had just happened between us. Something stronger and deeper, something I wasn't ready to put a word to.

Afterward, we dressed and held each other, content to exist in this perfect moment. Eventually, we returned the horses to the stable and rode back to his hotel suite, where we spent the rest of the weekend learning each other's bodies and never speaking a word of what seemed to be growing between us.

When Sunday night arrived, I gathered my things and stood by the door with a smile, trying to pretend that the thought of never seeing him again didn't officially crack something inside of me. It took everything I had to hold on to my resolve.

Especially when Jace approached me, arms folded across his chest, his body language radiating uncertainty as he stated, "Scarlett, I want to see you again."

I want to see you too. But that's the problem.

"We had an agreement." If I had any hope of keeping that agreement, I needed to get out of this hotel room. Now. Before my irrational feelings could take the reins.

"Just think about it," Jace suggested softly. "Remember, I added my cell phone number to your Contacts when we were at the bar."

Great. Now the temptation to break my own rule wouldn't be behind me. Maybe I needed to delete that contact.

"This was fun." I offered a weak smile. "Seriously, thank you. This was one of the best weekends ..." I was going to say for a long time, but it struck me that, in fact, this was one of the best weekends of my life. Not that I would admit that. "Anyway, thank you."

"Scarlett ..."

I stepped forward and kissed his cheek, trying to pretend like the feeling of my lips against his skin wasn't pure magic, like my body didn't pull to him, like my chest didn't ache as I locked eyes with him one last time and then walked out of his life.

Or so I thought ...

19

JACE

"I want to go to her place." I knew where she lived, thanks to us picking up that change of clothes. And thinking of her entering that building in the dark of night, unprotected (not that it was a bad neighborhood, but sadly, anywhere women went could be dangerous) corded my nerves into a knot.

"Don't." Axel's voice was flat, brooking no argument.

I ran a hand through my hair, pacing the length of the room. The city lights twinkled beyond the floor-to-ceiling windows, but they felt hollow tonight. Empty.

"I can't let that be the last time I ever see her. Maybe I'll just call, make sure she got home safely."

She did give me her number before she left ...

"That's a bad idea." Axel lounged in one of my leather armchairs, looking irritatingly calm while I was falling apart at the seams.

"Why? She took a rideshare home. I should've driven her myself."

A knowing smirk played at Axel's lips as he swirled the amber liquid in his glass. "From what you just explained about your weekend, if you'd driven her home, we both know you wouldn't have made it back to your car until tomorrow morning. And that's being generous."

I opened my mouth to deny it, then snapped it shut. Exhaled. "Fine. I would've tried to."

Axel studied me like I was a rare species discovered in the wild. "I've never seen you get this worked up over anyone before. It's like watching a documentary on mating rituals. Fascinating and slightly disturbing."

I glowered at him. *Jackass.*

"You've known her for, what, two days?" His eyebrows shot up to his hairline. "You can't possibly become this obsessed with someone in two days. That's not even enough time to figure out if she's a morning person or if she squeezes toothpaste from the end or the middle like a sociopath."

"That's what I thought too." I dropped into the chair across from him.

"Tell me why she's stuck in your head." He pointed his glass at me. "And if you say it's her eyes, I'll pour this drink on your head."

I pressed my fingers to my temple, trying to organize the chaos in my mind. The scent of expensive whiskey hung in the air between us.

"I suppose it started with how we met. She was this beautiful, delicate-looking woman, but fierce enough to plot revenge fantasies against someone who hurt her."

Axel's eyebrow arched so high, it nearly disappeared into his hairline. He pointed his glass at me. "See, to me? That right there would be a red flag the size of Texas. Some woman plotting revenge? That's not fierce; that's the prologue to a true crime documentary."

"She wasn't plotting," I shot back. "She was just blowing off steam."

"How do you know that? For all you know, she could be some psycho who keeps her exes' teeth in a jar. Or collects vintage bear traps. Or has a shrine to you already with candles and your stolen napkin."

A smirk pulled at my lips. "Funny, that's exactly what she said."

"She admitted to the shrine?" Axel clutched his chest in feigned shock, nearly spilling his drink. "Quick, check your hairbrush for missing strands."

"No, you idiot. She warned me she might be a psycho."

"So, she tried to talk you out of hanging out with her again?" Axel nodded approvingly, raising his glass in a toast. "Smart woman. Self-aware. I like her already. Maybe she's too good for you."

"She did." I leaned back, staring at the ceiling. "But it was too late. I was already infatuated."

"Infatuated." Axel rolled the word around like the ice in his glass. "That's all this is. It's lust. You told me yourself that she's beautiful, and I can only presume she was really good in bed. That's why you can't get her out of your head. It's not rocket science; it's biology."

Part of that was true. The sex with her was like nothing I'd ever experienced. But was that all this was? Just lust?

"Yeah," I said, the words tasting like lies, "that has to be what it is."

Because he was right, wasn't he? There was no way I could develop feelings for anybody within two days. Hell, I'd never even been in a serious relationship. How would I know what the early stages felt like?

So, why didn't that feel like the truth?

"Plus," Axel added, pointing his glass at me, "you're used to women throwing themselves at you like you're the last helicopter out of a disaster zone. It's probably refreshing, having someone who tried to push you away."

"Damn it." I took another sip of whiskey, letting it burn down my throat. "Whatever it is, I can't stop thinking about her."

"It'll fade," Axel said with the confidence of someone who'd never let anything stick long enough to leave a mark.

"How do you know?"

"Because it always fades. Trust me. This is just lust. It'll go away faster than that hangover she gave you."

I worked my jaw from side to side, trying to swallow the angry retort building on my tongue. Out of anyone I could've called tonight, I'd chosen Axel for a reason. He was nothing if not consistent in his disbelief in love, as allergic to emotions as anyone I'd ever met. The very notion of a relationship was like a flu to him. Something you avoided at all costs, something you took action against at the very first symptom. So, yeah, when I found myself pacing after Scarlett left, Axel was the one I'd called to talk some sense into me.

Why then did his words piss me off?

"I'm going to call her."

"It's midnight," Axel said lazily, checking his watch. "Even psychos need their beauty sleep."

My stomach twisted. Why hadn't she stayed until midnight, the sarcastic timeline I'd set early on, when she could run away like Cinderella? Why had she left earlier? When we'd been together on that bluff overlooking the lake, I thought I'd caught something in her eyes that told me she was feeling this too.

"Tomorrow then."

Axel glanced at his watch. "Don't you have the big announcement tomorrow?"

Holy shit. I hadn't forgotten about it exactly, more like it had been shelved to the back burner of my mind. Somehow, the entire weekend had flown by, and the only thing that had consumed my thoughts was Scarlett.

Tomorrow was the big announcement that my private equity firm had acquired a new company. We'd kept the identity of the acquisition private for several reasons. First, it was a hostile takeover, and I never counted my chickens before they hatched. Second, there was still that crucial signature missing on a page, which I would insist on having *before* I took that stage in front of thousands of employees—some in person, some on live stream—to let them know that I was now the one in charge. The person with control over the direction of their company and their jobs.

"Trust me." Axel's voice cut through my thoughts. "You'll wake up tomorrow and feel differently."

"Will I?"

Axel set his glass down with a decisive clink. "You know what I think? I think this is the first time you've managed to go two days without obsessing over work, and that's the real high you're chasing. Two days without being Jace Lockwood, corporate shark. Must be a personal record."

"I love my job," I protested.

"Even sex becomes a chore if you do it eighteen hours a day."

The words hit too close to home. Maybe he was right. Tomorrow was the biggest day of my career after all. I'd bet everything on this acquisition, put all my poker chips into the center of the table, so to speak. If it imploded, for any reason, my entire business could crumble.

It was only natural to have nerves, right? Only natural for anxiety to manifest in strange ways. Maybe that was all this was: displacement. Easier to obsess over a beautiful woman than face the weight of tomorrow's announcement.

Besides, even if these were true feelings, if Scarlett ever found out the truth about who I really was, what I'd done in my past, she'd never want to talk to me again ...

20

SCARLETT

"Okay, that was the last thing I expected you to say." Dakota's eyes were as wide as the coffee cup clutched in her hands.

I shifted in my tiny seat, hyperaware of the five hundred other people packed into this makeshift conference room. The air felt thick with tension and whispered speculation. Up front, the empty podium waited beneath stark fluorescent lights, its microphone standing ready for the person of the hour. Any second now, our new owner was going to walk onto that stage.

"What can I say?" I toyed with my employee badge. "It was a wonderful weekend."

"Right, I got that." Dakota leaned closer, her voice dropping. "But this is you we're talking about. You don't date people."

"I didn't say I was going to date him," I protested, though my heart wanted to punch me for it. "I just said it was the first time I was ever considering it."

"Which for you"—she snorted—"is as big of a deal as if you showed up here, wearing an engagement ring."

"Please." I rolled my eyes. "You think I'll ever get married?"

"Maybe you'll change your mind."

"I highly doubt that." I smoothed my skirt for the tenth time since we'd gotten down here. "A marriage is a legally binding agreement, and the vows, I'm pretty sure, say something along the lines of love, honor, and 'OBEY.' " I made air quotes around *obey*. "As if I would ever agree to that."

"I'm pretty sure most wedding vows are more modernized these days."

"Not the point." I drummed my fingers on my coffee cup. "Not getting into a legally binding agreement with a man."

"Remind me why you don't want a happily ever after with someone?" Dakota asked. Though I couldn't tell if she was asking sincerely or asking in that way friends did when they were trying to get you to see something in a different light. "From what you've told me, you've encouraged your friend Tessa to be with that Blake guy, so you must not be against relationships in general. But you're against them for you?"

I worked my lower lip between my teeth.

"Do you think you're not deserving or something?" she questioned.

"That's not it at all," I assured. Self-worth wasn't the issue. "It's a power thing. Dating gives a man power over me, and I refuse to give anyone that power."

"Power?" Dakota's worry line appeared between her brows as if my profession alone caused that wrinkle. After a few seconds, she waved her hand dismissively. "Okay, forget weddings. Let's get back to the point at hand. You had a fantastic weekend, he gave you his number, and you're thinking about calling him?"

"A little." The admission felt like pulling teeth, but calling him again didn't mean officially dating, right? Maybe we could find a way to spend time together, like we had this weekend, without it being a thing?

"Wow." She raised an eyebrow. "So, what makes this guy so worthy?"

I chewed my lip, considering. "He's incredibly disarming. Like, this weekend, at first, I thought he wasn't used to giving up control. That was the total vibe I was getting. I mean, he basically said as much." The memory of his fingers tracing my skin flashed through my mind. "But maybe he just wanted me to think he was in control at first because that's what most women go for. And he didn't realize that power was a complete turnoff."

But once he did realize it was a hard limit for me, he handed that control over without question. That one act said everything. He was confident enough to surrender the reins while respecting me enough to do it willingly.

"You know," Dakota said carefully, "power doesn't mean controlling. Not all guys are like your dad, Scarlett."

My cheeks burned. I could tell she regretted the words the instant they left her mouth. I didn't know why I shared so much about my past when Dakota was so guarded about hers. Hell, I felt like I knew everything about her life except the fundamentals. I was pretty sure she had a brother based on some comments, but there was something dark and twisty behind that relationship.

It was strange how you could know virtually everything about someone, know what made them tick, finish their sentences, and yet have huge gaps in their history. And more importantly, not know why they kept it hidden from everyone. Including you.

Then again, look at me. I'd only told her the broad strokes of my father. Abusive. Controlling. I'd never told her about specific examples. Like how he took Mom's keys the day she was sick so she couldn't go to the doctor. Or how he'd steal her wallet so she'd have no money. Or how he'd sometimes use a shoe to beat her. A boot, to be exact.

"Sorry." Dakota winced. "I didn't mean to bring up your dad."

"No, it's okay." I forced a smile. "You're right. I'm well aware of what land mines he planted in my psyche."

"So, back to Prince Charming." Her eyes sparkled with mischief. "If he's this unassuming guy, maybe he *is* someone you can explore a relationship with?"

"Maybe," I admitted, fidgeting with my badge. "I don't know. He's just ... different. Not trying to impress me or control the situation. Like this weekend, when I insisted we go horseback riding, he went even though it was the last thing he wanted to do."

I smiled despite myself, remembering how he'd looked up at me from the ground after falling off on the ride back.

"It was kind of nice, you know? Just being equals."

Because in the limited experience I'd had with dating, watching some relatives navigate relationships, not to mention my parents, there seemed to be an inherent power struggle that, all too often, favored men.

But with Jace, that power dynamic hadn't been there at all.

"Speaking of power," Dakota whispered, glancing around, "what time is your meeting with HR?"

I frowned. "This afternoon. Evidently, this morning is jam-packed with this announcement." Anxiety churned in my stomach. "Feels like I have to fight for my job twice as hard now. Once because of Grabby Hands saying God knows what before I have a chance, and again because whoever this new owner is, they might walk on that stage and fire all of us."

"That would never happen."

"Wouldn't it?" I arched my brow.

"Okay, it does happen sometimes, but I'm sure you're fine."

"I bet you've never been happier that your social media side hustle turned into an empire." I nudged her shoulder.

Dakota was putting in her resignation by the end of the year, waiting until her influencer career "stuck." She was a marketing genius who had amassed millions of followers in a short time. When the brand deals started rolling in, earning her more than her salary here, I'd once asked her why she hadn't already quit. Her answer was pure Dakota: "You don't jump off the train at the first glimpse of success. You time it to make sure the train doesn't crash."

"Ladies and gentlemen, if I could have your attention." A redhead in a pristine white suit stepped up to the microphone.

I'd never seen her before. Probably from the new company.

"I still cannot believe this is happening," I whispered. "I had to Google the term *hostile takeover*. I can't believe a company can be bought against its will."

Our current owners didn't want to sell, but it turned out, that didn't matter. Some new owner swept in and stole the company right out from under them.

"I mean, what kind of a terrible person does that? Purchases a company that doesn't want to be sold?" I couldn't imagine a bigger dick in the world. Like the corporate equivalent of the Grinch himself.

"I don't know, but whoever this guy is, I heard that he's a major bosshole. Legend has it that if he smiles, global warming will end."

I shot her a look.

While the new owner had successfully kept his name hidden behind an impenetrable wall of NDAs, his reputation apparently preceded him. Rich, obviously. Powerful, clearly. And one other nugget of intel women wouldn't shut up about: At every company he'd acquired, women fell at his feet, only to be rejected and turned away. That told me he was probably hot, but also that he thought no one was good enough for him.

Either way, it was time to meet our "god."

His silhouette emerged behind the lights, and as he stepped to the podium, he straightened his jacket until finally, the light hit his face.

"Holy shit," Dakota non-whispered.

Everyone in our row turned to look, but I barely noticed, too busy watching my weekend of freedom crash and burn.

Because there, standing at the podium in an impeccable suit, those green eyes scanning the crowd, was Jace. The man who'd spent the weekend making me feel powerful, in control, and free ... was, undoubtedly, the one thing I feared most:

My boss.

21

JACE

The marble floors of the room echoed with each of my measured steps. Another acquisition, another company to turn around. This was what I did best.

"This acquisition has to go flawlessly." Marcus ran a hand through his salt-and-pepper-tinted hair, his usual composed demeanor fractured. In all our years of friendship, I'd never seen him this rattled.

"The paperwork's signed," I said, adjusting my cuff links. Why wasn't he as relieved as I was that the guy had signed that missing page an hour ago? "What's got you looking like you just shot espresso straight into your veins?"

"You heard what he said when he signed. He'll be watching. Closely. We already have enough pressure from our investors and the board. We convinced them the leverage was worth it, but they backed it on the condition everything runs smoothly." Marcus pulled me aside, his voice dropping to barely above a whisper. "And with that morality clause—"

I clenched my jaw. "Which has been in other contracts."

"Not like this one." He glanced around the empty hallway. "The seller's out for blood, Jace. They're looking for any excuse to blow this deal up. So is the board for that matter; they didn't want this one."

"We've taken on low-profit projections before."

"If anything happens ..." He swallowed hard. "The board will replace you. The company you built from nothing will be gone."

The past clawed at the edges of my mind, but I shoved it back down.

A petite brunette from HR appeared. "Mr. Lockwood? They're ready for you."

I squeezed Marcus's shoulder. "We'll finish this later."

As I strode toward the stage, my head of HR buzzed in my ear like an anxious bee.

"They're nervous, Mr. Lockwood. And some are angry."

"Once they research my company, they'll realize we *save* jobs."

"Right, well, the current sellers haven't exactly painted you as their savior."

"Fantastic." I straightened my tie. "Because that's exactly what I need. All these people preprogrammed to hate me."

"Just ... reassure them. And don't give them a reason to dislike you more. We need them to be on your side. We want no complications. No problems."

"Understood."

I walked onto the stage, projecting the confidence of someone born to lead.

Until one set of eyes stopped me cold. *What in the holy hell?*

Scarlett. The woman who'd spent the weekend driving me absolutely wild, who'd blindfolded me and made me beg, whose taste still lingered on my tongue, was staring back at me. Her shocked expression mirroring my own.

22

SCARLETT

I swear to hell, my heart left the room. Ran away screaming, leaving my body behind to deal with this unimaginable new reality.

No. No. Dear sweet baby Jesus, no.

Any hope of becoming invisible evaporated when Jace's eyes found mine in the crowd, like out of five hundred people, his internal GPS had decided I was true north. Because of course it did.

Universe: 1, Scarlett: 0.

Some women might squeal at catching the hot CEO's attention. Maybe flip their hair, shoot knowing glances at their besties, and start planning their power-couple Instagram aesthetic. Me? I was calculating the fastest route to the nearest toilet before my breakfast made an unauthorized public appearance.

This was my worst-case scenario, wrapped in a nightmare wearing a designer suit. Because one weekend of no-strings-attached fun had just turned into a tangled web of *oh shit, what have I done*. The universe wasn't just laughing at me. It was rolling on the floor, crying tears of joy at my expense.

My carefully constructed world of independence was crumbling beneath me.

I'd spent my entire life calculating every single step with one singular purpose: to never let a man have any control over me. Having a successful career meant financial freedom, and financial freedom meant no man could ever hold power over me like my dad held over my mother, who lacked the financial resources to leave her abuser. My career was my freedom. My safety net. My everything.

And now? The guy who'd seen me naked less than twelve hours ago had the power to destroy it all.

He could take away my paycheck. He could take away my ability to pay for my rent, keep a roof over my head. Not to mention my mom's. He had the power to take away my ability to keep Buttercup fed and happy. Worst case, and this thought was making the instant thundering of my heartbeat slam even harder, I wouldn't even be able to find a new owner for her in time, and she'd get slaughtered because when people couldn't afford to take care of horses anymore, there wasn't an animal shelter on the corner you could drop them off at, and—

"Good morning." His voice carried through the room with wavelengths made of sex. "I'm Jace Lockwood."

"Holy crap." Dakota's eyes widened, and for a second, I swore there was something more behind her reaction than just shock about my weekend.

But I couldn't focus on it long enough to figure it out. I was too busy, you know, having a panic attack.

"Scar?" Dakota's voice was echoing in my head. A seriously bad sign.

So was the cold sweat on my forehead and the rebellion brewing in my stomach. I bet I wouldn't even make it to a countdown from ten before catastrophe happened.

Ten. I stood, eyeing the escape route through ten people on my left.

"Excuse me, need to get by."

Don't throw up. Don't throw up.

Nine.

"Scarlett?" Dakota whispered.

Sorry, can't talk. Emergency evacuation in progress.

Eight. I tripped over someone's legs. Fantastic. Nothing said professional like stumbling through a company meeting.

Seven.

I could feel eyes on me, so many eyes, but I couldn't bring myself to look up at that stage.

Six.

Finally, I broke free from the aisle and ignored the glowers as I speed-walked toward the door.

Five.

I hated that I was racing out of here. Because make no mistake, I was not racing out of here with my tail between my legs. It was just that the only thing more pathetic than the current state of my life would be vomiting in front of five hundred people.

Four.

I made it out of the room.

Three.

I opened the ladies' room door.

Two. I made it to the stall.

One.

Liftoff.

After my stomach finished its exorcism, I slumped against the cool tiled wall. Note to self: Ask Blake, Tessa's doctor boyfriend, why the stomach was basically anxiety's personal punching bag.

After cleaning myself up, I stared at my reflection in the mirror, wondering how the hell this happened. Here I thought the biggest problem at work today was gonna be a meeting with HR. Now I had a whole new problem:

That HR team now reported to Jace.

And I had no idea what was about to happen ...

23

JACE

SINNERS AND SAINTS GROUP CHAT

Blake: Congrats on the acquisition, Jace. Saw the press release. Another company falls to the Lockwood empire.

Ryker: I take it, you survived the weekend without committing felonies against your board members?

*Axel: More importantly, he spent the ENTIRE weekend with ONE woman. TWO DAYS. Same woman. *mind blown emoji* *calendar emoji* *question mark emoji**

Me: Shut up, Axel.

Ryker: The entire weekend?

Me: Have you nothing better to do than comment on my love life? Blake, don't you have someone's spleen to remove? Ryker, no legal briefs to alphabetize by shade of pretentiousness?

Ryker: Ohhh it's a "love life" now. Let me get my popcorn and sit back for this. [attaches GIF of man eating popcorn]

Blake: Don't listen to them, Jace. They don't know what true love feels like. Some of us remember what emotions are.

*Axel: True love? *barfing emoji* You've changed, Blake. I miss the emotionally stunted ER doctor who used to threaten my life with creative medical instruments.*

Blake: Only YOUR life, Axel. The CDC has a dedicated task

force with your photo and "approach with hazmat suit" stamped on it.

Axel: I'm careful, Dr. Buzzkill. My last STD test was so clean, they framed it at the clinic. Probably hanging in the lobby as inspiration.

Me: I have a problem.

*Axel: He has feelings for her. *laughing emoji* Someone check his temperature. Jace.exe has encountered an error. Have you tried turning yourself off and on again?*

Blake: After just one weekend?

Axel: That's what I said! Next, he'll be shopping for minivans and practicing dad jokes in the mirror.

Me: She works for the company I just acquired.

Ryker: Sexual harassment in the workplace is nothing to sneeze at. As your unofficial legal counsel, I advise backing away slowly while maintaining professional eye contact. As your friend, I advise changing your name and moving to Fiji. I know a guy.

Me: Thanks for the legal analysis, Counselor Obvious, but this is a bigger problem. I can't let anyone at work find out about us.

Axel: Notice he's talking about "us" like it's present tense. THAT's your problem, Jace. Make it past tense. Extinct species. Fossilized remains. Whatever they called failed relationships during the dinosaur age. Hieroglyphics of stick figures walking in opposite directions.

Me: Shut up, Axel.

*Axel: Whatever you say, CEO of Unwanted Emotions, Inc. Should I prepare the IPO for your feelings, or are you keeping them private for now? *smirking emoji**

Ryker: If you can't let anyone find out about you two, you know what you need to do.

Me: It'll hurt her feelings.

*Axel: Read your last text again. Now pretend you're the billionaire OWNER of a massive corporation who has a responsibility to his employees and investors. Oh, wait. You are. *mic drop emoji**

He was right. I did have a major responsibility here. But this weekend, I'd let her see my softer side.

Me: She hasn't seen my CEO side before.

Blake: That sounds vaguely terrifying.

Axel: Then put your shark fin on and get it over with, Jaws. Rip the Band-Aid off before you find yourself picking baby names and browsing real estate listings.

Ryker: For what it's worth, proper documentation of the relationship with HR could mitigate most legal risks. Just saying.

Axel: Or ... and hear me out ... he could NOT date an employee and avoid the entire dumpster fire of workplace romance. Revolutionary concept, I know.

Me: I'll handle it.

*Axel: I'll be over here with my popcorn, waiting for the inevitable fallout text. *popcorn emoji* *explosion emoji* *funeral emoji**

Blake: Good luck, Jace. And remember, some things are worth the risk.

Axel: Don't listen to him. He's been infected with the emotional virus. It's terminal.

Great. Ryker was right about protecting this company, and I knew what I had to do. The problem was, Scarlett wouldn't like it one bit. Worse, no matter how much a CEO like me shouldn't worry about it, I didn't want to hurt her.

Maybe she wouldn't be hurt though? Scarlett was a fierce, smart woman. Maybe she'd understand ...

24

SCARLETT

Operation Avoid Jace Lockwood was in full swing.

It started the moment I slunk back into that *hey, everyone, meet your new overlord* meeting, where I kept my eyes glued to the floor, which, as it turned out, was harder than I thought. In fact, I made the mistake of looking up once. You know, how you do when you drive past a car crash? And BAM. His eyes snapped on to mine with a sultry, dark look. Was that anger in his gaze? Shock? Delight? Didn't matter.

Nope. Not at all.

In Jace's defense, he worked the room like the corporate god he apparently was. All easy confidence and measured authority, his voice a perfect blend of *I'm definitely in charge* and *but I'm not going to be a dick about it*. The same voice that had whispered filthy promises against my skin just hours ago—

Focus, Scarlett.

The second that meeting ended, I channeled my inner speed walker (was that a thing?) past the water cooler, down the hall, taking the stairs two at a time (because elevators were death traps of potential Jace encounters). I didn't stop until I reached my tiny second-floor office—aka my fortress of solitude—where I collapsed into my chair and started mutilating my perfectly manicured nails.

And let me be crystal clear about Operation Avoid Jace Lockwood: I wasn't running away from him. I wasn't hiding. I was strategically avoiding, thank you very much. There was a difference. Running away was what you do when you're scared. Avoiding is what you do when your carefully constructed plan to handle a sexual harassment complaint gets detonated by the nuclear bomb of discovering your weekend fling is now your boss's boss's boss's boss.

A girl needed a minute to process that kind of plot twist.

And, no, I wasn't spiraling about any potential relationship with Jace. That ship had sailed, crashed, and sunk to the bottom of the ocean. A fact I could properly mourn later tonight with a bottle of wine. This was about my career. My future. My ability to walk into this building without wondering if today was the day everything imploded.

Because here was the thing about having your new CEO's tongue inside you: It really complicated workplace dynamics. Especially when said workplace had a strict no-fraternization policy. Sure, technically, we hadn't violated it. Unless *didn't know you were my future boss when we were doing unspeakable things to each other* counted. God, HR probably had a whole chapter about that somewhere.

But the sex wasn't even the worst part. No, the worst part was those quiet moments when I'd let my guard down. When I'd told him things. Real things. About loving animals because they'd never hurt you. About how I didn't do relationships. And, oh yeah, that tiny detail about being sexually harassed by someone at his company.

My stomach clenched. It was ridiculous to worry he'd side with Grabby Hands over me. I mean, what was I to Jace Lockwood? A weekend distraction. A complication in his bazillion-dollar merger. A girl who'd—

No. Stop. This isn't about feelings. This is about my career. Period. End of story.

I just needed to focus on my HR meeting. One task. Alert them about the slimeball in their ranks. I could do that. I had to do that.

Besides, Operation Avoid Jace Lockwood had one massive advantage: He was executing a major corporate acquisition. Day one. His schedule would be packed tighter than a Manhattan subway at rush hour. The fact he'd spent the weekend with me instead of prepping for today probably just proved how routine these takeovers were for him. How many companies had he consumed? How many lives had he casually reorganized over breakfast meetings?

But none of that mattered. The point was, he'd be too busy for random hallway encounters in this massive building. Thank God. Because with my world tilting on its axis, the absolute last thing I could handle was—

"Scarlett?" A redheaded woman materialized in my doorway like some harbinger of doom.

I stood, plastering on my best *I'm totally not having an existential crisis* smile and extended my hand. She ignored it.

All righty then. Maybe these new company people aren't the friendly type.

"Mr. Lockwood would like to see you in his office." Her tone could have frozen Antarctica over.

And just like that, Operation Avoid Jace Lockwood went down in flames.

25

SCARLETT

"He wants to see you in his office?" Dakota's eyes rounded.

"In fifteen minutes." I eyed the clock like it was a ticking bomb.

"What do you think he's going to say?"

I dragged a hand through my hair. "No idea. Based on the look he gave me from the stage, he was as shocked as I was about this little plot twist. Probably wants to do damage control. Tell me to pack my bags." My laugh came out hollow, the kind that belonged in a haunted house soundtrack. "That's the worst-case scenario bouncing around my panicking brain right now."

"He's probably panicking a little bit too."

"He has no reason to panic." I started reorganizing my desk for the third time because nothing says *I'm totally fine* like alphabetizing your paper clips. "He owns the company. I'm the one whose career is dangling by a thread. Would it have killed him to give me one day to process before summoning me to his office?"

Dakota tapped her fingers against my desk, a human metronome counting down to my demise.

"Was I imagining it, or were you more shocked than I was to see him?" I questioned.

Her lips thinned. "I should have recognized him at the bar,

but it's been so long. When he said his name onstage, it clicked. He's ... an old family friend."

"Wait, you *know* him?" I practically shrieked.

"Not really," she said quickly, shaking her head. "I think I met him a couple times, over a decade ago. Look, this isn't the headline here, and it's completely irrelevant to what's happening now." She shifted in her seat, clearly uncomfortable. "Back to you and your crisis."

I stared at her. Dakota knowing Jace, even barely, felt like too much of a coincidence. But something in her posture told me to back off, and honestly? I had bigger problems. Maybe I'd circle back to this when my world wasn't imploding.

"Anyway," she said, "maybe it's good to get the awkward conversation over with?"

It took me a second to fully focus back on the problem at hand.

"What if it's not just awkward?" I challenged.

"What do you mean?"

"I'm kind of a liability to him." My stomach rolled with a fresh wave of unease. "What if he's going to demand I resign?"

Note: She didn't say that'd never happen. Instead, she took a beat. A long one. The kind of pause that made you wonder if she was mentally updating your résumé for you.

"Okay, look." She finally spoke. "There's no sense spiraling through worst-case scenarios."

"I don't want this to be the reason I lose my career, Dakota." My voice cracked. "I've worked so hard, fought against so many obstacles. Put my heart and soul into this job. And now, what? It all gets stripped away because the one time—the ONE time!—I let myself have a carefree weekend, it blows up in my face?"

I slumped back in my chair, staring at the ceiling. "You know what's really messed up? I didn't even realize how much I needed that weekend until it happened. Last night, I went to bed smiling. Woke up smiling. Started thinking maybe I should let my guard down more often. Maybe even—God, this is embarrassing—

maybe even try actual romance." My laugh came out bitter. "What are the odds? Years I've worked at this company, and the one weekend I decide to live a little ..." I gestured helplessly. "It's like the cosmos waited for me to finally have fun just so it could point and laugh."

"I'm sure everything will be fine." Dakota leaned forward. "You said Jace seemed like a really nice guy. I doubt he's going to fire you over this."

I pressed my fingers against my temple, willing away the growing headache.

"Well, bright side? If Jace fires me, I won't have to stress about that HR meeting anymore. Though, at this point, that feels like choosing between a root canal and a colonoscopy."

"Speaking of which ..." Dakota straightened. "What are you going to tell them about Grabby Hands?"

It took me a second to get out of my own head and transition from my thoughts of Jace to the very important meeting I had in front of me with HR. The one I had prepared for with the diligence of someone planning a bank heist.

I pulled out my carefully crafted bullet-point list on my phone, trying to ignore how my hands trembled slightly.

"Everything." I tapped the screen with my pen. "Starting with how he strategically scheduled the interview for four forty-five on a Friday. He had three months to learn the culture of the organization, to learn that the office clears out by four thirty on Fridays, virtually guaranteeing no one would be here to witness anything."

Dakota's eyes narrowed. "Calculated bastard."

"Oh, it gets better." I started checking off points. "I'm going to describe every slimy innuendo, every lingering look that made my skin crawl. How he implied the promotion was mine if I did whatever he wanted." My throat tightened. "I'm going to detail exactly where his hands went, what he said while he was at it, and especially his charming parting threats when I walked away."

"Welcome back." Dakota smiled. "This morning after the

company meeting, you seemed rattled. It's nice to see you back to your strong self."

"I'm not stopping there," I clarified. "I want them combing through his employment history. Every company, every boss, every HR department." My finger tapped on the side of my phone. "Because I'll bet my next three paychecks, I'm not his first victim. But I'm damn well going to be his last."

Dakota shook her head in pride. "Thorough."

"Oh, I'm not done." I leaned forward. "I'm requesting interviews with every other candidate who applied for the promotion. Give them a safe space to come forward, you know? Because if he did this to me ..."

"You think there are others here?"

"I think we're about to find out." I tried to ignore the knot in my stomach.

"And if the company doesn't fire him?"

"Then I walk." The words came out firmly, despite the way my heart clenched. "I can't work somewhere that treats sexual harassment as a corporate perk. The higher up you are, the more responsibility you have to set an example. If they let this slide ..." I shook my head. "That's not a culture I want any part of."

Dakota stared at my list. "You've really thought this through."

"Hence the cheat sheet." I waved the digital list. "My memory tends to get spotty when I'm fantasizing about throat-punching someone."

"You're doing the right thing, you know."

"Yeah, well ..." My phone buzzed, and I froze mid-sentence, staring at the company-wide announcement. The blood drained from my face as I pieced it together.

That merger everyone had been whispering about? Turned out, several new hires were actually from our parent company, Lockwood Holdings.

Including one particular handsy executive who'd gotten way too familiar with my personal space.

"What?" Dakota leaned forward. "You look like you just saw a ghost."

I let out a sigh that sounded more like a wheeze. "Guess who's actually a Lockwood Holdings executive?"

"No." Dakota's eyes went wide. "Mr. Grabby Hands works for—"

"The company that literally owns us now? Yep." I stared at my meticulously crafted bullet-point list. All those perfectly planned words suddenly felt like a loaded gun pointed at my own head.

"But Jace wouldn't let—"

"Jace?" I barked out another hollow laugh, leaning in to whisper, "Dakota, all I really know about Jace is that he gives spectacular orgasms. A company that size? He's not running it alone. There's a board, probably armies of lawyers who specialize in making problems disappear."

"You're not a problem," Dakota hissed.

"No? Because from where I'm sitting, I'm about to accuse a high-ranking executive of sexual harassment right in the middle of a bazillion-dollar acquisition." My hands started to shake. "You know what corporations call people like that? Liability. Risk. Threat. The corporate equivalent of finding a cockroach in your fancy restaurant meal."

I slumped back in my chair, the weight of reality crushing down.

"And now the timing looks suspicious as hell. They'll say I'm trying to sabotage the merger, or extort money, or, God, I don't even know what they'll say. But guess which story's easier to believe: the lying opportunist trying to cause trouble or the poor, misunderstood executive who's just trying to smooth the transition of power?"

Dakota reached across the desk and grabbed my trembling hands. "So, what are you going to do?"

I looked down at my list again. The right thing to do was so clear an hour ago. Now? The list might as well have been titled The Complete Guide to Career Suicide: A Memoir.

"I don't know." My voice came out unsteadily. "But I have a feeling I'm about to find out exactly how deep this rabbit hole goes. And whether I'm Alice or the sacrificial rabbit."

The fact that she couldn't come up with something to try and reassure me was quite telling. She absolutely thought I was screwed. If not from Grabby Hands, then from Jace himself. Speaking of which ...

I glanced at the time.

"Crap," I said. "I have to head up to his office. Maybe I should stop by the bathroom first and practice my *I've seen you naked, but now I'm totally professional* face."

Dakota swallowed, trying to pretend she wasn't nervous for me.

"Good luck," she managed.

"Yeah." I stood. "I'll need it."

26

SCARLETT

The elevator doors whispered open to the top floor, and I stepped out like I belonged there. Like I hadn't spent the weekend with my legs wrapped around the neck of the man who now owned this building.

Professional. Confident. Pretending that inside me, my stomach wasn't a bundle of nerves.

Around me, the floor hummed with activity: phones ringing, papers shuffling, the click of expensive shoes on floors. Lockwood Holdings employees had descended like a well-dressed plague, already settling into their new kingdom. But all that white noise faded as my eyes locked on to the mahogany door at the far end of the hall.

My heels struck a steady rhythm against the floor as I approached. Click. Click. Click. The sound of inevitability. With each step, I pushed down the urge to smooth my pencil skirt, check my lipstick, or run nervous fingers through my carefully styled hair. Not because I cared how I looked. (*Liar*, my brain whispered.) No, this was about walking into that office radiating the kind of confidence that came with knowing your worth.

Even if, right now, I felt about as substantial as a dust speck in a hurricane.

"Excuse me, can I help you?"

I nearly stumbled as a petite brunette materialized in front of me, all pristine suit and arctic-blue eyes.

"Mr. Lockwood requested to see me."

She arched one perfect eyebrow. "You're Scarlett West?"

So, he looked up my last name. Something twisted in my stomach.

"Yes, that's right."

"Take a seat." She gestured to a row of leather chairs.

"I'll stand. Thank you." My voice came out cool, measured.

Fake it till you make it, Scarlett. He's just the boss, I told my thundering heart. *So what?*

So what? my anxiety screamed.

In the five minutes I'd spent frantically Googling him before Dakota had come to my office, I'd discovered that Jace Lockwood wasn't just powerful; he was basically a god in the corporate world. The man owned a multibillion-dollar empire and had acquired more businesses than I had treats for Buttercup (and trust me, that was saying something). According to every gossip blog and business magazine out there, he was one of the most-sought-after bachelors in the world. Though weirdly, I couldn't find a single reporter who'd ever uncovered an actual relationship. Not one.

So, either the guy didn't do relationships at all or he was so good at keeping them quiet that everyone involved disappeared into a black hole of silence.

And now here I was, the girl who'd spent the weekend discovering exactly what that mouth could do, about to walk into his office.

"He'll see you now," the brunette said, swinging the mahogany door open.

Okay ... looks like my throat has decided to go all dry.

Chin up. Shoulders back. I strode into the corner office—a space that could have swallowed my entire apartment whole. The massive glass conference table caught my eye, and suddenly, my brain decided to replay the image of Jace sprawled across a similar table, blindfolded, his muscles tensing as I—

Not. Helping.

I forced my gaze toward the desk at the far end of the room, just as Jace rose from his chair. The moment our eyes met, everything slowed to a crawl. Like someone had pressed slow motion on the universe, leaving only us, the air between us, and the dust dancing in the sunlight that stretched through the wall of windows. His emerald eyes sparkled, just a fraction, but enough to tell me he felt it, too, this crackling awareness that made it hard to breathe.

The sound of his steps echoed in the silence as he rounded the desk, and holy mother of God. Earlier, shock had short-circuited my ability to fully process what stood before me. Now? Now I could appreciate how that Italian suit hugged every hard plane of his body, how it barely contained those tattooed muscles I'd spent hours tracing with my tongue. And underneath all that expensive fabric? I knew exactly what kind of black boxer briefs—

Focus, Scarlett. Professional.

He settled against the edge of his desk, all coiled power and casual dominance. Much like when he'd leaned against that other table, and I'd taken him into the back of my throat and—

"Scarlett." My name rolled off his tongue like dark honey, hitting me low in the belly. "Thank you for coming." He gestured to one of the leather chairs. "Please. Take a seat."

"I'll stand." I moved forward, my heels silent as I stepped onto the plush carpet of what was probably a ridiculously expensive rug.

Those green eyes—the same ones that had darkened, watching me come apart beneath him—danced with something that looked dangerously close to amusement. His full lips, the ones that had mapped every inch of my skin, curved into the ghost of a smile.

"Suit yourself." Jace's gaze flicked past me to the door, presumably confirming it was shut, before settling back on me with an intensity that made my skin come alive with unwanted desire.

Don't fidget. Don't wring your hands. Don't show weakness.

But standing here, watching him watch me, I realized there was something far more dangerous than showing weakness: remembering exactly how powerful that body could be when it wasn't wrapped in designer suits.

Interesting. I thought I'd despise him, but apparently, my body hadn't gotten the memo. My vagina was staging a full rebellion, getting all hot and bothered, watching him lean against that desk, those long fingers drumming against the underside, ankles crossed with casual dominance. And that suit? That suit should be illegal in at least forty-eight states.

I did not like powerful men. So, why the hell was this turning me on?

Because beneath that suit is a labyrinth of tattoos and the man who worked your body like he had a PhD in pleasure. And whether you want to admit it or not, you can't just choose to make these unwanted feelings disappear.

Shut up, rational brain.

"I wasn't aware you worked for this company when I met you," he said, voice careful.

"Ditto." I matched his tone. Professional. Distant. Like I couldn't still feel the ghost of his hands on my skin.

He pushed off the desk and took two steps closer. I resisted the instinct to step back, to make myself smaller. Instead, I held my ground, but my traitorous gaze betrayed me by noticing how his shoulder muscles strained against that jacket as he slipped his hands into his pockets.

"I'm afraid this company has strict policies against us dating," Jace said.

"Good thing we're not dating then." I kept my voice light but firm. Not too assertive, but confident enough to make it clear that I wouldn't be intimidated.

"I'll have my lawyer draft an NDA. You'll sign it by the end of the day."

Anger shot through me, followed by what felt close to betrayal. Which was unfair. Why would I have expected anything other than him trying to cover his ass? We'd had sex. Great sex. Mind-blowing sex. But nothing more. Right?

Still, it didn't just hurt; it was insulting. He already held all the cards. Owned the whole damn deck really. He didn't need a legally binding agreement on top of it. One he commanded I sign rather than ask me if I would be willing to.

"Will I?"

"You will." There was a finality to his tone, so strong that it almost came off like a threat. It was jarring, the change to his personality. The guy from this weekend had smiled and let me take control. Held me, slept next to me.

"This is who you really are," I said carefully, keeping the anger out of my tone. "Controlling. Domineering."

"I own a multibillion-dollar company. I didn't get there by asking pretty please, Scarlett."

Heart, stand down. You have no right to be hurt.

"And the guy from this weekend. Who was he?"

Jace took several more steps toward me, until our faces were only separated by three feet. His eyes roamed over the planes of my skin, down my jaw as he tilted his head with that casual confidence that did something to my knees. Being in his presence, I realized, was going to be far more complicated than I wanted. Because my body was still not getting the message that this guy was now forbidden. That, if anything, he was my enemy. Someone that represented a threat to my career. And everything I'd fought against my whole life.

"The man from this weekend was a side of me I've never shown to anyone else."

What the ... I had no idea how to react to that, but a plethora of options started firing off votes. My heart had turned into a junior-high-school cheerleader, drawing hearts in my notebook and squealing. My soul was reaching for him, saying, *See? Those feelings that you're sensing? They are real!* My body was casting a unanimous YES while blushing furiously. And the way he was looking at me suggested he didn't want this to end either. But, thank God, my professional side muscled through the chaos and took the reins.

"I see. Well, I'll read over the NDA and ensure it protects both parties," I said.

Those beautiful lips curled on one side. "Both parties?"

"I don't sign any legally binding agreement without reading it first. This weekend poses as much of a problem for me, if not more, than it does for you. So, yes, ensure your lawyer has drafted a proper NDA that protects me as well."

He stepped closer still.

"And what protections would you like to see in that document, Scarlett?" The way he said it was seductive.

"You own a multibillion-dollar company. You didn't get there by having to ask people what belongs in an NDA." I repeated part of what he'd said before. "But if you need specifics, I want it in writing that I can't be terminated, passed over for promotions, or face any other professional repercussions because of what happened between us. I want assurance that any complaints I make about harassment or misconduct will be taken seriously and investigated properly, regardless of whom the complaint is against. And I want a clause that prevents either party from using this weekend as leverage against the other. Personally or professionally."

"You're immensely intriguing, you know that?" I hated the heart in his eyes and the way that his lips continued to curl slightly in apparent admiration. "I will have my lawyer send it to you by the end of the day, but before I do ..." He rubbed the side of his face. Which I totally ignored how sexy that looked. Nope. "As far as what happened between us, I suppose I'm curious what your thoughts are."

Even his word choices this morning were totally different. I guess your tone was very different when you were holding someone's sex to your face versus, you know, whatever this was.

"What my thoughts are?"

He looked at me. Guarded, apprehensive. "If there wasn't a policy against it, would you want this weekend to never be spoken of again?"

"It's the most professional course of action. In fact, after this meeting, we shouldn't be seen together again. Someone could get the wrong idea and cause a lot of trouble."

That part about us not seeing each other made his face tighten. "Is that what you want?"

This was exactly what I was talking about. This was what I wanted to avoid. Every conversation, every word was a power play.

"There is no good way for me to answer that question. If I tell you that I want to continue, that's inappropriate and violates company policies." *And puts the ball in your court to potentially reject me.* "If I tell you that I want to move on and never think of it again, your ego could get bruised. So, respectfully, I choose not to answer that question."

"In my presence, I prefer you to be unfiltered."

"That's unfortunate since you're the boss of the entire company. Every word I speak needs to be filtered."

"I disagree. I want you to be at ease around me."

"All right then. Consider me at ease."

But he looked displeased, sensing the wall that had come up around me. "You needn't be worried around me, Scarlett."

Needn't. The fact that this dude was someone who used the word *needn't* in a sentence told me I absolutely needed to be worried about him.

"Sure. Okay then." I smiled.

Again, he looked annoyed. It was like he could hear my professional words but was frustrated that he couldn't decipher what I was really thinking in my head.

"Is that all?" I asked in a very polite and friendly tone. "Because I have a meeting I need to attend to."

"Your meeting with HR."

I tried to keep my smile, but, goddammit, the blood decided to drop from my face. "How do you know about that?"

"I took the liberty of looking at your calendar."

"For what purpose?" I demanded.

"I wanted to see who you had meetings with today."

"Why?"

"Because you don't strike me as the type of woman who backs down from a fight. And after what you confided in me this weekend, I figured you would come in Monday morning swinging."

I wanted to tell him that he knew nothing about me. I had given little crumbs, that was it, and even that felt like a violation now. How dare he think he knew me well enough to know what I would do today about Grabby Hands?

It pissed me off even more that he was completely right.

"You're nervous about the meeting," he sensed.

"I'm not," I lied.

Jace looked down at my red nails, which had entire bites taken out of them. Seriously, a couple of them probably looked like I put them in a wood chipper.

"You don't chew your nails." His tone was soft.

I hated that he knew that about me. Every glimpse into my soul felt like something he could hold over me, evidence or an asset he could use as collateral. I didn't want him to know anything about me. I wanted to take it all back; every morsel of anything he'd garnered about me was mine and mine alone.

"Maybe I do," I suggested.

"You don't," he pressed, which had me clenching those nails into my palms. "You didn't chew them once this weekend."

Well, a) I was too busy having him lick my sex until I orgasmed all over his face. And b) FYI, *he* was the reason I'd ruined my manicure, not Grabby Hands. But I didn't say that.

Instead, I went with, "Well, if you'll excuse me."

"I'm not finished."

The formality and domineering tone of his voice stopped me cold.

"Give me his name," Jace insisted.

"Pardon me?"

"The man who put his hands on you. He works at this company. I want to know who that is."

I swallowed, shock and fear battling it out in my chest. My heart started pounding, and my palms started sweating. I had spent last night thinking about what I would say to HR, and already, there had been a huge complication, learning that Grabby Hands was actually part of Jace's organization. I needed to talk to somebody I trusted about this, somebody who didn't wield immense power over me the way that Jace did. In short, I needed to figure out my exact play because once I uttered the words, pointing an accusing finger, there would be no taking it back.

I'd have no control over what happened next. I was far too protective of my career to allow that to happen.

"You'll tell me who did this to you," Jace pressed.

"Will I?"

"Yes."

"Why? Because you're my boss?"

"Scarlett—"

"I don't even have an NDA protecting me yet," I pointed out. "Once I have that, I'll take this under advisement, but for the record, HR is the department responsible for fielding concerns over employees. Not the owner."

"HR reports to me."

"Then you can rest assured they will handle this."

"I don't want them to handle it. I want to handle it." Jace's jaw tightened, his voice bordering on anger.

"Why?"

"Because he did it to *you*. He put his hands on *you*."

Everything crystallized into a single, frozen moment. The air between us charged with electricity, time suspended, preserving his revelation as his eyes darkened to forest green, blazing with a possessive fury that stole my breath. My heart began thundering again, this time so hard that I wondered if he could hear it. Because that tone? That wasn't just a boss protecting an employee. That was pure, primal male, protecting what he considered his.

And, God help me, some deep, primitive part of me responded to it.

"I'll consider giving you his name after I have agreed to the terms of the NDA." The minute I reported the guy, Jace could find out anyway from HR. Hell, he might even have his entire HR team on alert for any complaints. You know, under the guise of smooth transitions.

The thing was, while I wanted to be offended by the power play, I liked how protective Jace sounded when he demanded the guy's name. I liked the look of vengeance that flashed through his eyes, the tension in his jaw, like he was imagining what he'd do to the guy when he found him. I liked that the thought of someone hurting me bothered him.

What did that say about me?

"I'll uncover the truth. One way or the other." His voice carried the weight of absolute certainty.

"Perhaps I'll reschedule my meeting with HR." I kept my tone light. "You know, until I have that NDA."

His chest expanded with a sharp intake of breath, jaw tightening. Poor billionaire. Probably the first time today someone hadn't jumped to fulfill his command.

"Even if you don't report him, how many bosses can you have?"

I smiled, slowly and deliberately, before raising an eyebrow. The old owner had loved his "horizontal" org structure, which meant, technically, I had quite the collection of bosses. Eight, if you counted "dotted line" reporting relationships. Seven of whom were men. And let's not forget, Grabby Hands, who wasn't even officially one of them.

The power shifted back to my court like a perfectly executed chess move.

"More than you think," I replied sweetly. *Good luck solving that puzzle, Mr. Lockwood.*

"I will find out who did this to you." His words came out like a promise. Or a threat.

We'll see about that.

27

SCARLETT

Tell her. Tell her what he did to you.

No. Protect yourself. You need to be careful, Scarlett. Now that Jace is the owner, you need to tread very carefully. You can't be the sexual harassment accuser AND the woman who slept with the owner, for God's sake.

I shifted in the chair across from Diana's desk, my heart hammering against my ribs. Seven years of working together had taught me one thing: if anyone in HR could be trusted, it was her. I'd seen her fight for employees when no one else would.

"I need to ask you a question," I said, forcing my voice steady. "Off the record."

Diana set down her pen, giving me her full attention. That was another thing about her: when she listened, she really listened.

"You and I have worked together for a long time," I continued. "I believe I can trust you with something off the record, even though you're HR. But I don't want to put you in an uncomfortable position, so if you can't field an unofficial question, just tell me."

She leaned forward, concern flickering across her features. "Okay ... off the record, what's your question?"

I cleared my throat, weighing each word carefully. "Hypothetically speaking, if a woman experienced sexual harassment and came to HR, what exactly would take place after that?"

Diana's body tensed with a micro-reaction that spoke volumes.

"Well," she said, her professional mask slipping into place, "the official company policy is that any sexual harassment needs to be investigated thoroughly, and appropriate disciplinary action will be taken against the perpetrator."

Oh, thank goodness. The relief lasted approximately half a second before her expression registered.

"But?"

She sighed, the sound heavy with years of experience.

"But, practically speaking, sexual harassment is ... difficult to prove." She met my eyes. "In my career, I've seen three instances of accusers come forward. All three of those accusers were on unemployment very shortly after their accusations."

My jaw hit the floor. The room suddenly felt too warm, too small.

"How can that possibly be?"

Diana leaned forward, her voice dropping. "There's always a supposed motive behind the accusation. Maybe the accuser didn't get the raise they believed they deserved. Maybe there's workplace conflict and it's a way to reclaim power."

Power. That goddamned word. My hands curled into fists.

"In any case," she continued, "there's always been reasonable deniability, lack of evidence, and an ulterior motive presented for why the accuser was making those claims."

"So, let me get this straight," I said, my voice tight. "One hundred percent of accusers have lost their jobs?"

"I've only seen three in my time here but ... yes, I guess you could say that."

"That can't be legal."

"People lose their jobs for all sorts of reasons." Her tone was gentle but firm. "It's not legal to terminate someone for making an accusation."

"But it happens anyway." My eyes stung with angry tears that I refused to let fall. Not here. Not now.

"The system isn't perfect," she admitted.

"Isn't perfect?" I barked out a laugh. "It's rigged."

My mind spiraled back to that night Mom finally gathered her courage and called the police. I could still see her trembling finger hovering over the phone, her split lip oozing blood onto her favorite yellow blouse. I could still hear Dad's smooth voice spinning his story about how she'd "fallen" while cleaning. I could still feel the suffocating silence after the officers left, the way Dad's footsteps echoed down the hallway toward their bedroom. The next morning, Mom's other lip was split too. She never reached for the phone again.

"I'm not saying it's rigged, but we do have a long way to go." She studied my face. "Is there something specific you want to tell me?"

I shifted again, my carefully constructed plan crumbling like a house of cards.

"What if, hypothetically, the perpetrator worked for the company that just bought us out?"

Diana shut her eyes, shaking her head slowly. "That would be … a very unfortunate and complicated situation. The accuser would have significant motivation to try to discredit a leader in the new ownership."

"Who said anything about a leader?"

"The only people who have been here from the new company, thus far, are leaders."

"Right." I stood abruptly, my chair scraping against the floor. "Well, thank you for this hypothetical conversation."

"Scarlett, wait." The use of my name stopped me. "I care about you. And for that reason, I'm going to tell you something I shouldn't. If you repeat this, I could be fired. But I'm telling you because I want to protect you. Okay?"

I sank back into my chair, nodding.

"Tread carefully," she said, each word measured. "The last woman who came forward wasn't just unemployed. She became unhireable."

"In the entire company?"

"In any company in Chicago. Maybe even farther. No one would touch her with a ten-foot pole. Once she made that accusation ..." Diana trailed off, letting the implications sink in.

"So, basically, once you make an accusation, you're like an infectious disease that everyone tries to avoid?"

"That has been my experience, yes." She held up a hand. "Maybe that's not the case every time. I can only speak to what I've seen. But from what I've heard, this company is one of the good ones. Three incidents in my seven years here says they don't happen here often."

"And that's supposed to make me feel better?" The bitter laugh escaped before I could stop it. "Well, this has been sufficiently demoralizing."

"I didn't say it was right—"

"No, you just confirmed what I already knew." I stood again, slower this time. "A perpetrator can do whatever he wants and never be held accountable."

"I didn't say that. He might be held accountable, but from what I've seen, the accuser will go down with the ship."

"Well, that's just fantastic." I winced. "Pardon my tone."

"Scarlett—"

"Thank you for your time." I met her eyes. "For the record, my anger isn't directed at you. Thank you. I needed you to be honest with me, and you were. Seriously. Thank you."

I walked out of her office, my legs somehow carrying me despite feeling like they might give out at any moment. Diana was good people. I trusted her. I'd seen her go to bat for employees like no one else ever had, so if she was telling me it was virtually hopeless ...

What would I do? Was I willing to blow up my entire career

just to try to take down someone who probably wouldn't face any consequences anyway? And not just my career *here*, but my career in general. All for what? To try and root out one bad weed? And probably fail anyway?

History really did have a sick sense of humor. Mom tried to report Dad, and look how that turned out. Now, here I was, ready to report another monster, only to discover that some things never changed. The victims still paid the highest price.

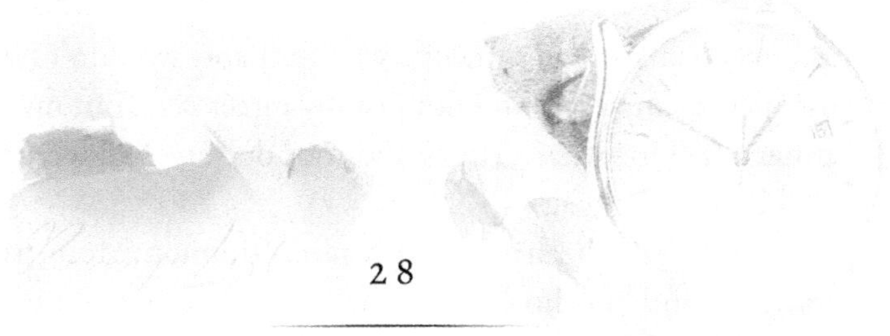

28

SCARLETT

"Fuck."

"Fuck indeed," I said, signaling the bartender for another round.

At this rate, Dakota and I would become professional drinkers with all the workplace drama. Being a Monday night, the bar was blissfully quiet, just a few lost souls drifting through while the sun made its slow descent in the evening sky.

"What are you going to do?" Dakota asked, her eyebrows tilted in concern.

I shoved a hand through my hair, probably making it look like I'd stuck my finger in an electrical socket.

"Think. Very, very carefully. This is like playing the most complicated game of chess ever, where one wrong move costs me everything." I took a long pull of my drink. "Morally? Yeah, warning the company about the vulture in their midst makes perfect sense. But then my practical side kicks in—the side that's worked her ass off, building this career—and asks if I'm really willing to torch everything just to do the right thing. Especially when said right thing might not even cost him his job. And could cost my mom her safe apartment."

"So, maybe Jace is the right person to tell?" Dakota suggested.

"If HR follows their procedures—and we both know how that usually goes—nothing good might come of it. But Jace ... if he's as good as you say he is ..."

"Maybe," I allowed, tracing patterns in the condensation on my glass. "But I need to see that NDA first. It has to spell out, in black and white, that I'll have absolute protection if I come forward."

"And if it does?"

I sighed. "I still have a metric ton of thinking to do. Maybe this makes me a terrible person, wanting to protect myself and my career. Maybe the noble, honorable thing would be to tell them about this creep, consequences be damned. Lord knows that's the kind of woman I've always admired when I see these kinds of stories on the news." I took another sip. "But I'm not the only one who'll be hurt if I lose my job, especially if it makes me unhireable everywhere else."

Dakota nodded, and I felt a surge of gratitude for her unwavering support.

"Still no NDA?" she asked.

I checked my email for the hundredth time. "He said I'd have it by end of day."

"Look, you had a great weekend with Jace. If he's half the man you described, he'll do the right thing."

"Maybe you're right." I straightened my shoulders, feeling a small spark of control return. "The most important thing, the only thing keeping me sane right now, is that the ball's in my court. No one else gets to decide when or if I pull this trigger."

My phone buzzed. We both froze, staring at the banner on the screen.

Subject: NDA from Jace Lockwood.

"Open it!" Dakota practically bounced off her barstool.

I opened it, scanning the legal jargon.

"So far, so good," Dakota mused, watching my face. But when I hit the bottom, her expression changed. "Oh shit. What?"

My heart plummeted to somewhere around my shoes.

"There's a legally binding clause we didn't discuss," I said, my voice hollow.

Ms. West agrees to a meeting tomorrow to disclose the name of an individual she has reported offline to have harassed her.

The realization settled over me like a cold shadow: the meeting requirement fundamentally changed our dynamic. Jace had taken my timeline, my decision-making power.

"He's giving me legal protection," I said slowly, trying to separate professional reality from my emotional response. "But he's also backing me into a corner."

My fingers tightened around the phone. The career woman in me understood his position. A predator in his company during an acquisition was a liability he needed to address. The woman who'd spent years building her career brick by brick, however, resented having choices made for her again.

I'd started to trust him, to believe he might be different. Now, I wasn't so sure.

"What if this isn't about protecting me at all?" I set my phone down like it might bite me. "What if this is just to protect his own ass?"

"What do you mean?"

"He's in the middle of this massive acquisition. He knows there's a harasser in his workforce." My laugh was bitter. "Maybe he's offering protection, but what if this is all about covering Jace's ass rather than actually giving a damn about what happened to me?"

"Isn't that good though? That he wants to weed the guy out?"

"Maybe," I whispered. "So, why then does it hurt so much? The thought that all of this was simply Jace covering his bases rather than actually caring?"

Dakota's face softened with pity. "You're protected though, right?"

"Legally? I think so. From getting fired for *this* offense at least." HR's off-the-record warning bounced around in my head.

"But they could force me out other ways. Bury me in so much work that I'd never keep up, then fire me for *performance* issues."

I mean, how could I trust Jace would do the right thing when I'd trusted him to not take away my choices like this?

"What are you going to do?"

I stared into my drink like it might hold the answers.

"I don't know. But looks like I only have until tomorrow morning to figure it out."

29

SCARLETT

"Mom?" I opened my apartment door to find her fidgeting in the hallway, rubbing her elbows the way she had since I was a kid. My stomach clenched. I knew that look, the toxic cocktail of desperation and shame that came with needing help. "I wasn't expecting you today."

"I'm sorry to bother you." Her voice was so quiet, I almost couldn't hear her. And her once-blonde hair continued to collect more grays, like this new chapter in her life was aging her faster.

"Hey, you're never a bother." I ushered her inside, noting how she still hesitated at thresholds, a leftover habit from years of asking permission to enter rooms in her own house. "*Mi casa es su casa*, remember? We've talked about this."

She stood in my living room, looking small and lost. "I was wondering if I could ..."

"Mom." I smiled. "It's okay. Just tell me what you need."

"Gas prices went up," she blurted, scratching her elbow raw. "And I have four interviews this week."

My eyebrows shot up. "Four?"

A tiny smile bloomed on her face. "I really think I'm getting close."

Pride and heartache bloomed in my chest. Look, if I was being completely honest, I was still struggling to figure out where that line was between helping someone and enabling them. Maybe I wasn't getting it right every time, but I was doing my best to help her get back on her feet. After all, I was really proud that she finally, finally left my father.

My feelings about her were like this kaleidoscope, all jumbled together, and each day, a different one might dominate. Like part of me was angry not just at him, but at her too. Sometimes, the resentment would bubble up like acid reflux. Why hadn't she protected me? Why had she just watched, silent and trembling, while he terrorized us both? Then the guilt would hit, making me feel like the world's biggest asshole. *Who gets mad at someone for being abused?*

I remembered how he'd controlled every penny, every decision. How he'd systematically dismantled her self-worth until she believed she couldn't survive without him. The master manipulator, convincing her that without a college degree, she'd never get a job, and without a job, the courts would take me away from her.

I was his ultimate trump card. The pawn that kept Mom trapped.

"At least he beat me instead of Scarlett," I'd once overheard her say. "At least Scarlett has food and a roof over her head." As if living with a monster was better than a homeless shelter. As if the bruises he left on both of us didn't go deeper than skin.

But today? Today, I chose gratitude. Mom was out. Safe. Living in an apartment Dakota had helped me rent under her name, creating a paper trail Dad couldn't follow. One more reason I couldn't lose this job. Mom would lose her apartment, Dakota's credit would tank, and the whole house of cards would come tumbling down.

But I wasn't going to let that happen.

"Of course, Mom." I grabbed cash from my purse, pressing it into her trembling hands before she could spiral into another apology.

Her eyes welled up. "I'm going to make you proud, Scarlett. I've kept track of every cent—"

"Stop." I squeezed her hands. "I don't want repayment. I want you safe."

She was taking steps with sharing her résumé, asking about job benefits, and learning how to exist in a world she'd been sheltered from for decades. In many ways, my mother was like a teenager, and I was her reluctant guide to adulting.

"Have you eaten?" I asked. "I was just about to make some food."

My mom joined me for dinner. We talked about lighter topics, and at some point, we even laughed. This was another thing I wanted Mom to experience: normalcy. Not everything had to be dark and heavy and about my abusive father. The more experiences she got that were normal, the more normal she would feel, I suspected.

Still, it was hard for my eyes not to wander to the scars that were visible.

After dinner, I walked Mom to the elevator, both of us riding down in comfortable silence. The lobby's fluorescent lights buzzed overhead as we pushed through the heavy glass doors into the night.

The evening was warm, the kind that drew people out of their apartments like moths to a flame, and streetlights cast warm halos on the row of parallel-parked cars, transforming puddles from yesterday's rain into pools of liquid shimmers.

"Look." Mom pointed to her car, wedged into a coveted spot between a fire hydrant and a moving van. "I parallel parked it in only two tries this time."

I grinned. "Soon, you'll be teaching me tricks."

We were almost to her car when I heard a fresh set of steps emerge behind us.

"I knew I'd find you."

That voice. My blood turned to ice in my veins, and Mom took a sharp intake of air.

Slowly, so slowly, we turned to find my worst nightmare.

I shifted automatically, pushing Mom behind me as a burly figure emerged from between the cars. The streetlight caught his face, and those familiar features twisted into something almost feral.

"Dad," I spat, my heart trying to hammer its way out of my chest. My palms were slick with sweat, but I kept my voice steady. I wouldn't give him the satisfaction of hearing my fear.

I'd always known this moment would come. Had rehearsed it in my head a thousand times. But standing here now, with Mom trembling behind me, I wondered if any amount of preparation could have been enough.

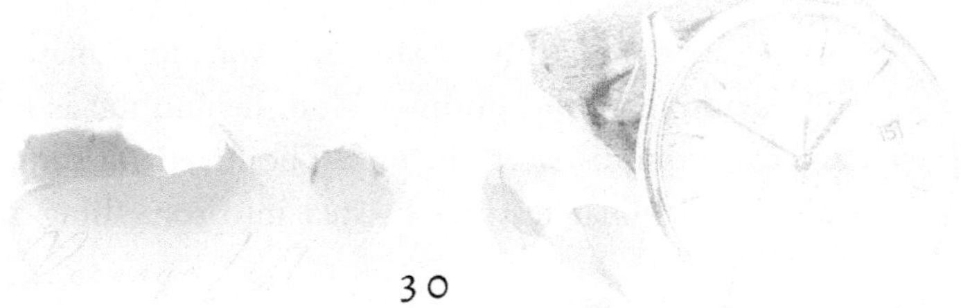

30

JACE

She never responded to my email.

I stood across from Scarlett's apartment building, watching windows glisten in the dark like a hundred judging eyes. What the hell was I doing here? The NDA terms could wait until tomorrow. There was absolutely no rational reason I needed to review them with her tonight, off company grounds, in private.

Except you're not here about the NDA, are you, Lockwood?

No. I was here because ever since my day concluded, my mind had been consumed with one thought: who had hurt her and what I would do to him when I found out. The rage simmering beneath my skin demanded action, demanded answer tonight, not tomorrow.

I'd told my driver it was a quick business matter. I'd only been here once before, for Scarlett to grab clothes before going horseback riding. Back before everything got complicated.

God, what was I becoming? Standing here like some obsessive stalker outside an employee's apartment. A woman's apartment. A woman who'd just endured workplace harassment, no less.

Walk away. Now.

The business side of my brain was screaming at me to leave before I crossed a line I couldn't uncross. Because if I went up to that apartment ... the image of Scarlett's lips, the memory of her laugh, the way she'd felt in my arms—

Stop.

That was it. I couldn't do this. Wouldn't do this.

I took a deep breath and turned to leave, to walk back to where my driver waited down the block, when suddenly, I saw her.

Scarlett was outside.

My gut dropped when I registered that something was wrong. Her stance was rigid, protective, as she positioned herself in front of another woman who was older and trembling. They were both facing someone. A man.

My body tensed, my instincts screaming that she was in danger, even if I didn't know why. There was something in the way he moved, the shift of his weight, the darkness in his posture that set off every alarm.

I cocked my head, watching the interaction, and as I did, I realized something in horror:

This guy was a predator.

And he was advancing toward Scarlett.

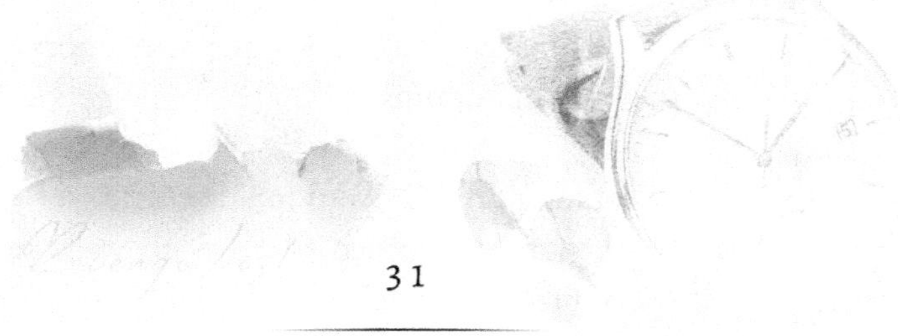

31

SCARLETT

Dad looked just like I remembered him. Brown hair in need of a trim, a beard peppering with gray, a soft body that hadn't seen the inside of a gym in years, and broad shoulders that seemed to block out all the light. Just like his presence had stolen the light from our lives for years. His eyes seemed thinner, darker, if that was even possible, like the brown had melted into ebony, surrendering to the shadow that had claimed his soul long ago.

"Get in the car, Nancy." Dad produced a small knife, holding it at his side so no one else could see it as he motioned with his chin to Mom's vehicle. Casual. Like he was offering her a ride home from the grocery store instead of threatening her life on a public sidewalk.

Flashes of my childhood invaded my thoughts. The times I'd been a little girl, hiding under my bed, covering my ears and crying at the sounds of pain and screaming, tears and terror. How I'd eventually crawl out to find my mother bloody and battered, and I'd say, "I'm so sorry, Mommy." Because I'd let him do that to her. I'd left her. Hiding, to protect myself.

It had taken years to find my inner strength, and I'd be lying if I said I didn't sometimes feel like that scared little girl again. But I'd never again hide under my bed from this monster. I'd never again abandon her either. The guilt of all those blood-soaked memories had almost done me in.

When Dad angled the knife, I took another protective step, planting myself firmly between them, shielding my mom with my body. My heart hammered against my ribs, but my voice came out steady.

"Don't," I said to her, not taking my eyes off him. "If you do, you won't survive the night."

"Don't be so dramatic," he sneered.

"Leave. Or I'll call the police." My hand inched toward my pocket where my phone sat. Truth be told, I'd be calling the police no matter what, but I didn't need to tell him that.

He smirked, the expression so familiar, it made my intestines knot. "It'll take them time to get here."

"Spoken like a domestic violence expert."

"Last warning. Get in the car."

"Scarlett," Mom whispered, trying to emerge from behind me. "I'll go with him." Her voice trembled.

"You won't," I said, pushing her gently back.

"Listen to your mother, Scarlett. Move aside."

"You don't want her," I accused, chin up despite the fear slamming around my rib cage. "You don't want a woman that rejected you."

His eyes narrowed. "You don't know what I want."

"You just want to control her. And now you want to punish her for leaving you."

"You've made it quite difficult to find you." He took a half step closer, trying to intimidate us.

"That was the intention." I straightened my shoulders. "Now leave before I call the police."

I tried not to tremble when he took another step, but the scent of his aftershave—the same cheap brand he'd always used—brought back a tidal wave of memories I'd spent years trying to drown. That smell. It had often mixed with the blood of my mother.

"Don't make a scene, Scarlett." His voice was low, menacing.

I let out a bitter laugh. "That was your favorite line to use in public. 'Don't make a scene, Scarlett.' 'Don't embarrass me, Nancy.' Doesn't work anymore. Leave. Now. And never come back."

He didn't move. Just stared at me with those dead eyes, calculating.

"There's an active restraining order against you," I continued, gaining momentum. "And there are cameras positioned there, there, and there." I pointed without looking away from his face. "Did you think I wouldn't do my own reconnaissance to make sure if you ever showed up, you would be caught? You use that knife, you're done. You'll spend the rest of your life in prison."

His nostrils flared. "You've always been a tumultuous little bitch."

"And you've always been the biggest coward." The words tasted like victory on my tongue.

His other hand, the one I hadn't been hyper-fixated on, moved in a blur. A flash of movement I didn't have time to counter. An explosion of pain rocketed across my cheekbone, sending me flying to the ground. The concrete scraped my palms raw as I caught myself, ears ringing, vision swimming.

Before I could even process what happened, a fresh blur—this time one from the street—flashed before me.

My father hit the sidewalk with a grunt, a tangle of limbs and curses.

A Good Samaritan had tackled him, I realized through the haze of pain. And that Good Samaritan was now punching my father. Repeatedly. Viciously. Each impact making a sickening sound that somehow felt like justice. The problem was, my father swung back, knocking the man off him and to the ground.

As I struggled to my feet, my father reached for his fallen knife, but I kicked it out of his way, sending it flying against the building.

The stranger wrestled my father to the concrete again, just

outside the glow of the streetlight. As I pulled my cell out, ready to call the police, I realized there was something familiar about the gait of the stranger. He was wearing a suit. Expensive by the looks of it, now being ruined on the dirty sidewalk.

One last punch. One last crack across my father's face that made him groan and finally stop fighting back. And then the Good Samaritan stood, fists clenched, chest heaving, before finally turning to me.

My stomach bottomed out.

"Jace?"

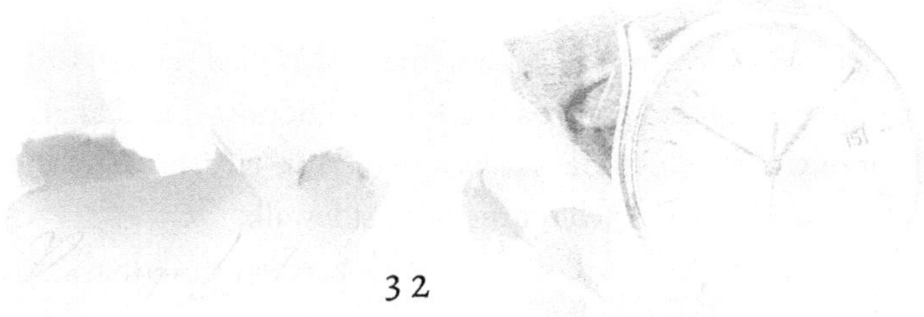

32

SCARLETT

After my father jumped up and fled (I told you he was a goddamned coward), Jace stood in his three-piece suit between me and where he'd vanished, arms at his sides, a human shield against whatever danger might return.

Strange. Even in this moment of absolute chaos, my heart registered his act of protection and how much he must care to have intervened. I mean, hell, I didn't know why he was here, but I was grateful he'd shown up when he did. That was for damn sure.

And appreciating his protection didn't make me weak. After watching my mother take a beating for years, I'd learned the hard way that sometimes, you couldn't keep yourself safe without support. Case in point, the help I was giving my mother.

In any event, I'd always felt like I had to be the shield. I'd never had anyone shield me.

Until now. And God help me, I liked it. Okaaay, file that under *Uncomfortable Emotional Revelations I'll Deal with Never.*

Jace's eyes blazed with a fury that wasn't directed at me but felt scorching, nonetheless.

"You okay?" His voice was steel.

I turned to find Mom shivering, arms wrapped around herself, but physically unharmed.

"Hey," I said, grabbing her by the shoulders. "It's okay, Mom. He's gone."

"He found us," she whispered, her voice small.

"It was only a matter of time before he found my apartment." I squeezed her shoulders gently. "You're safe. Your apartment isn't in our name, remember?"

Her eyes remained glued to the spot where my father had disappeared, shimmering with tears, her nose red, but after a moment, she nodded. Affording me the opportunity to turn back around and face our unexpected protector.

"What are you doing here?" I asked.

It was like he didn't even hear me. His attention was too busy scouring my body, presumably for any signs of injuries, until finally, his gaze halted on my cheek.

"Fuck." The single word carried concern and anger, and dare I say, it bordered on desire for vengeance. He brought his hand up, his lips hardening to a firm line as he swiped his thumb along my cheekbone.

I hissed, wincing away, but only for a moment. Because now that I was looking at him, I could see a red spot near *his* eye that was already starting to swell. Much more than mine.

"You're hurt," I said, reaching up without thinking. And then I scoured *his* body because, holy shit, my dad had a knife.

"Did he get you anywhere else?" Jace demanded.

"Did you get stabbed?"

"Your cheekbone might be broken."

I lifted his suit jacket, looking at his abs, his chest, his arms for any signs of a slice.

"*Your* eye's swelling," I said, my hand hovering near his face.

"We need to get this looked at." His eyes never left my injury.

"I'm fine," I said, but it seemed to go unheard. "Are you okay?"

Jace pulled out his phone, called a quick number, and relayed our situation and our address. Moments later, as if summoned by magic billionaire powers, a black sedan pulled up.

"Get in the car." Strange how those same identical words, spoken moments before from a different man, carried the weight of a threat while Jace's carried the weight of protection.

Jace opened the door, motioning for me to get into the back seat with all the patience of a man used to being obeyed instantly.

"I'm not leaving my mother," I said.

His expression softened. "Didn't intend for you to. Both of you, please get in."

An impatient driver pulled up behind the sedan, honking.

"I need to get my mom inside. And call the police," I protested, even as the adrenaline started to ebb, leaving my cheek throbbing in its wake.

"The police have already been called," Jace stated matter-of-factly. "They're meeting us at the hospital."

"What? By whom?" And *why* are they meeting us at the hospital? My eyebrows shot up, and then I immediately regretted the movement as pain lanced through my cheek.

HONK, HONK. "Move out of the way!" some dude shouted from his car.

Jace turned, and whatever look he flashed the driver must've been bone-chilling in its warning because the guy slumped down in his seat. Unfortunately, there was another car behind him, who joined in on the impatience train.

"My driver called them," Jace said, turning back to me. "Now, please get in, Scarlett." The way he said my name—not quite pleading, not quite commanding—did something to my insides.

Around us, the scene was unfolding like a bad movie: a line of cars honking, angry drivers waiting for us to move, while pedestrians slowed their movements, staring at us like freaks.

I looked at my mom, at Jace, at the growing spectacle around us.

"Get in, Mom," I finally said, guiding her toward the car.

As I slid in beside her, I caught Jace's eye. There was relief there and something else. Something that made me remember that not all men were created with my father's capacity for cruelty.

"How did you know to come here?" I asked.

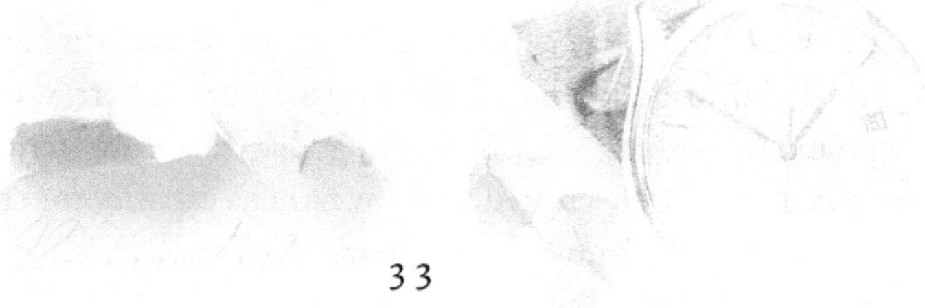

33

SCARLETT

"This seriously was unnecessary." I shifted uncomfortably on the paper-covered gurney that crinkled with every movement, the smell of alcohol wipes mingling with the slight tang of blood.

He'd refused to answer why he'd shown up at my apartment, too fixated on inspecting my injuries and making sure I was physically okay first.

"Humor me." Jace stood along the wall. Still wearing his three-piece suit, though his tie hung loose and his shirt was painted with a light splattering of blood. Whether it was his or my father's, I couldn't tell.

"You said that no less than ten times since I got in the car with you."

A distant code announcement echoed over the PA system, followed by the squeak of rubber-soled shoes rushing past our door.

"Evidently, you take a lot of convincing." The corner of his mouth twitched upward, despite the angry red swelling around his eye.

"The only reason I agreed to this is because you agreed to get looked at too. Your face looks far worse than mine." My attention flitted down to his knuckles, which were raw, split, and beginning to bruise. "So does your hand. God, I hope it's not broken."

"Even the police agreed with me," Jace reminded me, the overhead light catching on his cufflinks as he gestured.

The police interview hadn't taken as long as you'd think. *Ex abuser strikes again.* That kind of thing probably had pre-populated fields. I was grateful to the cops but worried no one could truly protect my mom from my father's dark side.

"I shouldn't have left my mother's side."

"There's a security guard positioned with her right now."

"What if my dad comes looking for her here? Makes it past him?" I ran my fingers along the edge of the bed.

"He'd have to get past hospital metal detectors, hospital security, and a security guard who, I assure you, is very good at his job." His tone softened. "Your mother is safe. If you'd prefer, I can have my security guard take her home."

"No," I said, wincing as the movement pulled at my throbbing cheek. "I want to spend the night with her." She'd be scared, and I wouldn't be able to sleep, worrying about her. "How do you have security at your fingertips at any hour, by the way?"

One phone call, and a dude with a gun showed up with an earpiece. Nothing says abnormally protected like that.

"In business, you can make big enemies sometimes."

Seriously? Did all CEOs have security on retainer like most people had DoorDash? But I had bigger things to worry about right now. Namely, the terror of replaying this night in my mind.

God, if I hadn't walked Mom to her car, what would have happened to her?

"Thank you," I said, the words feeling inadequate against the weight of what he'd done. "For what you did."

Jace tilted his head slightly, studying me. "I have questions."

"Figured you would."

"May I ask them?"

"You certainly earned the right to. You literally took a beating to protect me and my mom, so, yeah, ask away." I gave him a weak smile that pulled painfully at my injury.

Suddenly, the door to our emergency room opened, and a familiar set of eyes locked on mine.

"Scarlett?" Blake's eyebrows slammed together.

Dr. Blake Morrison was my best friend, Tessa's, boyfriend. Wearing blue scrubs and a white lab coat, he had a stethoscope strung around his neck.

"Blake." I knew it was a possibility to see him here tonight, of course, though the jury was out if that was good (comforting) or bad (he might tell Tessa about this before I could).

His eyes narrowed at the mark on my face, then shot to Jace.

"What the fuck happened?" he asked, accusatory. Very not doctorly, but as I said, this was my bestie's boyfriend.

"You guys know each other?" Jace asked, his gaze darting between us.

Wait. "*You* guys know each other?" I echoed.

But Blake was too busy examining my face to answer, his fingers gently probing the edges of what was surely becoming a spectacular bruise. After a few seconds of visually inspecting my father's handiwork, Blake's attention wandered over to Jace. Specifically, to his very swollen knuckles.

Blake looked between the knuckles and my face, then glared at my boss's boss's boss's boss with enough intensity to trigger a cardiac arrest.

"Jace, if this is a domestic violence thing, I'm going to kick your ass." His fingers flexed at his sides.

Jace's jaw tightened. "Really, Morrison? You know me better than that!"

"You have bruised knuckles. She has a bruised cheek. It's a fair conclusion. You'd better start explaining now. Because we might be friends, but violence against women? I'll give you a one-way ticket to the ICU if you did this to her."

"Did you notice the injury to MY face?"

"He didn't do this to me," I assured, jumping in before they could start measuring testosterone levels.

"Jesus, Morrison." Jace ran a hand through his already-disheveled hair.

In fairness, Blake was an emergency room physician, and this did look rather suspicious. And also in his defense, it would've been unethical for him to not at least ask, bro code or no bro code.

"Then what the hell happened?" Blake demanded.

"It would seem my cheek slammed into my sperm donor's hand." I replied.

"Your sperm donor?" Blake questioned.

"He doesn't deserve the term *father*. This isn't his first rodeo with violence against my face."

Okay, that appeared to have given Jace a full-on ... red face attack. Seriously, the guy needed to breathe, or he might pass out. The vein in his temple looked ready to erupt from his skin.

"Christ, Scarlett." Blake slapped on a pair of latex gloves with a snap that made me flinch.

Something Jace very much noticed, by the way.

"How do you two know each other?" Jace demanded again, gesturing between Blake and me with his injured hand.

"This is Tessa's best friend," Blake said, finally answering as he reached for an antiseptic pad from a metal tray.

Jace looked up at the ceiling. "You've got to be shitting me."

"Does Tessa know about your sperm donor's violent side?" Blake pulled up a rolling stool next to my bed, its wheels squeaking against the linoleum, and tilted my face for a better look.

"She didn't tell you?"

"Should she have?"

I smiled, cringing as it pulled at my cheek. I had asked her not to, and that meant the world to me that she kept my information private. Speaking of private ...

"Do not tell her you saw me here tonight," I said, fixing Blake with my best attempt at a threatening glare. "She'll freak out and overreact, and I don't have the energy to deal with that right now."

Blake began to clean my wound, the sharp sting making my eyes water. The little white swabs came back with small streaks of red, confirming that the skin was split slightly. I suspected a nurse could clean it just fine, but he was doing this himself because it was me. His girlfriend's best friend.

"Do not call Tessa," I repeated.

"If I don't call Tessa, she'll cut my balls off," he said matter-of-factly. "I'm fond of my balls."

"Blake ..."

"Sorry, but she'll want to know you're here."

It wasn't that I didn't want to tell Tessa; it was just that I was all talked out with this whole harassment situation at work (which, by the way, I also had to fill her in on), and now my father showed up, and my head was spinning, and—

"I'm exhausted, and all I want to do is go home and sleep, please."

"Scarlett, you were there for her; she'll want to be here for you." Blake applied butterfly bandages to my cheek.

"Tessa's heart stopped. My sperm donor slapped me. There's a big difference. Please. I don't want to talk about this right now. I promise I will call her and set up a drink for later. Okay? Just not tonight."

But Blake didn't say anything. I was about to shift the stance of my argument when Jace stepped forward.

"Don't tell her," he said.

Blake shot him a look.

"She's asking you not to tell her, so don't," Jace continued. "If you need a reason, you can cite those pesky HIPAA laws that'll have your nuts in a vise if you do tell her."

The doctor took an annoyed breath, standing up.

"Take a seat, Jace," he said. "I'll examine you next."

"So, you won't tell Tessa, right?" I touched his handiwork.

Blake took his latex gloves off with a snap and tossed them into a canister.

"Fine," Blake agreed. "But you'd better call her soon."

34

SCARLETT

My cheek throbbed as I opened the door to my apartment. Jace had insisted on escorting me home, inside, no less, to ensure I was safe. Police had found my dad and arrested him. I was shocked by how quickly a second restraining order was filed, this time on my behalf, but I was grateful for it all the same.

With Jace's tie now off and his shirt unbuttoned at the top, the exposed hollow at the base of his throat drew my attention, making my fingers itch to trace the smooth skin there.

Not helping this rush of unwanted feelings, by the way.

He looked around my microscopic apartment, which was approximately the size of a postage stamp. The living room was only big enough to fit a couch, a two-seater at that, and a television, and the kitchen brandished seriously small appliances that hummed and clanked at times, like a paper clip was doing backflips in them. It wasn't uncommon for Chicago residents to have a space management issue, but I could see the question circling in his eyes as he scanned the place. As the owner of many companies, he would know that someone in my position would have a salary that far exceeded these living arrangements.

"It's not much," I said. "But it's the only one I could afford right now."

He cocked his head, like he was beyond curious, but didn't want to offend me by asking about my financial distress.

"I pay for my mom's housing," I explained.

He swiped his lower lip with his thumb, and, God help me, that was sexy as hell.

"You pay for your mother," he repeated, making it half statement, half question.

"It's a long story."

"One I'd like to hear."

I sighed, trying to process everything that had happened.

"I don't normally tell people about this, but I guess you can pretty much piece together what's going on after what you witnessed downstairs ..." Which led me to question number one. The one that I'd been wanting to ask since the moment he showed up, the one that I sensed I wouldn't get a real answer out of him until we were completely alone.

Why did he witness one of the most intimate moments of my life? Strange that I didn't feel mortified by it. Somehow, in his presence, I never felt judged. Not in the car ride, not at the ER. Never.

"Why did you come here earlier?"

Jace's eyes met mine, uncertainty flickering across his face. "I told myself it was the NDA. But the truth is, I haven't been able to stop thinking about you, Scarlett." The raw honesty in his voice made my chest warm against my will.

I shook my head. "But you have to. Company policy states—"

"I know what it states." He grabbed the back of his head, fingers threading through his dark hair like this information was beyond distressing. And then he locked his eyes with mine again. "The truth is, I haven't been able to stop thinking about you since the moment you fell at my feet in that bar. I've never had these feelings for another woman. It's quite ... distracting."

It was adorable, watching this big, powerful man admit a loss of control. Mr. Billion-Dollar Spreadsheets, suddenly unable to explain his feelings with a neat formula or PowerPoint presentation.

"Why do you think that is?" I asked.

"I tried to convince myself it was just the circumstances," he said, gesturing vaguely. "Strangers meeting by chance, with no intention of ever talking again." His lips quirked up momentarily. "We both got to check our real identities at the door and just ... enjoy each other. No agendas, no games, no me wondering if you were after my bank account or company stock."

He sighed.

"Do you know how rare that is for me?" His voice dropped. "Not having to be Jace Lockwood, Wall Street's golden child, watching every word in case it ends up quoted in the *Financial Times*?" He shook his head. "With you, I didn't need the armor. I just got to be ... free."

Something shifted inside me as his guard dropped: a dangerous fault line opening where I'd thought there was only solid ground. Now threatening to unleash an earthquake.

"But that's not why I can't get you out of my head," he continued. "There was this ... moment ... when you fell to the ground at that bar." He paused, searching for words, frustration crossing his features. "I'm not usually this inarticulate. I run a multibillion-dollar company, for God's sake."

My mouth arched up. It was as strange as it was thrilling (and flattering) that I had this kind of power over him.

"The second we touched, the moment we locked eyes ... something shifted. Like that first subtle crack in the snow before an avalanche." His attention on me intensified. "And then every moment we spent together after that ... every touch, every conversation, it just gained momentum, gained intensity." He ran his fingers through his hair again, looking like he'd tried incredibly hard to outrun whatever this was. "I know how it sounds. I've spent three days telling myself I'm being ridiculous."

Jace took another step closer, close enough that I could smell his expensive cologne.

"Things don't just happen to me," he continued. "I make them happen. My life runs on forecasts, and five-year plans. Then you literally crashed into my life. Completely unplanned, totally unpredictable, and it's the best damn thing that's happened to me in years."

Me too.

"When Sunday night came"—he grimaced slightly—"when I had to honor that promise to never see you again, I couldn't sleep. Couldn't focus. Monday morning, I botched two calls with investors because all I could think about was ..." He gestured vaguely toward me. "And then I walked onto that stage, looked out at all those faces, and there you were." His expression shifted between guilt and undeniable excitement. "God help me, but for a split second, I was actually happy to see you there. An HR nightmare in the making, and I'm standing there, thinking, *I get to see her again.*" He rubbed the back of his neck. "Only to realize seconds later what an impossible position that puts you in. Your boss's boss's boss's"—he frowned—"boss."

The room fell silent. Jace's confession hung in the air between us.

"After we talked about the NDA, I told myself to let it go. Move on." He smiled, but it didn't reach his eyes. "Yet hours later, I showed up outside your place, using that same NDA as an excuse to see you again."

And then he saw the most intimate thing in my life: my dysfunctional family and the way my father used us as punching bags. I could see the shift in Jace's expression hardening, just like his voice did.

"One minute, I'm telling myself to leave, and the next, I'm seeing some man lay his hands on you." His jaw tightened. After what seemed like an eternity, he spoke again, his voice careful, measured. "How many times has your father hurt you, Scarlett?"

I flinched as his gaze seared through me with such fire that I looked away, walking to the window. Outside, Chicago sprawled before me in a runway of amber lights and dark shadows. A few floors down, a couple argued on the street corner, their gestures animated but voices lost to the night. Across the way, someone's lonely television flickered blue against their curtains. The "L" train rumbled in the distance, carrying people to their own complicated lives. It was easier to watch strangers navigate their problems than face the man behind me, waiting for answers I wasn't sure I wanted to give.

"I never talk about this. Not with anyone." Not anymore. My closest friends knew, of course, so I guess I should have said it was a subject I preferred not to share with others. But Jace saw my father hit me. There was no point in pretending anymore.

"My dad can be a really charming guy when he wants to be," I finally started. "And while he comes from a very broken place with his childhood, he chose to never get help."

I turned back to face Jace, needing him to understand.

"Not once in all the time my mom and I begged. As a young girl, I literally sobbed, pleading with him. It only made him angrier and more violent." My voice cracked. "Every day, I'd watch that front door, wondering which version of my dad was going to come home. The dad that hugged us or the dad that was looking for a fight." I swallowed hard. "I hated the power he held over my mother. He held all the cards. Financially, physically, emotionally, psychologically. Through their marriage, he wore her down to an absolute nub."

Jace hadn't moved, but his eyes never left my face, like he was absorbing and cataloging every word. Here was a man who, arguably, had far more important things to do right now with his major corporate takeover. But the only thing he seemed to care about in this moment was me. In fact, his phone had buzzed no less than ten times tonight, and he'd never even looked at it; instead, he kept his attention fixed on me.

I ran a trembling hand down my pant legs. "It was almost like my dad had puppet strings tied to different facets of my mom's psyche. She might finally get strong and decide that, financially, she would figure it out, so he would come after her with another angle." My breath hitched. "He always had something up his sleeve to press her back down, to keep her submitted to him."

Jace's expression darkened. "And he hit you too."

It wasn't a question. More like ... a veiled threat. Like anyone hurting me was of sudden extreme importance to him.

"I was in college the first time she officially left him," I continued. "It didn't stick. He convinced her to come back, and she stayed there, even after he broke her nose."

Jace made a sound low in his throat, something primal and angry.

"After that, she made various attempts to leave, but again, none of them stuck. Sometimes, she would go back because, financially, she was struggling. She would run out of money, or she would lose her job. But mostly, he just had this psychological hold over her that I could never seem to cut, no matter how hard I tried." My voice hardened. "This is the longest she's stayed away from him, and I swear to God, I'll do whatever it takes to make sure she never goes back. Not this time. Not ever again."

I walked to the couch, but didn't sit, just leaned against it for support. "I know this isn't my fight. I know that she is the one that has to leave him, and she has. But I can't let something as small as finances get in the way."

I raised my chin, defiant, despite the bruise forming on my cheek.

"That's why this job isn't just a career to me. It's a lifeline. A single missed paycheck isn't an inconvenience; it's the difference between my mother's safety and her returning to him and his escalating abuse. I can't gamble with that. I won't." I met his gaze directly, something fierce in my own. "So, maybe you look at me and say I'm not a very brave person because I'm reluctant to give up the company harasser's name without some forethought. But you don't understand the complicated chess match that I'm in. One wrong move, and it's not just me that will suffer the consequences."

"Scarlett." Jace stepped forward, his voice turning raw.

"You've got to be the bravest person I've ever met. You stood between your father and your mother, faced down a man twice your size, holding a knife, knowing exactly what he was capable of." He shook his head, eyes never leaving mine. "That's brave as hell, so don't you dare think for one second I see it any other way."

My eyes burned with unshed tears as I realized how much his confession mattered to me.

"Every day of my life, my biggest fear is answering a phone call from an unknown number because I'm terrified that it will be the morgue telling me that my dad finally got to her, and this time, he finished her off." A tear finally escaped, tracking down my injured cheek. I brushed it away angrily. "I will not allow that to happen."

Jace crossed the room in three long strides, stopping just short of touching me. "Let me help financially."

I took a step away, shaking my head, recoiling from the idea.

"I won't transfer power from one man to another, Jace. You seem like a really nice guy, but the truth is, I really don't know you very well. My dad was very charming in the beginning, too, and then once he had all the power, everything changed."

His brow furrowed, his muscular arms crossing over his broad chest.

"I hate him for doing this to you," he growled. "For making you suspicious of any man who cares about you." I swallowed. "But you don't have to be afraid of me, Scarlett. I would never do that to anyone. Especially not you."

"Well, I will not accept that kind of help from anyone, especially not a man. And especially not someone who holds an immense amount of power over my life already."

Jace's expression softened, the tension in his shoulders easing slightly. "You know, my favorite book as a child was called *The Keeper's Compass*," he said. "It's about a child entrusted with an ancient compass that always points toward those in need." His voice grew quieter, more vulnerable. "My mother read it to me when I was feeling lost after we moved to a new town. She taught me that helping others provides direction when you feel adrift yourself. It's a virtue she instilled in me."

He took a careful step back, giving me space. "I'm not trying to control you, Scarlett. I just ... see someone in need, and everything in me wants to help. It's who I am."

"I appreciate it," I said. "But no thank you. I'll figure this out."

For a long moment, he just looked at me, and the fury toward my father began to waver into something different. Something like awe.

"For the record, you're the strongest woman I've ever met," he said finally.

I felt my defenses lower, just slightly. "For the record, you don't know me ... not really."

"I'm starting to," he insisted. "And I want to know more."

I looked down at my hands, feeling suddenly vulnerable, the image of him fighting my father unleashing all kinds of confusing feelings.

"No one's ever stuck up for me like that before," I admitted.

Okay, that seemed to bother him. But to his credit, he swallowed it and cleared his throat.

"What if I want to keep doing it?"

Squaring my shoulders, I replied, "I don't need you to."

Jace took a careful step closer, the heat of his body igniting my own. There was something wonderfully jarring about being near him, like little cells in my body had come alive with electricity, their light fading when they were no longer in his presence.

"Need has nothing to do with this." His eyes held mine, intense and searching. "You've kept yourself safe and successful for years. I'm not suggesting you need saving. I'm saying I want to help shield you. From your father. From whoever hurt you at work."

Something fluttered in my chest, a feeling I'd long ago buried, and now, that NDA paragraph requiring a name felt very different. Protective rather than controlling. Like maybe for once, someone with power wanted to use it to defend rather than dominate.

"What if I said I want you to be mine?" His voice was almost a whisper.

I stood there, stunned, the word *mine* bouncing around the chambers of my heart. Trying to plant seeds and grow and rise in a sun that I'd never experienced before.

"You said company policy—"

"What if I don't care about the policy?"

The question hung between us, charged with possibility.

I felt my defenses waver further. "That would be ... complicated."

"I'm good with complicated." He was closer again, one hand lifting cautiously to hover near my uninjured cheek, giving me time to pull away.

I didn't.

His palm cupped my face, thumb brushing gently across my skin. "And I meant what I said earlier ... I want to know more about you. All of you."

My heart hammered against my ribs as he leaned in, his eyes asking permission. Despite every warning bell in my head, I found myself tilting my face up to his, my lips parting slightly in invitation.

When our lips finally met, it was like coming home. To a good home. A warm one, with baked cookies and a normal family.

Jace slipped his tongue along my lower lip, coaxing me to open for him. When I did, the kiss deepened into something primal. Electric. My toes curled, and my heartbeat drummed in my ears as I reached up and threaded my fingers through his thick hair.

He winced slightly.

"Sorry," I whispered against his mouth, feeling a small lump beneath my fingertips. I couldn't tell if it was from my father's fist or his collision with the concrete sidewalk. Either way, it was evidence of what he'd done for me. The bruised knuckles. The cut eyebrow. This lump. Injuries he'd sustained to protect me.

As our kiss evolved, heat pooled low in my belly. I wanted more. So. Much. More. I wanted to pull Jace into my bedroom, peel off that expensive suit, trail my fingers along the tattoos that I knew were hidden beneath, and feel him inside me, his lips on my neck, his body bringing me to the edge of oblivion.

But reality crashed through my fantasy. Hard stop.

This was happening too fast. Yes, I wanted him, but I'd managed to go through my entire life blocking out feelings for any man, and if I was going to date anyone—and that was properly cataloged in my *Never Going to Happen* folder—I really didn't want that person to be someone so powerful. Rich. Connected. A man who could alter lives with a single phone call.

Specifically mine.

Even though Jace had stood up for me, had somehow unlocked something inside me—a possibility I'd kept firmly bolted—I hesitated at the threshold. Tonight had drained me completely. The last thing I needed was a reckless decision haunting me in the morning.

So, I pulled back, and even though the absence of his warmth was freezing, I said, "I should probably get some sleep."

His emerald eyes searched mine. "I don't want to risk leaving you alone."

"My father is in jail."

"What if they mistakenly let him out?"

I tried not to let my lips curl at how far-fetched that sounded, but it was adorable. Jace worrying about me when there was no risk. "You heard what the police officer at the hospital said; he's behind bars until his bail arraignment tomorrow."

Jace gently tucked a strand of hair behind my ear, his bruised knuckles ghosting across my cheek. "I'm still leaving Red here. He's a top-notch security guard." Since I'd lost every battle over the whole bodyguard situation, I simply nodded, unable to fight the knot forming in my throat. "How about I pick you up in the morning and take you to work?"

I smiled and placed my hand against his chest, feeling the solid wall of muscle beneath. "That's not necessary." A thought suddenly struck me. "But we do have something we need to figure out."

His uninjured brow arched upward.

"I think we need a cover story." My finger traced the edge of his bruised eyebrow, careful not to apply pressure. "We can't show up at the office tomorrow with matching shiners. People will get suspicious."

His slow smile revealed a dimple I hadn't noticed before. "And we wouldn't want that, would we, Trouble?"

The way he said my nickname, like a secret he was keeping for himself, made my heart stutter in my chest.

"Cover story," Jace repeated as his eyes lit with something that was both mischievous and calculated. "Actually, I have just the right guy for this job."

"You do?" I asked, suddenly wary.

His smile turned dangerous. "You're looking at the man who once convinced the board I got a black eye from a charity boxing match that never happened." He leaned closer, his breath warm against my ear. "Trust me, by tomorrow afternoon, our matching bruises will be the most boring topic in the office."

The tension in my shoulders eased, just a fraction. But then his expression shifted. The playfulness vanished, replaced by something darker. More intense. His jaw tightened as he studied my face.

"There's one other person I want to protect you from, Scarlett."

My breath caught when I realized who he was talking about: Grabby Hands. In the chaos of tonight, I'd momentarily, and blissfully, forgotten about him.

"I won't pressure you about it right now. You've been through enough." Gently, his fingers brushed mine, despite the rage I could see simmering beneath his surface. "But tomorrow, you'll give me the name of the man who violated you."

The sudden shift in his tone caught me off guard. The playful banter from moments ago had vanished, replaced by something cold and precise. Something dangerous. Before tonight, I'd assumed if I gave him the name, best-case scenario, Jace would fire the guy. But the darkness in his eyes suggested he might have other plans.

"And if I tell you who did it," I said carefully, "what will you do to him?"

Jace's expression gave nothing away, a perfect CEO poker face sliding into place. "Let's just say, he'll understand boundaries better after our conversation."

"Jace." I pulled my hand back.

I should have been horrified by the implication of possible violence. Should have recoiled from this dangerous edge he'd revealed. Instead, a small, dark part of me—the part that still woke up screaming some nights—whispered that sometimes, just sometimes, it might be satisfying to have someone else use their power for good.

His phone buzzed, breaking the moment. He glanced at the screen, then back at me with an expression I couldn't read.

"Tomorrow," he said, the word somehow sounding like both a promise.

And a warning.

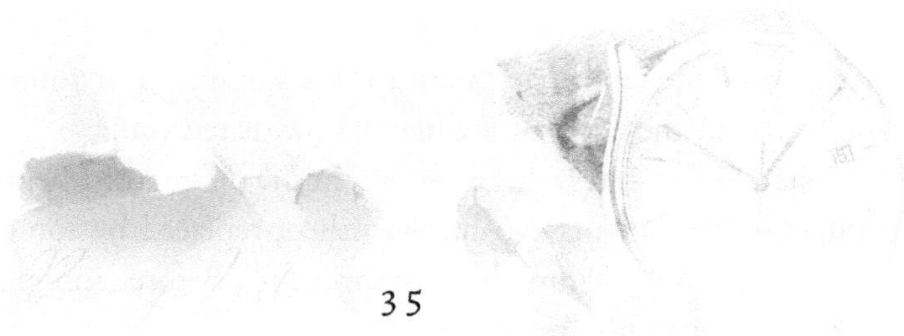

35

SCARLETT

"Holy shit," Dakota said, leaning in the seat across from my desk. "What did you do when you left the emergency room?"

"After Jace left, I stayed at my mom's place."

I held up the compact, dabbing my red cheekbone with more powder. I'd done a decent job of hiding this, but, damn it, I could still see the mark, and if I could, that meant other people could too. The last thing I wanted was to get Jace in trouble for being with me last night. It wasn't like we exactly had a professional explanation for him being at my apartment and getting into a violent confrontation with my father ...

"And the security guy? Did he stay there too?"

I nodded. "He was positioned outside the entire night. And he followed me back to my place, where I changed and got ready for work this morning."

"Well, I have to say, it's pretty hot that Jace came to your defense." Dakota wiggled her eyebrows suggestively.

Speaking of which ... I eyed her. "You can't tell anyone what happened."

She cocked her head. "You know I would never do that."

"I know, but it makes me feel better to have said it. You work at this company, too, so you can't say anything."

Now that I was thinking about it, maybe I shouldn't have told Dakota what happened. The nondisclosure agreement refrained me from discussing the romantic weekend with anyone, but it didn't stipulate what to do if Jace showed up and, you know, punched my father in the face and wrestled him to the ground. *Details.*

Grabbing a pen, I flattened the NDA on my desk and signed the bottom of it.

"So, you're going to tell Jace who Grabby Hands is," she deduced in a relieved tone that suggested I'd finally come to my senses after wandering in the desert of indecision.

"It won't take him long to figure this out on his own. Might as well do it on my terms." I tapped the pen against the paper. "Protecting me."

"Still, this is a big deal. It means you trust him."

"I trust that he'll believe me." Rising, I folded the paper in half to remove the risk of anyone seeing its contents.

"Good luck," she said.

"Thanks."

Why was my heart thundering in my chest? The hardest part, being believed, was virtually a sure thing. I'd spent the entire weekend with Jace, so he knew me well enough to know I would have no reason to lie about this. Right? So, why then was this so nerve-racking?

I got into the elevator, and just before the doors closed, a hand shot between them, forcing them back open. My stomach dropped to my toes. Clad in a black suit that was fitting for his dark soul, Grabby Hands appeared. He had the nerve to smirk at me as he entered the elevator, trapping me alone with him.

Fantastic. Just ... fantastic.

"What happened to your cheek?" he asked, eyeing the mark from last night. "You mouth off to somebody else?"

Mouth off. Wow.

"No, I got it from dodging questions as absurd as that one." I stared straight ahead at the elevator doors, refusing to give him the satisfaction of seeing me rattled.

"I'm on my way to deliver my recommendation for the job. The one you interviewed for."

"Good for you." I kept my voice flat. Dead. Unimpressed.

"It's not too late to bump your name to the top of the list."

I glared at him. He smelled like cedar and misogyny.

"We can meet tonight if you'd like." His voice dropped into a sleazeball octave.

I took one deep breath to calm my absolute boiling rage at this man. He probably expected me to either comply or cower away from him, but I would do neither of those two things.

"In case it wasn't clear when you were sexually harassing me the last time, your advances are unwanted and unprofessional. Stop."

He smiled at me with condescension and said, "Last chance. You want the job or not?" As if his perverted tone wasn't bad enough, he moved closer.

I could not believe the balls on this guy. Having the audacity to sexually harass someone during an interview was disgusting enough. Taking another chance at it was repulsive. But being this brazen, this vile? That took the cake.

Too bad for him, this document in my hand was about to destroy his ass. Within minutes, Jace would have this guy's name, and his career would be professionally cremated.

The elevator doors dinged open, and I gave him a smirk back.

"It was nice working with you," I said, making my exit.

The fact that Grabby Hands was nervous enough about my veiled threat to follow me all the way down the corridor toward Jace's office gave me all sorts of satisfaction. Outside the closed door, a crowd of executives had gathered for what had to be a massively important meeting, but when that door opened, Jace locked eyes with me.

And only me. Other people might not have noticed the way he looked down at my hand, at the paper clutched in it, or the way his mouth lifted slightly on one side as he met my gaze once more. But I did. And seeing as how Grabby Hands might be standing behind me—the creep—I squared my shoulders and played the role of confidence. Pure confidence.

Jace greeted the other men and women quickly with handshakes, making his way through the crowd of leaders until he got to me. My pulse quickened as he approached, that intensity in his eyes making it clear he had only one destination: me.

Grabby Hands walked around me, extending his hand with a confident smile. My stomach twisted as I watched him approach Jace, anticipating the interaction between my protector and my harasser.

Jace looked at him for a moment, his expression shifting in a way I couldn't quite read. Then, to my absolute horror, instead of just accepting the handshake, Jace clasped his hand, pulled him halfway in, and gave him that familiar one-armed pat on the back that men reserved for old friends.

Seeing this, my brain decided to turn into sloth-level slow motion as I witnessed the scene unfolding before me. Witnessed the intimacy that these two guys clearly shared. Jace hadn't bro-hugged any of his other executives. In fact, he didn't strike me as a hugger at all, and even though it was a very masculine, pat-on-the-back kind of hug, it was a hug nonetheless. Any doubt about its significance evaporated when Grabby Hands shot me a victorious look, his villainous eyebrow arched.

Total power play, flapping his proverbial dick on the table, as if to silently say, *See, Scarlett? I'm super close with the owner. So, good luck getting anyone to believe you.*

My throat ran dry. And that pounding heart decided now was a great time to do full-on cartwheels, bouncing around my ribs like it was auditioning for Cirque du Soleil.

Maybe they weren't *that* close though. Maybe, I don't know, Grabby Hands had rescued Jace from a flat tire or something? Okay, my mind needed to come up with better explanations. And fast. Because the alternative, that they were close friends, could not be reality.

"What happened to your face?" Grabby Hands asked Jace, who was sporting a bruised eye. "Second person I saw today that looks like they were on the losing end of a bar fight."

Grabby Hands's dark brown eyes snapped to mine with silent accusation. As if I didn't have enough to worry about, him suspecting Jace and I had been together outside of work, let alone in some kind of violent struggle, was not something I could deal with.

"Stumbled in the dark," Jace said quickly. "Mind giving us a minute?"

"Of course." Grabby Hands placed a hand on Jace's shoulder, shot me an antagonistic smirk, and then ambled off with the confidence of a man who'd already won the game he'd dragged me into.

"You two are close?" Could he hear the tremble in my voice? The disbelief? The absolute horror? I hoped not. I was half smiling, playing the role of a woman who had not just met her harasser.

"Marcus?" Jace looked back at Grabby Hands for a moment. "Oh, yeah. We go way back. He's actually one of my best friends."

Houston, we have a catastrophe.

"That the NDA?" Jace asked, reaching out his palm.

What I wanted to do was rip it up in front of him and throw it in the air like confetti. I wanted to scream at him, *How could you be friends with someone like that?* And what did that say about Jace? Was he really the stand-up guy that I thought he was, or was he somebody who would protect his "best friend" above all else?

He'd certainly never believe some fling he'd shared two days with over his best friend—that was for damn sure.

But I had to play it cool. I needed time to digest what just happened, and until I knew my next move, secrecy was my greatest asset.

"I can't sign it." I pulled the paper closer to my chest.

Jace's eyebrows pulled together, and he shoved his hands into his tailored pants pockets. After glancing at the doorway and the conference table full of people, he sighed in frustration.

"I didn't realize you had a meeting," I said. "We can talk when you have time."

"I never have time," he said. "My calendar is booked. We're talking now."

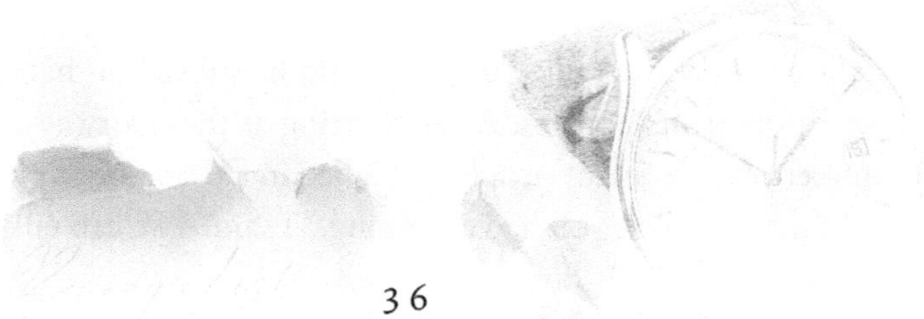

36

SCARLETT

Oh my God, so many thoughts were racing through my head. First of all, this NDA, *theoretically*, protected me against losing my job or suffering unfair consequences if I revealed the name of the sexual harasser. Even if Jace turned around and believed him over me. But that was theoretical.

Practically speaking? Jace had an army of lawyers and HR experts at his disposal. He was Goliath, and I was David with a slingshot loaded with accusations that had bounced off men like him a thousand times before. If Jace believed his best friend over me, I was, to put it bluntly ... screwed. Royally screwed. Majorly screwed. Like *update my résumé while crying into a pint of ice cream* screwed.

And let's just talk about that for a moment. Sure, so far, Jace had seemed like a really good guy, and if the bad guy was anybody else, I would venture to say he would believe me. But he'd only known me for a few days. This was one of his best friends. Best. Friend. If someone accused Tessa or Dakota of something, you bet your ass it would take more than a few days with her accuser to *ever* make me question or second-guess my best friend's integrity. So, chances were, Jace would absolutely side with his best friend.

Or, even worse, what if Jace *knew* that his best friend was shady as hell? In which case, had Jace been, or currently was, complicit in Grabby Hands's behavior? Maybe I didn't really know Jace. I mean, sure, he'd swooped in and protected me from my father and protected my mother, but I'd learned the hard way that people could have multiple faces. Hero in one moment, but covering for his bro the next. Not only did that spell very bad news for me and my prospect of not getting fired over this, but also that kind of guy would be somebody I wanted nothing to do with.

"Follow me," Jace demanded, his voice leaving no room for argument.

"Mr. Lockwood"—his assistant rose from her desk, pen hovering in midair like she was about to conduct an invisible orchestra—"I'm afraid Mr. Camdon has to leave shortly for a flight."

"I'll be there in a minute," Jace replied, his tone clipped.

"Sir ..." she persisted, her eyes darting nervously between the office of waiting leaders and Jace, who continued striding in the wrong direction.

"A minute," Jace repeated so firmly that she said nothing more.

He led me to the small conference room, holding the door open until I walked inside. My pencil skirt felt suddenly too tight as I squeezed past him, the fabric brushing against his perfectly tailored pants. Even in my highest heels, I barely reached his chin. He shut the door behind him with a soft click that sounded like a prison cell locking.

"What do you mean, you're unwilling to sign the NDA?" He turned to face me, his broad shoulders blocking the exit like the world's sexiest bouncer.

I swallowed, trying not to notice how his custom suit curved his body perfectly.

"You have people waiting for you. We can talk about this later."

"They can wait." His eyes darkened. "Explain."

"I mean ..." I cleared my throat, attempting to look anywhere but at the way his jaw clenched. "After careful consideration, I have opted against legally binding myself to this document." Look at me, using big lawyer words, like I hadn't been fantasizing about fleeing the country five seconds ago. "You don't have to worry. I won't talk about our relationship to anyone in the office. In fact, if you draft another NDA that strips out the paragraph where I have to report who harassed me, I'll happily sign it immediately."

"So, that's what this is about." Jace folded his arms across his broad chest, his biceps trying to stage a prison break from the fabric locking them in. "You're refusing to give me the name of the man who harassed you."

"That's correct." I lifted my chin, trying to summon confidence I absolutely did not feel.

"Why?" The single word sounded like it had been chiseled from granite.

The door cracked open, and his assistant poked her head in. "Mr. Lockwood, they—"

"I will let you know when I'm ready," Jace cut her off, his voice glacial. "Do not interrupt us again."

Based on the widening of her eyes, she wasn't used to him taking this tone with her.

"Yes, sir." The door closed with a snap.

I took a deep breath. "The *why* doesn't matter."

"Like hell it doesn't." He took a step closer, and I caught a whiff of his musk cologne that made my knees wobble. "Did he threaten you?"

"No." I shook my head. "In fact, he doubled down." *Okay, great job, Scarlett. Why the hell did you say that?*

Jace's expression darkened. "He did *what*?"

"It doesn't matter." I glanced at my shoes, suddenly fascinated by the scuff on my left heel.

"What did he do?" Each word was measured, dangerous.

"Look, the point is, if you draft the NDA without that paragraph—"

"So, this happened today then?" Jace's voice sharpened. "He did something else today?"

I opened my mouth, but wasn't sure what to say. Especially not when Jace took another step forward, close enough that I could feel the heat radiating from his body. My heart and hormones betrayed me, buzzing with electricity in his presence. These feelings needed to stand down ASAP. This was officially way too complicated.

"Scarlett," he said, "I have been patient. I have been understanding. But there is a predator in this organization. You will tell me who it is."

"Why?" I blurted out.

His eyebrows shot up. "Excuse me?"

"Why, exactly, do you want to know who it is?" I forced myself to meet his gaze.

"Is that a trick question?" Jace looked genuinely bewildered. "He doesn't belong in this organization."

"Have you ever had someone in your organization accused of sexual harassment before?" I asked, surprising myself with my boldness.

"The CEO doesn't field complaints of harassment. That's HR's department."

"So, you don't know then."

He said nothing, the silence stretching between us like a ticking clock, counting down to something I wasn't sure I could stomach.

"Have you ever been aware of someone in your company sexually harassing anyone before?" I pressed.

My rebellious heart waited with bated breath for his answer because his answer would determine if, in my eyes, Jace was a good guy or a bad guy. And I needed him to be a good guy. Even if nothing else ever happened between us, I needed to remember him as the guy who heroically showed up and protected me and my mother from my father. Not a wolf in sheep's clothing because, so help me, I couldn't handle that. Not after what we'd been through. Not after I'd unwillingly given him a fragment of my heart.

"Where are you going with this?" His voice was dangerously soft.

"Information flows two ways, Jace." I crossed my arms, mimicking his stance. "You want to know his name, and I want to understand why you want to know it and if he's the first or if he's just the first in a long line of harassers that you've ignored."

His eyes flashed. "Are you accusing me of fostering a toxic work environment?"

"I ... no. I ..." I stammered, suddenly aware of how far I'd pushed.

"Then what exactly are you accusing me of?" He stepped closer still, the heat between us ratcheting up several degrees.

"I'm not accusing you of anything! I just want to know if ..." *If you know that your best friend is a total slimeball. If you're in on it. If you've been covering for him.*

"Let me make this perfectly clear. HR handles all complaints in my organization, and they have protocols and procedures. But if you're asking about me specifically, about where I stand on this, I do not tolerate harassment of employees in any of my companies. If I was ever made aware anyone had done that, they would have been escorted out by their ear without severance."

After studying him for several seconds, I realized, with immense relief, that I believed him. I could see it in the fire in his eyes and the anger in his posture. He would not be complicit in it, and he would not cover it up, which left one option: he had no idea that his best friend was a complete douchebag. It was the best option because it meant that Jace really was a good guy.

But that didn't make this any easier. Good guy or not, Jace would still require a lot of convincing to believe his best friend was a predator. Especially when said predator knew Jace well enough to sow seeds of doubt.

Plus, I'd done some research on Grabby Hands and discovered he'd been a leader in Jace's organization for years. And let's be clear: a leader in a billion-dollar private equity firm made bank. His entire identity online was wrapped up in it—from the sports car that he drove to the models and actresses that he dated.

Grabby Hands had everything to lose.

And so did I.

"Scarlett." Jace's voice softened just enough to remind me of how he'd spoken to me in bed. "I understand you're afraid, but I will not accept no for an answer. You will give me his name."

"I won't." I straightened my spine, trying to ignore how his proximity made my skin tingle. "There is nothing that you can do to make me tell you."

His jaw moved from side to side, a muscle ticcing in his cheek. Something in his expression shifted, and his lips flattened into a firm line that was both challenging and devastatingly sexy.

"Then you'll force me to get that information from you some other way."

Heart hammering against my ribs, I managed to ask, "Such as?"

With one last glare—and, dammit, how could angry look sexy?—he turned and left me alone in the conference room, the door clicking shut behind him with finality.

I sank into the nearest chair, the realization hitting me like a hangover: this was far from over.

In fact, this was just the beginning of a war.

37

SCARLETT

"Me?" I asked, my coffee cup freezing halfway to my lips.

"Yes," an HR executive I'd never met before said with a professional smile that revealed absolutely nothing. "At one o'clock."

I set my cup down carefully on my desk, buying myself precious seconds. "Today?"

"I know it's short notice," she continued, inspecting her immaculate manicure, "but this is an incredible opportunity. Can you make it work?"

"Of course," I replied, mustering every ounce of corporate cool I could fake.

Meanwhile, a tiny version of me was doing jumping jacks on my shoulder, screaming, *Of course I can't make this work! I've never presented to the board of directors before! And you're only giving me three hours to prepare what could be the career-defining presentation of my life? Why not just ask me to scale Mount Everest in flip-flops while you're at it?*

I mean, my God, even under normal circumstances, this would be the opportunity of a lifetime, but with everything going on with Grabby Hands, this was a chance to get in front of leaders and show them who I was: a capable, valuable asset to this organization. That way, if he tried to spread rumors, they'd have something else to base their opinion of me on other than the word of one lone man with octopus tendencies. This was a dream.

Right?

Except for the timeline. I'd prefer to spend three *weeks* preparing for this kind of opportunity.

"What do they want me to present?"

"Truly, you can pick what you want."

I tilted my head, suspicion crawling up my back. The incredibly busy board of directors was inviting me to present, but had no specific goal for the meeting? Nothing suspicious about that at all.

Perhaps reading the skepticism on my face, the HR woman said, "They're interested in learning more about some of the employees from the company they've acquired."

Right. Okay ... I wanted to say, but why *me specifically*?

Instead, my frazzled brain replied with, "Sure. That sounds perfect." *Gold star for professionalism, Scarlett. Maybe next time, you can respond with finger guns and a wink.*

"Great." Her smile widened a fraction. "They'll see you at one o'clock."

She clicked away on her designer heels, leaving me standing there with my stomach performing a flag presentation. Specifically, waving red flags all over the place.

I didn't know what was going on, but my internal alarm system was blaring like a five-alarm fire. Tapping my pen against my desk, my brain sprinted through scenarios of what this might mean.

Was this like one of those scenarios out of those movies where it was not a presentation at all, but a corporate execution squad waiting for you to justify your existence? The kind where if you didn't come up with a good enough presentation or didn't field the whole "what would you say you do here" questions, you'd walk out with your personal items in a cardboard box and security breathing down your neck?

Oh crap, what if there was no meeting at all? I'd learned through other fallen colleagues that when companies performed mass firings, they never put it on your calendar like: *Hey, come to your termination meeting at one o'clock! Bring tissues!* No, it always came disguised as something that would ensure you showed up.

Or maybe this was a good thing? An opportunity even? Jace's doing perhaps? Trying to throw me a bone by giving me visibility to leadership after our argument? His way of making it up to me? What if it was the opposite though? What if Jace was so pissed I'd refused to give him Grabby Hands's identity that he'd had enough and orchestrated a way to get me fired?

Or ... or perhaps this was simply what that HR executive said it would be: an opportunity for new blood to learn what old blood did here.

Standing up, I paced in my office for two minutes before finally telling myself to stop obsessing over hidden agendas and get to work. No matter what this was, no matter how bad of a feeling I had about this, I had no choice but to show up prepared.

I could only hope that after this mysterious meeting, I'd still have a job.

Sitting at my desk, I cleared my calendar, created PowerPoint slides faster than an IT coding genius on a Red Bull bender, practiced my talking points until my mouth went dry, touched up my makeup and hair (because I read that looking good while getting ambushed was important), and finally, I walked upstairs, took one last steadying breath, and stepped inside the conference room.

And promptly forgot how to breathe.

Because there, commanding the room like he owned it (which, technically, he did), was another party I hadn't expected to join this board presentation or whatever this was: Jace. He sat at the center of an oval glass conference table because, of course, it had to be glass, taunting me with memories of what we'd done on one, while his eyes laser-focused on me with an almost-predatory intensity. Predatory in the best way, to be clear, and dammit if that wasn't infuriating. Also infuriating was how he somehow looked even more gorgeous today than yesterday, when we'd had that argument over the NDA. The light streaming through oversize windows highlighted those eyes—the unusual shade of absinthe, equal parts danger and temptation—and his black suit with the white button-down was impeccable, complete with a blue tie.

Wait. That wasn't just any blue tie. Was that ...

Yep ... that was the same tie I'd fastened around his eyes while he lay naked on another glass table entirely, the one where I'd straddled his face and he'd licked and sucked me into oblivion.

Did he wear it on purpose? To remind me that I could refuse him all I wanted, but we had an intimate relationship whether I liked it or not? Was it a message of some sort?

It took me a full three seconds to tear my gaze away from him and notice what should have been immediately obvious. The table was surrounded by over a dozen business people. All my bosses (minus the lone woman, suspiciously), a sprinkling of executives I worked with, plus a couple from the new organization, including Grabby Hands, who occupied one of the seats next to Jace.

All men. Every. Single. One.

Move, Scarlett. Play the part of the unaffected professional.

I forced my feet toward the only open chair, the pieces clicking together in my mind as I digested the scene before me with a horrible realization.

This wasn't a presentation.

It was a trap.

38

JACE

Goddammit, she is beautiful.

That pencil skirt hugged her hips, ass, and legs that I wanted to spread wide open and feast on until she screamed my name. I wanted to bend her over this table and grab that blonde hair in my fist and pound into her, maybe give her ass a slap or two and tell her she'd been a bad girl, defying my orders yesterday. How was it possible that each time I saw her, she only grew more gorgeous? If anyone looked beneath the table, they'd see my pants struggling against my growing erection. Which was the absolute opposite of a professional response for someone who was actively staging a battlefield to uncover who had harassed Scarlett.

Someone in this room was a predator. Someone had laid hands on her. Someone had teased out Scarlett's painful and deep-seated insecurities about men with power.

I couldn't help but wonder, *If I had met Scarlett before this man had violated her trust, might she have been more open to me? Might she have felt less intimidated, less threatened by my power, and thus more willing to surrender to the idea of us?*

It was a selfish thought. Yet one that fueled my wildfire of rage.

I watched her face as she took in the scene, noting the exact moment realization dawned in those expressive eyes of hers. While I'd carefully rounded out the occupants to include various executives, both old and new in an effort to make it a little less obvious what I was actually doing here, she clearly knew this wasn't just a presentation. I could see it in the way her professional mask slipped, just for one glorious moment. A heartbeat of time, when I could see the anger behind her eyes. No one else would be the wiser because she was exceptional at concealing that anger behind a mask of professionalism.

But I knew her better than anyone in this room.

All I needed was a flinch. A slight grimace. The tiniest tell when she got close to the right man. Then I'd take the bastard down so hard, he'd never work anywhere again.

I kept my eyes fixed on her, tracking every micro expression, every subtle shift in her posture. I wasn't just looking at her. I was reading her.

"Ms. West," I started, leaning slightly forward in my chair. "Thank you for taking the time to meet with us today."

Folding her hands on the table, she plastered on a smile that didn't reach her eyes. "Of course, Mr. Lockwood. I was rather excited when I was told I'd have an opportunity to present to the board." Her attention flicked around the table, a calculated scan. "Will they be joining us shortly?"

"I'm afraid there was a misunderstanding." I held her gaze, letting the words hang.

"Oh?" One perfectly shaped eyebrow arched. Translation: *What game are you playing?*

"The board won't be joining us today." I kept my voice even, professional.

"I see." She tapped her index finger twice against the table. "Well, it was my intention to educate the board on my roles and responsibilities. Most of the people in this room are already quite familiar with my ... work."

The slight pause before "work" was imperceptible to anyone who hadn't heard her voice break during intimacy.

"I'd like you to present all the same." *Trust me*, I tried to convey with my eyes.

Anger flashed across her features in a micro expression only someone who'd studied every inch of her face would catch.

"Of course," she managed, smoothing her skirt with a deliberate motion that reminded me of when I'd pulled another off of her. "I emailed the slides to Jessica, per the email I received." *But this isn't what I agreed to*, her eyes said.

A flicker of guilt flashed through me for using my power like this against her.

"Your copies, Mr. Lockwood." My assistant entered the room, placing a stack of stapled copies of the presentation in front of Scarlett. Just as I had ordered her to do. "Will that be all?"

"Yes. Thank you."

I waited until my assistant left the room.

"Ms. West, would you be so kind as to hand out those copies?"

Make no mistake. This wasn't a sexist thing. This wasn't because she was the only female in the room and tasks like that belonged to the female population; I wasn't a chauvinistic douche. This was a test. A deliberate move in our silent chess match, requiring her to get close to each and every man in this room. There was no way she'd be able to do that without some kind of tell.

I know exactly what you're doing, her gaze seemed to say.

I arched an eyebrow with a silent, *Did you honestly think I'd let this go?* My fingers adjusted the blue tie at my throat—a calculated reminder of our intimacy.

Her subtle frown deepened for just a split second, followed by a sharp, precise movement as she rose from her chair. Her posture communicated clearly: *You want to play games? Fine. But you're not getting anything out of me.*

I cocked my head slightly, maintaining eye contact a beat too long. *We'll see about that.*

Whether she realized her cheeks were flushing slightly, I

wasn't sure. But that little tell confirmed it: she was nervous, not just angry. And that meant the suspect was, in fact, in this room. I'd wondered if perhaps I had gotten the roster right. It looked like we had all the players. Fifteen people sat in this room. Thirteen, aside from me and Scarlett. Seven of her bosses, four executives I'd confirmed she interacted with regularly, two new executives from my team, including Marcus, to throw her off the scent (evidently, it didn't work).

And one of them was the asshole.

I watched her swallow as she picked up the stack of papers and made her way slowly around the table, carefully placing one in front of each man. Her movements were deliberate. Professional yet guarded. A tiny bit rough when she set my copy in front of me. Each time she leaned forward, I tracked the space she maintained, the angle of her body, the tension in her shoulders. And while I watched her face, her mannerisms, and the small betrayals of her true feelings, I also watched *them* react to her. Some followed her movement with their eyes. Others barely acknowledged her presence. I didn't need much. Just a flinch, a hesitation, anything.

When she made it all the way around the table, passing out the copies without one hint of who the guy was, I clenched my fist.

Even harder when she sat back down and gave me a slight swivel of her head, silently saying, *Nice try. Won't work.*

Clearing my throat, I shot her a look too: *If you think that was my only tactic, you underestimated me.*

"Ms. West, I'm sure you have an incredibly insightful presentation prepared." I leaned forward, resting my elbows on the glass table. "However, I would like to focus on your projects and work from last week."

A nearly imperceptible pause interrupted her breathing, along with a flash of understanding in her eyes.

Last week, someone had grabbed her thigh. So, who had she worked with? What had she done?

"Last week," she repeated, with a bite to her tone. Her fingers traced the edge of the folder before her. "Is there something specific you are interested in?"

Yes. You. All of you. And which of these assholes' cheekbones I'm going to break.

"Tell you what." I leaned back in my chair, all casual CEO confidence. A posture I'd perfected over years of boardroom battles. "Why don't you just go over everything you did last week?"

She started clicking the mouse that controlled the presentation on the front screen, fast-forwarding through what appeared to be an incredibly impressive presentation. The slight tensing of her jaw told me she'd spent hours on this.

"The projects that I worked on last week—"

"Forget the PowerPoint," I said, trying not to smirk at her *seriously? do you know how hard I worked on these damn slides* look that flashed across her face. "What I'd rather do is learn this organization from the inside out. Walk me through your days last week."

So far, no one in the room seemed any wiser. Why would they? This was just a new owner trying to get to know the new organization. Right? Wrong.

"Okay. Well, the main project I worked on was for the Agma contract."

I set my pen down deliberately, making sure it aligned perfectly with the edge of my notepad.

"Forgive me for what might sound like an unusual request." I kept my voice measured. "But if it's not too much trouble, I'd like you to stand at the front of the room. It'll make it easier to see you without everyone having to crane their heads," I claimed. "And each time you're discussing a project you're working on, anyone who was working on that with you, I would like to have them join you at the front and add additional context."

Look at that slight flash of anger, her fingers tightening

around the pages for a beat before relaxing. Her eyes held mine for a dangerous moment.

You're pushing it, they said.

Try and stop me, mine replied.

"Of course," she said with professionalism.

"Let's start with Friday." *The day you stumbled into that bar with a revenge list.*

She cleared her throat, smoothing her skirt as she walked to the front of the room. I let my gaze sweep across the table, watching for anyone to slip up and stare at that fine ass. An ass that could make a married man crash his car from being unable to look away, but no one took the bait. They all sat there, some with their fingers steepled, some flipping through the presentation, all still thinking this was a legitimate meeting.

Scarlett, on the other hand, stood at the front of the conference table and shot me another subtle glare. Her weight shifted to one hip in a stance that told me she was preparing for battle.

"Friday morning began with a comprehensive marketing analysis that I performed for our main Q3 campaign," she began.

"Impressive," I said, tapping my finger once on the table. "Did you review this analysis with anyone?"

"Yes, sir," a guy whose name I'd learned was Thomas said. "She reviewed it with me."

Did she now?

"Please," I said in my friendliest tone, gesturing toward the front. "I would love to have your insight."

The guy stood up, buttoning his jacket like he thought he was getting picked as the teacher's pet. Scarlett cocked her head slightly and then almost imperceptibly rolled her eyes at me.

This is ridiculous, she seemed to say.

But look at her body language when he got close to her, this time without the distraction of passing out slides. Not flinching. Not grimacing. And not at all blushing. If anything, she relaxed slightly, her shoulders dropping a fraction of an inch.

I allowed them to quickly review her analysis, noting how

naturally they interacted. Professional. Comfortable. No hidden tension.

"Thank you, Thomas," I said, tentatively checking him off my mental list. "What other work did you do on Friday, Ms. West?"

One by one, I pulled them up. One by one, I watched. Each time, her posture remained professionally neutral, sometimes even genuinely engaged. Not once did I catch the wariness, the subtle recoil I was looking for.

After repeating this until we had gone through her entire week of work, I was gripping my pen so tightly, I wondered if it would snap. I massaged my hands together beneath the table. She had given up nothing. Not one damn thing, and look at her standing up there, her lips threatening to curve up in the barest hint of victory.

Told you, her raised eyebrow seemed to say.

Inhaling an incredibly frustrated breath, I said, "This was insightful, but I still have not gleaned the information I was hoping to get." The admission cost me, and from the slight tilt of her head, she knew it.

"I'm sorry you're disappointed, Mr. Lockwood." The way she said my name—formal yet intimate—sent a current through the room that only I could feel. "If you'd like me to create another presentation—"

"This isn't over," I said, my tone making two executives straighten in their chairs.

39

SCARLETT

I stared up at the sky, the warmth of the setting sun caressing my face, and I couldn't help but smile with the surge of relief that washed over me. I'd survived that conference-room showdown without revealing Marcus's identity to Jace.

At first, I'd been furious that Jace staged that meeting, but you know what? Maybe I needed it. It proved I could keep this secret. This was within my control. The first semblance of control I'd felt since the harassment happened. Now, I was confident I could get through this without destroying my career. Without failing to pay Mom's rent. Without giving Dad the chance to get his hands on her. All I needed to do was keep my head down, do my job, and this nightmare would fade to black.

Another thing that had me smiling was the outcome of my father's bail hearing. I'd learned my father would not be released from jail while awaiting his day in court. Instead, he'd be detained, and he was facing felony-level charges rather than misdemeanors, which carried significant jail time. It seemed the tides had turned on the dark storm of my father, and for the foreseeable future, the threat he posed to us was gone.

I walked along the sidewalk, my high heels click-clacking against concrete as I headed up the staircase to the "L" train that would take me home. For a fleeting moment, I caught movement in my peripheral vision that made me turn, but no one was there. And, hello, even if there was, this was the busy "L" platform. People came and went all day, so why had that flash of movement put me on edge?

Why was my body still firing off warning shots? Unsure, I rode the public transportation to my usual stop, then quickened my pace, crossing the last intersection before reaching my apartment building. Practically diving inside. It wasn't until I stepped off the elevator into the safety of my hallway that I exhaled the breath I'd been holding hostage.

Walking toward my apartment door, I heard the ding of the second elevator signal its opening. Then heavy, deliberate footsteps behind me.

I spun around, ready to face whatever random neighbor was innocently heading to their—

Holy shit.

The man standing before me was none other than Grabby Hands himself: Marcus.

"Did I frighten you, Scarlett?" His tone was creepy AF, like he was hoping the answer was yes. But even though my heart jammed itself into my throat, I refused to give him the satisfaction.

"Stalking is a crime, you know." I crossed my arms, channeling my best impression of *you don't scare me.*

"Stalking." He smirked, shoving his hands into his pockets so casually, the movement itself was disturbing. "If you think this constitutes stalking, you clearly are unfamiliar with the term."

A veiled threat. Lovely.

"So, by the sound of it, you must be an expert." I cocked my head. "What's your specialty? Workplace harassment with a side of home invasion?"

He took a step forward, broadening his shoulders to block the light behind him. Which was when I suddenly realized just how alone we were. I mean, in theory, one of those elevators could open at any moment, or a neighbor could emerge from their apartment, but I knew the patterns in my building. My immediate neighbors didn't typically get home until late, so they wouldn't be here to interrupt ... well, whatever the hell this was.

Breathe, Scarlett. He has nothing to gain by attacking you. This is just intimidation tactics 101.

"Why are you here?" I demanded.

"After that dog and pony show, it seems you and I have something to discuss," he answered.

"You think that was a dog and pony show? Wow." I cocked my head, trying to look more annoyed than terrified. "What exactly do you and I *need* to discuss that couldn't happen at the office?"

"You told Jace someone sexually harassed you," he accused.

My heart expanded in my throat.

"And," Marcus continued, "there's something else I learned from that meeting."

"Well, I can't wait to hear this." I raised my chin, trying to pretend I wasn't mentally scrolling through self-defense YouTube tutorials I'd watched at two a.m. "Is it that your cologne makes you smell like you bathe in discount aftershave?"

"Jace likes you."

"I'm a very competent employee. Most leaders I work with appreciate my competence. And they *respect* me," I added, hoping the insult landed like a slap.

"You know I'm Jace's best friend."

"Strange. Because I thought Blake was one of his best friends, and I've never heard him mention you." I scrunched my nose. "Like, ever."

Marcus raised his eyebrows. "You know his other friends?"

"I want to give you one last opportunity to tell me what the hell you want before I start screaming loud enough that all my neighbors will call 911. Oh, and Johnny over there?" I nodded to a door. "Keeps a baseball bat behind his front door." Lies. There was no Johnny, no bat.

"You're a feisty little thing, aren't you?" He smirked, taking yet another step closer. The way his filthy eyes raked over my body made me want to power-wash my skin.

"So, you're here to, what, intimidate me into silence? By threatening to assault me again? Because that worked out so well the first time."

"Who's threatening?"

"Get to the point. What. Do. You. Want?"

He cocked his head, studying me as he licked his lower lip in what I assumed he thought was seductive but actually resembled a lizard with food stuck in its teeth.

"Jace is obviously trying to figure out who 'harassed' you," Marcus said, using air quotes around the word *harassed* like sexual assault was some made-up concept, right up there with unicorns and men who put the toilet seat down.

"Is that so? What, pray tell, makes you think that?"

"He didn't ask anyone else in the company to present to him today, so I knew it meant something. And when all of your *male* superiors were in the room, but not the female one, I suspected what he was up to." His voice dripped with smug satisfaction. "I know him. Any last shred of doubt evaporated when you walked in and Jace's entire demeanor changed. He was like a shark circling for blood, trying to figure out who it was." He leaned closer. "But here's the very interesting part: I did some due diligence, and as it turns out, there's no complaint on file. So, how is it that the owner of the company is aware of some supposed sexual harassment that was never even reported?"

His eyes flickered to the mark on my cheek, the one that looked similar to Jace's injury.

"That's a whole hell of a lot of hypothesizing," I said. "Maybe I'm just the first victim of your harassment who didn't go along with it, so you're becoming completely paranoid, reading into everything. Or, shocking thought, maybe you should keep your hands to yourself and your conspiracy theories in your pocket, right next to your apparently nonexistent moral compass."

"I know my friend."

"Then talk to *him* about your theories. And get out of my apartment complex before I call the police and tell HR in the morning about your failed intimidation tactic. I'll make sure to mention the stalking. Very professional touch, by the way."

"It's quite puzzling, isn't it? That Jace Lockwood knows about the harassment, but HR doesn't?"

"That he supposedly knows, according to you," I clarified.

"And based on how angry he seemed in that meeting, he cares about you *a lot*."

"Any owner would be displeased if he suspected sexual harassment in his company. It's called being a decent human being. You might want to Google the concept."

He shook his head. "I know my friend. Those weren't business emotions."

Crap. The no-fraternization policy flashed through my head. While Jace was the owner and CEO, he also had a board of directors to report to. The last thing I wanted was to get him in trouble. Not after what we'd experienced together and not after he'd protected me from my father.

"Jace and I are not dating, if that's what you're implying. But thanks for the fan fiction. Very creative."

"He obviously has feelings for you. Which creates quite a complication."

"A complication," I repeated. "Is that what we're calling your inability to keep your hands to yourself now?"

"How well do you know Jace?"

"You tell me. You seem to be the one with all the hypothetical answers to all the hypothetical questions."

He smirked. "Well, let's just say, if someone hurts someone Jace cares about, the man can be quite ... unreasonable."

Unreasonable. He said it like he was saying the word *bullet*, but meant *nuclear weapon*.

"Then assume all his employees are people he cares about. Or here's a thought: don't sexually harass anyone, ever, because you know ... laws. Rules. Basic human decency. Stuff they usually teach in kindergarten right after *don't eat glue*."

"If you were to claim that what happened in your interview was harassment—"

"It was."

"To Jace, that would create significant problems."

"I see. And you thought stalking me and harassing me would make me LESS likely to rat you out? Wow, college really failed you, didn't it?"

His face tightened. "You will not tell HR," Marcus declared, his voice dropping to a dangerous whisper. "And you will not tell Jace."

"Is that so?" My eyebrow shot to my hairline. Now it was my turn to put my body language into full-on offensive mode.

See, here's the problem with my control issues: Sometimes, when someone tries to back me into a corner, all the rational reasons I have for staying quiet evaporate. The only thing that matters becomes reclaiming my power. Because sometimes having a man tell me exactly what I was going to do? That made me want to do the exact opposite, consequences be damned.

"Well, seeing as how you've followed me home and peppered me with implied threats, I think maybe it's time I do tell everyone what you did. I'm thinking company-wide email. Maybe an Instagram post. How photogenic are you? I hear fluorescent lighting in police stations is particularly unflattering."

His movement was so fast, I barely registered it. I pulled away at the last second, but it was too late. My arm was in his grasp. A painfully biting, vise-like grip that would leave finger-shaped souvenirs by morning.

"You think *I'm* such a bad guy? Well, Jace isn't the clean-cut man you think he is."

I jerked my body free. "Screw you. With a cactus. Sideways."

Digging around in my purse, I pulled out my cell phone, unlocking the screen to call 911. But it exploded out of my hand with the force of his fist.

It took a couple of seconds to register what had happened, to evaluate the shadows crossing the planes of his face, the dark turn this encounter had taken. And to register that Marcus wasn't just a creep.

He was dangerous.

"If you need more incentive to keep your mouth shut, allow me to give it to you." He stepped closer, towering over me, and it was everything I could do to not step back, to give him the satisfaction of showing him I was afraid.

But, holy hell, I *was* afraid. Too afraid to scream, too afraid he'd choke me to death or something before I could alert anyone for help.

"I'm protecting Jace's darkest secret," he continued. "One that no one knows about except for me. Not even his other so-called friends."

"You expect me to believe you? What's next? You're going to tell me you're actually a Nigerian prince who needs my bank account details?"

His eyes darkened into a predatory glare reminiscent of my father before his violent episodes.

"If you expose me, I'll expose him, and he'll lose everything. His career, his reputation. His freedom. Hell, his safety would be on the line. That secret could dig up enemies that would also endanger people he cares about too. People like his buddies that you seem to know so well."

I didn't know them well. I mean, I knew Blake reasonably well, but that wasn't the point here. The point was, I had no idea what to make of Marcus's claims. But I trusted my intuition about Jace being a good person. Marcus, on the other hand, had already proven himself to be human garbage.

"Sexual harassment is just a symptom of who you really are," I said. "And if you're capable of sexual harassment, you're capable of lying. So, forgive me if I don't take your word as gospel."

He smirked. "Then call my bluff, Scarlett West. But if you

care about Jace at all, you'll keep your mouth shut and watch your back."

As he turned and walked away, I stood frozen, reeling from his words. The outright threats. The implied ones. The accusations about Jace and his supposed dark secrets.

I picked up my fallen phone, swiped it over, and hovered my thumb over the Emergency Call button.

But something stopped me from pressing it.

What if Marcus wasn't bluffing? What if Jace did have secrets that could destroy him? And what if, by trying to protect myself, I ended up destroying the one man who had made me feel safe for the first time in forever?

The taste of fear filled my mouth as one terrifying thought solidified. I was caught between two dangerous men: one I feared and one I was falling for. And I had no idea which one would hurt me worse in the end.

40

SCARLETT

"Holy crap," Tessa gasped.

We sat in Blake's dining room, crystal wineglasses catching the amber glow from the recessed lighting above. Well, technically, this was Blake *and* Tessa's place now since she'd moved in shortly after they'd fallen in love. It was at this very penthouse that I had first met Blake, back when I was the spitting image of confidence. Sitting on his countertop, giving him advice like I had my life together.

And now here I was, with my world crumbling, and I was trying to stop it before it turned to dust. I'd filled her in on my weekend of fun with Jace. A weekend Blake probably knew about, too, after the ER visit. But most pressing at the moment, I'd filled her in on Marcus.

"You can't let this guy get away with that," Tessa insisted, her small frame practically vibrating with indignation as she leaned forward across the table, which smelled of sandalwood and wealth.

My best friend was right.

"I have no intention of letting him get away with it." I took a deliberate sip of the cabernet and savored its rich bite against my tongue. Liquid courage. I'd need it.

"You have to tell Jace."

"Agreed. But I have to be smart about it." I traced the rim of my wineglass, buying time to organize my thoughts. "Marcus is a slimeball. He clearly knows Jace very well and will probably know just what to say to convince him that he's innocent."

"I'm sure Jace will take your side," Tessa said, taking a sip of her own drink.

"If there's even a small chance that what Marcus is saying is true, if Marcus has some dirt on Jace that could destroy his company and endanger everyone he cares about ..." I swallowed hard. "If I tell him before I have my ducks in a row, this will go south. Fast."

When I told Tessa how Marcus had essentially threatened people like Blake, her face went through a complete emotional journey. First stop: wide-eyed shock. She'd stared into her drink for several silent seconds. Then, step two. With a sharp intake of breath, shoulders squaring, nostrils flaring, she'd gone into anger mode. Now, it looked like we'd graduated to step three: an unexplained gleam in her eye.

"What?" I demanded.

"You realize what just happened, right?" Tessa's eyes lit up like she'd just solved a murder mystery.

"My growing venomous hatred for a sexual harasser?" I arched an eyebrow, reaching for my drink. "Or the fact that I'm now fantasizing about Marcus mysteriously falling down an empty elevator shaft?"

"When you caught me up on everything, it was all *my career this* and *my job that*. But now?" She leaned forward, voice dropping to a dramatic whisper. "Now you're worried about *Jace*."

I blinked. "Huh?"

"You. Want. To. Protect. Him." Her smile stretched wider with each word, her eyes twinkling, like she'd just caught me writing his name, surrounded by little hearts. "Just like he protected you from your father."

Yep. I'd told her that whole debacle, too, including the ER visit.

"And," she added, "you said the sex was HOT."

"Are you hearing me?" I straightened my shoulders. "Did you miss the part where this sociopath might come after Blake? Your boyfriend? The love of your life? The guy whose face is literally your phone background?"

Tessa waved her hand like I'd mentioned a minor inconvenience. "Which is exactly why you need to warn Jace. Once he tells the guys what's going on, it's Marcus who should be shopping for a bulletproof vest."

"She said with disturbing murderous implications." I squinted at her. "Should I be concerned about your browser history?"

"Back to the point," Tessa sang, tapping her nails against her glass. "You, my friend, want to *protect* Jace."

"It's the decent thing to do."

"It's the *romantic* thing to do," she countered, practically serenading the words.

I glared at her. "You know, for someone who just found out her boyfriend might be in danger, you're disturbingly cheerful. Did you replace your blood with champagne when I wasn't looking?"

Tessa's smile fell, and she stared at her wineglass as she swirled the red liquid around, creating a miniature burgundy tornado.

"You're right. Sorry." She squared her shoulders. "Okay, back to the plan. What is the plan exactly?"

"First of all, I've already applied for two other jobs."

"You're quitting? That's your grand plan?" Disbelief dripped from every word.

"My plan of attack has multiple levels," I explained, setting my glass down with a soft clink. "I need to be smart here and protect myself *and* Jace. So, parallel to the big plan, I'm going to be looking for another job, just in case."

"I guess that's smart ..." She fiddled with the delicate silver bracelet on her wrist.

"Which leads me to the second part." I leaned in. "I need proof. I need to bring Jace evidence that Marcus is the one who harassed me and is now threatening him."

"Maybe we should ask Blake how to approach Marcus?" Tessa suggested. "Maybe he's met him before?"

"If you ask Blake, he'll go to Jace, and then Jace will be tipped off, and Marcus will have an opportunity to weasel his way out of all of this." I shook my head firmly.

"But if this guy is dangerous, I want to warn Blake."

"Give me a day or two." Surely, Marcus wouldn't have a reason to turn into a serial killer within forty-eight hours.

"So, what is your plan to get this proof?" Tessa mirrored my posture.

"I'm going to wait until the office is mostly cleared out. And then I'm going to tell Marcus that I want to meet with him."

A crease appeared between her brows. "Trapping yourself alone with a guy who might be dangerous sounds risky."

"When he left me, he gave me a choice: to drop this or face the consequences. So, it stands to reason that he's waiting for an answer." I tapped my nails against the table. "I'm going to give him that answer. But I want to be recording audio when I do it. All I have to do is catch him saying one thing that corroborates my story, and then I can take that to Jace."

"But what if he—"

"Tessa?" Blake's voice boomed down the entryway, interrupting whatever objection she was about to raise.

"In here!" she chirped.

"I thought he wasn't going to be home tonight?" I whispered.

Not that I minded seeing Blake. He was a really good guy. It was just that this was a very private conversation, one that I did not want her to share with her boyfriend right now.

She shrugged, lips quirking apologetically. "His hours are unpredictable sometimes."

Right. ER doctors.

"Remember what you promised: that this conversation was just between the two of us," I said, my voice low but firm.

Based on Tessa's pursed lips, I could tell she didn't like this, but her slight nod told me she would oblige. At least for now.

"Scarlett." Blake entered the room, wearing black pants and a fitted black shirt that emphasized his broad shoulders. "I didn't know you were coming over tonight." His voice had changed in the time since I'd first met him. Before, it had been gruff and grouchy. Now, there was a lighter side to it, like someone had finally adjusted his settings from *brooding hero* to *actual human being.*

Case in point, he walked over to Tessa and kissed her on her forehead like a lovesick puppy. He might be huge and muscular and smart enough to save lives, but he was seriously becoming a bit of a golden retriever if you asked me.

Which, yes, was beyond adorable. And he treated Tessa like a queen, so Blake was golden in my book.

"I was just about to leave," I said, already gathering my purse.

"No need." Blake waved a dismissive hand. His doctor eyes settled on my cheek. Stepping closer, he put his finger beneath my chin and tilted it toward the light to get a better view, his clinical assessment mode apparently never fully off.

"It's healing nicely," he said approvingly.

"It was a minor injury," I reminded him.

"Sometimes, even minor injuries can get infected. You ladies hungry? I can have Maria cook up—"

"I'm fine," I interrupted with a forced smile. "I was actually just about to leave."

"You don't have to—" Tessa started.

"I'm tired," I cut her off with a smile that, hopefully, didn't look as fake as it felt. "Thanks for the wine, Tessa."

She followed me to the elevator. Yep, Blake lived in a penthouse with an elevator because of course he did—and waited until she seemed sure Blake was out of earshot.

"You look great, by the way," I said, genuinely meaning it. I should have led with that, for crying out loud, rather than droning on about my problems. "You still feeling healthy?"

She'd battled a medical mystery, one that Blake had been there for every step of the way. Another reason I adored Blake; had it not been for him, Tessa wouldn't be here right now.

"Never better," she said, glancing over her shoulder to make sure Blake wasn't within hearing range before whispering, "Are you sure about your plan?"

"I'm sure." I stood straighter, channeling my inner warrior princess.

"What if he does something?" Worry etched across her face.

"That's why I'm doing it in the office. The building has twenty-four-hour security on the first floor."

The elevator doors opened with a soft ding, and I stepped inside, summoning every ounce of confidence I could muster.

"Scar, I don't think you need to go through all that to tell Jace the truth. I'm sure he'll believe you."

"But this isn't just about me anymore, and this is too important to take any risks. It's only one conversation in a carefully controlled environment."

What could go wrong?

Spoiler alert: everything. Everything was about to go horribly, worst-case scenario wrong.

41

JACE

The mansion's main room was a testament to luxury: walnut paneling, leather chairs, and a custom poker table. The Sinners and Saints Club, aptly named for the mix of sinners (primarily, Axel) and reluctant saints (debatably, Blake) that made up our brotherhood.

I shuffled poker chips between my fingers—click-click-click—a nervous habit from college finals that now surfaced whenever my mind was a category-five hurricane. And lately, that hurricane had a name: Scarlett.

Blake walked in, hanging his hoodie on the rack with the surgical precision you'd expect from a man who regularly held lives in his hands. "Just saw Scarlett," he announced casually, like he hadn't just detonated a bomb in my chest.

My heartbeat accelerated at the mere mention of her name. Like a teenager. Like a goddamn lovesick puppy.

"You did?" I tried for casual disinterest.

"She and Tess were drinking that new cabernet I imported." He settled across from me, rolling up his sleeves. "She seemed ... guarded."

"Did she say why?" The chips moved faster. Click-click-click-click.

Blake's doctor eyes diagnosed my pathetic condition instantly. "I presume it's because of her sperm donor situation. Why? Did something else happen with the guy from work?"

I'd dumped the whole situation into our group chat at two a.m., seeking advice but getting only variations of *just talk to her* and *you're screwed* from these three emotional geniuses.

Before I could answer, Axel sauntered in with a bottle of scotch. "Please tell me you two aren't going to talk about women all night? I came to take your money, not audition for the Lifetime Movie Network."

I watched him, resentment building in my chest. How did he do it? How did Axel float through life, sampling women like wine vintages, while I was over here, drowning in feelings I'd never wanted?

Ryker poured himself a neat whiskey and smirked. "Rich, coming from you. Last week, you spent three hours describing a bartender's, and I quote, 'transcendent legs.' "

"I talk about the beauty of women," Axel clarified, dealing cards. "Emotions are ugly. Like Ryker's attempt at a beard last summer."

The chips stilled in my hand. Must be nice, treating emotions like an optional side dish. Meanwhile, I'd cannonballed into the deep end for a woman I could never have.

"Besides," Axel added with his trademark smirk, "those were exceptional legs."

"Will you shut up?" I snapped. "We all know the emotionless-playboy act is bullshit."

Axel's trademark smirk vanished, and something flashed in his eyes I rarely saw. Something raw and unguarded. The transformation was so quick, I almost missed it before his walls slammed back into place.

"You know, that's the second time you've said that recently," he said, voice quiet but tight. "If you have something to say, Jace, just say it."

The room went silent. Blake and Ryker exchanged glances,

suddenly very interested in their cards. We'd rarely ever heard that tone from Axel before. It wasn't his usual defensiveness or sarcasm. This was different. This was real.

That was when I realized I'd stumbled on to something he didn't want anyone to see. The carefully constructed image of Axel—the carefree playboy with a different woman every night, the guy who joked about everything and took nothing seriously—had cracked, just for a second.

I'd always suspected his exaggerated womanizing was a shield. It was why I'd said that, twice by his count, but now, I was certain. The more outrageous his stories, the fewer questions people asked. The more he played up being shallow, the less anyone looked for depth. It was brilliant really: hide in plain sight behind a reputation so consistent, no one bothered to look past it.

Who the hell was I to throw that in his face, especially when I had my own problems?

I ran a hand over my face. "Sorry," I managed. "I'm on edge."

His eyes held mine like he was deciding whether to let me off the hook or finally have it out with me. Then the moment passed, and Axel was back to smirking and shuffling cards.

"This is exactly why I avoid dating. Emotions make you lose all sense, dude. Look at Blake." He nodded to him. "He texted from the jeweler, wanting our approval, picking out an engagement ring."

"Opinion," Blake corrected, placing a small velvet box on the table. "I've never bought one before. I want to make sure it's perfect."

"You came to the wrong club if you think we'll have the first clue," Ryker said, examining his cards with exaggerated interest. "Half of us are emotionally stunted, and the other half are ... well, Axel."

"Screw you very much," Axel replied cheerfully, then picked up the box with a low whistle. "Better not take her on a boat. She'll sink to the bottom of the lake with this rock weighing her down."

"Too much?" Blake looked legitimately concerned.

"Depends. Does she like being able to lift her hand?" Axel arched a brow.

Ryker snatched the box from Axel. "It's nice, man. Tessa will lose her mind."

"Speaking of losing minds," Blake said, reclaiming the ring. "Scarlett. She doing okay? Tess mentioned something about a tense meeting at work between you two."

I sighed, letting my cards fall face down. "Scarlett's turned out to be a worthy adversary. I knew she was fierce, but, damn ..." I shook my head, remembering the fire in her eyes. "I just had a conference-room showdown with her that made me fall even deeper."

Fall even deeper? Did I just say that?

"Oh?" Blake asked, a hint of genuine curiosity breaking through his usual reserve.

"She stood up to me—to ME—in front of the entire team. Played a game of chess and won. Most people can't even maintain eye contact with me in those meetings."

"So, she yelled at you, and that made you horny?" Axel asked, raising the bet. "That's some next-level masochism. I'm both disgusted and impressed."

I glared. "It wasn't like that. She was brilliant. Fierce. It was ..."

"Hot?" supplied Axel.

"Impressive," I corrected, though the heat crawling up my neck betrayed me.

"Should we be worried?" Ryker asked, studying me. "I've known you for years and never seen you this ..."

"Pathetic?" Axel offered helpfully.

"Invested," Ryker finished, shooting Axel a look.

"Still haven't figured out who hurt her?" Blake asked.

I shook my head. "Thought she'd tell me by now. The fact that she hasn't makes me admire her more. It would be easy for her to tell me, but she's so damn private." I collected my winnings absently. "Maddeningly inconvenient, but I respect the hell out of it."

"Maybe you should give up," Axel suggested, refilling his glass. "Some battles aren't worth fighting. Some women aren't worth the heartburn."

"Like that brunette from the charity gala who stole your watch?" Ryker asked innocently.

"We agreed never to speak of that again," Axel said through gritted teeth.

"Never," I said, answering Axel's suggestion. "I'm not giving up on her."

Blake's eyebrows rose slightly in a silent acknowledgment.

"All right, let's address the elephant in the boardroom," Ryker said, leaning forward. "What's your endgame? She works for you. You've got your no-fraternization policy. Where exactly do you see this going?"

I ran my hand down my face. "I really thought she was going to tell me everything the other day. She had that NDA in her hand, and I swore she was about to give it to me. Then she just ... pulled the rug out. No explanation."

"You really like this woman," Blake noted.

"I do." The admission felt like jumping off a cliff without knowing if there was water below. "But I don't know if she feels the same. And even if she does ..."

"Even if she does?" Blake prompted.

"Even if she does, I'm not sure she'd ever act on it." The truth ached in my chest. "She's built walls so high, I'm not sure anyone's meant to scale them."

"Does she know how you feel?" Blake asked.

I grabbed my lip angrily between my teeth. "I've never ..." I stopped. How could I explain that in the boardroom, I could command armies with a few words, but with Scarlett, I was suddenly illiterate?

"You've never what?" Blake pressed.

"I've never felt this way before," I admitted quietly. "I don't know the protocol. There's no business strategy for this. No contingency plan."

Blake nodded, as if confirming a diagnosis he'd suspected all along.

"Show her," he said simply.

"Show her what? My emotional incompetence?" I asked, shuffling chips again. "Not sure that's the wisest move. We're still forbidden to date, remember?"

"You're the boss," Blake pointed out. "You make the rules. And I'm not saying break them, but ... sometimes, people need to see action, not just words."

"What Blake's trying to say," Ryker translated, "is that you need to find a way to show her you care."

"Do something meaningful that shows you've been paying attention," Blake continued, his voice softening. "When I found out Tessa had never seen the ocean, I flew her to Malibu for the weekend. It wasn't about the money or the private jet; it was about showing her I'd listened when she talked about her dreams."

"Dude, you falling in love is giving me hives," Axel complained, but something almost wistful crossed his face. "Next, you'll be telling us how the sound of her laugh makes flowers bloom or some shit."

Falling in love. The thought should've terrified me, but instead, it felt like putting a name to a condition I'd been suffering from.

"Show her," I repeated, the wheels already turning.

"Think about what she cares about most," Blake advised. "What lights her up when she talks about it?"

As Axel dealt another hand, a plan began forming. Scarlett deserved something big, something that would show her I understood what mattered to her.

"All right," Axel conceded, pouring me another drink. "If you're going to be disgustingly romantic, at least do it with style.

Make it big enough that when she inevitably breaks your heart, we can mock you for years."

"Your support is touching," I said dryly.

"That's what brothers are for," he replied with a grin. "Now, are we playing poker or planning your emotional demise?"

"Both," Ryker said, raising the bet. "We're excellent multi-taskers."

As chips clacked and cards flew, I couldn't focus. My mind was filled with Scarlett. Her fierce intelligence, her guarded heart, and what it might take to finally break through.

For the first time in my life, I was all in on something that had nothing to do with business. And for the first time, I had absolutely no idea if I was going to win or lose everything.

42

SCARLETT

"I didn't expect to hear from you so soon," I said, unable to keep the surprise from my voice as I paced the small confines of my office, phone pressed to my ear.

"Are you kidding me?" Mary replied with a laugh. "We would be lucky to have you."

Mary was a coworker from two years ago. We had gotten along really well and worked on several projects together. When she was offered a position outside our company, she took it for better work-life balance. Something that existed in fairy tales and HR pamphlets, as far as I knew.

"Between you and me," she continued, her voice dropping to a conspiratorial whisper, "there are a lot of other applicants, but—"

"Define a lot?"

"Um ... I think, like, thirty-two?"

"Seriously?" Thirty-two applicants?

"But," she continued, "I have a good feeling that *you'll* get an offer."

I stopped pacing. "Because you're vouching for me?"

"Because you're amazing. And, of course, I'll put in a good word for you!"

Wow. My muscles immediately softened, tension melting away. Anxiety that had evidently been knotted into steel cables began to loosen. This whole time, I had been terrified of losing my job, of derailing my career, and after just two applications, would it be this easy to find something else? Thirty-two applicants warned me not to get my hopes up, but Mary sounded so confident.

Maybe the universe had thrown me a lifeline. Maybe I could escape Marcus's threats *and* still have a career.

"Now, I thought I'd give you the lay of the land before your interview," Mary said, her voice shifting into professional mode.

"I would love that." I sank into my chair and swiveled to face the wall so no one walking by could see my absolute glee.

I smiled, twirling a pen between my fingers as I listened to Mary's tips and tricks. As it turned out, Mary was quite happy in her current position and loved the company she worked for. She had branched into HR and also knew about other companies in the area, which explained why this particular company was such a great one to work for. When she was done summarizing the role, the people I would be working for, the culture, and everything else, she cleared her throat.

"Now, I should warn you," she said, her tone shifting slightly, "there are a couple things about this organization that aren't perfect."

I leaned back in my chair, confidence surging through me. "Of course. No company is."

Famous. Last. Words.

"Well, at this company, people tend to stay in their roles for five or more years. There's not as much upward mobility." She paused, letting that sink in. "This company values people who learn from the ground up slowly."

"So, it would be a long time before I would ever see a promotion," I clarified, my chest tightening.

Okay. Not the best news. I really did want to move up in a company, but at least this one seemed like a great place to work. I could handle that. Career advancement wasn't everything, right? Sometimes, stability was worth more.

"There's one more thing." She used a tone that told me whatever she was about to say was a big one. And the way she let a long silence pass made me nervous.

What could it be? So help me, if she told me that while the culture was generally kind, there were reports of sexual harassment in the work—

"The salary," she said quietly.

My pen stilled mid-tap.

"Back when I decided to leave for work-life balance purposes, I interviewed with many different companies in the area," she explained. "I was really fortunate at the time to receive several job offers." She took a breath. "All of them were at least thirty percent less."

My stomach bottomed out like I'd just hit the first drop on a roller coaster, only there was no exhilarating rush, just nausea and dread.

"Thirty?" I balked.

I knew our company paid very well; it was something that people talked about incessantly, but I had never done market research to know just how much they paid above other companies. I supposed it made sense since we also weren't known for good work-life balance, but thirty percent? That wasn't a pay cut; that was financial amputation.

"But the good news is, you'll have better work-life balance," Mary chirped, as if that would somehow make up for losing nearly a third of my income.

"I ... um ..."

The sad truth was, I was living paycheck to paycheck right now. Between my rent, my mom's rent, and helping her get back on her feet, I was already staring down the barrel of the heartbreaking possibility of having to sell Buttercup and the financial responsibility she came with. But with a thirty percent pay decrease, even selling my beloved horse wouldn't make the math work.

I dropped deeper into my chair, despair spreading through my body, contaminating every hopeful thought I'd had just minutes before.

Maybe I could just move in with my mother? But the whole purpose of our current arrangement was to hide her from my father, and until I knew exactly how long my father would serve in jail, I didn't want to risk it. If we lived together, there was a higher probability he'd find her. Plus, doing so would only close some of that financial gap. And I'd be sued by my landlord for breaking my lease.

As if that weren't bad enough, we weren't talking about a short-term problem. At thirty percent of a pay decrease, it would take at least a decade to get back to my current income. If ever. All while rent prices and the cost of living would rise. The math was brutal, unforgiving.

"You still want to interview, right?" Mary asked hopefully, oblivious to my internal financial meltdown. "I mean, I'm sure you could probably negotiate two to five percent over whatever they offer. But again, think about how nice it'll be to work less hours!"

Yeah. It would be great. Almost as great as having electricity and running water.

"Thank you," I said, forcing brightness into my voice that I absolutely did not feel. "I really appreciate it, Mary. Yes, I'd love to interview for it."

I hung up the phone and stared at the ceiling, the reality of my situation crashing down on me like a ton of very expensive bricks.

Plan B had just imploded. I needed to make plan A work, which meant confronting Marcus and making sure I got him to confess.

I straightened my spine, resolution hardening. *Time to gather evidence.*

43

SCARLETT

"Other jobs? Really?" Jace slapped a file down on his desk with enough force to make his Montblanc pen roll across the polished mahogany. He leaned back in his leather chair, steepling his fingers beneath his chin, his custom Tom Ford suit jacket pulling just enough across his broad shoulders to remind me why I should be looking at his face instead of the delicious curves to his muscles.

"How did you find out?" I kept my voice measured, professional, even as my pulse quickened under his scrutiny.

"Chicago is a very small city," Jace said, his green eyes flickering with something dangerous while a muscle twitched in his jaw.

The way he looked at me—like I was a puzzle he was determined to solve—sent an unwelcome flash of heat down my spine. The air-conditioning hummed quietly in the background, but it did nothing to cool the tension between us. I didn't appreciate being summoned like this just to get an attitude. I had enough on my mind. Namely, Marcus's vague-ass threat that he could hurt Jace.

"What did you expect after the conference-room showdown?" I challenged, adjusting the cuff of my blouse, acutely aware of how his gaze tracked the movement of my fingers. "A thank-you note and a fruit basket?"

"Tell me his name," Jace said, his voice dropping to that quiet, menacing tone that somehow managed to be both threatening and inappropriately arousing, "and he'll be gone within the hour."

No, he won't.

Because as far as I could tell, I had two scenarios in front of me. Door number one: Jace would have to pick between me and a longtime friend. And he would most likely pick his longtime friend every day of the week, making him vulnerable to the wolf in sheep's clothing that Marcus was to Jace. The guy was a trusted adviser and close friend, and I had to figure out how to do this in a way that wouldn't put Jace in a precarious position. Door number two: Marcus wasn't bluffing, and he would pull the trigger on that dirt he claimed to have on Jace.

My plan, the one I'd told Tessa about, was the only one that would work. The only way Jace would be left with no doubt that Marcus was not only my harasser, but he was also a threat to Jace himself, was if I could capture Marcus saying it.

"If you have any other questions for me, I'll be in my office." I pivoted and started to walk away, wondering if his eyes followed the sway of my hips.

"You will have dinner with me tonight," he declared in a firm, controlled tone, making me stop in my tracks. It wasn't a request. Not even close.

I turned slowly, one eyebrow arched with precision. "That wasn't a question, Mr. Lockwood. Perhaps we should revisit the corporate handbook section on workplace communication."

"A work dinner," he claimed, walking around his desk with the grace of someone used to getting exactly what he wanted. His cologne drifted into my space as he approached, triggering memories of how that scent had clung to my skin after we'd sweated in that meadow, doing a very non-meadowy thing. "Strictly professional."

"Anything you would like to discuss, we could do so here," I countered, gesturing to the perfectly adequate conference table in his office. Which was *for sure* not reminding me of the one he'd lain naked on, sucking on my sex until I shattered on his face. I adjusted my legs, hoping he didn't sense the flash of heat shooting through them. "Where there are witnesses."

"Please." His voice softened unexpectedly, and for a split second, I caught a glimpse of something vulnerable behind that billionaire armor. His fingers twitched at his side, as if fighting the urge to reach for me. "Have dinner with me. There's something I need to talk to you about."

"If this is about getting a name out of me ..." I narrowed my eyes.

"No name."

Jace held up his palms in surrender, the gesture drawing my attention to his hands. Hands I knew were equally skilled at closing business deals and unraveling my composure. Those fingers—my Lord, what they could do to my—

"It's about something else, I promise."

Then what? What could it be? And why did his eyes look ... borderline sparkly? If it wasn't about us (was there even an us?) and it wasn't a new tactic to extract information from me, what else could possibly warrant this dinner routine? My curiosity was officially piqued.

Dammit.

"Seven o'clock. Le Bernardin." He moved closer, close enough that I could see the faint shadow of stubble on his jaw despite his morning shave. Stubble that had left the inside of my thighs deliciously raw. "I promise to be on my best behavior."

"Your best behavior probably makes the *Wall Street Journal*'s gossip column," I pointed out, fighting the urge to step back—or worse, forward. "And I prefer establishments where the menu actually lists the prices."

A ghost of a smile tugged at his lips, the same lips that had mapped every inch of my body. "Fine. You pick the place."

"I pick the place; we split the bill," I countered, chin raised, my breath catching slightly when his gaze dropped to my mouth.

"The bill will be paid for by the company," he challenged. "It's a work dinner. Splitting the bill implies it's personal."

Mental note: Next time, bring better arguments to a verbal sparring match with a man who negotiates billion-dollar deals before breakfast.

"But I admire your defiance all the same," he added, having the nerve to smirk and look sexy as hell, doing it, the heat in his eyes making it clear he was remembering exactly how that defiance had played out between us in private.

"Seven thirty. Rosebud on Taylor." I took a step back, reclaiming my personal space before I did something ill-advised, like remember how his mouth tasted. "And this had better be worth sacrificing my evening of true crime documentaries and takeout."

"It will be." The confidence in his voice was infuriating.

And it had me all sorts of curious ...

I bit my lip, failing to tame a smile as I exited his office. Funny how just last night, I'd felt so heavy, and now I felt so light. Excited even to spend the evening with Jace.

Hopefully, I'd be armed with some damn evidence against Marcus by then.

44

SCARLETT

The candlelight cast a warm glow across Jace's face, highlighting that jaw that could cut glass. We'd been at Rosebud for an hour, our appetizers long gone, our entrees half eaten, and the conversation flowing as easily as the wine. Something about this felt different. Safer somehow. As if the outside world couldn't touch us here.

But safety was an illusion I couldn't afford to indulge in. My failed attempt to meet Marcus today lingered in the back of my mind, a persistent shadow over our elegant dinner. He'd given a vague possibility of meeting tomorrow, but the uncertainty had my nerves on edge. Was I doing the right thing by sitting here, smiling across candlelight at Jace instead of warning him? Was waiting for concrete evidence the safer move? Or would delaying another full day, taking the risk he might dismiss Marcus's threat as empty posturing, become the more dangerous play here?

"So," I said, taking a sip of my cabernet, "you've spent the entire meal avoiding the topic you claimed was so important. Are you going to tell me what this is about, or should I order dessert first?"

Jace's green eyes danced with something I couldn't quite

place. Excitement? Pride? He reached into his suit jacket and pulled out a business card.

"I wanted to wait for the right moment." He slid the card across the table toward me, his fingers lingering just a moment too long.

"What's this?" I asked, curiosity piqued despite my best efforts. "If it's another NDA printed in size two font, I should warn you, I'll renegotiate that one too."

He laughed, the sound rich and genuine. "Just read it."

I smiled, but when I read the lines on the paper, my heart thudded like a drum, my mouth ran dry, and bile roiled around in my gut. On this business card was my name, embossed in elegant silver lettering, followed by *Vice President, Creative Development.*

I tried not to vomit, clenching my chair until my knuckles turned white.

Jace's smile faltered when he saw my reaction. "I thought you'd be happy. I heard you didn't get the promotion you recently applied for."

So, it was official then. I'd lost the promotion I'd earned, and even though Jace didn't know why I'd lost out on it, he thought he could what ... invent a consolation prize? How insulting.

"Do you know how many women get sexually harassed at work?" My voice came out steadier than I felt, and it took serious effort to not let it slip into a cutting edge. "None of *them* have a rich boyfriend who owns the company to make it right for them."

"Scarlett," Jace started, but he cocked his head. "Wait, the incident involved your promotion?"

"When I get a promotion, it will be because I earned it."

Jace's eyes narrowed. "You did earn it. You spent years earning it, in fact, clearly robbed of the promotion you should have gotten. Which I'll be circling back to, by the way. Meanwhile, consider this a way of correcting that awful bullshit."

The waiter approached with a fresh bottle of wine, took one look at our faces, and wisely retreated.

I lowered my voice to a whisper. "Did you even stop to think how this sounds? I got passed over for a job because I wouldn't do sexual favors for a guy, and then when I finally get it, it's because I happen to be sleeping with the boss? Do you realize how devaluing that makes me feel?"

Jace's eyes flashed with anger, hurt visible around the edges. "The boss? Is that all I am to you?"

"Do you not see why this would upset me?" I demanded incredulously.

"Honestly? No!" He leaned forward, his voice intense. "I'm trying to do the right thing here. And I thought this was something that would make you happy."

"I want to be treated like everyone else."

"Scarlett—"

"I have to go." I stood up, grabbing my purse, my chair scraping against the floor. My heart hammered in my chest as tears threatened. *No. I will not cry in this restaurant.* "I respectfully decline the promotion."

"Scarlett, wait—"

"You want to know the real problem here?" I leaned down, palms flat against the table. "It's about power. And who wields it. And maybe, just maybe, the person you supposedly loathe is a lot closer than you think."

His expression shifted, confusion replacing anger. "What is that supposed to mean?"

Marcus. The name burned on my tongue, desperate to be spat out. I should say it. Tell him now. He'd believe me. He had to. My lips parted, the confession teetering on the edge of revelation, when the unmistakable electronic click of a camera pierced the moment. The sound hit me like a bucket of ice water, a stark reminder of my original plan to catch Marcus red-handed, to deliver indisputable evidence to Jace on a silver platter and finally be done with this whole twisted game.

I straightened, suddenly aware of our audience. Phone cameras flashed around us. Perfect. Corporate America's favorite billionaire playboy was creating a scene in public, and I was the unwitting costar in this tabloid drama.

"Wait!" Jace demanded.

As I dodged between tables, whispers and stares following in my wake, I heard the scrape of his chair, the rustle of bills being thrown carelessly onto the table. By the time I pushed through the restaurant's heavy door, the rain had picked up, pelting the sidewalk in angry bursts that matched my pulse.

I made it three steps before his voice cut through the downpour.

"Scarlett."

Just my name. Nothing else. But something in the way he said it—raw, demanding, stripped of all the polish that normally coated his words—made me freeze mid-stride.

I didn't turn around. Couldn't. Because I knew that if I faced him now, with rain streaming down my face, masking what might or might not be tears, whatever came next would change everything.

His hand closed around my wrist, and he slowly turned me to face him. Lightning flashed overhead, illuminating his face in stark relief. Jaw clenched, eyes blazing, hair plastered to his forehead by the rain.

He looked nothing like a billionaire CEO now.

He looked like a man on the edge of something dangerous.

45

SCARLETT

I looked up at Jace, standing there in his almost-drenched suit. His green eyes were fixed on me, attentive and questioning. That *Forbes*-cover-worthy haircut framed a face that was just unfairly handsome. All of it dripping wet from the thunderstorm raging as much around us as in my heart.

"This is uncharted territory for me," Jace started. "I never intended to hurt you or diminish your worth. I see your talent, your drive; you're more than deserving of that promotion. I thought I was helping by moving quickly, but I never meant to upset you."

His words washed away some of my anger, but good intentions didn't erase the reality check I'd just received. Jace wielded the kind of enormous power that could create a new position with the stroke of a pen while I'd sacrificed weekends and sleep just for a chance to be considered.

"You know this is something that no matter how hard you try, you'll never understand," I began, my voice steady despite the tremor in my chest. "You've always had power. You were born with it because of your money, your family's influence. One phone call from your parents could probably make most problems disappear."

Jace's shoulders tensed slightly, but he remained silent, giving me space to continue.

"I shoved a kid once and was suspended for three days. My grades suffered," I said. His jawline tightened, the first hint that my words were landing. "In high school, my friend shoplifted a shirt worth one hundred and one dollars—one dollar over the felony threshold. She's been a convicted felon ever since, struggling to find work." I faced him directly. "But if your friends had done something similar, their parents would've probably called the prosecutor or judge. Any charges probably would have disappeared entirely."

"Scarlett," he started, his deep voice soft.

Lightning illuminated the sidewalk, cars sloshing past with the scoop-slap of their wipers.

I held up my hand. "We live in different worlds, Jace. You're swimming with a current rushing you forward. I'm not saying you don't face obstacles or hardships, but the current works for you, not against you. Your chances of landing where you want to be are high. When you speak, people believe you."

His eyes never left my face, conflict evident as recognition dawned that I might be right.

"I grew up fighting against a current designed to push people back and hold them down. My father held me down. Even an abuser was believed more than my mother."

Jace's hand twitched at his side, as if wanting to reach for me but thinking better of it.

"I finally break free, put myself through college, get my mom out, build a career from scratch," I said, words tumbling faster, "and then some privileged man who probably never heard the word *no*, whose problems magically disappeared, who never learned you couldn't abuse power ... he and I ended up in the same room, and he tried to take it all away."

Jace stepped forward, his muscled frame rigid.

I shook my head. "That's something you can't understand. I know you'll try, and I appreciate that. But you'll never fully grasp what it's like to know that if you raise your hand against someone powerful, the most likely outcome is that your career will end while he gets nothing but a slap on the wrist. That's the power you represent to me now. And I don't know if it'll ever be something I can get past."

He ran a hand through his hair, momentarily disrupting it before it fell right back into place.

Even his hair obeys him, I thought bitterly. Even when he was in the middle of the thunderstorm, his hair did exactly what he probably wanted it to do.

"Let's look at more examples. How many times did you go to bed hungry? Did you wonder where your next meal would come from?" I stepped closer. "I did. My father would raid the cabinets as punishment."

Jace's neck tightened, a vein popping out.

"How about college? Did you wonder how to pay for it? I worked three jobs, applied for every loan and aid possible. It was almost impossible. I bet funding wasn't even on your to-do list."

He opened his mouth, then closed it again.

"And consequences? Does the world throw the book at a Lockwood, or do they appreciate your family's donations?"

Something in his face darkened. His Adam's apple bobbed with ... was that guilt?

"Then job interviews. Have you ever had a boss threaten your promotion by putting his hand on your thigh, making it clear there was only one way you'd get it?"

Pure, controlled fury crossed Jace's face, though not at me. His shoulders straightened, and I glimpsed why people followed him.

"Have you ever had to consider reporting said incident and having to weigh all the consequences of what might happen if you did? Don't believe me? Why don't you look up the last three people who raised their brave hands to alert the company that they had a predator in the mix? And find out where those three women are now and where the three men are."

Jace took a step toward me, his movement purposeful but gentle. "Scarlett—"

"Extra credit if you look deeper at those three men and see if any other complaints had ever been filed against them—because my bet is, the answer is yes. And my bet is, those three women had their careers destroyed when they raised their hands to try to do the right thing."

I could see each of my words hitting him like punches, even as he maintained his composure.

"*This* is why power turns me off, Jace."

As I turned on my heel to leave, Jace's impassioned words hit me from behind, halting my retreat.

"You're right. The world is messed up and unfair. But you're blaming me for things outside my control!" he snapped. "Admittedly, I've lived a privileged life, but that privilege didn't leave me unscathed. Money couldn't save my mom from cancer or protect my dad from being murdered. And money is why I've shielded myself from relationships. I learned the hard way that it makes people pretend to care. So, yes, money and power have provided me many things, Scarlett, but those things also came at a cost. And no amount of money and power could guard me against the world's brutality or give me my parents back."

My heart softened, and I turned back to face him. "I can have compassion for what you've faced, Jace, but life's odds are still stacked in your favor. The obstacles between us are just too high."

He stepped closer. I stepped back.

"So, that's it?" he challenged.

"I guess so."

"Tell me you don't have feelings for me," he demanded, his voice dropping to that dangerous, velvet tone that had undone me before. "Tell me you don't want this."

I opened my mouth to lie, to protect myself. But the words failed me. My heart thumped traitorously against my ribs.

His eyes caught my hesitation, and something triumphant flashed across his face.

"You don't get it, do you?" I whispered, a new coldness settling in my chest. "It doesn't matter what I feel. It never has."

"Of course it matters—"

"No," I cut him off with finality. "As long as you're holding all the cards in the relationship, I can't see us ever working out."

With a deep breath, I walked up to him, kissed him on the cheek, and with fresh tears in my eyes, turned and walked away.

46

JACE

"What's with the long face?" Axel questioned. "Did your stock portfolio drop a whole percent today?"

My mind wasn't here, in this room of the mansion, with my fellow Sinners and Saints brothers. I'd known it the second I pulled up to the gates, the gargoyles looking down at me like I was someone new. The brick, the luxury of it all, ignited guilt within me. Here we were, using a goddamned mansion as a club of sorts, while other people like Scarlett were probably out there right now, struggling financially.

"Hello," Axel repeated, snapping his fingers in front of my face. "Earth to Jace. Are you going to play or sit there, looking like someone keyed your favorite car?"

I glared at him. He sat with his usual confident demeanor next to my other chosen brothers, Blake and Ryker.

"I just ..." I paused, looking at my cards without really seeing them.

"He's calculating how many companies he can buy before lunch tomorrow," Ryker joked, tossing chips into the center. "I'll raise fifty."

"I see your fifty," Blake said, tossing his chips into the center.

Blake didn't grow up with privilege. He'd grown up in the

foster care system, and Ryker grew up middle class. Axel's family were business owners who had oscillated between poverty and upper middle class. These guys weren't handed privileges like I'd been.

"Let me ask you something," I said, absently folding my cards down in front of me.

"Are you folding, as in you're out?" Axel asked.

"When you guys grew up," I continued, ignoring him, "if you got in trouble, what would happen?"

"Is this your version of Never Have I Ever? Because we need more tequila for that," Axel said, reaching for his drink.

"Let's say a"—I hesitated, thinking of the pervert boss Scarlett had mentioned—"teacher had done something inappropriate. What would have happened?"

"Dude, we're playing poker. What the hell?" Axel snarled, throwing his cards down. "Did you get into some kind of philosophical edibles?"

"Where is this coming from?" Blake wondered, studying my face. "You've been weird since you walked in. Usually, you're trash-talking Axel's receding hairline by now."

"My hairline is not receding, asshole," Axel retorted, running a hand through his hair self-consciously. It wasn't receding, but Blake loved to make him think it was. He even cited (fake) medical "evidence" to goad him.

"Did a teacher do something to you, but you waited until your mid-thirties to tell someone?" Ryker asked with a smirk. "Should I get my doll so you can point to the parts?"

"Just answer the question," I said, my tone sharp.

The guys looked at each other like I'd lost my mind.

"Is this about a woman?" Ryker asked, his eyes narrowing. "You actually look like you give a damn about something other than the next acquisition."

"He's got that look my parents' dog used to get when they left for work," Axel chimed in. "Complete confusion and existential dread."

"Okay ... in your strange hypothetical question," Ryker answered, steering us back on topic, "if a teacher did something like that when I was younger, I'd probably just want to shut my mouth."

"Why?"

"Why? Because I'd want to pass the class. It would be pretty foolish, pissing off the teacher responsible for my grade by ratting them out."

"I'd get my ass beat if I brought trouble home," Blake added casually, arranging his chips. "Foster dad number three wasn't big on 'making waves.' "

Jesus. Scarlett was right. I knew she was right, of course; everything she had said to me made complete sense. But it was still hitting me in waves, the unfairness of it all.

"If the teacher had done something inappropriate to me, my family would've made one phone call and gotten them fired," I said quietly.

The guys exchanged a look.

"Can we please get back to poker? I raise you twenty," Axel said, pushing chips forward. "And, Jace, if you play that sad puppy face as a bluff, I swear to God ..."

"Dude, what is up with you tonight?" Blake asked, studying me.

"Privilege," I said, the word tasting strange in my mouth. "Power. And all the things that it impacts. But, specifically, how it affords me the opportunity to hold other people accountable for their actions while simultaneously letting me off the hook for my own."

"Jesus, dude, I didn't come here for a therapy session," Axel groaned, reaching for his drink. "I came here to take your money and make fun of your designer shoes."

"If I wanted to feel bad about my life choices, I'd call my mother," Ryker added, downing his drink.

"Jace, what is going on?" Blake asked, his tone shifting to genuine concern.

"I'm falling in love with Scarlett." There ... I said it out loud.

Another look was exchanged.

"That's what this is about?" Axel said. "You're ruining poker night because you have feelings? God, you're worse than Ryker when he discovered poetry in college."

"That was a phase," Ryker defended. "And I still say my sonnet about beer pong was underappreciated."

"She's making me realize that we come from two different worlds," I continued, ignoring them. "When I want something, people help me get it. And when I speak, I'm believed. And if I do something wrong, people will be there to try and clean up the mess. All while she's afforded none of those things."

My God, did that make me respect this woman even more than I already did. Fully understanding what she'd had to go through to get where she was in life, to see what she'd overcome, it made my feelings even deeper for her. Respect. Admiration.

"Jace, you didn't ask to be born into a wealthy family," Blake said seriously. "It's not your fault. It's not something you should be ashamed of. She's making you feel ashamed—"

"She's not." At least, she wasn't trying to. "She's just trying to help me understand the differences between us. It's pretty pathetic that it took me this long to see it."

"So, what, you're going to start feeling guilty every time you use your platinum card?" Axel asked. "Should we meet at McDonald's next time instead of the mansion? Will that help your conscience?"

"This isn't about money," I said, frustration rising in my voice. "It's about consequences." No, my life hadn't always been easy ... but it'd been a helluva lot easier than Scarlett's and many others' who had to pay for consequences that my privilege enabled me to avoid.

Before that conversation, I had convinced myself that Scarlett's aversion to powerful people was confined to her experience with her father who had abused that power. But now, I realized it went much deeper than that, and it was a huge roadblock that we might never be able to overcome.

Here was someone who was already grappling with the power dynamics between us, who didn't want to be with someone who would never be held accountable for his own hypothetical actions simply because he came from a place of privilege.

And here I was, a man who'd done something unspeakable, something I had gotten away with.

If she found that out, she would never talk to me again, let alone ever consider a relationship.

"Jace, you're a good guy," Ryker said, his joking tone gone. "You literally acquire companies to save the employees. You're like a white knight in a Mercedes."

"People like me don't suffer the penalties of our actions," I said, my voice low. "Scarlett didn't even do anything wrong, and she's facing consequences that could destroy the rest of her life. Meanwhile, I've done something repulsive, and I never faced a single consequence for it."

The room went quiet. The joking atmosphere evaporated.

"What are you talking about?" Blake asked cautiously.

"You respect me because I've taken my business skills and done something good with it," I said, looking at each of them. "I buy companies and save people from unemployment and hardship. People commend me, put me on the covers of magazines, but do you want to know why I've always been on the mission to save as many jobs as I can? To save as many people as I can?"

They waited. They had asked me this so many times through the years, and I had never answered. Until now.

"To ease my guilty conscience," I said finally. "Because I killed someone, and I was never held accountable."

47

JACE

I followed Scarlett's challenge and tracked down every man in this company who'd had an HR complaint filed against him about sexual harassment over the past ten years. Seven men. Three still worked here. Of the four who no longer worked here, only one had been fired for it. One. All four now worked elsewhere, so I'd taken the liberty of calling the owners of those companies and letting them know my thoughts.

Power. I had it. Might as well try to use it for good.

The file in front of me made my blood simmer. This woman, Rebecca Collins, had filed a detailed complaint. Reading between the bureaucratic lines—the sanitized corporate speak that turned "he groped me" into "inappropriate physical contact was alleged" —I could sense her fear, her humiliation. How many Scarletts had suffered in silence in this building? How many women had these men tormented, knowing they'd likely face no consequences beyond a strongly worded lecture about "workplace etiquette"?

This guy's days were numbered, no matter what, but I wanted a face-to-face. I wanted to do it myself. I wanted to wrestle a confession out of him so I could go back to that woman and tell her he'd admitted it, that he'd been fired. So I could give her closure and a fat recommendation to any job she wanted, here or at another company. HR liked to call it "creating a positive separation experience." I called it the bare minimum of human decency.

I could only hope I wouldn't resort to violence. That was the thing I worried about most. The board frowned upon CEOs who broke employees' jaws, no matter how richly deserved.

Toby entered my office with an infuriating swagger, straightening his tie as he approached my desk.

Look at his smug mouth. I wanted to smash his teeth into the table so hard, his dentist would need four assistants to rebuild it, but I forced my hands to remain relaxed on the desk.

"You wanted to see me, sir?" His tone was casual, probably expecting this to be about a promotion or some new opportunity.

The nerve. This man had made a woman feel violated, made her afraid to come to work, and here he was, strutting into my office like he owned the place.

I gestured to the chair across from me. "Have a seat." After enduring small talk to lower his guard, I got to the point. "I'd like to discuss the events of March 14, 2018."

The change in his demeanor was immediate. His shoulders tensed, and that easy smile faltered. It was like watching a cockroach when the kitchen light flicked on.

Good. Let him squirm.

"March 2018?" He rubbed his hands on his thighs. "I'm not sure what you're referring to."

Liar. My pulse quickened as I thought of this woman, Rebecca, who'd been brave enough to file a complaint that ultimately went nowhere.

I opened the folder on my desk, making a show of reviewing the documents inside.

"There was an HR complaint filed. I'm reviewing all outstanding issues as the new owner."

His voice had an edge now. Defensive. "That was resolved years ago."

Resolved? My teeth ground together. It was "resolved" because there was not enough evidence, so it, apparently, had come down to who was more believed: a low-level employee or a leader with a country club membership. The injustice of it burned in my chest.

I leaned back in my chair, deliberately casual.

"You know how it is these days. Everything needs to be documented properly. HR's been all over me about company culture." I released a strategic smile, watching his reaction.

He relaxed slightly, misreading my signals. "Between us, it's getting impossible to even have a conversation with female colleagues anymore."

My stomach turned at his assumption that I'd be someone who'd protect the status quo. The urge to leap across the desk, grab him by his tie—a hideous silk number with tiny sailboats—and drag him around my office like a dog on a leash was almost overwhelming.

"I hear you," I said, standing to pour two glasses of water, needing the moment to compose myself so I didn't paint my walls with the blood of an entitled asshole's split lip. "Everything gets misinterpreted."

He accepted the glass with a nod. "Exactly. One compliment, and suddenly, you're the bad guy."

"So, what actually happened that night?" I asked, keeping my tone conversational. "The after-hours meeting? By the sounds of it, she blew it completely out of proportion." The lie tasted vile, but I had to get him on my side. Believing he was just clearing the record with me.

"Nothing worth writing up," he said with a dismissive wave. "We were working late on a project. Just the two of us. I thought we were having a moment, you know? Friendly chat, a little flirting."

I nodded, encouraging him to continue while simultaneously wondering what he'd look like with a broken nose.

"All I did was touch her leg to emphasize a point." He shrugged. "Next thing I know, she's filing a complaint. Total overreaction."

Gotcha, you self-incriminating moron.

I set my glass down slowly, my expression hardening. "So, you did touch her inappropriately."

His eyes widened, then narrowed as he realized his mistake. "No, that's not—"

"You just admitted it, Toby." My voice was ice now, the facade dropping away like a shed skin.

His face flushed with anger. "She was asking for it, the way she—"

"You're fired," I cut him off. "Effective immediately."

"What?" He stood up abruptly. "You can't do that over some misunderstanding from years ago!"

"It wasn't a misunderstanding. It was harassment." My voice rose now, sharp with controlled anger. "And based on the pattern I've seen in your department, it wasn't an isolated incident."

"This is bullshit," he snarled. "You have no idea who you're messing with. I'll sue for wrongful termination."

I took a step closer to him. "Please do. That way, everything—and I mean, everything—will become part of the public record. They'll depose all your former employees, under oath."

Look at him, at a loss for words.

"Security will escort you to clear out your desk."

Part of me—a primal, vengeful part—hoped he'd try something. Give me an excuse to take just one swing. Was that too much to ask from the universe?

"That little—" he started.

"Choose your next words very carefully," I warned, my finger hovering over the intercom. "Security is one button away, and I don't mind adding *threatening behavior* to your file."

He glared at me, then stormed out, slamming the door behind him.

I should have felt relieved. Getting into a fistfight would be frowned upon by the board and would be a violation of that damn morality clause in the contract that might as well read, *CEO shall refrain from physically assaulting employees, no matter how punchable their faces may be.* But it was such an empty victory.

Firing him wasn't enough. Spreading the word through every contact I had in business about him and the liability he'd pose to companies—and, yes, I'd do that—wasn't enough. Breaking his cheekbone ... that was what I'd wanted to do. That was what would have felt like justice.

I flexed my fingers and buzzed my assistant.

"Send in the next one," I said.

The following meetings went on similarly: strategic conversations that led to damning admissions. By the end of the day, the company had three fewer problems. Three fewer predators hiding in plain sight. It wasn't enough, but it was a start. People would not be abused on my watch. Not at my company.

I should have felt triumphant. Powerful. Instead, I felt hollow.

I stared at my phone, at all my unanswered calls and texts to Scarlett. How could she walk away like this? I hadn't meant to insult her with a promotion. I was trying to give her what she deserved. What she'd earned.

At least she'd given me more intel to figure out who had done this to her, letting it slip that it happened during her interview. Six interviews, according to my sleuthing, and HR was assembling the names of those interviewees.

Still, even the knowledge that I was one step closer to finding out who hurt her couldn't erase the pain slicing through my insides.

I poured myself a scotch, downing it in one burning swallow. It didn't help. Nothing did. Not the satisfaction of cleaning house, not the knowledge that I'd done something good today. None of it mattered if she wasn't here with me.

The truth hit me like a wrecking ball. It was no longer a possibility: I was absolutely falling in love with her. Completely, irrevocably in love with a woman who might never speak to me again.

My hand tightened around the empty glass, her final kiss still burning on my cheek like a goodbye I couldn't accept. I'd lost people before—my mother to cancer, my father to violence—but this was different. This was someone walking away by choice. Someone deciding I wasn't worth the risk.

Maybe she was right. Maybe the power imbalance between us was too fundamental to overcome. Maybe some differences couldn't be resolved with determination and good intentions. Not everything could be fixed with money or influence—a hard lesson I learned early on in life.

But for the first time in my professional career, I faced a problem I couldn't solve. A battle I couldn't win. She didn't just distrust my power; she resented it. And I couldn't shed who I was any more than she could erase her past.

I drained the glass, feeling hollow. Empty. All those years of protecting myself from exactly this kind of pain, and in the end, I'd finally let someone in. And now, she was walking away from me.

No. Fuck that. I hadn't built an empire by accepting defeat. I hadn't survived everything life had thrown at me by giving up when things got hard.

I wasn't going to lose her. Not like this. Not without a fight.

She always worked late. She'd probably still be here, hunched over her desk, that little crease between her eyebrows indicating she was deep in concentration. And she was going to get a piece of my mind this time. I'd tell her how I felt, how I couldn't eat, couldn't sleep, couldn't breathe without thinking of her. How she'd somehow become the center of a universe I'd never meant to create.

I put my glass down, shoved my phone in my pocket, and stormed out of my office.

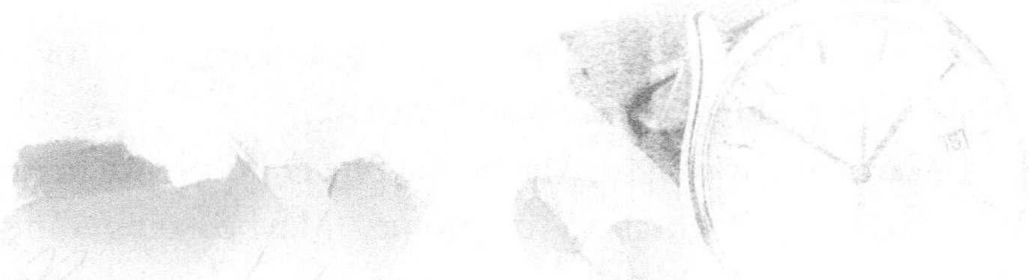

48

SCARLETT

Operation Trap Marcus into a Confession was in full swing. My cell phone was carefully hidden on the desk, its camera lens facing outward, recording already initiated. Even if he moved out of the video frame, all I needed was one shot of him, and the rest could be audio. I'd sent him an "urgent" message. Bait that his ego didn't let him ignore this time.

Meanwhile, I positioned myself on the opposite side of the room, deliberately distant from my phone, arranging items on my bookshelf with calculated nonchalance. The perfect cover. When he arrived, when he sat down in one of the chairs beyond my desk, he shouldn't suspect a thing.

Once I had this proof, I'd make a copy at home, stored somewhere impenetrable. Then I'd finally face Jace. I'd been ghosting him all day, declining every call, ignoring every text, but with evidence in hand, there'd be no disputing Marcus's true nature. Together, Jace and I could determine our next move: HR? Legal action? Whatever it took, I'd ensure Marcus couldn't hurt Jace.

And then ... then maybe I could untangle these messy feelings for Jace that kept my mind racing. Tessa was right; I was feeling wildly protective of him. If not for that, I might not risk everything on this sting operation.

A shadow darkened my doorway. Marcus stepped inside, his demeanor suggesting that being summoned to my office registered somewhere between a mild curiosity and an inconvenience.

"Close the door," I said, my voice steadier than the thundering pulse in my throat.

Marcus regarded me for a long moment, his eyes calculating as they swept over me. He obliged, pushing the door shut with a soft click before sliding his hands into his pockets, assessing me as if I was a curiosity in a museum display. For a fleeting second, I could've sworn there was a flicker in his eyes—a momentary consideration that perhaps I'd reconsidered my stance on his "promotion offer." That I was about to do whatever it took to secure it.

Fat. Chance.

"Calling me to your office after-hours?" Marcus clicked his tongue, eyebrows raised. "That won't look very good to HR, you know. Innocent people don't invite supposed perpetrators into their offices when the building's practically empty."

Yep. That's why there's a recording device on my desk, you handsy harasser.

I folded my arms across my chest, widening my stance to project confidence I didn't entirely feel.

"I called you down here because I want assurances."

"Assurances," he repeated, a smirk playing at the corners of his mouth as he rubbed the side of his face. "What kind of assurances?"

"You gave me an ultimatum. I want to negotiate the terms."

His expression hardened. "I'm afraid I don't know what you're talking about."

Panic fluttered in my chest like a trapped bird. I glanced at the closed door, realizing he might not feel secure enough to incriminate himself. My eyes darted to the window separating my office from the hallway, where anyone could walk by. I crossed the room and closed the blinds with a quick snap.

"There." I turned back to him. "No one can see us now. So, drop the bullshit. I want to negotiate."

Marcus checked his watch with exaggerated impatience. "If you could get to the point, I have dinner reservations."

I wanted to recite every vile thing he'd said, to box him into a corner where all he'd have to do was utter one damning word. But this snake was too slippery. I needed to play it slower, more strategically.

"If I keep my mouth shut about what you did," I started, voice deliberately vulnerable, fingers twisting together, "I want you to promise you'll never hurt Jace like you threatened to."

Marcus sighed, fingers already wrapping around the doorknob. "Miss West, I don't have time for immature theatrics."

"I care about him," I blurted out.

The words froze Marcus mid-turn, his body tensing in a way that sent warning bells clanging through my mind. Something shifted in his posture. Something predatory.

"I like him. A lot," I continued, sensing I'd struck something important. "And I don't want him to get hurt. So, I need guarantees that you won't do anything to harm him."

He pivoted slowly, a victorious and creepy-ass smirk spreading across his face. "You care more about him than your promotion?"

The realization hit me with startling clarity. "Yes. I do."

The smug look of triumph that transformed his features sent ice cascading down my spine. Why did it feel like in this chess game, I'd just sacrificed my queen?

"That's good to know, Miss West," he purred, the words dripping with menace.

"I want assurances that you're not going to hurt him," I repeated more forcefully.

"Why would I hurt one of my closest friends?" His face was the picture of innocence.

Damn it. I was getting nowhere. Not yet. But I could see his mind racing, that my confession about Jace had taken him off guard, so maybe, just maybe, he'd slip up. Especially if I managed to rattle him even more.

"Because you're a predator. And I don't trust your word, so like I said, I need assurances, or I'm not going along with your plan."

He turned and closed the distance between us in three measured steps. It took every ounce of willpower not to retreat, not to give him the satisfaction of seeing me cower.

"You seem to be under the impression you have leverage," he sneered.

"And you seem to be under the impression you're holding all the cards," I countered. "But you're not."

"Your future promotional opportunities could go up in flames like that." The sharp snap of his fingers made me flinch. "Your entire career could implode faster than that." Another deliberate step forward. "I hold all the cards, Miss West, and you'd better damn well get used to it."

I'd hit a nerve. Power was his currency, his addiction. Maybe that explained his grudge against Jace.

"It must be hard," I said, the words poised like a dagger, "to play second fiddle to another man. Jace has more power in his pinkie finger than you'll ever have in your entire lifetime."

The transformation was instantaneous, darkness flooding his eyes like spilled ink. Warning bells weren't just ringing; they were screaming, *Run! Run! Run!*

He advanced, and this time, I *did* back away.

"He thinks he holds all the power," Marcus snarled, "because I let him think he holds all the power. But he doesn't hold anything." His voice dropped to a venomous whisper. "I'm the one with all the power. I'm the one keeping his secret. With one phone call, I could orchestrate his collapse. He would lose it all—his money, his freedom, everything. And you?" He jabbed a finger toward my chest, taking another step closer while I stepped back. "You think you're any kind of match for me? You have no idea who you're messing with."

"I'm messing with someone who sexually harasses women," I shot back, "then stalks them and shows up at their apartments to threaten and intimidate them. You think they'll go along with whatever you say just because you're, what, flexing your alpha-male bullshit?"

His nostrils flared. "You will do as you're told, Miss West, or you will lose everything. And now that I know you care about Jace this much?" His lips twisted into a cruel smile. "That's a handy piece of intelligence to have."

I swallowed hard. I might not have a full confession, but I had enough to show Jace who Marcus really was.

"Get out," I said coldly.

My cell phone rang.

God help me, the sound drew Marcus's attention directly to it. I lunged toward the desk, but he was faster. Maybe he grabbed the phone to prevent me from answering it and telling whoever it was that he was currently in my office, threatening me. Or maybe he noticed how it had been propped up slightly, but either way, he got to it first, and when he swiped to decline the call, his eyes locked on the screen.

He froze. His dark gaze snapped from my phone to me, realization dawning. He saw that I'd been recording him. His jaw tightened to granite as his fingers jabbed at the screen, deleting the evidence I'd gathered.

"You think you're a crafty little bitch, don't you?" he growled.

With a vicious flick of his wrist, he hurled my phone across the room. It crashed against the wall and clattered to the floor, the impact making me flinch. Before I could react, his hand shot out, fingers clamping around my throat. I instinctively grabbed his wrist, trying to pry it away.

"You just made a big fucking mistake." His grip tightened.

I drove my knee upward into his groin. "So did you," I choked out.

His hold loosened with a pained grunt, but when I tried to

dart past him, his fingers tangled in my hair, yanking me backward with such force that stars exploded behind my eyes.

Time slowed to a nightmarish crawl. I recognized that look on his face. That same unfathomable rage that had transformed my father's features into something inhuman decades ago. Pure malevolence stared back at me, a desire to hurt, to punish, to dominate radiating from every pore.

Marcus clearly saw himself as untouchable, and I had nearly toppled his house of cards. Had the phone call not interrupted, he would have been destroyed.

With a guttural sound, he slammed me against the bookshelf. Volumes rained down around us as his expensive leather shoe drove into my rib cage, sending me sprawling to the floor. Any hope that someone outside my office would hear that crash and come running in passed. Confirming I'd waited too late in the day to make this happen. I should have done it earlier. At a safer time, when the office was filled with potential witnesses.

Instantly, my mind fractured, past and present colliding in a kaleidoscope of terror.

"No, Daddy! Stop!" I squealed, clutching my teddy bear against my chest like a shield.

Marcus advanced toward me, that familiar evil twisting his features. I scrambled onto all fours, heart thundering against my ribs, trying to crawl away.

"Daddy, stop hitting Mommy!"

"You bitch." Marcus's fingers closed around my ankle like a vise.

I thrashed wildly, breaking free.

"I hate you, Daddy!"

Daddy stopped beating Mommy, who was lying on the ground, too still. His eyes flashed to me, darker than I'd ever seen as he redirected his attention. To me. He stomped closer, and I ran screaming.

I was a terrible daughter because in that moment, I regretted shouting at him to stop hurting Mommy. I don't want to be hit. *Last time, I thought I was going to die and—*

"Ow!" My head jerked backward violently.

Marcus fisted my hair, wrenching me toward him. "You think you're so smart, don't you?"

Daddy flipped me onto my back. I kicked my little Mary Janes against his chest, but his fist came up, and I knew, even in my nine-year-old mind, that this was it. Mommy and I would never make it to the ocean, never feel warm waves lapping against our ankles while sunshine warmed our finally-free-from-Daddy smiles. We'd never escape. His fist slammed into my temple, and everything went dark.

"No!" I cried, scrambling beneath my desk, making myself as small as possible, the way I always did when I hid under my childhood bed.

What had I been thinking? Marcus had proven he was dangerous when he'd stalked me to my home and threatened me, so why the hell did I think I could control this? It was naive and reckless, and I'd let my desire to protect Jace cloud my better judgment.

As Marcus's polished shoes stepped closer, I retreated further under the desk. He reached for me, but I kicked wildly at his grasping hands.

"You tell anyone about this," he hissed, backing away slowly, "you're dead."

His footsteps receded. The door squeaked open with a groan, and then there was silence, the only sound my broken, ragged sobs.

I didn't know how long I sat there, shivering, crying, trying to reclaim the adult Scarlett I'd painstakingly built from bruises and scars and determination. My ribs throbbed with each shallow breath, and my scalp burned where he'd pulled my hair.

Then a sound. Footsteps in the hallway, growing louder. Closer to my office.

My entire body went rigid with terror. The pattern of those footfalls was familiar.

Marcus had returned.
To finish what he started.

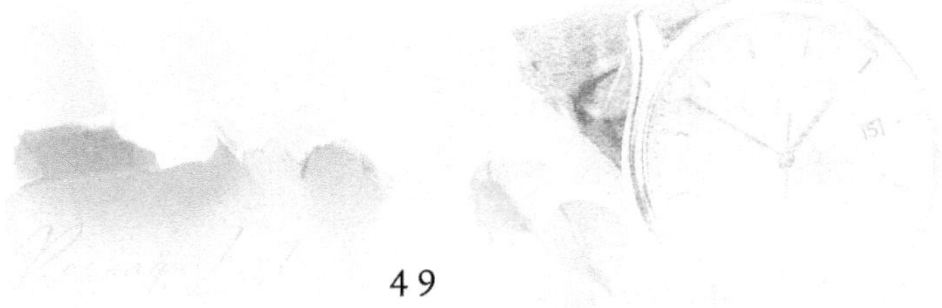

49

JACE

I glared at my phone, finally striding toward Scarlett's office. If she wasn't here, so help me God, I'd show up at her apartment.

Avoiding me? Really?

What surprised me most was how deeply it bothered me.

The realization was unsettling, how I was at the mercy of her choices. If she decided to never speak to me again, I wasn't sure how I'd handle it. Somehow, I knew she'd haunt me, that I'd never stop wondering what she was doing, who she might be with. The thought of her with another man had me swiping my thumb over my lip as irrational jealousy surged through me.

Worried I'd find her with another man, at this exact moment, no less, was as illogical as it was unrealistic. It probably spoke to how unhinged I was feeling right now. Scarlett had made it painfully clear she didn't date.

Plus, there were plenty of rational reasons she'd be avoiding me, but my heart was a jealous, possessive beast striding toward her office, praying I wouldn't find her with some other guy. Because if I did, I'd slam him against the wall and make these bruises on my knuckles look like child's play.

As I approached her office, my unease deepened when I saw that the blinds that separated her space from the hallway were closed. There was absolutely no reason for that unless she was trying to hide something.

God help me, I steeled myself as I rounded the doorway and stepped inside. The office appeared empty, but instantly, my gut twisted as goose bumps prickled across the back of my neck. A framed photo of Buttercup lay on the floor, alongside several awards Scarlett had received. Books from the shelf were scattered along the ground, some splayed open with cracked spines.

What the hell?

Jealousy and possessiveness evaporated, instantly replaced by cold, suffocating panic. It looked like there had been a struggle, one that left Scarlett's phone lying haphazardly in the corner.

Holy shit. Did her dad get released from jail and attack her? No. He'd never make it past security into this building, but what the hell happened, and where the hell was she?

I pivoted on my heel, swiping open my phone to call security when something stopped me dead.

A sound. Faint, almost imperceptible.

I stilled, straining my ears, recognizing what it was when it came again: a whimper.

Scanning the space urgently, I heard it again. Striding deeper into the room, I rounded the desk, spotting her high heels lying on their sides, one broken at the base. My gut clenched, and when I heard the soft sob again, I finally caught a flash of skin.

Scarlett.

She was under her desk.

"Scarlett!"

When I dropped to my knees, she flinched violently, throwing her hands up, as if to ward off a blow, eyes wild with terror.

"It's me," I said as gently as my rage-infested body would allow, holding my palms up in surrender. Making it visually clear I'd never harm a hair on her head.

My throat tightened at the sight of her. Scarlett was hiding, tucked beneath her desk, trembling so hard that I could hear her teeth chattering. Mascara trailed down her cheeks in jagged black rivers, her lipstick smeared across one cheek. Her usually immaculate blonde hair was tangled, strands stuck to the sweat beading on her forehead.

Long gone was the fierce woman who'd bravely confronted her father, putting herself between danger and her mother. Long gone was the razor-sharp professional who'd commanded that conference room, playing mental chess with a business tycoon and winning. In her place was a quivering, fractured human being.

And that ... Christ, that unleashed more rage than I'd experienced in my entire life. I wanted to leave right now, find whoever did this to her, and beat him until his heart stopped beating. I wanted to break every bone in his body twice over. Rip off his arm and shove it down his throat. Violent crimson fantasies I'd never entertained before surged through me with alarming clarity.

I would kill for her, I realized. Without hesitation. Without remorse. All these years of feeling immense guilt for the time I'd taken a life by accident, and now, I'd do it willingly. Gladly.

The intensity of that epiphany shook me, but I pushed it aside. I needed to focus.

"Are you hurt?" I managed, my voice a controlled rumble.

Her wide eyes fluttered shut, and she exhaled deeply. A relieved breath, perhaps, that whoever had done this couldn't get to her. Not with me here now.

"Who did this to you?" I asked, my fingers flexing involuntarily.

When Scarlett opened her eyes, her gaze was unfocused, staring through me rather than at me. She wasn't here, not fully.

"Scarlett?"

No response. No change to her almost-catatonic state.

"Scarlett, it's okay if you don't want to talk." *For now. But soon, you'll tell me who fucking did this to you, and they'll wish they'd never been born.* "But I need to know if you have physical injuries that require medical attention."

Her gaze flickered slightly, recognition seeping in. She wiped her cheeks with quivering fingers, leaving gray smudges across her skin as she shook her head.

Relief flooded my system like adrenaline, leaving me momentarily lightheaded.

"Can you come out, please?" I asked, extending my hand slowly, as if approaching a wounded animal.

She shook her head, shrinking further into the shadows beneath the desk.

"Scarlett, we need to leave. Whoever did this to you might come back."

Her eyes widened, pupils dilating as her panicked breathing returned—quick, shallow gasps that made her shoulders heave.

"It's okay," I soothed, keeping my hand outstretched. "I won't let him hurt you again." *He can't do that without a heartbeat.* "Can you come out, please?"

She bit her lip, torment etching itself across the planes of her face as she calculated her options: remain hidden where it felt safe or risk exposure to potential danger.

"You used to hide under furniture as a child, didn't you?" I said, the realization dawning on me.

A slight, almost-imperceptible nod.

"It makes you feel safe."

Another nod, her eyes brimming with fresh tears.

"You're safe, Scarlett." The conviction in my voice surprised even me. "I won't allow anything to happen to you. But I need you to come out so we can leave. Because if that man comes back ..." My voice dropped to a dangerous whisper. "I will kill him."

Her eyes snapped into focus then, truly meeting mine for the first time. Wide and worried, but present. She seemed to digest this for several seconds, staring at my outstretched hand as if it might disappear. And then, hesitantly, she gripped my palm.

My God, the flood of emotions that washed through me when her skin met mine. Her fingers were ice cold, but that small contact burned through me like wildfire. The trust she placed in me at a moment when she was so terrified she couldn't even bring herself to leave the shelter of her desk, it humbled me and ignited something fiercely protective deep in my chest.

I'd need to take her to the police. Get security all over this. But we could do neither of those things if she remained too traumatized to speak. Somehow, I needed to stop her panic attack.

And I knew just how to do it.

As I guided her gently from beneath the desk, her fingers tightened around mine like a lifeline. A silent plea not to let go. And in that moment, I made a silent vow that I wouldn't.

Not today, not ever.

50

SCARLETT

For the record, I wasn't silent on the long drive to wherever the hell Jace was taking me because I was upset he'd taken control and insisted I come with him. I was silent because I was furious with myself for allowing Marcus to reduce me to that pathetic little girl who hid under furniture. I'd sworn I would never be her again. I'd been proud of the woman I'd become.

A professional woman paying her own bills and matching powerful men in conference-room showdowns. And let's not discount how I'd handled my best friend, Tessa, dating a very powerful man. Blake was an emergency room physician who made serious money and lived in that ridiculous penthouse, taking control of her medical care. Did I warn her away from that? No, I did not. Because I recognized that my own demons weren't mine to spread like an infection through society and certainly not into my best friend's heart. And during my encounters with Blake, was I nervous? Hell no. I leaned into my confidence and sarcasm with ease, comfortable around his presence because, deep down, I sensed he was a good man. That my best friend had nothing to worry about.

I'd made so much progress becoming the Scarlett I wanted to

be, stuffing down that pathetic, whimpering version of my childhood self.

And then it all just evaporated right in front of me with one wolf in a suit. One. I was so angry with myself. So disappointed for letting him break through that invisible wall and yank out my inner scared child by her hair. And beneath that anger and disappointment was a giant fresh wave of fear.

What if I would never be whole, would never be one hundred percent *new Scarlett*—the Scarlett I chose to be rather than the one I'd tried to leave behind? What if this vulnerable version of me would always be lying beneath the surface, waiting for the right moment to break through? I thought I had shoved her down deep enough where that could never happen.

So, why then did it happen today?

Because some pathetic excuse for a man had attacked me? I was safe when it happened. All I had to do was scream, for crying out loud. The building had security, so logically speaking, there was no reason to let myself feel that afraid. It was pathetic.

Maybe I'd fallen into the dark hole of vulnerability because tonight was the first time in years my resolve had been tested to the breaking point. After all, other than my father, I had never had a man lay hands on me.

Still, I hated myself for it.

In fairness, I guess it was only human to be rattled by that whole Marcus attack. It'd probably rattle anyone, let alone someone with my past.

I took a deep breath, forcing my shoulders to relax. What I needed was clarity. Focus. I needed to pivot away from this spiral of shame and think about my next move.

Marcus was going down.

In. Fucking. Flames.

"You don't need to look at me like I'm some broken person because I'm not," I said. It was the first thing I'd said in almost an hour. Pathetically, it had taken that long for this shock, or whatever the hell it was that silenced my voice, to finally break.

"I can tell you're not," Jace said softly.

He flipped his hand open on the space between our seats, while he alternated between looking murderous and worried. I glanced down at his palm, surprised by how much I wanted to take it. Even more surprised by how soothing it felt when I finally laced my fingers with his.

His hand was warm, steady. Strong in a way I needed right now.

"My mom didn't intend to get pregnant with me," I rambled, the words tumbling out now that the dam had broken. "She got married really young. By the time she realized her husband was a raging asshole, two pink lines appeared on a pregnancy test. She stayed for me. She wanted to make it work, wanted to go to therapy, wanted to get help, but you can't fix somebody who doesn't think they need fixing. He's an arrogant asshole, but I'm not a victim. I've never been a victim. I've simply been the daughter of a complete raging narcissist."

I glanced out the window, watching the lane markings blur beneath the car as we sped along the highway. The sky was beginning to take on that golden-hour glow, making everything look deceptively peaceful.

"I'm not weak." Maybe if I said it enough, it would feel true tonight. "It's very important to me that you see that I'm not weak."

"Scar," Jace said, shifting in his seat, gripping the wheel with only one hand. His other remained firmly entwined with mine, his thumb absently tracing circles against my skin. "We've talked about this. I don't see you as weak."

"Yeah, well, we talked about that before tonight." Before I'd cowered under a desk, trembling like a child.

"Can we talk about what happened?" His voice was careful, measured.

My heart thundered in my chest, nausea swirling in my gut. My throat tightened, and I felt the cold sweat break out across my forehead again.

He must have sensed my panic because he squeezed my hand gently and said, "It's okay. Take some time."

Some. But Jace wouldn't wait long to hear the horror that had unfolded. The horror that was lodged in my chest.

"We're here," Jace said gently.

I blinked, pulled from my thoughts. Then my mouth fell open in shock as realization dawned, and instantly, a soothing balm spread over the raw wounds in my heart. Our tires crunched along the gravel driveway, my eyes burning with unexpected tears of gratitude.

Despite being barefoot and still in my disheveled work attire, I jumped out of the car as soon as Jace threw it into park and ran. Ran with the wind blowing through my tangled hair, tiny stones biting at the soles of my feet.

Unsurprisingly, Jace knew exactly what I needed.

Needed. Not wanted. Needed.

I ran into the stable, the amber glow filtering through open panes on the walls, making everything inside look warm and safe. The familiar smell of hay and oats washed over me, instantly calming my frayed nerves. Throwing open the stall door, I wrapped my arms around my horse's neck, burying my face into her warm, solid presence as I finally let myself sob openly.

"Buttercup," I whispered against her mane, feeling her solid strength beneath me.

She nickered softly in recognition, dropping her head over my shoulder, as if returning the embrace. As if to say, *I'm here.* As if to say, *You're safe now.*

I felt Jace watching from a respectful distance, giving me this moment. And in that instant, something shifted between us. Something profound that I wasn't ready to name yet.

Because, without my specifically telling him, he had known exactly where I needed to be, known the one place I'd feel safe. He had seen the real me beneath the mascara-streaked face and trembling hands. He had seen past the scared woman hiding under her desk to the heart of who I was.

51

JACE

I watched Scarlett nuzzle her face into her horse, their connection pulsing like a visible heartbeat between them. Unbreakable. Elemental. I'd been right in taking her here, this magnificent beast the exact prescription her wounded soul needed when everything else in her world felt toxic.

Thank God. For the first time since I found her trembling under that desk, looking small in a way Scarlett West should never look, I could finally breathe again. And with that breath came space—space to examine the complicated web of thoughts and emotions tangling themselves into a goddamn knot in my head.

This woman had spent every waking moment since I'd known her overcompensating for having been vulnerable during her childhood. Scarlett "I Don't Need Anyone" West. Queen of steel spines and take-no-prisoners smiles. So, seeing her surrender to fear earlier did two things to me: First, her pain ignited a white-hot rage that scorched through my veins. Second, it made me fall for her even harder than I already had. And trust me, I was already in dangerous territory.

Don't get me wrong; I worshipped her confident, take-no-prisoners side. That sass could power a small city. But witnessing her brokenness cracked something open in me too: the ridiculous hope that maybe, just maybe, I wasn't beyond repair after all. Perhaps she could glue me back together, and we could hold our fragmented souls in place.

The truth was, beneath my billions, beneath the empire and designer suits that cost more than some people's mobile homes, when I went home at night and stared up at my ceiling, I felt completely hollow inside. Empty. Broken.

That brokenness had started when I was a kid, when my father was murdered in cold blood, and whatever fragments remained shattered even more when cancer took my mother years later.

The only time I'd felt even close to whole again was with Scarlett. It was like my soul had been infected with some terminal disease, and she was the experimental medication slowly spreading its antidote through my veins. One sarcastic comment at a time. One smile at a time. One touch at a time.

No matter how hard I tried, I'd never understand the science of it. But then I suppose that was how it worked with things that didn't fit themselves into Excel spreadsheets or PowerPoint charts. The unspoken, invisible forces made someone pure magic while others remained just flesh and bone.

Maybe I'd never understand how love worked. But I understood three very simple things:

One, I would find the man who hurt her.

Two, when I was done with him, his heart would no longer beat.

Three, so help me God, I would never allow anyone to hurt her again.

There was just one pesky detail complicating my vengeance plan. My intuition told me if I confronted Scarlett right this second, she would retreat, and I had no clue how long it might take for her to emerge from her shell again.

I wasn't sure how long to give her though, but I knew some guys who might ...

52

JACE

SINNERS AND SAINTS GROUP CHAT

Me: I have a female question.

*Axel: My specialty. *trophy emoji* What part of the female anatomy is confusing you today? I charge by the hour, but will give you the friend discount. First fifteen minutes of mansplaining absolutely free.*

Me: If a girl has been scared shitless but you need information from her, how long do you have to give her before you demand answers?

Blake: Reread your text. Note the word "demand." That word suggests you have no concept of the female mind.

Me: And now that you're with Tessa, you're suddenly Dr. Phil?

Blake: It doesn't take a medical degree to tell you that women don't respond well to being ordered around.

Me: Someone hurt her. I want his name so I can fucking destroy him.

*Ryker: HELLO! It's me, your friendly neighborhood criminal attorney who doesn't want to visit YOU in prison too! May I kindly suggest you refrain from making felony threats in WRITING? Judges tend to find premeditated murder confessions in group texts compelling evidence. *face smacking emoji**

Me: I was obviously exaggerating. By destroy, I meant professionally.

Ryker: Still terrible. You know what defendants always say? "I didn't mean it literally." Right before they're convicted. These texts can be subpoenaed, and the jury won't care about your "just kidding" follow-up. They'll be too busy calculating how to divide your fortune in the subsequent civil suit.

Me: Can we get back to my question? Some guy scared the hell out of a woman, and I want to know who did it.

Blake: Scarlett?

Me: Someone hurt her.

Ryker: Call the police.

Me: I'm not 100% sure what happened. I don't even know if a crime has been committed. Thus my question, which I will ask AGAIN: How long do I have to give her before interrogating her?

*Axel: Dude, you're talking about her like she's a witness on a TV drama, not someone you care about. No wonder you're still single. *smirking emoji* Even I know better than that, and I'm professionally allergic to commitment.*

Ryker: My experience with traumatized witnesses is that it varies. Sometimes, they're ready to talk immediately. Sometimes, it takes more time. Almost like—and this might shock you—women are individual humans with different processing capabilities and not robots with standardized recovery protocols.

Me: Define "varies." I need more. Provide a specific timeline.

Blake: Did you just ask for a recovery timeline? For trauma? With bullet points and a Gantt chart?

Axel: Classic Jace. Probably wants to schedule her emotional breakdown between his 2 p.m. and 3 p.m. meetings.

Me: You're all useless.

Axel: Dude, just use your gut instincts. Does she look like she's ready to talk?

I ground my molars.

Me: No.

Axel: Then wait.

Me: The guy could show up at the office tomorrow.

*Axel: So, stand guard outside her office. Women probably love shit like that. Nothing says "healthy relationship" like a brooding billionaire with boundary issues. *superhero emoji**

Me: I'm not letting this guy get away with this!

*Axel: Fine, then try to berate it out of her. Good luck with that. Women love being pressured when they're already traumatized. *eye roll emoji**

Blake: Shockingly, I agree with Axel, but for the record, I highly recommend you discard his advice on a go-forward basis. I saw the third woman on his arm on Instagram THIS WEEK.

Axel: Blake's officially checking Instagram? The apocalypse must be near.

Blake: I like seeing Tessa's business page, but your posts keep interrupting my feed, jackass.

Axel: Please, seeing me on your feed is the best part of your day. Which woman was I with in the last photo you saw?

Blake: You're disturbing.

Axel: Red dress?

Blake: Have you nothing better to do with your time than grow your conquests?

*Axel: You're just jealous because you made the mistake of settling down with one woman. Some of us haven't surrendered to domestic "bliss." *devil emoji* My condolences to your manhood. May it rest in peace.*

Me: HELLO? Can we circle back to MY problem? How long?

Blake: Maybe Tessa could encourage Scarlett to open up to you?

Me: Maybe. But that will take time to get those two together. I want to know tonight. Tomorrow morning at the latest.

Ryker: Give her space, but make it clear you're there when she's ready. And for the love of God, when she does talk, don't make more threats that I'll have to explain away in court while wearing my "please don't convict my idiot friend" tie.

Me: Fine. I'll TRY to wait. For now.

*Axel: Our boy's growing up. Next thing you know, he'll be asking about proper dinner date etiquette. *tear emoji**

Blake: Miracles do happen. Should we start planning the intervention now or wait until he starts using words like "feelings" without breaking out in hives?

Ryker: I'll clear my calendar for the inevitable bail hearing either way.

Great. It would seem I was going to have to find another way to get the guy's name tonight. Luckily, I had an idea ...

53

SCARLETT

"The hell is wrong with this horse?" Jace snarled as Snickerdoodle came to a complete stop, huffed dramatically, and then trotted forward just enough to make him grip the reins like they were the last parachute on a plummeting plane.

I bit back a laugh. Seeing Mr. Fortune 500 out of his element was better than front-row tickets to my favorite concert. With backstage passes. And an open bar.

"This one is defective," he muttered, adjusting himself in the saddle for the fifteenth time in ten minutes. At this rate, his designer pants would be worn through by sunset.

Thank God the sun didn't set until nearly eight thirty this time of year. If today's after-hours drama had happened in winter, the sky would already be pitch black. Instead, it was cotton-candy pastel, the sun dipping toward the horizon.

"She's perfect."

"If I had an employee with this kind of performance, they'd be fired before lunch."

"She's not an employee. She's a soul with four legs, and you need to treat her like that."

"She's plotting to buck me off." He narrowed those green eyes at the horse's innocent ears. "I can't very well run a company with a broken neck. I knew it was a bad idea to let you talk me into riding again."

In his defense, the last time, he rode a different horse. Snickerdoodle was more spirited.

"If it makes any difference, you look super handsome, doing it." And he did. Unfairly so. Like someone had Photoshopped a *GQ* model onto a horse calendar. *December, featuring Billionaire Who Can't Ride But Looks Damn Good Trying.*

Jace glared at me, which only emphasized his chiseled jawline. Still wearing his suit pants and button-down, he'd abandoned his tie and jacket back at the stable. So, at least half of his "seven-thousand-dollar Brioni suit"—his words, not mine—was safe from Snickerdoodle's shenanigans. But still, it wasn't every day I saw a man in tailored pants riding a horse. Let alone riding one so ... spectacularly badly.

Me? I was comfortable and riding well, thank you very much. It didn't hurt that I was wearing the change of clothes I kept at the barn. My body knew these trails like my fingers knew a keyboard: effortlessly, instinctively.

"I shouldn't have let you talk me into this, Trouble," he grumbled, shifting his weight again as Snickerdoodle sidestepped like she was avoiding paparazzi.

"You didn't need much convincing."

"Seeing that smile on your face, I would have boarded a rocket ship to the moon to keep it there," he said absently. Like it was nothing. Like casually admitting he'd hurtle himself into space just to see me happy was as ordinary as ordering coffee.

My heart did a flip in my chest, and suddenly, I had to fight the urge to launch myself onto his horse and wrap my arms around his ridiculously ripped body. And say thank you.

Thank you for knowing exactly what I needed.

Thank you for agreeing to go for a ride when I'm one thousand percent sure that is the last thing on your corporate agenda.

And thank you for not ruining this moment by demanding Marcus's name right now.

I got the impression that Jace was normally a fist-pounding CEO who snapped his fingers and expected information to materialize in front of him. Patience? Not in his vocabulary.

But this Jace? This Jace placed my needs, all my needs, far above his own.

Make no mistake. Marcus's name wasn't staying secret anymore. I just needed a moment to catch my breath, like a boxer on the canvas who needed to stand up on her own terms. After feeling as vulnerable as I did in that office, hiding under my desk like a frightened child, I needed to feel in control again. HR and police would hear his name tomorrow, guaranteed, but I'd be the one telling them—not because someone forced my hand, but because I chose to.

Bonus if I could somehow do damage control with my career in the meantime. Should I tell Jace before HR? At this point, I doubted he'd think I'd made it all up, but it was still complicated, and my bank account wasn't exactly overflowing with *quit your job on principle* money.

I shook my head. Those were tomorrow problems. Today, the sun was beginning to set, painting the sky in watercolor strokes of amber and gold around the trees and gorgeous foliage as we ambled along the trail.

"Damn horse!" Jace snarled as Snickerdoodle came to a complete halt out of nowhere, nearly sending him flying over her head.

"She senses your anger," I said, patting my own horse's neck. "Animals sense feelings. You need to relax."

"My feelings have nothing to do with a giant ball of fur misbehaving."

"She's mortally offended you said that." I smirked. "Look at her ears. That's horse for *I can't believe this guy*. And FYI, horses have hair, not fur."

"Horses are basically big, fuzzy dogs with hooves. You train them. You feed them. This one is failing spectacularly at part one."

"Snickerdoodle is one of the best trained horses in the stable. It was nice of the barn manager to let you take her out. Most beginners get Turtle." I paused. "He's named that because ... well, you get it. He makes glaciers look speedy."

Snickerdoodle huffed again, trotting forward so suddenly that Jace jerked backward. I briefly wondered if whiplash was covered under whatever platinum-diamond-encrusted insurance plan billionaires had.

"Fucking horse!" he snapped.

I couldn't help but laugh. The mighty Jace Lockwood, who probably made grown men cry in boardrooms, was being absolutely owned by a horse named after a cookie.

"Jace, I can tell you're upset, and if I can tell, she can definitely tell. She's basically a twelve-hundred-pound emotional sponge with a tail."

His eyes darkened to a forest green as they slammed into mine, the fury he was clearly trying to keep at bay unleashing as he growled, "I found you quivering under a desk. Of course I'm upset."

Okay. I'll just pretend your fury didn't do all sorts of unwanted things to my heart. My hormones ...

"Take a deep breath in, hold it for two seconds, and then breathe it out through your nose," I instructed. "It's what I do when my laptop crashes right before a deadline."

Jace cocked his head, and dammit if he didn't look even sexier doing it. The man could make annoyance look like a cologne ad. "Deep breathing exercises? Really?"

"Do you enjoy having your spine in one piece? Because I'm pretty sure Snickerdoodle here is taking mental measurements for a full-body cast."

Jace pouted—actually pouted—looking every part a sexy hero on a horse in the process. I considered telling him it was his shirt that was the problem. Seeing his muscles and abs covered in tattoos, clenching with each horse movement would be ... educational. For the local wildlife. And me.

Instead, I watched him close his eyes, taking deep breaths that made his chest rise and fall. He looked as peaceful as a billionaire in the throes of a complicated acquisition could, and then, after a few seconds, Snickerdoodle calmed down. Either that or she was just recharging for her next attack.

"See?" I said, not even trying to keep the smugness out of my voice. "Horse psychology 101."

"If it's all the same to you, I'd like to take a short break before this four-legged menace decides to test gravity with my body."

I gave Buttercup a good rub between her ears. "Good girl," I whispered. "At least one of us knows how to behave around pretty boys."

After dismounting, I pulled some food from the satchel I'd secured on the back of my horse and gave the ladies something to munch on. Including Snickerdoodle, who, despite her antics, was still a very good girl.

"I'm sorry you didn't enjoy the ride," I said as Jace approached me, his hair adorably disheveled from his battle with equestrian dignity.

"Wouldn't go so far as to say that."

I eyed him, smirking. "You seemed miserable."

"With the horse's behavior," he clarified, his lips quirking into a half smile. "The company was perfect."

My eyes stung again for the umpteenth time since Jace had brought me here.

"How did you know to bring me here?" I asked, handing a carrot to Buttercup, who accepted it like the lady she was. "How'd you know what it would do for me?"

Jace closed the distance between us, his strides rustling along the grass in his bazillion-dollar shoes that, before tonight, had probably never seen actual dirt.

"When you brought me here, you said horses never hurt you the way people do. I could see you had a connection to this horse that was deep. Healing." He paused, his jaw tightening. "Figured after what you went through today ..." Jace swallowed and clenched his eyes shut, like the memory of seeing me trembling under that desk was one he couldn't bear. "I was hoping she would make you feel safe again."

Sucking in a sudden breath, it struck me how well he knew me. And how, in that moment, he'd wanted to make me feel better. More than anything. I mean, my God, this was a CEO who had a predator in his company. Others in his position might've prioritized his needs: uncovering who had done this so he could protect his precious company image. But instead, he prioritized me.

Stepping even closer, Jace allowed his gaze to travel around my face, like it physically pained him, imagining what I had gone through. Then, he drew his knuckles up and traced them down my jaw, the touch sending my skin aflame.

"Are you okay, Scarlett?" He said the words softly, his voice a mixture of concern and something deeper, as if my well-being had somehow become crucial to his own.

When I nodded, his chest dropped a couple of inches. Relief, I guess, housed behind a breath he'd been holding this entire time.

"I don't ever want to see you like that again," he declared.

"Me neither." I tried to say it lightly, but my attempt at humor was lost on him as he cupped my cheek, stroking my skin with his thumb.

"I have something for you," I said, nervous energy suddenly fluttering in my chest.

"For me?" His eyebrows rose in genuine surprise.

I nodded, crossing over to grab my purse from the satchel, grateful Jace had grabbed it before we'd left the building. I pulled out a small package wrapped in simple brown paper and twine. Nothing fancy, but somehow, that made it feel more significant.

"It's not much, but ..." I trailed off as I handed it to him.

Jace carefully unwrapped it, revealing the worn cover of *The Keeper's Compass*. His fingers froze on the book, and for a moment, I worried I'd made a terrible mistake. Then I watched his throat work as he swallowed hard. When he opened the cover to find the handwritten signature inside, his composure cracked just enough for me to see the boy who'd once found direction through its pages.

"eBay has everything," I said softly. "Found this signed first edition and had it expedited. I ordered it as a thank-you for punching my father in the face and intended to give it to you sooner but ..." I smiled. "This moment felt right."

He ran his thumb across the signature, a gesture so tender that it made something in my chest ache. I'd seen Jace confident, powerful, even angry, but never vulnerable like this.

"You remembered." His voice was hushed with wonder.

"Your mom used to read it to you when you felt lost," I said, echoing his earlier explanation. "I worried you might already have a copy, but I thought maybe not a signed one."

"I don't—" His voice caught. "Didn't."

He looked up at me then, and I saw something shift in his eyes. This man who could buy anything, who controlled billion-dollar deals with a single word, was holding this battered children's book like it was made of gold.

"Thank you, Scarlett," he said simply, but the weight behind those three words felt heavier than any flowery speech could have been.

A silence fell between us. His expression shifted, like he was wrestling with some internal decision. Probably wondering if he should keep pressing me for a name or let me decide when to bring it up. After a sigh, I figured he'd opted for the latter, thank God, but a fresh wave of anxiety flooded his face. His eyes, usually so confident and direct, flickered away toward Snickerdoodle and then back to mine.

"I hate riding horses," he announced with the solemnity of someone confessing to tax fraud.

I tilted my head, wondering if I'd heard that right. "What?"

"I hate riding horses," he repeated, looking relieved to have this terrible burden off his chest. "I love that you love doing it. And I'll bring you to the barn anytime you want, and I'll watch you and buy all the treats for the furry beasts that you desire. Hell, I'll buy you a hundred horses if that's what you want. I want to support you in the things that you do and love. Especially things that make you happy, but I don't want to do the same things you do. I don't like riding horses. They're scary and unruly, and they don't listen. And they chomp. With very large teeth."

His face was so earnest, like he'd just confessed to the crime of the century rather than admitting he wasn't keen on horseback riding.

"Okay?" I managed, trying not to laugh at his adorable confession.

"I hope it is okay. Because I want to spend a lot of time with you, Scarlett." His voice dropped lower, more serious. "And you deserve to know up front what you're getting yourself into if you date me. I don't like riding horses. If you want some cowboy, I'm not your man. I think the horses can even sense I'm an imposter in the barn, but I adore you, and I hope that counts for something."

"Date?" I repeated, the word feeling foreign on my tongue. Like trying to speak a language I'd sworn off years ago.

"I know," he said, running a hand through his hair. "You said you don't date, but here's the thing: We don't have to call it dating. We can just call it spending time together. And having sex."

"Sex," I echoed, holding back a smile.

"Lots of it." His eyes darkened as they swept over me. "I just ... I can't stop thinking about you."

The truth was, I couldn't stop thinking about Jace either. I had never had a guy stuck in my head like this before. But in fairness, I had never experienced a guy so attentive to my needs either. I had never had a guy go out of his way to help me and my mom in her time of need. And I had never known anyone that knew exactly what I needed like Jace knew what I needed tonight.

The thing was, that realization was starting to feel a lot less terrifying and more exhilarating. Like standing at the edge of a cliff and realizing you actually wanted to jump.

"I thought there was a no-fraternization policy at work." *Practical to the end, Scarlett. Well done.*

"I know," he sighed. "There'll be some kinks to work out for sure. I want you to consider it, Scarlett, but ..." He trailed off, struggling to find the words.

I wasn't sure where all this apprehension on his face was coming from. Fear of being rejected maybe?

The scary thing was, I felt like he didn't need to be afraid. And I didn't need to think about it. I wanted him. Not just his body, which, let's be honest, deserved its own zip code, but him.

I dropped the food in my hands to the ground and threaded my fingers through his hair, pulling his body against mine, savoring the warmth and firmness of his chest against my own as I pressed my lips to his.

Around us, the pastel sky was orange with hues of purple, the green leaves of the trees rustling in the breeze, and the slight sound of horses blended with birds chirping. The smart thing would be to ride back now, before darkness set in, but with his hands trailing down my back, the thought of abandoning this moment for anything seemed impossible. Like trying to leave a warm bed on a cold morning: theoretically doable, but why would anyone do something that atrocious?

Especially when our kiss evolved and deepened. Especially when Jace's lips kissed a line down my jaw, down my throat, and heat began to coil in my lower belly. The kind of heat that made me forget about horses and barns and everything that wasn't his mouth on my skin.

Tugging at his shirt, I was taken off guard when Jace grabbed my wrist with his non-book-holding hand to stop me. The sudden halt made me blink up at him in confusion.

"I don't have protection," he said, his voice strained. Like the words physically hurt to say.

"Oh." Right. But ... "I'm on the pill." For menstrual cycle

reasons, not that it mattered right now with his hands holding mine so firmly.

"I've never had sex without protection before." He said it apologetically, the implied *and I'm not going to start now* hanging in the air between us like an invisible wall. Which made sense. After all, a man worth billions could never afford to place his trust in anyone who might lie to him. One runaway sperm would link his fortunes to her forever.

"Okay." I released his shirt, settling for kissing him instead. Because kissing was wonderful, even if it was torture of the sweetest kind.

Our hands explored each other's hair, our faces heating with each touch. We would pull apart and stare into each other's eyes and smile, only to crash back together with increasing desperation. He trailed his thumb along my lower lip and then opened his mouth to allow our tongues to connect over and over. All the while, I tried to ignore the heat pooling between my thighs, the hunger of wanting so much more than he could give me right now.

His hands slid down to my waist, fingers digging in slightly before he suddenly froze. I could feel him fighting his own desire, his body rigid with restraint.

Eventually, I pulled back, trailing my fingers along his jaw. His eyes were dark, pupils wide with want.

"We should get back," I said, the words tasting like disappointment in my mouth.

With a tight jaw, chest heaving with quick breaths, Jace nodded, like this was the last thing he wanted to hear. But he stepped back, letting his arms fall to his sides, staring at me as if he needed me to be the one with the willpower between us.

The air between us crackled with desire as we stood there, neither one of us moving. I could almost hear the ticking of some invisible clock, counting down the seconds until the spell broke completely.

I turned before I heard it: a single, guttural phrase that sent electricity straight down my spine.

"Fuck it," he growled, his hand shooting around my wrist and spinning me around, slamming his mouth to mine again with newfound urgency.

I moaned as he dropped the book, pulled my shirt over my head, followed by the rest of my clothes. The cool air hit my skin for only a moment before the heat of his body pressed against mine, the contrast making me shiver. Or maybe that was just him.

Good Lord, I didn't realize just how much I'd needed this until I was unbuttoning his shirt, sliding it over his broad shoulders. The sounds of his belt clinking came next, followed by him abandoning me for a moment to lay our clothes down next to each other, quilting together our shirts and pants into a makeshift blanket covering the grass.

And then he grabbed me and lay me down on it, my fingers threading through his dark hair as he kissed down my throat to my collarbone. Each touch was a promise, each kiss a declaration that maybe, just maybe, some people were worth the risk.

"You have any idea how beautiful you are, Scarlett?" Jace kissed down my breast, taking my nipple into his mouth.

Heat shot from my chest to my sex, which started to throb with need. He swirled his tongue around the sensitive bud, the heat of his mouth abandoning it for cool air when he moved to the other side.

His touch was like fire and ice, all at once, scorching yet making me shiver. As his lips traced patterns across my body, I saw something in his eyes that terrified and thrilled me in equal measure. This wasn't just desire; it was worship.

"I want you, Scarlett," Jace declared, and I knew what he meant. He didn't just want me physically. He wanted all of me: my heart and soul, my laughter and tears, my past and future. The realization should have sent me running. Instead, it fused me to this moment, to him.

I swallowed, locking eyes with him as he kissed down my

stomach and positioned himself between my thighs. Which he spread wide open, holding my gaze for another moment before taking in the sight of me.

"So beautiful," he murmured, kissing my inner thigh. Torturing me by bringing his mouth so close to where I needed it, the throbbing becoming unbearable.

"Please," I whispered, unable to contain the need in my voice. With any other man, I would have been embarrassed by my desperation. With Jace, it felt like strength. The strength to ask for what I wanted.

"Tell me what you want, Trouble." More kisses, just out of range. More throbbing.

"I want you to lick me."

"Good girl." Jace flattened his tongue and made one long stride up my sex, making me buck when he reached the sensitive bundle of nerves at the top.

Moaning, I gazed down at him over the curve of my breasts, drinking in the scene before me: a secluded meadow, deep within the wilderness trail, wildflowers swaying gently around us as the setting sun cast golden light across our skin. The tattooed billionaire, all lean muscle and focused intensity, with his face buried between my thighs. I could already feel a wave climbing inside of me.

He licked down my folds and penetrated me with his tongue this time. I sucked in a sharp breath, watching him pump his tongue in and out of me, my inner thighs quivering harder and harder with each thrust.

"Jace ..." I groaned.

He pulled his tongue back up my sex and sucked my sensitive bud into his mouth. The wave rose higher and higher as he licked and swirled my body, knowing the perfect pressure and tempo. I loved hearing his groans, watching the hunger in his eyes as he'd alternate from closing them to savoring the beautiful glistening folds before him.

"Jace ..." I tugged his hair hard between my fingers.

"Come for me."

That was all it took. I crashed around him so hard that he had to hold my hips to keep from being dislodged, and through every ripple of pleasure, he pulled more out of me, teased even more ecstasy. Only when I stopped trembling did he finally sit up.

With a smile, he climbed on top of me and lined himself up at my entrance.

"That was amazing," I said, panting, gliding my fingers down his arms.

"You haven't seen anything yet," he promised. And then, with one thrust, he plunged deep inside of me. "Oh fuck ... you feel amazing."

My mouth fell open, my breath escaping at the sensation of him buried to my core. My body stretched around him, filled by him, as he kissed my neck and began to move.

And move he did. He rolled his hips in a circular motion so that with each thrust, he was stimulating the bundle of nerves outside of my body while simultaneously hitting that sensitive spot inside. All the while, his eyes never left mine, silently asking if I was okay.

Silently, I answered him by running my fingers through his hair and pulling his mouth to mine. His tongue slipped past my lips, and then his kisses trailed down my jaw, my neck.

"You feel so good," Jace murmured, the words vibrating against my skin. "Perfect."

Bare skin against bare skin, he thrust and pumped into me, making a fresh wave climb higher and higher.

"Roll over," he demanded, pulling out and sitting back on his knees.

I happily obliged, anticipation coiling through me.

Jace paused for what felt like an eternity. Then, with unbridled abandon, he thrust himself deep inside of me. I cried out, and he stilled, letting my body stretch around him, letting me take in the fullness of him. As he pulled back and found his rhythm, I was taken again by how we must look. Me on all fours, a muscular, gorgeous guy taking me from behind.

"You're perfect—you know that?" He growled.

My sex throbbed around him, a fresh orgasm coiling in my lower belly. And as he moved, as he gave me a mix of angry thrusts and gentle words, he pulled my head back and to the side so he could claim my mouth with his own.

"I'm coming," I said against his lips.

He growled, thrusting harder into me to ride my wave, ripple after ripple. Until finally, he stilled with a climax of his own.

After, we lay there in the meadow, in each other's arms, my body still humming from what we'd just shared. It was remarkable, how one person could take me from the trembling ball of terror, through the valleys of happiness and passion, and now into a place of complete contentment. All effortlessly.

"I've never met anyone like you," I admitted. "You're pretty damn admirable—you know that?" In every way. Bedroom, emotions, you name it.

Jace stiffened beside me. Not the subtle kind of tension. We're talking full-on marble statue mode. The silence stretched between us, elastic and threatening to snap while I was trying to figure out what in the world made the temperature drop between us.

I propped myself up on my elbow, studying the fresh apprehension on his face.

"Why did you deflate like an expired balloon when I said I find you admirable?"

His jaw tightened, eyes fixed on some distant point above my head. "I'm not the white knight you think I am." He paused, and I swear, even the birds around us stopped chirping, straining their little ears to see if we'd heard him right. And then he added, "I've done something unforgivable."

I froze. "What is it?"

He bit his lip while alarms began to blare. Whatever this was, it was big. Catastrophic.

"Another time," he said.

"Fat chance. I'll spend all night wondering what horror you're keeping from me, and I've seen enough true crime shows to conjure some truly creative scenarios. Spill it. Now."

Jace looked like he was mentally calculating the odds of winning an argument against me, then surrendered with a sigh. He knew me well enough by now to gauge my stubborn streak. I wasn't letting this go. This man had just been inside me. If he was keeping something from me, I damn well deserved to know what it was.

"Fine," he said, voice flat. "But let's get dressed first."

"Why?"

"Because after I tell you, you might want to get away from me as fast as possible."

54

SCARLETT

"Scarlett, there's something I haven't told you ..." His voice faltered. "And once I do, you might never want to talk to me again."

I adjusted my shirt, my mind racing with horrible possibilities.

"I should have told you sooner. I ... let myself get lost in finding out who did this to you while also fighting my feelings, but I should have told you before I asked you to be mine."

It took Jace several seconds to speak. Seconds where I held my breath until my lungs burned, until finally, his voice emerged, soft and laden with guilt.

"After the death of my father, I felt like I had to be the strong one in the family," Jace began, pacing slowly. "The one who never got in any trouble. I kept my grades up and tried to be the easy kid for my mom. Lord knows she was dealing with enough grief of her own, and my brothers ..." He ran a hand through his hair. "Let's just say, they didn't handle the death of my father well. So, I tried to be a good kid for her sake."

He paused, his attention sweeping over me. "You might want to sit down for this."

My heart stuttered. What was he about to tell me? Jace was the first guy I had completely let my guard down with, the first guy I had let myself fall for, the first guy I actually wanted a future with. In short, I'd given him power over my heart.

If he turned out to be someone I should never have trusted, I'd never ever try again.

"I'd rather stand," I said, bracing myself.

A night breeze rustled through my hair, the horses making snickering noises that felt inappropriately cheerful for the moment.

Jace chewed on his lip but nodded.

"When I was in college, I found out that my mom had cancer." His voice grew rougher. "The night I learned her treatments were failing, I was at a bar with Marcus that served underage kids. I was twenty, below the legal drinking age, and I don't remember most of that night, but I do remember drowning my anger with alcohol."

He moved to the nearby tree, twisting a branch between his fingers until I thought it might snap, just like my composure if this conversation continued in the direction I feared.

"I remember coming to on the ground, staring up at the sky, wondering what the hell I was doing, sleeping outside in the middle of the night. That's when I heard the hiss of the engine and saw steam rising from the crunched hood of the car. I had been ejected when it hit a tree."

"Were you hurt?" I asked, already stepping toward him.

Jace shook his head. "Your first question shouldn't be if I was hurt, Scarlett. It should be if I hurt someone."

My mind attempted to catalog his words, unsure if I really wanted to hear whatever he was about to confess. Some truths changed everything. Some truths couldn't be unheard.

"I had a head injury," he said, his voice flat. "So, the paramedics prioritized stabilizing me. By the time the police came to talk to me, they had already gotten a statement from Marcus, who took the fall. He claimed he was driving that night."

"Was he?"

Jace shook his head, not meeting my eyes.

"In the hospital, he told me what happened. He said I was belligerent and beside myself at the bar, that I had gone to my car to drive. I don't remember leaving the bar. I don't remember being in that car."

"I don't understand. If you crashed, why did Marcus say he was driving?"

"He didn't know how much longer my mom would live, and whatever time I had left with her, he didn't want me to spend it on trial or in jail. So, he took the rap."

I tried to reconcile this with what I now knew about Marcus. Had there been a time when he was actually decent? How could a man who took a criminal fall for Jace be the same man who hurt me tonight? How could both men inhabit the same body?

Then again, look at my dad. Charming. Funny. Violent. Dangerous. Loving. People weren't simple creatures with on/off switches for good and evil.

"But a few days later, circumstances changed," Jace continued, his voice tight. "We hadn't just hit a tree; we had hit another vehicle. At the time, the woman driving didn't have life-threatening injuries. But she had a complication. A blood clot went to her lungs and killed her." His voice lowered. "So, Marcus was charged with vehicular manslaughter."

"Oh my God." I drew my hand to my mouth.

"I tried to recant my statement to take responsibility. I went to the police station. I called a lawyer. I did everything I could, but they didn't believe me. They thought I was just trying to cover for my best friend."

My mind was reeling. A woman died? Because of Jace's terrible decision? I was glad he at least confessed to the police because I didn't know that I could have respected him otherwise. But still, he was responsible for a death.

And Marcus had saved Jace from certain prison?

"Did Marcus go to jail?"

"Almost. I went to my uncle and confessed everything. He secured the best lawyers in the country who, somehow, managed to make the problem go away. But that only left me with more guilt." Jace's shoulders slumped, appearing to recognize how much this reinforced the talk we'd had in the rain. "I sank into a deep depression after that," he continued. "Ashamed that while my mother was fighting for her life, I had gone out drinking and caused someone else to die. And I was ashamed that we had used our wealth and connections to get away with it."

Oh God. And then I threw things like that in his face outside the restaurant about the privileged not suffering consequences. No wonder he'd looked so destroyed by that talk.

He took a ragged breath. "If the police had listened to me, if they had charged me instead of Marcus, I would've surrendered to whatever punishment they sentenced me to. But I couldn't let Marcus spend his life in prison because of my mistakes."

He looked at me, his eyes haunted. "I never even told my other friends about it at the time. I was so disgusted and ashamed. I didn't want anyone to know my darkest secret."

This was a lot to digest. That poor woman—someone's daughter, maybe someone's mother—gone forever because of one reckless night. That family left with a gaping hole no explanation could ever fill. Cold fury and disbelief warred inside me. How dare he get behind the wheel? Grief-stricken or not, drunk or not, it wasn't just a mistake. It was a selfish, devastating choice that cost someone everything.

My throat tightened. Part of me wanted to scream at him, to make him feel every ounce of that family's pain. We all had a responsibility to ensure our actions didn't hurt others. No amount of guilt or subsequent good deeds could ever bring that woman back.

And yet ... looking at the haunted shadows in Jace's eyes, I could see he'd been serving a life sentence of his own making. The prison he'd built for himself had no walls, but the punishment had been no less severe.

"For a while, I had no real purpose in life," he continued. "I didn't feel deserving of happiness, and I felt especially unworthy of love. So, I chose to put up walls and steered clear of relationships."

My stomach twisted at his words because I could tell he'd believed that. All those years, he'd been hating himself, forcing everyone away because of a terrible decision he'd made years ago. Maybe I didn't know exactly how this would all land in my heart, but I did believe people deserved second chances, and Jace ... Jace was a good man. That much I knew.

He moved closer to me, close enough that I could see the pain etched in every line of his face.

"But after a while, I realized self-loathing wasn't enough. I needed to take this guilt and turn it into fire, into fuel to do something good."

His voice grew stronger. "I later learned that the woman had been driving on the road that night because she was working a late shift at a job she'd taken after her primary employer laid her off. Turned out, her company had cut hundreds of employees for no other reason than corporate greed."

Jace's eyes lit with a familiar passion. The one I'd glimpsed whenever he talked about his business philosophy.

"I realized maybe there was something good I could do with my wealth." His voice softened. "But I never changed my mind about relationships ... until you. I let you into my world, and I developed feelings for you, Scarlett. In fact, I'm falling in love with you."

Strange how my heart could still react with a hiccup, as if his profession wasn't imprisoned in a jail of complications.

"But you deserve someone far better than a man who caused the death of an innocent woman. Not someone who was never held accountable for taking another life."

I had no idea how to process all of this. It would take time. Hours, days, maybe weeks to digest what Jace had told me he'd done, to see how that settled into my soul. The woman. The cover-up. The wealth that made it all go away while another family buried their loved one. I couldn't offer absolution, not today. Maybe not ever. But I also couldn't deny the ache in my chest when I looked at him, the tangle of feelings that wouldn't simply dissolve because of this revelation.

My father had hurt people deliberately, systematically, without a shred of genuine remorse. What I saw in Jace was different. This wasn't just guilt; it was a man who'd spent years trying to atone. Who'd built a company that protected thousands of jobs. Who'd turned his darkest moment into a mission.

"I ..." I started, then stopped, searching for the right words. "I can't tell you how to feel about what happened." His eyes met mine, vulnerable, expecting rejection. "But my father ..." I swallowed hard. "He never felt sorry for what he did. And he sure as hell never tried to make anything better." I took a shaky breath. "You've dedicated your life to helping people, Jace. That doesn't erase what happened, but it says something about who you are."

"You don't see me as a monster?" he asked, his voice barely audible.

I shook my head slowly. "What I see is someone who's been punishing himself for years ... who's convinced himself he doesn't deserve a second chance."

I stepped closer, my heart hammering. "You have a choice. You can keep shutting people out, or ..." My voice caught. "Or you can forgive yourself enough to let someone in."

Hope took flight in his green eyes.

"When this is over ..." He gestured vaguely, words failing him. His gaze searched mine, asking the question he couldn't bring himself to voice. "Would you ... I mean ... I'd understand if you needed time. Or if you couldn't ..." He trailed off, jaw working, the vulnerability in his expression almost unbearable.

This powerful man, who built empires, reduced to incomplete sentences and unspoken questions. Afraid to ask directly for what he wanted. Afraid even to name it. He was asking if there was any hope that he and I could have a future together.

"You opening up to me makes me feel much closer to you," I assured. "But after everything that's happened tonight, I'm in a vulnerable, fragile state of mind and shouldn't be making any life-altering decisions until I've had time to process it all."

There was something more urgent pulsing beneath my shock. Something that made the hairs on my neck stand up.

If Marcus was this good, honorable man, so selfless that he'd taken the fall for Jace all those years ago, why was he behaving so terribly now? By the looks of it, Marcus had made out like a bandit. He'd gotten off any criminal charges and been a loyal right-hand man to Jace ever since, benefiting from what was probably an outrageous compensation package, power, and endless opportunities. Why blow it all?

And more pressing, why on earth would he threaten to hurt Jace tonight? *This* was the dark secret Marcus was alluding to, the one he was holding over Jace's head.

Knowing what it was now, I could see he'd exaggerated a bit. Jace probably wouldn't lose his freedom; I'd have to believe the statute of limitations had run out, but that wasn't the point. Marcus wasn't the loyal friend Jace believed him to be. He thought Marcus was on his side, all while his "so-called-friend" was threatening him behind his back.

"You owe a lot to Marcus," I managed, trying to keep my voice flat. Playing the role of understanding friend as I attempted to tease out what Jace might know. Did he have any clue that Marcus was a snake coiled to strike?

"I owe him everything," Jace said, the raw conviction in his voice making my stomach twist.

And just like that, I had my answer. Jace had no idea Marcus was a monster. He was oblivious to the danger lurking in his inner circle, tethered by gratitude to the very man who wanted to destroy him.

I opened my mouth to tell him the truth. But then I pictured Jace's face when he'd found me earlier tonight with that cold, unfiltered fury in his eyes. If I told him it was Marcus, Jace might do something rash, something he couldn't take back. Something that would destroy his life as thoroughly as Marcus intended.

The "good" news, if you could call it that, was that this wasn't just an HR problem anymore. Marcus had committed a crime by attacking me. I thought of my father, who'd been arrested and sitting in jail ever since he'd assaulted me. There was a system for this. A process.

I'd go to the police first. File a report. Once Marcus was safely behind bars, where Jace couldn't blow up his life by beating him senseless, then I'd tell Jace everything. This way, I could protect both of us.

But that created another problem: Marcus had explicitly threatened to expose Jace's past if I went public. The accident. The cover-up. Everything Jace had just trusted me with could become headline news if Marcus made good on his threat.

I had to choose: protect Jace's secret or protect Jace from himself?

55

SCARLETT

"You took her for a ride." Maggie, the barn manager, smiled as I put Buttercup back into her stall for the night.

"I did." The grin that spread across my face wasn't forced, not like the ones I'd been wearing at work all week. "It was exactly what my soul needed."

I locked eyes with Jace. His confession had surprised me, but so far, on the ride back to the barn at least, it hadn't launched my knee-jerk reaction to push him away, like I would have done in the past.

"I'm glad," Maggie said, but her tone made me pause.

"Is everything okay?"

Maggie leaned against the stable door. "Well, I'm keeping an eye on her. She's eating less and seems lethargic. Nothing serious yet, but something's off."

Suddenly, all my complications—Jace, Marcus, my father—seemed irrelevant.

"Why didn't you tell me?"

"I was planning to on Saturday." She hesitated. "I think she's depressed since her stable mate left. Horses form strong bonds."

My eyes burned. Buttercup was suffering, trapped in a situation she couldn't understand or escape. Just like I had been with my father, just like I was now with Marcus.

"And the horse bullies?" I asked.

"I'm trying to keep them away, but she's alone out there now."

"She has a fresh bite," I noticed.

"Didn't need stitches."

But she was being hurt. Just like me, only I had the power to make her pain stop.

"I think maybe I should sell her," I said. The words felt like bullets in my heart.

"Scarlett ..." Maggie's voice softened.

"She's with her stable mates twenty-four hours a day. She only sees me once or twice a week." I forced out words that were breaking my heart. "If we could replace one person in her life to give her the best quality of life, it would be me."

"You love this horse."

"Exactly." I rubbed Buttercup's neck, looking into her eyes. "And I have a responsibility to do what's best for her. Can you start making some calls?"

"Maybe you should think about it," Maggie suggested.

"Just make the calls. I want an owner who can afford to move her to Valley Creek Stables, where her friend is. I'll only sell to someone who contractually commits to it."

"Scarlett, I'm sure in time—"

"Make the calls," I interrupted, my voice breaking. I touched Buttercup's velvety nose. "I won't wait for her to get hurt badly by those horses."

I knew what it was like to feel trapped. I wouldn't let her suffer that fate, even if it meant breaking my own heart to set her free.

And now, with what I was about to do, Buttercup might not be the only one I'd risk losing ...

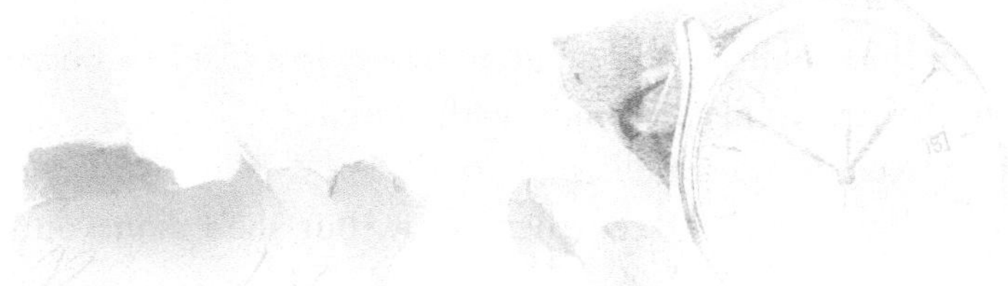

56

JACE

The security guard shifted uncomfortably in his chair as I loomed over his desk. The fluorescent lights cast harsh shadows across his face, highlighting his growing unease.

"How could there be a hundred men that left the building?" I demanded, my knuckles turning white as I gripped the edge of his desk.

The guard cleared his throat. "It's a big building, Mr. Lockwood." He gestured at the monitoring screens behind him. "It normally occupies two thousand people. I thought you'd be happy to find out there were only a hundred."

"A hundred," I repeated, shoving a hand through my hair, already calculating how many hours it would take to investigate each one. "Is there any way to isolate who came from which floor?"

The guard grimaced. "We don't have surveillance cameras inside the building." He pointed to a monitor showing the main entrance. "Just in the foyer on the front doors by the security system."

I leaned in closer, my voice dropping to a dangerous whisper. "There's got to be a way to narrow down who was in Miss West's office around six o'clock this evening."

The security guard's eyes flickered with curiosity. "Do you mind if I ask what this is about, sir?"

My jaw clenched. "Yes, I mind." I straightened to my full height, letting my CEO persona slip fully into place. "Now, do your job and narrow down the goddamned list."

The guard flinched, then quickly turned to his keyboard, fingers suddenly very busy. "Right away, Mr. Lockwood."

"How long will it take?"

His fingers stopped moving. "Er ..."

"For God's sake, call me when you have something."

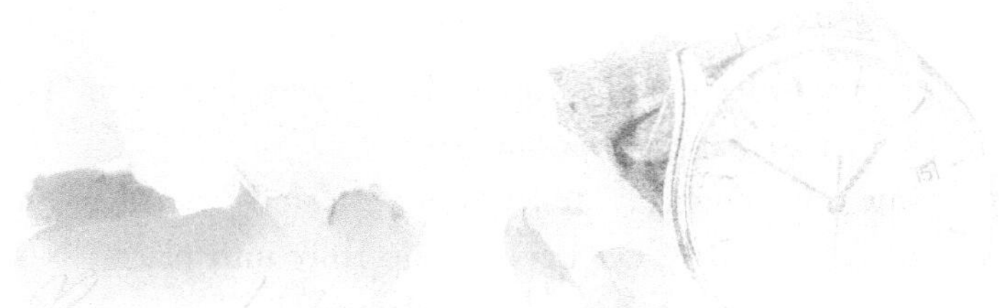

57

SCARLETT

"You had hot sex in a meadow?" Dakota whispered, her eyes wide.

"Shhhhh!" I glanced frantically at my office door before shutting it with a decisive click.

It was surreal, coming in this morning. Someone had already cleaned up all the mess in my office and put it back together like nothing had ever happened. For all I knew, Grabby Hands might've done it to cover his tracks, but my money was on Jace, wanting me to come in and have nothing triggering me.

"That wasn't the highlight of what I just told you!" I hissed.

Dakota waved her hand dismissively. "I hear you. I'm saving my barrage of questions about Grabby Hands for a minute, but for right now ... you and Jace? Are things getting serious between you two?"

"Seriously? Why is that your focal point?" I dropped into my chair, bewildered by her priorities.

In her defense, I'd left out another headline: the confession Jace had made to me. I didn't need an NDA to know that was a private thing he'd shared in confidence. It wasn't my place to broadcast his darkest secret, and frankly, I wasn't even sure how I felt about it yet.

My heart begged me to move on from his past. It whispered

that everyone made mistakes, that he hadn't meant it, that he'd been only twenty, that he'd spent years tormented by guilt, that it had been one terrible decision in a lifetime of helping people.

But my brain countered that his actions, drunk or not, had cost someone everything.

Then my heart would circle back, asking if people should be defined by one terrible mistake? Or should they be defined by the whole of their lives? And who was I to judge anyway? People in glass houses and all that. Was I seriously considering pushing away the first man who'd made me feel safe and seen? The first man I'd trusted enough to let past my walls? My feelings for him ran too deep to simply walk away, didn't they?

I shook my head, forcing the mental tug-of-war to pause. Focus. I could untangle my complicated feelings for Jace later. Right now, I needed to take down Marcus and somehow get Dakota to stop fixating on my love life.

"Well?" I prompted, waiting for her response to my question about why my possibly dating Jace was the headline in her mind when there were actual crimes to discuss.

"Okay, fine, you're right. Grabby Hands turning violent is definitely the headline. But we're going to circle back to this whole Jace thing eventually." She sat back. "So, what's your plan?"

I squared my shoulders. "I filed a police report."

"Holy crap." Her jaw dropped.

"What he did yesterday meets the definition of assault." I fidgeted with a pen on my desk. "In hindsight, I should've gone straight from the office to the police station, but I can't change that now."

"Good. That asshole deserves to be arrested." Her nostrils flared with righteous anger.

"There's a chance he won't be arrested," I clarified, tapping my pen against the desk in frustration at the words the officer warned me. "Unfortunately, there's not a lot of evidence."

"What? That's bull." Dakota's cheeks flushed red.

"I know. I'm not saying it's not possible. I'm just trying to brace myself for that potentiality."

"Then why did you go to the police first? Why not rat him out to HR? The guy doesn't deserve to have a badge after how he acted."

I gave her a knowing look. "If I went to HR first, there's a chance they'd try to bury this. This company is in a massive acquisition with a lot of investors' eyes on it. Having a sexual harassment accusation backed up by an assault involving one of their leaders would cause them major problems." I ticked off points on my fingers. "They'd have every incentive to bury it, fire me, and paint me as a disgruntled employee."

"I'm sure Jace would intervene and insist they fire him or whatever," Dakota countered.

"I think you're right, but I'm not taking any chances." My voice hardened. "I'm not placing that kind of control in anyone's hands except for mine."

Not even the hands of a sexy billionaire who made my toes curl. Especially not his.

Dakota leaned back in her chair and arched her eyebrow. "Damn, girl. Smart." She tilted her head.

"With any luck, he'll be arrested by the end of the day."

I could only pray that Marcus was bluffing about telling Jace's dirty secrets. Or hope that Jace had enough protections in place where it wouldn't destroy his company.

That guilt, that fear, had kept me up all night. And now, there was no going back.

"Today's going to be a very interesting day," Dakota said.

58

JACE

"Sir, we have a problem," my assistant said, hurrying to match my stride as I barreled down the hallway.

I had no idea what problem she was referring to, but *mine* trumped everything else.

"I want every HR leader and all of building security in my office within the hour." Surely, HR would have that damn list of interviewees by now, and we could compare that to the footage.

"Sir—"

I stopped short when I got close enough to see that the conference room table in my office was unexpectedly occupied by a familiar set of faces. Eight pairs of eyes locked on to me.

"What the hell is the board doing here?"

"This is what I was trying to tell you, sir." My assistant's voice dropped to a whisper. "They took the red-eye and flew in for an emergency meeting."

"An emergency meeting for what?" I muttered through clenched teeth.

Seriously, what the hell could they have a problem with now? These guys had been a thorn in my ass since I first *created* this board of directors. At the time, the concept made sense. Lockwood Holdings was expanding rapidly, but my capital was completely tied up in acquisitions. I needed outside investment to fund the growth. Investment that came with strings attached, like a board of directors.

The private equity firm had insisted on board seats in exchange for their capital infusion. I'd thought I'd found like-minded individuals who wanted to do good with their money, thought I'd vetted them thoroughly, but as soon as the ink dried on the contracts, as soon as they had their official seats, they showed their true nature.

And their true nature was like most every other corporate shark I'd ever met: opportunistic. It was all about the bottom line. And don't get me wrong; I was a businessman, so I understood the importance of profits. But not when it came at the expense of doing what was right.

I mean, honestly, what happened to people's souls on this planet?

And why didn't it occur to me until now that out of the eight people on the board, only one of them was a woman? Was I unknowingly contributing to the misogynistic culture that Scarlett had experienced?

"Mr. Lockwood." Randolph Whitmore stood, deliberately buttoning his suit jacket. The guy's hair had gone gray long ago, his middle soft from too many expense-account lunches.

"Randolph." I stepped into my office, shoulders tensed, sensing an ambush, though I couldn't pinpoint its source.

"Please, take a seat," Randolph said, gesturing to my own damn chair like he owned it.

At least Marcus, my right-hand man, was here.

I made eye contact with him, silently asking, *Any idea what this is about?*

His response was immediate. A slight shake of his head and a deep breath told me Marcus was as exasperated by these guys' tactics as I was.

"I was unaware we were meeting today," I said, keeping my voice neutral despite the tension knotting in my intestines.

"We weren't." Randolph's lips curled into something that wasn't quite a smile. "Take a seat."

The tone of his voice pissed me off. I was the CEO of Lockwood Holdings, and he would be well advised to remember that.

"What do I owe the pleasure?" I remained standing behind my chair, gripping the backrest until my knuckles whitened, eyeing the board. Their body language screamed trouble: angry glares, and tense postures.

"It seems we have a problem," Randolph announced.

"Another one?" I arched an eyebrow. *Shocking*.

Randolph folded his arms across his chest and leaned back in his seat, eyeing me like a father scolding his son. If he thought that would intimidate me, he'd clearly forgotten who he was dealing with.

"Something has come to our attention."

"Don't drag it out, Randolph." I wasn't normally this short with the board, but I'd had it with them.

They had set up roadblock after roadblock about this deal in particular, making it clear they hated it. And that, I'd decided, was what showed me in blaring lights what their true colors were. Because this deal was more financially stressed than the prior two we'd done. The previous owners were so in debt that it was going to require an ass ton of cash to turn the company around, and patience was, evidently, something this board lacked.

Money, money, money. Ticktock.

"Are you or are you not dating Scarlett West?" Randolph asked curtly.

I froze, though I wasn't sure if it was shock or anger that suspended my movements.

"Pardon me?"

"Scarlett West. She is an employee here. It has come to our attention that you're dating her."

I quickly glanced at Marcus, who looked just as surprised as I felt. He shifted in his chair in that way he always did when he was formulating a plan to have my back.

"Come to your attention how?" Marcus snapped, leaning forward.

"That doesn't matter." Randolph dismissed with a wave of his hand.

"I disagree." My voice dropped dangerously low. "You serve as the board of directors for *my* company. If someone is coming to you with information about *my* personal life, you will tell me who did it."

"It's a yes or no question," Randolph pressed, scrubbing that gray excuse of a beard.

"What difference does it make if Jace is or is not dating an employee at this company?" Marcus pushed back, his loyalty a shield I was grateful for.

I shot him a quick glance of appreciation. The only person in this company who had my back one hundred percent of the time was Marcus.

"The difference is the morality clause," Randolph said, tapping his finger against a folder in front of him. "Which clearly states it is against company rules to date an employee."

"Oh, please, Randolph." I balked. "Your son got his assistant pregnant. With twins. Your *married* son." I let that sink in for a beat, watching his face turn an impressive shade of corporate crimson. "So, I can appreciate why fraternization in the workplace is such a hot button to you, but don't pretend this is about dating. With your funeral face and stoic tension, you look like you're accusing me of skinning puppies and selling them on the black market." I shook my head in disgust. "Let's cut the bull. You're just looking for an out." I lowered my voice.

His jaw tightened. "We're executing the morality clause," Randolph announced, his eyes cold.

"Over a hypothetical relationship?" Marcus shot out of his chair. "This is bullshit. That clause is a technicality, a loophole.

You don't expect us to believe that you actually give a shit who the hell Jace might be dating."

"You've been trying to sink this acquisition for months. This has nothing to do with who I might be spending time with."

"This deal is a fraction of the profits we could have made," Randolph snarled. "We had four other deals that had at least five times the profit potential of this company. The fact that you went for *this* one has us questioning your competence as a CEO."

"This company was about to go under," I said, struggling to keep my temper in check. "We didn't have the luxury of waiting. It was now or never. I personally didn't want to see six thousand people lose their jobs."

"Oh, it's always about the goddamned *jobs* with you," Randolph snapped, his composure cracking.

"I was very clear from day one when you joined my board of directors, was I not?" I moved my chair out of the way so I could stand right up against the head of the table. "Yes, I turn a profit with these deals, but my intention is to save these companies so that we can save the employees. And now you're acting like you're surprised by it?" I shook my head in disbelief. "I've always been up front about my intentions. You, on the other hand"—I pointed my finger at Randolph—"pretended to be on board, and then once you signed the documents, you have been a thorn in my side ever since. It's nothing but the profits to you."

"Welcome to private equity, Jace." Randolph's smile didn't reach his eyes. "I have a news flash: private equity firms are not charitable organizations. We are in the business of making money. It seems you're the one who is misaligned with those objectives."

"You have tried to sabotage this deal from the beginning." I stopped talking, a realization dawning. That legal document that started all of this, the one that drove me into that bar where I first met Scarlett, the one with the missing signature. "It was you, wasn't it? Somehow, you managed to convince him to 'forget' to sign one of those pages."

Randolph's lips thinned into a line that confirmed my suspicion.

"Unbelievable," I breathed. "That goddamn piece of paper almost took down the entire deal."

"He wasn't supposed to sign on Monday," Randolph barked. "So, I don't know what dirty tactics you employed to get him to sign that piece of paper, but this deal was never supposed to happen!"

"You want to know how I got him to sign it?" I leaned forward, palms flat on the table. "I laid out my intentions, Randolph. That man had a lot of pride, as many owners do. He should be proud of the company he built. He suffered hard times and made some mistakes, but he cared about his company, and he cared about his employees. All I did was remind him that my intention was to save all of their jobs. That's how I got him to sign." I straightened. "Some people employ dirty tactics, but that person isn't me. It's you. Frankly, I'm disgusted by it."

"Disgusted?!" Randolph shot out of his chair, pulled up something on his phone, and slid it across the table to me.

When I realized what it was—a picture of me and Scarlett making love in the meadow last night—my body reacted in a domino of sensations. First, my gut dropped to the ground. This poor woman had been photographed having sex. Had been violated by some creep who'd been close enough to see it all. Who captured an image of it. Even though all of Scarlett's private parts were covered, it didn't lessen the humiliation of having our intimate encounter photographed and then delivered into the hands of the board of directors, no less.

The second thing that reacted was my heart. It began pumping like a jackhammer, sending adrenaline surging through my veins, along with blinding rage that made my fists clench so tightly that I swore they were about to draw blood from my palms.

"Someone is tracking me?" I kept my voice deceptively calm, a stark contrast to the fury boiling inside.

"I have no idea," Randolph claimed.

"You'd better have an idea. You have the evidence on your phone." My eyes narrowed to slits. "Marcus, take his phone, turn it over to the IT department. I want to know what IP address sent that photo, and I want it traced down within the hour."

Marcus stood up and reached for the phone, but Randolph was faster, snatching it back. "You will do no such thing."

"Give me the phone," Marcus demanded.

"I don't know who was following you. Frankly, I don't give a crap." Randolph held up his phone like a trophy. "But whoever did, they've done us a favor, sending us her name, along with this photo. Because we are executing the morality clause."

"You can't do that," Marcus said, his jaw tight.

"Draft up the paperwork," Randolph ordered one of the other board members. "I want it signed within the hour."

"You're a businessman. Think about this long-term," Marcus urged, switching tactics. "Your disdain for this deal is shortsighted. You can't sabotage a deal under the accusation of bad behavior by the CEO and *not* have the CEO and his ability to run a company permanently affected by those accusations. Sure, you can go public and say it was just because he had a relationship, but when a half-billion-dollar deal goes belly up and over six thousand people lose their jobs, no one is going to believe it's over something as benign as a forbidden relationship. They're going to think that Jace is dirty or corrupt and that the relationship with the employee is the cover story. No one will do a deal with Jace again, and Lockwood Holdings will go under. You guys will be out a shit ton of money, and you'll never find anyone who knows this company well enough to save it."

"That's why we want you to take over," Randolph said to Marcus.

Marcus's head snapped back. "What the hell are you talking about?"

"We don't trust Jace's judgment anymore."

Visions of slamming my fist into Randolph's face flashed through my mind.

"That's ridiculous," Marcus spat.

Randolph turned to me. "First, you buy this bad company, missing out on the much higher profits of the other companies we had the opportunity to buy. Now, you're dating an employee when you know it has the power to take down a half-billion-dollar deal."

"I didn't know she worked at this company when we started dating," I said through gritted teeth.

"Did you know last night?" Randolph asked, and so help me, he might as well have had a handlebar mustache that he was twirling. "Marcus will take over as CEO."

"So, you're going to sabotage the deal, bankrupt this company, put over six thousand people out of work, and try to steal my company out from under me?" My voice was deadly quiet. "You think I'll let you get away with that?"

"You seem to be under the impression that we don't have the power to do it." Randolph's smug expression made me want to put my stapler through his esophagus.

Power. The word stopped me cold, and I realized that in this moment, this was what Scarlett was talking about. When other people held power over you and wielded it against you like a weapon.

"This is absurd," Marcus said, shaking his head in disbelief. "I will not become the CEO. In fact, if you do this, if you oust Jace? You'll have my resignation by the end of the day."

Randolph nodded to his fellow board members as if this was the response he'd expected.

"Tempers are hot in this room," Randolph said, feigning reasonableness. "We'll give you some time to think it over. I implore you to reconsider, Marcus. Because if you don't take over this company, we will find someone else to do it."

"Jace is the best leader I've ever worked with," Marcus insisted.

"And you've been his right-hand man this entire time," Randolph countered smoothly. "You know this organization inside and out. You know how companies are turned around."

"Jace is the CEO," Marcus said firmly. "I will never oust him."

"We'll give you thirty minutes to reconsider," Randolph said, gathering his things. "Otherwise, Lockwood Holdings will likely go under."

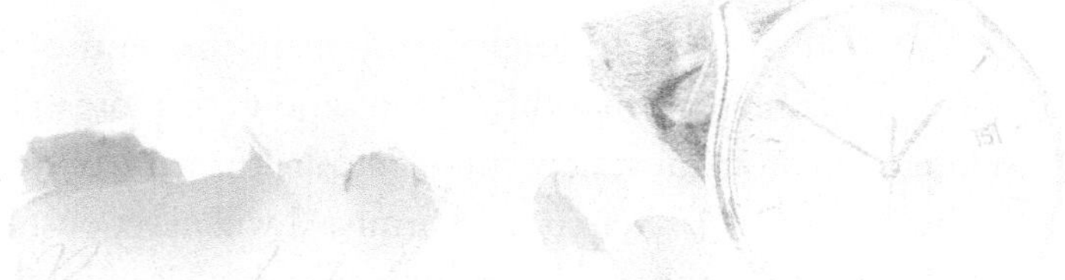

59

JACE

"He's bluffing," Marcus said, running a hand through his hair, his jaw clenched tight.

I sank into my chair, the weight of reality crushing down on me. "He's not."

"They can't do this." Marcus paced the office. "We have a team of lawyers. We'll go over that contract with a fine-tooth comb. Both the purchase agreement and whatever bullshit rights these board members think they have."

"Marcus—"

"Did you even see that photo?" His tiny eyes narrowed to slits. "I caught a glimpse before he snatched it away. It was grainy as hell. There's no way they can know for sure that's Scarlett in that photo." He hesitated, and I watched him slip from colleague to friend. "Is it true? You two dating?"

When I said nothing, he dragged a hand over his face. "You could date anyone, Jace."

The unspoken words hung between us: *dating her, of all people, jeopardizes everything we've built.* He had every right to be pissed, every right to remind me what was at stake. But being the friend he was, he swallowed the lecture. My stomach twisted into knots. *Poor Scarlett.*

"I can't believe someone was following us."

"So, all we have to do is convince them that it's not an employee in that photo." Marcus snapped his fingers, the sound sharp. "We could even hire someone to play the role of your girlfriend. If there's no proof it's an employee, there's no morality clause to execute. If Scarlett is willing to deny this relationship and deny it's her in the photo, they have no ground to stand on."

"I just admitted to dating her," I reminded him.

He flicked his fingers, like this was a minor detail. "We'll retract that statement, say you misspoke. To execute the clause, they'll need cold, hard proof. Witness statements."

A strange feeling washed over me. Not the familiar burn of anger at being betrayed or the cold calculation of business strategy. This was different. Protective, fierce. "I won't put Scarlett in that position. I won't ask her to lie for me."

"Look," Marcus said, his voice gentler now. "I know you're honorable and noble or whatever—"

"Am I?" I asked, snapping my eyes to him, the weight of my past pressing down on me.

Marcus thinned his lips. "Now is not the time to bring that up."

"They're executing the morality clause." A bitter chuckle escaped me. "They're just picking the wrong thing to do it over."

"Jesus, do not do this." Marcus dragged a chair across from me and sat down, leaning forward. "Do not do that thing where you go into your downward spiral of self-hatred and feel like you deserve this."

"Maybe I do," I murmured, memories of choices I'd made long ago surfacing like ghosts. But how could I ever forgive myself when the jobs of six thousand people might suffer because of it?

"You don't." Marcus's voice was steel. "That guy has been a total dick, and he's trying to steal your company from you over a few sentences in a contract. You need to see that for what it is. This is nothing more than a power grab. And you cannot give into it because, if you do, those sharks are probably going to run your company into the ground."

"Not if you're at the helm," I said, meeting his gaze.

He shook his head. "I will never do that to you. I will never take that position. Especially not under these goddamn circumstances."

"You're the only one I trust, Marcus." The words came out heavy with resignation. "If we can't find a way out of this, you're the only one I trust to take over Lockwood Holdings and not let it come at the expense of people. Unlike them, you care about the employees."

"You sound like you've already given up!" His voice rose. "Where is that fire?"

"I just need a minute to think about this," I said, walking back and forth to burn energy. "I won't put Scarlett in the uncomfortable position of having to lie."

"Deny," he hedged, rubbing his chin. "We just need her to deny it before this goes any further. Or convince Randolph to change his mind. He can convince the rest of the board."

I clenched and unclenched my fists, my thoughts racing. All my life, my company had been my priority, my purpose, my identity. But now, standing here with everything I'd built on the line, all I could think about was Scarlett. Her face when she told me about her past. The way she'd trembled. The strength it took for her to trust me.

The realization hit me like a hurricane, shattering everything that once mattered: I cared more about protecting her than saving my company. And I wanted to do right by her, not escape the consequences of my actions.

"Where are you going?" I asked when Marcus headed for the door.

His voice was tight with frustration. "I've protected you for years, and I'm going to protect you from this now."

"Wait—"

But Marcus was already out the door before I could stop him.

"Goddammit."

I paced for a few minutes, trying to decide my next move, then suddenly stilled. What if Marcus was going off on Randolph right now? Or, God help me, what if Marcus had gone straight to Scarlett's office to ask her to lie for me?

Bolting out of the room, I pushed past my head of legal and my assistant, both of whom had been present in the tense meeting, and both were urgently vying for my attention. Instead of talking, I jogged down the hallway, down several flights of stairs, and finally neared her office.

But when I got close enough to see her, something stopped me cold: that look on her face.

60

SCARLETT

Marcus slid into my doorframe, all smooth confidence and toxic shine. His eyes immediately went to the bookshelf, where items had been scattered during last night's violent encounter, now cleaned up.

"Get out." I stood up from behind my desk, squaring my shoulders and jutting my chin forward.

My gaze darted past him, relieved to see people milling about nearby. Witnesses. Safety in numbers and all that.

Theoretically.

"Do you know where I just came from?" His lips curled into something that wasn't quite a smile.

"Hell? Crawling back up through the floorboards must be exhausting." I kept my voice steady, refusing to show weakness. Refusing to show any part of that scared woman he'd seen yesterday. Today, he'd get defiant Scarlett. Strong Scarlett.

I watched his disgusting lips curl higher on one side. "It seems our friend Jace is in a lot of trouble."

Trouble? The worry hit me like a sledgehammer, but I wasn't about to give Marcus the satisfaction of seeing me react. For all I knew, this was just another game, another trap.

"Funny that you still use the word *friend*. Does he know you're actually a snake?" *Because he will today, you creep.*

Whew. My last little bite of venom did not go over well with Marcus. He stepped further into my office, shoving his hands into his pockets with that same flash of darkness in his eyes that I'd seen last night.

Unfortunately for me, my heart had the same reaction: trying to run right out of my chest and escape without me. My throat instantly dried, and I put my hands on my hips to conceal their trembling.

"I have to say, I was rather surprised today," he said, gaze assessing me.

"Were you expecting your horns to grow overnight, or did you think Satan's points would take longer to come out?" I tilted my head, mock concerned.

"Figured you would have run right to him last night and told him what happened."

I opened my mouth to tell him that the police already knew everything, but snapped it shut. Information was power. Now was not the time to reveal any part of my hand.

"You know better than to tell anyone what happened last night," he said.

But something in his expression shifted, something I sensed was important. Why was he taking a different tone than last night? Why show your violent self, only to come in here with more sternness and less hair-grabbing? I supposed one could argue it was due to all the witnesses, but my gut said otherwise.

"Something's changed."

He didn't deny it.

"Interesting." I walked around my desk, trying to pretend all of my organs weren't completely panicking and curling into the fetal position at the mere presence of him. It turned out that while my brain was on board with taking Marcus down, my body was still reacting like that scared little girl running from her father.

"I'm not here to talk about last night," he said dismissively.

"And yet it's pretty clear that what happened between us would cause you much bigger problems today than it did yesterday."

"And what makes you say that?" His eyes narrowed.

"Easy. I see something on your face that I didn't see yesterday."

"Do tell." His voice was dangerously soft.

"Fear," I said, finding strength in the observation. "You look afraid, Marcus. Tell me, is it because you thought about what you did and realized your entire career could implode?"

I mean, what else could have happened in a matter of hours that would raise the stakes for this man? Wasn't the fear of losing his job or being arrested always there?

"*My* career isn't the one you should be worried about," he said.

"Right, it's mine. Because you thought that threatening me would stop me from revealing what a disgusting piece of trash you are." The words were out before I could stop them, my anger overriding my fear.

"You might want to be careful about speaking to me like that. You never know when things could change around here, Scarlett."

"Wow, threatening me again? That's so creative and unexpected. Do you have any original material, or are you just recycling the same tired bullying tactics from yesterday?"

"I just came from a board meeting," Marcus declared, ignoring my taunt.

"And what, you expect me to be impressed by that? Did they give you a gold star for attendance?"

"The board is convening about executing a morality clause against Jace. He's in hot water. It seems someone let it slip that you and he have a relationship."

Okay, I thought it was impossible for my heart to beat any faster, but it turned out that wasn't correct. It was thundering so hard that the edges of my vision started to go black.

"What would give them the idea that we were in a relationship?" I kept my voice neutral, though my mind was racing.

He smirked, like whatever the answer was provided all sorts of satisfaction to him. It made me squirm, wondering what it could be. Assuming it was even real, mind you.

He could be bluffing.

"The board is circling for blood," Marcus explained. "If anything else comes up that spooks them off, the acquisition will be canceled, and everyone in this company will be out of a job."

Oh. So, that was what he was doing. Trying to warn me that it wasn't just Jace who would suffer the consequences if I spoke out against Marcus; everyone at this company would suffer.

"And you expect me to believe all of that? Do you pinkie promise it's true?" I held up my little finger, sarcasm dripping from every word.

"It is true. Whether you want to believe it or not is irrelevant."

"You don't care about Jace or the employees. You only care about yourself."

He cocked his head, as if waiting for me to put the pieces together. It took me a second, and I had to say, I wouldn't have guessed it if he hadn't come in here playing the part of evil villain, but Marcus was an executive. Jace was in hot water. Marcus was here, looking like he'd won, and that must mean ...

"They want you to take over." I prayed he'd deny it. Or at least give me a flash of something on his face that told me it wasn't true, but with sickening awareness, I realized it must be true. "So, you're here to beg me for my silence? For Jace's sake, right?" I added sarcastically.

"No." He took a step closer and sneered at me, letting ten seconds pass. "I'm here to make it look like I did."

My eyes darted between his, my mouth falling open as the pieces clicked into place.

"You did this," I realized, searching his face for any flicker of guilt. "You got him in trouble because you want to take him down."

Marcus's jaw clenched, but he remained silent, his eyes never leaving mine.

"You've been resentful of him, haven't you?" I continued. "Being second-in-command." I circled him slowly, the way he'd circled me countless times before. "You've probably watched him make decisions and thought you could do better."

A muscle twitched in his cheek, telling me I'd struck a nerve.

I leaned in, close enough to catch the scent of his expensive cologne. "Jealousy is a dangerous emotion, Marcus."

He exhaled sharply through his nose, hands curling into fists at his sides.

"But this?" I gestured between me and upstairs, in the direction of Jace's office. "This opportunity fell in your lap unexpectedly." My lips curved into a bitter smile. "Taking him down, seeing him replaced—that was the goal. But they offered *you* the role, didn't they?"

Marcus's facade finally cracked, his eyes widening just enough for me to know I'd hit the mark.

"Which you didn't expect," I continued. "Typically, when a board asks a CEO to step down, they bring in their own, but they're offering you to become the CEO of Lockwood Holdings."

I stepped closer, riding the wave of newfound power. "So, now all your dirty little secrets are going to be a gigantic problem if they come out, aren't they?"

"Stop talking," Marcus hissed.

I crossed my arms, unmoved by his command.

"Because the NEW CEO of Lockwood Holdings? He can't be entangled in a sexual harassment scandal now." I paused for effect, watching his face drain of color. "Let alone an assault charge."

Marcus barked out a laugh. "They'll never believe you."

"Maybe not," I conceded with a shrug. My fingers traced the edge of my phone in my pocket, drawing comfort from its presence. "But if they're willing to fire Jace over a possible relationship with an employee, what will they do when they discover a written police report detailing your assault?"

His mouth twisted into a sneer. "They'll think you were trying to get back at me for taking Jace's job."

I couldn't help the triumphant smile that spread across my face. "Well, there's just one little problem with that, isn't there?"

"And what's that?" he growled, taking a menacing step forward.

I stood my ground, chin lifted. "I filed the police report this morning. It's time-stamped," I said, the words landing between us like a grenade. "Sounds like you just found out about replacing Jace, so how is it that I would've woken up this morning with, what, psychic capabilities?" I spread my hands wide. "And decided to try to take you down as a preemptive strike?"

I shook my head slowly, watching realization dawn in his eyes. The air in the room chilled a thousand degrees with that look on his face. His jaw clenched, his eyes darkening to something primitive and dangerous.

"You went to the police?" He stepped closer.

"Leave." My voice didn't waver, but inside, alarms were blaring. "Now."

"What did you tell them?" Another step.

"I'll scream." My hand inched toward my phone.

"You little ..." Marcus snapped, his composure cracking.

"You're so charming. It's any wonder you're able to fool anyone at all." I forced a brittle smile. "Though I guess toxic masculinity and a nice suit can hide a multitude of sins."

"You'll be discredited to the board, the police, everyone."

"Your name is in black and white on an official police report, and pretty soon, some detectives are going to come talk to you."

Marcus's leer sent a cascade of goose bumps over my skin. It was the type of leer that had my gut forming knots, had my alarm bells screaming to run. That I was in the room with a predator, a predator who looked like he was coming unhinged.

So terrifying that this time, when he took a step toward me, I instinctively held my palm up. Unfortunately, my hand was shaking. Worse, when he took yet another step, I stepped backward, slithering around my desk like yesterday's frightened woman again. Now both of my hands shot up defensively.

He pursued me, backing me steadily toward the wall.

"You can't touch me now," I said. "There's a police record of you. If anything happens to me again ..." I let my thought trail off.

Marcus stopped, his eyes flicking to my hands before settling on my face with a glare so intense that it felt like he wanted to reduce it to nothing but blood and skin.

In that moment, I wondered what Marcus was truly capable of. In all the years I'd witnessed my father beat my mother, I'd never seen the kind of darkness now emanating from this man's eyes. They seemed to turn completely black, as if a demon had been hiding behind that expensive suit and charming smile all along.

And I'd just unleashed it.

His gaze shifted to my open door, perhaps reminding himself that he couldn't harm me physically. Not with the office full of people at least. Yet his hunger for violence was palpable in the air between us. I swore, I could freaking taste it.

"Well," he said, his voice unnervingly calm as he straightened his cuffs, "that's assuming you're alive to tell them."

I froze. He couldn't actually be threatening to *kill* me over this.

Could he?

With one last silent warning, Marcus turned on his heel and left, shutting the door behind him, trapping me alone with my spiraling thoughts.

I sagged against the wall, legs trembling, breath coming in shallow gasps. Last night's violence had shown me how dangerous Marcus was, but now, I realized he was far more lethal than I'd understood. He wasn't just threatening to kill me; he was practically promising it with those eyes. All he needed was to get me alone, just once. Maybe he'd follow me home or find a way to break into my apartment. I couldn't explain it, but every instinct screamed that I now had a deadly target on my back.

And Marcus had every reason, and more disturbingly, the intention, to eliminate me.

But that was preposterous, right? My intuition had to be wrong.

People don't just murder each other like this.

Do they?

Suddenly, the door to my office flew open with such force that it slammed against the wall, making me gasp.

"Is it him?" Jace snapped.

61

JACE

Great. The good news was, Marcus hadn't gone directly to Randolph to defend my honor with punches. The bad news was, he'd done the only thing worse: he'd gone to talk to Scarlett.

Worse still, thanks to being stopped several times on my way here, I was several minutes behind Marcus, so God knew what he'd said to Scarlett already. Judging by their body language, whatever it was, it definitely wasn't landing well with her.

God. Dammit.

Between the workplace harassment and the trauma she suffered last night, Scarlett had enough to deal with already. The last thing she needed was to be confronted about something that could land me in hot water. Nor did I want her pressured into lying to protect my ass.

Dammit, Marcus. I know you mean well but—

I froze. Standing just outside her office—close enough to see through the glass partition, but far enough that neither spotted me—I felt my stomach plummet. My heart rate launched into some kind of a sprint while my brain tried to register what it was that sent adrenaline soaring through my system.

Maybe it was how upset Scarlett looked. Maybe it was how she stiffened and was backing away (why was she backing away like that?). Maybe it was the way that Marcus matched her step, either oblivious or callously indifferent to her body language, which demanded her personal space.

Maybe it was the tension in his shoulders, the anger I knew far too well.

Rationally, I could try to convince myself that their behavior was nothing more than a disagreement. A frustrated one at that. After all, Marcus wanted her to lie for me, and with how upset Marcus had been in that board meeting, perhaps he wasn't asking nicely. Perhaps he was demanding, and a man demanding anything of Scarlett would not be met with happy compliance. Their animosity-filled body language and postures could theoretically be attributed to all of that.

Yet, somehow, I knew, at the cellular level in my body, something else was going on. Something darker. There was something about Scarlett's body language, the look on her face, that shot a warning flare into the night sky.

And any doubt that my sixth sense was wrong evaporated when Scarlett made her next move.

She raised her palm up.

Her *shaking* palm, in a defensive move reserved for a predator. And her eyes. Even though I couldn't see their fine details from my position, I could absolutely see the fear in them. Fear that trembled down her arm as she continued backing away from Marcus.

My fingers balled into a fist.

I had only seen Scarlett West quiver two times. Last night, when I'd found her trembling under her desk. And briefly, the night her father, a dangerous abuser, had shown up.

Even then, she'd done a great job of swallowing that fear because after everything Scarlett had been through, this woman was not easily frightened. In fact, she railed against terror like it was a cancer that threatened her very identity.

And yet she was clearly afraid of Marcus.

Marcus. Who was advancing toward her as she backed away,

now holding two palms up in a plea for him to stop. Marcus, who didn't hold *his* palms up in a silent assurance that he wasn't going to hurt her.

I took a step forward, only to be blindsided by my assistant materializing in front of me, babbling about the board waiting for my return. Her voice faded to white noise as I fixated on the scene unfolding through that glass window. Something primitive and protective roared to life inside me, drowning out everything but the sight of Scarlett's fear and Marcus's predatory stance.

Luckily, he'd stopped advancing toward her, but he looked every part the hunter cornering prey.

And in that moment, a sequence of memories crashed into my consciousness like dominoes, each one triggering the next in a devastating chain reaction. Tiny little moments that had occurred throughout the years where I had cocked my head or arched an eyebrow. Things that had felt off, but never big enough to suspect the man who had protected me, the man who had saved me from prison, might not be the savior I'd cast him as on that dark night in college.

Or maybe he was my savior. But maybe he was also a predator. If there was one thing I learned from having the complicated brothers I had, uncovering the secrets they thought they'd hidden so well from me, it was that a human being was perfectly capable of having two sides to their personality: light and dark. Hell, I was the poster child for that duality. So, why had I been so willfully ignorant when it came to Marcus?

Like how Marcus could never seem to keep a girlfriend. As soon as they would get close to him, they would break it off, block him from social media, and cast him as a pariah. I'd chalked those incidents up to angry ex-girlfriend behavior. And I'd dismissed his subsequent derogatory, condescending remarks as those of a jilted ex-lover who had been dumped.

And then there was the way that he would look at women. Constantly. Chronically. Un-freaking-ceasingly. Luckily, he'd always kept his eyeballs in check at the office, but anytime we went anywhere public, it was like his gaze was an addict looking for its next fix in the curves of a female. But all men looked, I'd told myself. It wasn't like I had some universal metric for the appropriate percentage of time someone should spend looking at the opposite sex.

But there were other incidents. Like the time he walked up to the bar, and while he waited for his drink, he turned his attention to that redhead to his left. I watched from afar as he said something to her and put his hand on her shoulder. I remembered thinking it was pretty bold to touch someone he didn't even know, but I had chalked that up to how flirtatious he could be, and I chalked up her recoiling from him and walking off to a humorous rejection of Marcus. When he returned and called her a "frigid bitch," I'd slammed my glass down on the table and told him to never talk about women like that. For a second, there had been a fire in his gaze, like how dare I chide him, but he'd quickly apologized. And he had been drunk, I told myself. But that night, that one little episode had bothered me more than the others. It had almost felt like he had let his mask slip, and I had seen a side of him that he had tried to hide from me.

But by the next morning, I convinced myself that it had been nothing more than a bad night. He'd been drunk, had said something he didn't mean. End of story. Further, I reminded myself that Marcus had been a loyal friend to me, had forgiven me for the unforgivable. So, who was I to claim a moral high ground? Even thinking about it had made me feel like an arrogant asshole, so I'd stuffed that down too.

And there were other more recent moments that also clicked into place. Like how Scarlett changed her mind about the NDA clutched in her hand. In hindsight, it had happened shortly after Marcus made an appearance. Or how one of Scarlett's interviewers for that promotion would likely have been Marcus. How unfathomably tight-lipped Scarlett had been about identifying her tormentor ... almost like *who* it was, was more important than what they'd done.

This was when all of those pieces finally fell into place. Moments that I shouldn't have dismissed.

Because standing here now, with all those thoughts going through my head in the space of a few heartbeats, I knew something with absolute clarity: Marcus was the one who hurt Scarlett.

62

SCARLETT

"It's him, isn't it?" Jace's voice cut through the air. His eyes burned with a mixture of fury and fear as he stalked toward me.

"Jace?" My heart raced at his unexpected appearance.

Today, he wore a charcoal suit, a white shirt, and a crisp black tie.

He crossed the room in a few long strides, his gaze never leaving mine as he cupped my cheek. His thumb traced my cheekbone, the gentleness of his touch at complete odds with the lethal tension radiating from his body.

"Tell me the truth. Was it Marcus?"

He was looking for one hundred percent confirmation, I realized. Before ... before what?

I opened my mouth, tempted to reassure him that one of his closest friends wasn't the monster in my story, but I could find no words. The truth was already in black and white at the police station anyway, so there was no point in denying it anymore.

Something dark and dangerous flashed in his eyes at my silence.

"I'll fucking kill him," he growled.

"Jace—"

"Did he hurt you?" His eyes swept the length of my body.

"Not today."

That was all the confirmation Jace needed. His fingers coiled into fists at his sides as he took a step backward, closer to the door.

"It was him last night," Jace realized, his voice dropping to a deadly tone. "And he's the one you made that list about," he continued, taking several more steps toward the exit.

I moved quickly, placing myself between him and the door. "Jace, wait."

"He's the one who put his hands on you before we met." His voice was so low, it sent ice crawling down my spine. "What else has he done?" Jace demanded, his entire focus locked on me despite his body language screaming his intent to leave.

I sighed, giving up on holding any more secrets. "He followed me home," I said. "To intimidate me. He threatened to destroy you and everyone you care about."

Jace's nostrils flared, his breathing turning sharp. "He threatened everyone I care about?" The words came out like a growl, the true scope dawning on him that this was more than just harassment. This was personal, calculated to hurt Jace. I watched the realization ripple through him, his muscles coiling as he no doubt replayed every interaction, searching for signs he'd missed "All this time, I thought he was on my side."

I grabbed his wrist, holding him in place physically as I spoke. Maybe if I could get him talking, maybe I could hold him here until he calmed down.

"Why is Marcus threatening you? Why now?"

Jace licked his lip in frustration. "Because he resents me. Always has since that night he took the fall for me. He's never forgiven me for allowing him to do it and for all of the hardships he's faced because of it." His voice hardened. "And now I know just how deep that resentment runs."

"But he's the one who told police he was driving, not you," I pointed out, still trying to keep him in place.

"A moment of protectiveness that poisoned his life ever since."

Jace stepped to the left. I matched it, blocking him, but I was fighting a losing battle. With panic, I continued babbling, hoping to keep him here.

"Let me come forward," I said. "I'll tell them who he is."

But Jace's mind was elsewhere now. Namely on the hallway to my back, where Marcus had vanished after leaving my office.

With a muscle ticcing in his jaw, Jace growled, "I can't believe he laid his hands on you."

Fire burned in his eyes, and I knew in that moment I was witnessing the transformation of a businessman into something much more primitive. A protector. A warrior.

"He hurt you too," I said, desperate now, walking back with another step he took forward. "He's trying to take your company."

"The only thing that matters is that he hurt you."

Another step. Another from him.

"Jace, listen to me," I pleaded, placing both hands on his chest now. "Marcus is more dangerous than I realized, and now he has everything to lose."

His eyes finally focused fully on me.

"I wanted to believe he was partly bluffing, but he's not. He threatened me and everyone you care about." I swallowed hard. "He's dangerous, Jace. More than either of us knows."

I'd hoped my words would stop him. But it looked like it had the opposite effect, fueling his fury even more, because Jace pivoted and finally made it past me, storming down the hallway with predatory intent.

"Jace, wait! He's not just dangerous; he's unstable. He told me he'd destroy everything you love if I said anything!"

He paused, turning back to me with such dark intensity, it made my breath catch.

"Not half as dangerous as I am when someone touches what's mine." The possessive growl in his voice sent a fresh wave of ice water over my body. "When I see him ..."

And with that, Jace's footsteps thundered against the floor.

I bolted after him, heart hammering against my ribs. "Jace!"

He didn't slow, didn't turn. A missile locked on its target. The employees scattered in his wake, pressing themselves against walls, as if they could sense the violence radiating from him.

"Don't try to stop me, Scarlett." His voice was dangerously quiet, the calm before a Category 5 hurricane.

The muscles in his forearms corded while his hands curled into white-knuckled fists as he approached the elevator.

"He thinks I'm still that twenty-year-old kid," Jace said, slamming the elevator's button. "He thinks I'm still afraid." His eyes met mine. "But he's about to find out he's the one who should be afraid. He's about to learn what happens to anyone who hurts a hair on your head."

The elevator arrived with a soft ding that seemed obscenely normal amid the tension.

When Jace stepped inside, I tried to follow him, but he held his hand to my stomach. Gently. But firmly.

"Stay here," Jace ordered, his eyes finding mine as the doors began to close. There was something in them: a flash of tenderness amid the storm, a silent promise that cut straight to my soul.

He pressed the Close Door button, trapping me out before I could stop him from whatever he was about to do.

63

JACE

I knew my only focus right now should be saving my company, salvaging what remained of my position to ensure my employees were protected.

Instead, an assault of images flashed through my mind.

Marcus's hand sliding up Scarlett's thigh. Him following her home like some deranged stalker. Intimidating her. Threatening her. Escalating until the violent confrontation last night.

The way she had put her palm up, backing away from him, her eyes wide with fear. And the way that he pursued her like an arrogant man drunk on power he had stolen.

How dare he touch her? How dare he hurt her? So help me, the next time I saw him—

Only one floor up from Scarlett's office, the elevator doors slid open with a soft ding. And there, standing alone, was Marcus, eyes glued to his phone.

Time immediately froze.

What he was doing on this floor—a meeting, a quick conference—I didn't care. All I cared was that he stepped inside. Alone. With me. The walls of the elevator were large panes of mirrors, cleaned to such perfection that every pore on his traitorous skin reflected back in high definition.

Here I was, dressed in dark gray, and he in cream, almost white. But the colors should have been reversed. Evil wearing white. How poetic.

When he lifted his attention from his screen, our gazes locked. The moment recognition flickered in his eyes—the instant he realized I *knew*—all pretenses crumbled away. His lips curled into a smug, knowing smile.

I slammed my fist into his smirk before he had the chance to duck. Someone's shriek registered nearby, but they were outside this elevator bank. And here, it was just me and him, the universe delivering its second gift when the doors closed.

With a hum, the elevator began its ascent to the top floor, but that short ride wasn't enough for what I was about to do to him. Not even close. Pulling the emergency alarm, the car jerking into place, I trapped Marcus with me.

Who wiped his lip with the back of his hand, a smear of crimson against his pale skin.

"It was you," I growled.

"Careful." His voice was silky with threat. "I'd hate to see you sharing a prison cell with Knox."

His knowledge of Knox, one of my closest real friends, was like salt in an open wound, reminding me of how much I'd shared with Marcus over the years. All those late nights, confessions over whiskey, vulnerabilities exposed to a traitor who was just pretending to care about me, pretending to care about my employees. I had trusted him with everything.

And he hurt Scarlett.

Something primal snapped inside me. I slammed my fist into his temple, my knuckles instantly screaming in pain, but the rage numbed it all. Marcus grabbed fistfuls of my suit jacket and slammed me against the side wall, the mirror cracking in an elaborate spiderweb pattern, then dropping shards of glass all around us in a symphony of tinkling clinks against the elevator floor.

I kneed him in the groin, and when he bent over, gasping, I slammed my elbow into his ribs, knocking him to the ground.

My kicks landed in his stomach, his back, his ass, so violent that I wondered if bones were cracking beneath my Italian leather shoes.

Suddenly, my balance gave out, and I landed on the floor of the elevator with a thud. He'd grabbed my ankle, and now I was the one on my back. Worse, my right arm was pinned beneath me as Marcus straddled me, holding a broken fragment of glass to my jugular.

"Why?" I snapped, voice rough with rage. "Why her?"

He smirked, blood staining his teeth.

"*That's* the question you're asking right now? Not: *Why am I taking your company? Why did I betray you? Why did I make you think you were the one driving that night?* You just want to know about her?"

Think you were the one driving that night. The phrase echoed through my head, begging me to home in on it, screaming that the past was nothing like what I thought it was.

Problem was that my jugular rightfully reminded me that it was about to be sliced open.

I grabbed his wrist with my left hand and tried to pry my right arm out from under me, but the movement seared pain across my shoulder like it was ripping through tendons. I growled in frustration.

"Why her?" I screamed.

Marcus cocked his head, a cruel smile playing on his lips.

"Originally? Scarlett has a nice ass. I wanted to see what it looked like bent over my desk while I pounded her from—"

I bucked him off me with a roar, rolling on top of him and landing an assault of punches to his head and face. Blood sprayed from his nose onto the mirror like abstract art.

"Little bitch should've kept her mouth shut," he spat through bloodied lips, swinging back.

That landed him a punch to his mouth, his front left tooth cracking in half. He spat the fragment onto the floor and looked up at me, the rest of his teeth streaked in even more red.

"This is what you never understood," he said as I grabbed him by the throat. He clutched my jacket in two fistfuls of fabric, pulling me closer. Not backing down, even now. His smile was almost serene, a madman's peace. "The world isn't fair, Jace. Never was. You play at business like it's some noble calling, but it's just the modern jungle." He winced as blood bubbled at the corner of his mouth. "Power is all that matters. Everything else is just ... pretty lies we tell the weak."

I tightened my grip around his esophagus, but he kept talking.

"You think I crossed a line with Scarlett?" His eyes gleamed with something like pity. "If she didn't want the attention, she wouldn't dress the way that she does. She's probably been playing this game for years, prancing around the office and pretending she doesn't want men to touch her. She should be grateful that I gave her my attention." His voice dropped to a confidential whisper. "And then she threatens me? Me?" A cold laugh. "I made this company what it is while you were playing philanthropist."

Blood dripped down his cheek onto the pristine elevator floor, bright red against sterile white.

"Men like me make the real decisions, Jace. Always have. While you've been trying to save the world, I've been running it."

I cracked him one last time in the eye, my knuckles splitting from the impact, digesting the words he'd said to me. He'd obviously resented me for years, aggrieved that I had gotten away with what I'd done all those years ago. Yet that phrase implied I'd never been the one to kill that woman.

"What did you mean?" I demanded, chest heaving. "You convinced me I was driving?"

He laughed again, almost maniacally, like the wolf was finally, finally free from the charade of being on my side, of playing the role of my friend. The sound rippled across my skin like a disease.

"I tried to get you to drive," he said, eyes wild. "I wanted to see the great Jace Lockwood with a mug shot on the news. Figured a DUI would knock you off your fucking pedestal."

You were never my friend, I realized, the truth hitting harder than any kick to the ribs. *You've always been jealous of me and wanted to take me down.*

"You were born with a silver spoon in your mouth," he sneered. "I was born with food stamps."

"I had always been good to you," I said, disbelief coloring my words.

"You rich people always act like treating people with dignity makes you a superhero." He coughed, spraying blood. "But your grandfather's company put my grandfather's company out of business. And cost my dad his job. *That's* the reason my family lost everything. Our home went into foreclosure. We had to move school districts, go hungry at times. Maybe if you had done due diligence on the friends you let into your life like you do with business, you'd have discovered that connection. I managed to get accepted to a prestigious university on scholarships based on hard work, not a handout from my daddy. And then there you were, the grandson of the man who ruined my family."

"My grandfather was a good man," I growled.

"You know how many small businesses died because of him?" Marcus snarled back.

"My grandfather offered employment to anyone that went out of business because of his growing success."

"He just expected everyone to accept his crumbs with gratitude. My family refused to work for the guy who'd destroyed us, and we suffered because of it." His eyes narrowed to slits. "So, there you were in college. And I thought maybe a DUI would be a nice little black eye for you and your perfect family."

"I was devastated that night," I said, memories flooding back. "I had just learned my mother was dying."

"We all lose people. You billionaires act like your pain is more than ours, but it's not."

"*You* were behind the wheel," I realized, the horrifying truth dawning on me.

"When you refused to get behind the wheel, I had no other choice," he explained. "I guess I shouldn't have had that fourth beer." His eyes widened in mock regret before his lips curved into a smile. There was no remorse in his gaze for costing a woman her life. He was the one drinking and driving, he was the one who hit her, and I helped this man get away with it.

My stomach rolled with bile.

But something didn't add up ... if the goal was to screw me, why did he take the fall?

"If you wanted me to get arrested for a DUI, why didn't you claim *I* was driving?" I asked, trying to make sense of his twisted logic.

"Surveillance cameras are a pesky thing," he replied with a shrug.

"There were no references to security cameras in the police report."

"Cops didn't have a reason to doubt who was driving and pull the footage." Footage he never told our lawyers about because Marcus tried very hard to get away with it, to tell my high-priced attorneys I was the one driving. "Trust me, I tried to recant my statement later. Didn't work."

"I kept you out of prison," I said, incredulous. "I gave you a job."

"There's that superhero complex again," he mocked.

"You're so clouded by resentment," I said. "But I have news for you. Your father might've lost his job, but plenty of people suffer hard times, Marcus. They don't become sociopaths. That was all you."

"Stop flattering me," he drawled.

"Were you planning to try and steal my company all along?"

He chuckled, the sound dark and hollow. "I planned to use every opportunity that presented itself to take whatever I could from you. The more you confided in me, the more information I had and the more I could take from you." His eyes gleamed with malice.

So, Marcus taking the blame was a power play on his part. Yes, he probably hadn't counted on that woman dying, but he wanted me to owe him my loyalty. He wanted some kind of leverage to use down the road ... which he obviously had over the years. All while playing the good, supportive, dutiful friend to my face while stabbing me in the back when I wasn't looking.

"But that little girlfriend of yours ruined everything. I had a good thing going for me until she came along. Now, I'm going to ruin her for you. Make her pay until she's screaming my name. I'm going—"

My fist slammed into his temple so hard, he groaned. Suddenly, he bucked, and we were wrestling again on the ground. The elevator jerked as it began moving again, warning me we'd bumped the emergency switch back off, and my time to hurt him was coming to an end far too soon.

To my horror, Marcus gained the upper hand, straddling my hips, pinning my arms down with his knees as he held the jagged blade of mirror to my jugular again and said, "I'm going to take your company. I'm gonna destroy everything you built, and I'm going to kill that woman after I've made her pay."

His eyes grew wild, pupils dilated with bloodlust, and I knew in that instant, it was all over. I tried to buck him off me, but he had the weight, he had the advantage, and he smirked, knowing this was the end for me.

He'd probably claim this was self-defense. After all, Scarlett had watched me storming to the elevator. Other people probably had seen it too. There might even be a witness that I was the instigator, slamming Marcus into the glass wall before the elevator doors closed. If I got stabbed in the process, well ...

He pressed the blade harder against my neck. I growled in frustration, writhing, trying to get away from it. I could feel the first prick of its cut, the first drops of blood seeping down my neck. And then I felt it puncture deeper and slice.

A crimson spray erupted like a mini volcano, painting Marcus's pristine cream shirt with red patterns and splattering against the mirrored wall. Suddenly, the elevator doors opened with a cheerful ding that mocked my dire situation, and something flashed through the air. Marcus jerked off of me with a howl and landed on his side, a bright red stiletto heel wedged deep into his ear.

"Jace!" Scarlett's panicked voice echoed through my fading consciousness, her hands clamping down on my throat. "Oh my God! Someone call 911!"

"What the fuck?" Randolph's voice boomed outside the elevator.

A crowd began to gather, witnessing their CEO bleeding out on the floor. Marcus moaning, trying to yank Scarlett's high heel out of his eardrum.

My assistant materialized, pulling the emergency stop so the elevator doors wouldn't shut.

"Get Marcus out of here!" Scarlett demanded, authority ringing in her voice.

I wanted to tell her how proud I was of her for protecting me from a possible second attack. Look at her, taking command of the situation, everyone following her orders. Randolph wrapped his arms around Marcus and pulled him out of the elevator, laying him on the ground while Scarlett hovered over me, her eyes blazing with tears.

"Don't leave me," she begged, pressing harder on my wound. "Please. Hold on, okay? An ambulance is coming. You just need to hold on."

If there was only one last piece of information that Scarlett West could ever learn about me before I died, I wanted her to know that I wasn't the killer after all. I wanted to die with honor. I wanted my family to be proud of the man I'd been.

And I wanted to be worthy of her love, if only in the moments I had left.

"I wasn't the one driving," I managed, blood bubbling between my lips.

"Shh," she cried, pressing harder.

"I ..." I started, voice barely a whisper.

Blood sprayed through her fingers, making her shriek until she covered the wound effectively.

"I love you," I murmured, realizing the truth behind the words that I'd never said to anyone before.

"Stay with me, Jace," she pleaded, her voice breaking.

But I couldn't stay. I could feel myself fading. Her little hands were doing nothing more than slowing the bleeding, but I was hemorrhaging out right here on the elevator floor. The very heart of my empire—stories of steel and glass that had once been my greatest triumph—now reduced to nothing but the cold surface where I'd take my final breath.

How fitting that my life would end here, in the monument to ambition I'd spent years building, only to discover it was hollow compared to what I'd found in her. As consciousness ebbed away like the crimson pool beneath me, the pain mercifully receded, allowing me one final, perfect clarity: to see her beautiful face without distraction. The empire would crumble to dust, but her tears falling on my cheeks were the only legacy that mattered now.

She looked like an angel, really. If I had to go, at least I had felt the warmth of love.

The edges of my vision went black, and the sound of Scarlett's voice crying, "No ..." dissolved into nothingness as darkness claimed me.

64

SCARLETT

Jace's lifeless body lay beneath me, his blood—sticky, warm, and smelling of iron—drenched around my trembling hands. I fought back the sobs that racked my body because each one shook my shoulders, and I couldn't risk moving my hands. Not even an inch.

I won't let him die.

Please, please, please let help get here before it's too late. His skin looks so white already.

It felt like an eternity before the paramedics finally arrived, an eternity measured in heartbeats. Mine racing while his grew fainter. An EMT took my place, securing his jugular and performing critical life-saving measures, and then loaded him onto a stretcher.

Around us, a larger crowd had gathered. People crying, sobbing really. It wasn't every day you witnessed an attempted murder in your workplace, but all I could focus on was Jace's ghost-like face, the frightening stillness of his powerful body. I closed my eyes and begged the universe, God, or anyone who might be listening to not take him from me.

Something he had said ... how he wasn't the one driving ... it should have mattered, but I realized in that moment that I would have looked past any wrong he had ever done. I would still choose to be with him. I would surrender everything to him forever if he just didn't leave me.

"The helicopter landed!" someone called out, voice cutting through the chaos.

"I want to go with him," I said, rising on unsteady legs, my shirt and neck and hands stained with sticky blood.

"You can't," the paramedic replied.

"Where are you taking him?" I managed.

"We're airlifting him to Mercy Harbor."

Mercy Harbor. A level-one trauma center. The hospital where Blake, an emergency room doctor, worked.

Thank God for small mercies.

Then, I watched with horror, as the paramedics ran—actually ran—with Jace's lifeless body, rushing toward his only hope of survival.

Move, Scarlett. Move.

I snatched up my fallen phone with blood-slicked fingers and began running down the hall, abandoning my remaining heel as I sprinted toward the stairs toward the parking lot, grateful I'd driven here today rather than taken public transportation like I normally did to avoid traffic. If I hadn't had to stop at the police station this morning, I wouldn't have my car here.

With trembling fingers, I dialed the number Tessa had given me.

"Scarlett?" Blake answered on the first ring, his voice cautious.

"I—" I choked over my tears, chiding myself for wasting precious seconds.

"Scarlett, what's wrong?" Alarm had replaced caution.

"Are you at the hospital?" I managed.

"I just arrived. Why?"

"It's Jace," I cried, the words finally breaking free. "A medical helicopter is taking him to Mercy Harbor right now. His jugular's been cut. Please, Blake—please save him."

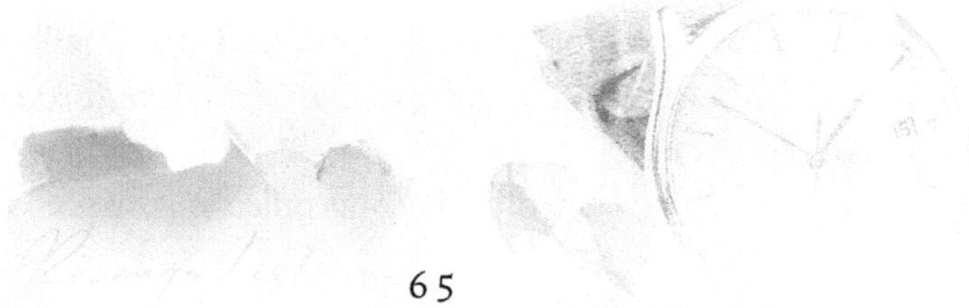

65

SCARLETT

I charged through the doors of the emergency room, delirious with panic. It had taken an eternity to get here, Chicago's unforgiving traffic conspiring against me at every turn. Luckily, there was no one in line at registration, so I ran right up to the desk, the woman's eyes widening at my bloody mess of an appearance.

"Nurse!" she shouted, half rising from her chair.

"I'm not bleeding," I assured her, holding up my hands. "This isn't my blood."

Her gaze swept over me again, not looking convinced in the least. For all she knew, I could be in shock, not registering my injuries.

"We should check you out to be sure," she insisted, reaching for the phone.

"I'm not hurt." I fought to keep my voice steady. "I just need to know if Jace Lockwood arrived. If he's ... is he here? Is he alive?"

"Ma'am, I'm going to have our triage team check you out."

"I'm fine!" My voice rose, desperation clawing at my throat. "Please, I don't have time for this. Can you tell me if a patient named Jace Lockwood is here?" I pressed my palms against the counter, the blood long dried or it would have left crimson smudges. "He should be here." Then again, what if the helicopter changed course for some reason? "Can you tell me if he's okay?"

I was causing a scene. Whispered conversations in the waiting room had come to a hush, and I could feel eyes boring into my back.

Despite my pleas, a nurse materialized and attempted to usher me away. I stepped back, refusing.

"I'm. Not. Harmed," I said, punctuating each word. "And I'm not going anywhere until you tell me the status of Jace Lockwood."

The nurse exchanged a look with the reception lady, who sighed begrudgingly, and then finally asked, "What is your relationship to him?"

"I'm ..." I hesitated. "His girlfriend."

She pursed her lips in pity. "I'm afraid I can only disclose information to family members."

"But—"

"Now, we'll check you out, and if you're *not* injured, you're free to have a seat over there if you'd like." She gestured to the waiting area.

"Can you at least tell me if he's alive?" My voice cracked.

"Like I said, family members only. I'm sorry."

My entire body sank with defeat for a moment.

"Dr. Blake Morrison. Can you tell him I'm here?"

Her shoulders pulled back. "You know Dr. Morrison?"

"Yes, I'm a friend of his. Can you tell him that I'm here?"

The ladies exchanged a look.

"We'll get the message to him."

Only then did I allow that nurse to check me out. I was pretty sure she inspected my skin for gashes, took my vitals, but I was in too much of a fog to register it. When she was convinced I wasn't dying, she let me go to the waiting room where I decided pacing was the answer to all my prayers. So was massaging my bloodied hands, evidently, and so was replaying what had happened.

After Jace had vanished into the elevator, I bolted up the stairs and waited for the elevator to arrive on Jace's floor. Proud of how fast I'd run. But when the elevator didn't open right away, I worried he'd outpaced me. That he'd already made it into his office and was already in a confrontation with Marcus. But then, suddenly, I heard a muted battle coming from the elevator. A battle that grew louder with each press of the button.

Finally, those elevator doors opened, and there was Jace, lying in a pool of his blood.

"Scarlett?" A familiar voice broke my train of thought.

I turned.

"Blake." I ran up to him as he emerged from a pair of double doors that led back to the treatment area. "Is Jace alive?"

"Scarlett"—Blake's attention scanned my bloody clothes—"are you hurt?"

"I'm fine. Is Jace alive?" My voice rose an octave.

"Are you cut?"

"No."

"Why are you barefoot?"

"Because running down a flight of stairs and through a parking lot is much slower with only one high heel on." I grabbed his arm. "Is. Jace. Alive?"

My heart stopped beating. In the space of one breath, my entire world paused and waited for the verdict that would change my life forever.

"He's alive."

I let out a huge gust of air, my knees weakening so much with relief that Blake had to grab my arms to steady me.

"Are you sure you're not bleeding?" His medical fingers lifted my hair, looked for any sign of injury on my body.

I shook my head. I couldn't stop the tears from flowing down my cheeks as my throat clenched.

"This is Jace's blood."

After a moment, Blake guided me by the elbow to the side of the room, theoretically out of earshot of everyone else who was staring at me like a woman who'd escaped a horror movie.

And then, in a low growl, he asked, "Who the fuck did this to him?"

"Marcus," I said, feeling nauseous from my heart beating so fast.

"Marcus," Blake repeated, as if trying to remember who I was talking about. "The guy he works with?"

I nodded. "Is Jace okay? Is he going to be okay?"

Blake put his hand on my shoulder and switched to a soothing tone. "He's lost a lot of blood. They've taken him up to surgery. I'll bring you back to a room where you can wait. I already called his family; they're on their way."

"His brothers?"

Blake nodded. "I have more questions for you."

"I'll tell you anything you want, but please, please save him."

I'm not sure how long I stood in that room after Blake left me. Chewing my thumbnail, which was really gross since it was still coated in blood. The taste of iron lingered on my tongue, and on more than one occasion, a nurse came in and offered to help clean me up. But I didn't want to do anything until I knew Jace was okay. I didn't want to be in the bathroom. I didn't want to be in the cafeteria. I wanted to be right where Blake had left me, right where he would look for me when he had an update.

The door opened.

Blake's large frame ambled into the room, but surprisingly, he wasn't alone. Ryker, I recognized: that was my best friend, Tessa's, brother. But I'd never met the third guy.

"Is Jace okay?" I asked Blake, my heart lurching.

"Still in surgery," he answered.

"Is he ... is he going to make it?" I couldn't keep the tremor from my voice.

"They're doing everything they can." Blake's voice carried that doctor calm, but beneath it simmered rage. "Scarlett, we'd like to ask you some questions."

I scanned the men, noting their demeanor. Clenching and unclenching fists, broad shoulders, tight jaws.

"You know Ryker." Blake motioned to him. "And this is Axel. If it's okay with you, they'd like to hear your answers," Blake started.

"Okay?"

"Tell us what happened," Axel said, his voice low and controlled.

And so I did. Through it all, the guys glared with what could only be described as controlled fury as they listened to me recount their friend being attacked.

"His jugular was punctured, but the cut stopped abruptly," Blake said. "That pattern suggests he intended to slice the entire throat."

I wasn't sure why this mattered. Medically, they had to repair whatever damage there was, so who cared? That was when I realized that these men, these friends of Jace, must want every horrid detail.

"Who stopped the attack?" Axel wondered aloud, his eyes narrowing.

"Um ... I guess I did?"

"How?" Ryker asked.

"I kicked Marcus."

Kicked. Perhaps wondering how a small woman could stop a murder without wearing something like steel-toed boots, the men glanced down at my feet and seemed to realize I was barefoot.

"I lost one of my high heels," I explained, gesturing vaguely at my exposed toes. "It lodged in Marcus's ear canal."

The guys exchanged a look, a ghost of a smirk brushing across their faces.

"Well, if I'm ever being attacked, I want Barbie as my bodyguard," Axel said, his tone lightening just a fraction.

Despite myself, I nearly smiled. There was something so calming about their presence. I felt their love for Jace, felt how much they had his back.

"I called Tessa," Blake said, squeezing my shoulder. "She's on her way."

"So, this Marcus guy"—Axel's tone turned serious again—"any idea where he is?"

"Um …" I blinked, suddenly realizing I had no idea what had happened to him after the chaos. "I would assume either in a jail cell or in an emergency room."

Blake exchanged a loaded look with the other guys. "I'll go check."

"I'll come with," Axel said, a dangerous edge to his voice.

"Me too," Ryker added with a glint in his eye that made me almost feel sorry for Marcus.

Almost.

66

SCARLETT

Blake appeared in the room, along with Axel and Ryker. I rose to my feet, clutching my chest as I waited for the news.

"He's out of surgery. He's alive, but it's too soon to know how much damage his body might've sustained from the blood loss. Next twenty-four hours will be critical."

"Can I see him?"

"Soon," Blake promised. "But, Scarlett ..." He paused, looking toward Tessa, who'd arrived to comfort me. "You need to prepare yourself."

I shook my head. "No."

"He lost a lot of blood. Even if he survives, we can't be certain what kind of damage his body has sustained from lack of oxygen."

"Brain damage."

"Or organ damage," Blake said gently.

"But he survived." Tessa squeezed my arm. "Let's focus on that and take this one step at a time."

My heart sank. All I wanted to do was celebrate the fact that Jace had lived, but the look on Blake's face, his body language, screamed of a doctor trying to prepare a loved one for the worst.

I wanted to ask more. I wanted to ask him if there were any signs of permanent damage. And suddenly, my pain took on a new form: rage. How dare Marcus do this to Jace! How dare he pretend to be his friend when underneath he'd hated him! And how dare he—how dare he!—try to kill him!

I dug my fingernails into the palms of my hands.

"Did they find Marcus?" I snarled.

The three men exchanged a look. Something unspoken passed between them. I could be misreading it, but it felt like Axel and Ryker were furious, throwing glares at Blake, who cocked his head slightly, as if to say, *We've talked about this.*

"He's in the emergency room," Blake replied.

"Here?"

"Yes."

"I'd like to see him," I demanded.

Blake glanced at Tessa, at the boys, then back at me. "I'm afraid I can't allow that."

"Why?"

"For one, it's family only. The only reason you're going to be able to see Jace later is because I cleared it with his brothers. Two, respectfully, you look like you're going to hunt down another high heel and shove it into his eye socket."

"I'll pay one hundred bucks to see that," Axel said.

"He sliced his neck open. That's not a fistfight gone wrong," I said. "That's intentional homicide."

"I'm sure the police are taking that into consideration with his charges."

"He doesn't deserve to be alive."

"See?" Axel motioned to me with his hand, arching an eyebrow to Blake.

I sensed some kind of a disagreement between these three men, but I didn't care what it was about.

"I know you're angry," Blake said.

"Angry?" I stepped closer to Blake, feeling the eyes of Axel and Ryker on me. "That man is a traitor. He pretended to be Jace's friend, and then he tried to kill him. Why should he have the resources of the doctors and nurses in this hospital trying to save his life when the victim of his attempted murder is fighting for his?"

"I like this girl," Axel said. "I'm going to advise Jace to keep her around."

"They had a violent fight," I said. "Please tell me Marcus's injuries are just as severe. Better yet, tell me Marcus will leave here in a body bag."

"Okay, I *love* this girl," Axel said. "When Jace wakes up, let's invite her over for poker night."

"Come on," Tessa said, placing a hand on my back. "Let's get you cleaned up. I brought you a change of clothes."

"I want to stay here."

"When you see Jace, you don't want to scare him with all this blood. Let's get you cleaned up and get you something to eat so that when you visit him, you can take your time."

"It will be at least an hour before you can see him," Blake added.

Hesitantly, I nodded and then looked up at the tall, muscular doctor in front of me. "Thank you, Blake. For everything."

My cell phone buzzed with a text message from my barn manager, of all people. It read, *She's so happy!* with a picture of Buttercup attached. While a sliver of my heart was happy that Buttercup happened to be having a good day today, especially after all the agony she had been through, that little seed of happiness didn't take root. I didn't even click on the picture to see it full-size either. Because all I could think about was that the last time I had seen Buttercup, I was with Jace.

"Come on." Tessa wrapped her arms around my shoulders. That was when the light caught something sparkling on her finger.

I took her hand, turning it over to catch the diamond's brilliance under the harsh hospital lights. "Is that what I think it is?"

"We can talk about it later," she murmured, gently pulling her hand back with a quick, apologetic glance at Blake.

"I want to hear about it now." My voice cracked. "It'll take my mind off ... everything."

Tessa shook her head, her eyes soft but determined. "Later."

I thought about pushing it—my stubbornness usually won these battles—but I could tell she had her mind made up. Besides, I didn't have the energy. That conversation deserved champagne toasts and squealing and jumping up and down like idiots. I was, at best, a muted version of myself. At worst, a black hole of fear threatening to collapse in on itself.

Plus, I was still covered in blood. Not exactly the Instagram-worthy moment you want when congratulating your best friend on her engagement. Some things, even filters couldn't fix.

So, I let her guide me out of the room, my feet moving mechanically across the squeaky floor. Behind me, I could hear whispered voices rising into a small disagreement about Marcus. Something about "two in a short period of time ... prison." Just another thing I was too exhausted to care about right now.

67

SCARLETT

I followed Blake down a long hallway as he continued to prepare me for what I was about to see.

"He's in intensive care, being closely monitored for complications, including blood clots, brain hypoxia, or excessive bleeding. He's been intubated, due to the swelling and damage his neck sustained, so he won't be able to talk to you when he wakes up. But hopefully, we'll be able to remove the intubation soon."

I nodded, feeling like each of my steps was weighted down with terror.

"His brothers have already seen him; we don't allow a lot of people in here, so they went to the cafeteria to give you some time, but I'm afraid you can't stay with him too long. They want to come right back."

My eyes stung. It was selfish, wanting to be the one to stay with him. Because the thought of leaving him ripped my heart out of my chest.

Blake suddenly stopped and turned to face me. "You ready?"

No. "Yes."

He motioned toward an intensive care unit room, where Jace's lifeless body lay on a white bed, covered with a white sheet up to his chest. His arms lay above the crisp linen, taped up with an IV, his neck wrapped in some kind of thick bandage. Even after being warned, it was still jarring to see the tube coming out of his mouth. A soft hissing sound pushed air into his lungs, pausing and then repeating.

I guided myself to his bed and placed my hand in his.

"His skin is cold," I said. "And so white."

"I'll give you some privacy," Blake said.

And then he left me alone with him.

Jace Lockwood. The powerful billionaire tycoon was reduced to this fragile, ghostly pale version of a human being. His designer suit had been traded in for an ordinary hospital gown with faded blue dots, one that every other mortal had to wear. All the businesses he could buy with a phone call, all the people whose lives he could change with a signature, and his was hanging by a thread because of something as mundane as blood.

And as complicated as betrayal.

I knew that no matter how this turned out, in the coming weeks and months, I would replay my every move and wonder if I should have done something differently. If I had told him who had harassed me sooner, if I had told him how Marcus had followed me home that day, might this have been prevented? Or maybe I shouldn't have told Jace at all. When he came into my office, I could tell he already knew, but I had confirmed it. Which pushed Jace into an all-encompassing rage.

Rationally, I knew Marcus was responsible for this. Yet I couldn't help the thought from invading: *What if this was my fault?*

My throat swelled, my eyes blurry with tears.

"I'm sorry," I whispered. "I'm so sorry."

I leaned down and brought his hand to my lips, kissing his skin. He didn't smell like Jace. He smelled like medical disinfectant, and his skin felt clammy against my mouth.

"Blake warned me that you might never regain consciousness," I said, wiping a fresh stream of tears from my cheek. "But here's the thing. You have to wake up. Because I can't wake up tomorrow in a world where you don't exist. I can't take a single ride on my horse without remembering you riding next to me. I can't stand in the meadow without thinking about you kissing my skin. I can't look at a glass table and not think of you." I smirked. "You're everywhere, Jace. You're in office buildings that have your name on them. You're in legal contracts that require signatures. You're in the beats of my heart. So, you can't *not* wake up. Okay?"

I watched his face for any kind of reaction, but there was nothing. His eyelids remained closed, the hiss of the ventilator mocking me with its cruel rhythm.

"You have to wake up," I repeated.

I squeezed his hand, my heart thundering in desperate panic.

"You have to wake up because you are the person that made me feel powerful. You're the person that made me realize that romance isn't about power. When we give our hearts to each other, we're both vulnerable, no matter how much money we have, no matter how many businesses we may own. You handed me your heart, and I'm giving you mine. All you have to do is open your eyes and take it."

But he didn't move. His eyelids did not flutter. His fingers did not flicker.

Blake had said that if he didn't regain consciousness soon, that was a bad sign. Sometimes, someone's organs could be deprived of oxygen for so long that even if they replaced it, even if they stopped the bleeding, the damage could be irreversible.

My whole life, I had fought against feeling vulnerable. I'd run from love, convinced it was nothing but a weapon men could use to break me. I'd built walls, established rules, and kept my heart locked away where no one could reach it.

I sank to my knees, bringing his limp hand to my forehead.

"Please," I whispered to the universe. "Please don't take him from me."

The truth hit me with painful clarity: I had never been in control. Not really. Sure, I'd avoided romantic entanglements, but in doing so, I'd only been running from my own power. The power to choose *this*. Because that was what this was. Not weakness or surrender to another person. But surrender to something far greater than either of us: love.

It wasn't about giving someone else control over me. It was about acknowledging that some forces couldn't be controlled at all. That loving someone meant accepting the possibility of loss, of pain, yet choosing them anyway.

I pressed my lips to his knuckles, tasting the salt of my tears. I had spent my entire life avoiding this very feeling, believing I was protecting myself.

But in this moment, with Jace's life hanging by a thread, I finally understood: *Love is the most powerful thing of all.*

"Come back to me," I whispered against his skin. "I'm not afraid anymore."

And I wasn't. Because love wasn't the weapon. Fear was. And I was done letting fear make my choices.

I lifted my head, studying his eyes. *Was that ...*

"Did your finger just twitch?" I asked, my heart taking off in a gallop.

I looked down at his hand in mine, panting with anticipation and hope.

"Yes!" I cried when his finger moved again. "I'm here, Jace." I rose to my feet and gently drifted my knuckles across his cheek, avoiding his bandaged neck.

Finally, his eyelashes fluttered, and his lids slowly opened.

His green eyes struggled to focus in the brightly lit room, but after a few seconds, they found me.

"You can't speak," I said. "Not yet. So, for once, you'll have to listen to me."

His eyes crinkled in the corners slightly.

And then he looked down at my hand, and with his index finger, he traced a sign: a heart.

68

JACE

"Dude, you looked like the Cryptkeeper." Axel popped another potato chip into his mouth. How the guy managed to keep his physique in check while eating like that was beyond me.

"Can you stop chomping?" I snapped. "I'm pretty sure there are quieter ways to consume food."

Ryker smirked.

"Thank God you're getting out today. Hospital rooms make you cranky." Axel grinned, completely unaffected.

"Listening to your incessant chewing makes me cranky."

Axel locked eyes with me and, with the deliberate slowness of a man who knew exactly how to push buttons, popped another potato chip into his damn mouth. He crunched it between his teeth with open lips, curled into a smirk that screamed, *What are you gonna do about it?*

Most days, I adored the man I considered family. But some days, I wanted to shove potato chips down his throat.

"How's our favorite patient?" Blake strolled into the room.

"Any update on the ETA?" Scarlett asked, her delightful voice full of hope that made something in my chest warm.

"Discharging takes time." Blake took a stethoscope from around his neck. "Paperwork, signatures, more paperwork ..."

"Dude, we talked about this," I said, batting away his hand. "There are plenty of other doctors in this hospital who can listen to my heartbeat."

"But none of them are as handsome as me." He pressed the cold metal against my skin anyway. "Besides, some of your nurses started a betting pool on when you'd finally snap. I've got twenty bucks riding on *makes it to discharge*."

I glared at him. He was making me sound like a mean patient. I wasn't. I was just beyond done with this whole *stabbed in the jugular, poked and prodded, woken every thirty-four seconds to check vitals* situation.

"Strong as a horse," Blake announced with a wink at Scarlett.

Her smile lit up the entire room. Every time someone came to check my vitals, I could see her tense with fear that this might be the moment they found something bad. But they wouldn't.

"These bedsheets are uncomfortable," I grumbled.

Blake tossed his stethoscope around his neck. "You know, for a patient who made a miraculous recovery, you sure find a lot of things to gripe about."

"What'd you expect? A billionaire probably never endured anything less than thousand-thread-count Egyptian cotton," Axel said, popping. Another. Fucking. Chip. Into his mouth.

Crunch. Crunch. Crunch.

I swore he was amplifying the sound just for me.

"I've spent more nights in this hospital bed than I care to. I would like to go home to sheets that don't feel like they were woven from the hopes and dreams of sandpaper."

"We're working on it," Blake assured me.

"Dakota will be here shortly with your car," Scarlett chirped.

From across the room, Axel looked up from his chips while I snapped my attention to her.

"You let her drive my Mercedes?" My prized Mercedes. The one I had custom-ordered? The one with hand-stitched seats made from leather so fine, it probably released oxytocin?

"Er ... I didn't want to leave your side." Scarlett shrugged with a sheepish smile that somehow made it impossible to be genuinely angry.

"Why didn't you call my driver?" I asked.

"Why would I?" Scarlett replied.

"It's his job."

Her mouth fell open. "It ... didn't cross my mind."

God. Fucking. Dammit. Scarlett wasn't used to this lifestyle, I realized. In her world, if you needed a ride, you called a friend, not one of the several employees I kept on payroll. I'd have to train her how to call my staff—correction: our staff—for help. But for now, Jesus fucking Christ, her friend was driving my prized car.

As if reading the horror on my face, she assured, "Dakota's a really good driver."

"Has she ever been in a car crash?" I asked, sitting up straighter, ignoring the twinge in my side from where Marcus had landed a good blow. "Even a fender bender? A parking lot incident? A near miss that made her gasp?"

"Dakota?" Axel stepped forward, thankfully halting his next round of chip terrorism. His voice had changed, carrying an edge.

"She probably lives downtown," I realized in horror. "Does she even have a car of her own? Because if she doesn't, she probably doesn't drive that often, which means she could be out of practice with how bad people can drive downtown." The thought of my baby in inexperienced hands made my heart monitor beep a little faster.

"What's her last name?" Axel's tone was borderline panicked.

But Scarlett was too busy patting my hand to notice. "Relax. She's a really good driver. She's doing me a favor so that I can stay by your side and help you downstairs."

Bloody hell. It was impossible to get mad at Scarlett when she was being this damn thoughtful, but so help me, if Dakota so much as scratched my car ... oh, who was I kidding? I wouldn't do anything. But I would be annoyed. In capital letters. With exclamation points. ANNOYED!!!

That car was my baby. My chrome-and-leather firstborn.

"Dude, tell me Scarlett's friend isn't Dakota *Blackwood*." Axel's voice had dropped an octave, like he was invoking the name of a demon.

Blackwood. That was why Dakota looked familiar to me when I'd met her and Scarlett that night at the bar. It had been years since I'd seen Knox's sister, and she'd only seen me in court back then.

Recognition swept through the room. I could feel it in the sudden stillness, see it in the way Blake and Ryker stilled.

How had I missed this? With everything spiraling around us, I should have connected the dots the moment I saw her. That nagging sense of familiarity, the way something about her face wouldn't let go. I'd brushed it off instead of digging deeper.

It had been over a decade, sure, but still. Dakota Blackwood. *The* Dakota.

The last name also drew Scarlett's attention. "How did you know her last name?"

Axel threw his head back and growled, "You've got to be kidding me."

"You know her too?" Scarlett's eyes darted between us—from Axel to me. Evidently, Scarlett knew that I'd met Dakota in the past. But based on the shock on her face, she'd been under the impression our history was small. "How do you know her too?"

Before I could reply, Axel ignored her question and said, "Dude." He tossed his bag of chips onto his chair and brushed off his hands. "Super glad you're not dead. I gotta run."

"Wait, you can't rush off!" Scarlett stepped in front of him, evidently putting a pin in her line of questions to focus on the more pressing matter first. "You guys said you'd help me get Jace into his place."

"I'll be fine without him," I assured her, suddenly fascinated by this development.

Axel, the man who once told a Victoria's Secret model she wasn't his type, was practically vibrating with anxiety as he tried to make another break for the door.

"No." Scarlett planted herself in front of Axel like a tiny, determined roadblock. "You promised to help me. God forbid I get him up to his penthouse and he falls down or something."

"The guy's a billionaire. He can probably order a custom robot to lift his ass off the ground and have it delivered within the hour. Now move." He tried to sidestep her.

"No." Simple. Definitive.

Axel tried to step around her again. I cocked my head, watching him. I couldn't remember the last time I'd ever seen him this flustered. After his antagonistic chip chomping, it was all sorts of satisfying.

"You promised, and you are not backing out of that promise." Scarlett put her hands on her hips.

Axel towered over her. He could probably pick her up with two fingers and set her aside if he wanted to, but Scarlett was acting like she was ten feet tall, glaring at him with the ferocity of someone three times her size.

"Yeah, that was before you dropped a little bombshell." Axel's eyes darted to the door like he was calculating his chances of escape.

"How do you know Dakota Blackwood?" she asked, not budging an inch.

Axel glared at me. "How did you not tell me about this, dude?"

"I was busy being stabbed in the neck." I gestured vaguely to my bandages.

"*Before*. Before you got stabbed in the neck. Why didn't you tell me that she's friends with Dakota Blackwood?"

"Didn't know her last name until this moment. And even if I did, believe it or not, you're not the first thing on my mind when I wake up in the morning, Axel. I have other things going on. Like running a company. And occasionally getting stabbed. Besides, if I tried to connect the dots with all the women you have problems with, I would run out of string before I hit the halfway mark."

"She's not *some woman*. She's THE woman. The only one I

want to avoid more than I want to avoid the plague, tax audits, and my mother's date setups combined."

I arched my eyebrows. "Axel Pierce is trembling at the mention of a woman? How, pray tell, did she work this magic, and more importantly, can she teach me?"

"I've been friends with Dakota for a long time," Scarlett said, a calculating look crossing her face. "She never mentioned you."

"Bahahahahah." Ryker slapped his knee, appearing from wherever he'd been lurking. "That's brutal, man."

"Shut up, dude." Axel looked like he might tackle Ryker next.

"Ouch," I said, wincing in exaggerated sympathy. "That has to hurt worse than my stab wound."

"Good," Axel said. "I don't want her to talk about me because I never want to talk to her again. In fact, I never want to see her again, so if you could just move aside, I want to get out of here before she—"

"Oh. My. God." Dakota stepped into the room, her eyes trained on Axel with laser-like focus.

Axel shut his eyes, letting out a deep exhale with curses like a man facing execution. "Kill me now."

"Can someone hand me that bag of chips that Axel discarded?" I smirked, settling back against my pillows. "I think I'm going to enjoy this."

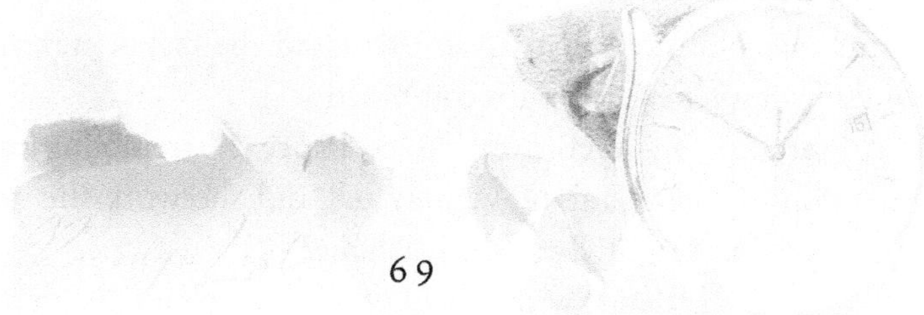

69

SCARLETT

"You know Axel?" My eyes darted between Axel and Dakota, feeling like I'd stumbled into the middle of a Western standoff.

Wearing a pair of blue jeans and a white T-shirt, Dakota should have looked every part the casual woman. But casual wasn't in the dictionary when her tiny arms folded over her chest, her eyes narrowed to lethal slits as she tried to assassinate Axel with her glower.

"You mean Satan's spawn? Yes. Unfortunately, I do know him." Her voice dripped with the kind of venom usually reserved for tax auditors and people who talked during movies.

"How?" I asked, suddenly fascinated by whatever cosmic joke had connected these two.

"He was my brother's best friend," Dakota said, each word clipped.

"Is," Axel snarled, leaning forward. "Present tense. Knox is still my best friend."

"Can someone hand me that bag of chips?" Jace interrupted, extending his hand. "This is a show that deserves treats."

"Knox?" I questioned.

"My brother," Dakota clarified, her eyes never leaving Axel.

"Your brother?" I repeated like some deranged parrot.

"Seriously, that bag of chips, please." Jace waggled his fingers impatiently.

"I don't think you should be eating potato chips yet," Blake said, slipping effortlessly into doctor mode. "Your digestive system is still—"

"Since when does a stab wound affect my cholesterol level?" Jace countered. "Did they rewire my arteries while I was under?"

"Your body is healing," Blake insisted. "Maybe start with something less—"

"Save the lecture. Pass the chips."

Ryker rolled his eyes and finally made himself useful by grabbing the chips and tossing them to Jace. "Here. Die happy."

"Finally." Jace opened the bag with the reverence of a man unwrapping a priceless artifact. He popped one into his mouth, making sure to chomp loud as hell.

Axel shot him a death glare, so Jace smirked. And chomped louder.

"Maybe we should give them some space," Ryker suggested, eyeing the door.

"Absolutely not," Jace said between crunches. "I'm not missing whatever this is." He gestured between Dakota and Axel with a chip, dropping crumbs on his hospital gown.

"You never talked about your brother with me." I tried not to feel hurt by Dakota's revelation. She knew virtually everything about my life—from my father's abuse to that mortifying incident with the mechanical bull last year (which we'd sworn never to speak of again). So, why wouldn't she share something this basic about her family?

She met my eyes, her expression apologetic and haunted, the anger momentarily replaced with something raw. "Because he's in prison. For murder."

Holy. Shit.

The room went silent, except for Jace's crunching.

"Dude, read the room," Ryker hissed, smacking Jace's arm.

Suddenly, everything about Dakota's behavior over the years

clicked into place: how she'd dodge questions about her family, changed the subject whenever siblings came up. Maybe this even explained why she was so careful about her social media empire. One headline about her murderer brother, and her business could crumble overnight.

"Why didn't you tell me?" I asked softly.

"It's not exactly easy to drop into conversation." She gave a bitter laugh. "*Hey, want to grab lunch? Oh, and by the way, my brother's a convicted murderer. The spinach artichoke dip is amazing here.*"

"Did you think I'd judge you?"

"God, no." Dakota waved it off. "I didn't keep it from you because I was worried about how you'd react, Scarlett. I kept it from you for the same reason I keep it from everybody. It's just ..." She took a breath. "The only way I can get through my days sometimes is by shoving that information into the darkest corner of my mind. Because if I let myself think about what my brother did to another human being, I become frozen. Okay?"

Well, when she put it that way, how could I not understand? It wasn't dissimilar to all the years I'd refused to talk about my father.

"Okay." I nodded, feeling bad for a moment that I had made this about me.

In fact, I admired Dakota even more than I had before. This was a woman who'd created an empire of her own (she'd finally given her notice to focus on her mega-successful empire) and managed to get through all the days without talking about something incredibly dark. Something dark that could have held her back, but she didn't let it.

"Jace, you knew Knox too?" I asked, the pieces finally clicking together. This must be why Dakota had recognized his name, why she'd called him an "old family friend" she'd only met a couple times. "That's how you two know each other?"

Jace nodded. "Met Dakota a few times during Knox's trial."

Right. A murder trial that Dakota had clearly tried to block out of her memory.

"I guess I can understand why you don't want to talk about your brother," I said to Dakota, turning back to the matter at hand, "but why do you hate Axel?"

"We have a history." Dakota's jaw clenched. "And not a delightful one."

"She's my sworn enemy," Axel added, as if clarifying an important detail on his résumé.

"Did you two date?" I asked, unable to keep the curiosity from my voice.

"No," they both said in unison, their faces contorting like they'd both simultaneously bitten into lemons.

"I avoid him at all costs," Dakota said, her tone suggesting Axel was less a person and more a communicable disease.

"Well, tough luck, Sunshine," Axel said. Gone was his panicked demeanor, and in its place was an antagonistic smirk that seemed designed specifically to make Dakota's blood boil. "Looks like we're going to be stuck spending some time together."

Her chest swelled like she was preparing to breathe fire.

"You can go," I said to her. "Thank you for bringing the car."

"Did you scratch it?" Jace asked, panic momentarily overriding his chip mission.

"No," Dakota answered him before turning her fiery glare back to Axel. "And, no, I don't run from vermin. I said I'll help, and I'll help. If he wants to run off like the coward he is, he can do that."

Axel huffed. "Run? From *you*?" He rolled his eyes with such dramatic flair, it was a wonder they didn't get stuck in the back of his head. "Don't flatter yourself. You're not even a blip in my universe."

"That's not what your face said when I walked in," Dakota countered. "You looked like you'd seen a ghost. Or your credit score."

“I was surprised to see you—that’s all. Like finding a hair in your food. Unpleasant, but not life-altering.”

And with that, Axel sat back down in his chair, his posture rigid enough to make a drill sergeant proud. Dakota remained standing, arms still crossed, as they entered a glaring competition intense enough to melt steel.

“If anyone needs me, I’ll be ... anywhere but here,” Ryker said, inching toward the door.

“Stay,” Jace commanded, pointing a chip at him. “We might need the help. If these two finally snap and try to kill each other, Blake can only save one of them at a time.”

70

SCARLETT

"Jace, what did you do?"

But I didn't wait for an answer. I took off running through the sprawling meadow, the crisp air whipping my hair behind me like a banner. My heart pounded against my ribs, not from exertion, but from something wilder, something that felt dangerously like hope.

The moment Buttercup spotted me, she lifted her head and nickered, turning to trot in my direction. She paused only momentarily, waiting for a dappled gray mare to join her, as if to say, *Look who I found! Look what I have now!*

"Buttercup!" Tears blurred my vision as I finally reached her, burying my face in her warm neck, breathing in that familiar scent of hay and sunshine. "Yes, I see! You're back with your best friend!"

She made that soft, happy whicker, nuzzling against my shoulder.

"When you love someone, you never want to be without them, do you?" I pulled back, stroking her velvety muzzle.

She looked right into my eyes with that deep, knowing gaze that horses sometimes had—like they understood more about the universe than we ever would—and her eyes were brimming with unmistakable joy.

It wasn't until this moment that I truly took in my surroundings. The rolling pastures seemed endless, offering more space than any stable I'd ever seen. The barn itself was magnificent, a cathedral to equine comfort with soaring ceilings and sunlight streaming through perfectly placed windows. Inside, I could glimpse spacious stalls and a staff complete with its own full-time veterinarian. It was as if someone had plucked the image of horse paradise from my dreams and built it here on earth.

"How?" I asked as Jace approached, his steps unhurried, giving me this moment with Buttercup.

Without the bandage on his neck, the red raised line across his skin caught the sunlight. A reminder of how close I'd come to losing him and how close we'd come to never having this moment.

"I actually arranged this before I went to the hospital," he said, running his hand gently along the other love of my life's neck. "Made some calls and had her moved. I was hoping you wouldn't be angry."

"Angry?" I balked. "Why would giving Buttercup the life of her dreams make me angry?"

He looked up at my magnificent girl, then locked his beautiful green eyes on mine. Something vulnerable flickered there, something I was still getting used to seeing in a man who commanded other CEOs.

"Don't take this the wrong way, but the last time I tried to do something big for you, you walked out of the restaurant and yelled at me in the rain." My cheeks burned at the memory of him giving me that promotion, the night that had started with champagne and ended with mascara-streaked accusations. "Plus, you tend to push back hard when people do things for you. Pay for things, for example." His voice held no judgment, just careful observation, his eyes studying me like I was a puzzle he couldn't quite solve.

I laughed softly, wiping away a stray tear with the back of my hand.

"Yeah. I guess I've been pretty strict about that."

"But when I heard you were willing to sell her to try to give her a better life here, I made up my mind. I was going to pay to have her moved and fund all of her expenses for the rest of her life. You would never have to leave your horse or feel guilty about keeping her for yourself."

"That was before you were stabbed?" Something warm took flight in my chest.

He nodded, as if that specific detail behind his grand gesture wasn't significant.

"So, you did this, not knowing if we would even be together?"

He shrugged, like it was no big deal. Like he hadn't just found the key to my soul. And, sure, I could take a moment to appreciate how much I'd changed. The old me would have been ten levels of upset at someone "solving my problems" for me. Would have seen it as control, disguised as kindness.

But the new me? The new me grasped on to joy and happiness like a drug I couldn't get enough of. The new me savored professions of love in whatever form they took. And loved to return them.

I wrapped my arms around Jace's back, pressing my mouth to his. He stiffened in surprise for just a moment before melting into me, his lips curving into a smile against mine. Our kiss evolved and deepened until Buttercup nudged us apart with her nose, as if reminding us we weren't alone.

How lucky was I that he lived? Our lawyers were confident that Marcus would be found guilty of assault with a deadly weapon. A class three felony would put him behind bars for fifteen years. I caught the dangerous glint in Jace's friends' eyes—that hunger for vengeance—but either they'd found the strength to resist or Blake had talked them down from doing something reckless in his ER to Marcus. Either way, I didn't care anymore.

My heart had found its home in Jace, and I couldn't imagine a life more perfect than this one. A life I'd nearly lost forever.

After what happened in the elevator, the board of directors had come around. They realized they'd been manipulated by Marcus, who was the one who had sent that grainy photo, which had since been destroyed. They traced it back to his IP address, and once they realized they'd been played, they put their trust back in Jace. Where it should have been all along. The company was thriving under his leadership now. It was still early days, but everything was headed in the right direction.

And then there was my mom, who finally had a job. My father, meanwhile, sat in jail on assault charges, where he'd be for quite some time. And while one day, he'd be released, I had seen my mom's confidence grow with each day that she stood on her own two feet. It was as if my father's words had tunneled their way into her self-esteem, and each independent step she took slowly rebuilt it, one brick at a time. Making her realize she was, in fact, better off without him. And she could absolutely do this on her own.

As for Jace and me ... we were gloriously, impossibly happy and in love. I didn't know what I'd done to deserve this, but I knew one thing for certain: I would never take a single moment for granted.

I pressed a soft kiss to his cheek, breathing in his familiar scent.

"I can't wait to dance with you at Blake and Tessa's wedding."

He smiled that smile, the one that still made my stomach flip, trailing his knuckles down my jaw.

"They're getting married fast."

I laughed. "You'd think a wedding planner would want some elaborate yearlong extravaganza, but no. She's practically ready to elope in sweatpants if it means being Blake's wife sooner."

"It's good, seeing Blake like this," Jace said, his voice softening. "Never thought I'd see the day."

"Tessa too. She's practically glowing."

"So, you'll be my date at the wedding then, Trouble?" His eyes held mine, still carrying that hint of vulnerability that only I got to see.

I kissed him slowly, deliberately. "Wouldn't miss it for the world. Though fair warning: I cry at weddings."

After, despite him previously saying how much he didn't want to do it, he went horseback riding with me. The new barn manager helped me pick one of her slow, older horses, so this time, Jace didn't hate it. I appreciated that even though he wouldn't always go riding with me, he was willing to sometimes.

When we returned home, Jace stared at his phone, squinting at the screen with adorable confusion.

71

JACE

SINNERS AND SAINTS GROUP CHAT

Ryker: Dude. WTF. I just lost 10 points of respect for you, Jace.

Blake: 10? Try 15 at least. Maybe 20. My clinical assessment shows terminal dignity loss.

Me: The hell are you talking about?

Ryker: Your girlfriend just posted this on Insta ...

[Ryker sends image]

Me: What the—

The picture was of me. On a horse. Staring thoughtfully into the sunset with that golden light hitting my face just right. The kind of shot I never knew was being taken.

It had been edited into a romance novel cover though. Professionally done, down to the glossy finish and embossed lettering. For one suspended second, I thought maybe this was some kind of publishing deal my PR team forgot to mention.

Until I read the title.

DOUCHEBAG COWBOY

Book One in the Men Who Surrendered Their Balls Series

After quickly confirming what I already knew—Scarlett had simply posted a raw photo on social media, and one of the guys had done the editing—I continued with the text.

Me: Which one of you immature jackasses did this? How long did this take you to create in Photoshop? Are you fucking obsessed with me?

*Axel: Oh, please, have you ever heard of easy editing apps? Took 30 seconds. The sound I imagined your soul making when you saw it was all the motivation I needed. *chef's kiss emoji**

Ryker: The font choice really sells it. Very Fabio-meets-Wall-Street douchebag.

Blake: I'm saving this forever. This is going up in the hospital break room.

Me: Delete it. Now.

Axel: Never. It's going in my will. My dying wish will be to have it projected onto your corporate headquarters.

Me: Keep it up, and I'll send Dakota to your house.

Dakota was the human equivalent of a Category 5 hurricane who somehow had Axel—the most unmanageable man I'd ever met—cowering in unease.

Axel: That's not funny.

Me: Oh, but it is. Wish I could see your face right now. I bet even your hair is nervous.

Axel: You wouldn't dare.

Me: One text. That's all it would take.

Blake: What just happened? Did someone actually find Axel's off switch?

Ryker: I can feel his anxiety through my phone. What is your deal with Dakota, and how do we nominate her for a Nobel Prize?

Axel: She's a soul-destroying she-devil in high heels. And NOT in the fun way.

Blake: I can feel your blood pressure spiking from here.

Me: The mere mention of her name made your throat close up at that hospital. You know why? Because unlike the rest of us who've developed immunity to your bullshit, Dakota would apparently dissect your soul and serve it back to you on a silver platter just for fun.

Ryker: Dakota sounds like my kind of woman. Does she offer lessons?

Axel: Gotta go. Working on the sequel—Corporate Cowboy Catastrophe: His Manhood Galloped Away When She Batted Her Eyelashes.

*Blake: *skull emoji**

Ryker: I preordered.

Me: I hate all of you.

Axel: That's not what the dedication in Douchebag Cowboy says. "To my friends, who supported my journey from uptight billionaire to whipped boyfriend."

Blake: I'm framing this entire conversation. Featured prominently at our wedding reception.

Ryker: Speaking of which, the shortness of your engagement is what lawyers call "suspicious." If I find out you knocked up my sister before the wedding, I'll relocate your balls.

Me: I'm buying all your companies and firing every one of you.

Ryker: Worth it.

I put my phone back into my pocket but could still feel it buzzing with their messages, just as I could feel Scarlett watching me with those knowing eyes.

Because, damn it, I'm smiling.

72

SCARLETT

Jace and I returned to his penthouse. *Our penthouse.* We showered away the scent of hay and leather, letting hot water glide over us as our hands explored familiar territory with new appreciation.

We sipped wine by the fire, getting lost in lazy kisses that tasted of cabernet and contentment. But I had something up my sleeve tonight, something I'd never done before—a gesture to show Jace how much everything had changed between us. How much I had changed.

I led him into the dining room, my pulse quickening with each step.

"You hungry?" he asked.

"No." I pulled my shirt off in one fluid motion.

"Oh." His smile was slow and magnetic, eyes darkening as he followed my lead.

After we stripped out of our clothes, I grabbed the blue silk tie I'd placed on the chair earlier today. The same blue tie from our first weekend together.

"You want a repeat of the hotel room?" He arched an eyebrow, that half smile already launching hormones.

"Something like that."

Climbing onto our dining room table, completely naked, I locked eyes with Jace as I lay down on my back. Understanding flickered across his features right before I pressed the tie over my eyes.

I knotted the silk around my head and surrendered to the darkness. Surrendered to whatever he wanted to do to me. With me. For me. I could hear his breathing change, could almost feel the weight of his realization as he whispered my name.

My skin hummed with electricity, desire and anticipation pulsing between my thighs. I could sense his presence surrounding me, but I had no idea exactly where he was.

Not until his hands gripped my ankles and slid me further down the cool surface. He hooked my thighs over his shoulders, his stubble grazing the sensitive skin as he kissed the inside of my legs. I arched my back, waiting for what I craved. But I wouldn't ask for it. Wouldn't try to control it. I simply savored his kisses, his gentle attention making the throbbing between my thighs grow into a persistent, demanding pulse.

Finally, his tongue traced a path up my center, making me gasp and grip the edges of the table.

Jace knew my body better than I knew it myself. He knew how to swirl precise circles around the most sensitive part of me, knew exactly when to apply pressure and when to ease off, prolonging my pleasure. He knew when to pull back when I was getting close, drawing out the exquisite torture until I was trembling, wordlessly begging.

There was something incredibly beautiful about that, about how much pleasure he gave me in every facet of my life. Something profoundly intimate about having one of the most powerful men in the world on his knees, worshipping me like this. I pictured it in my mind's eye as he groaned against me, the vibrations sending shock waves through my body. My breathing became more ragged, and he read the tempo like sheet music, knowing exactly when the crescendo was building.

When I finally shattered around him, he gripped my thighs with delicious force, holding me to his mouth, drawing out every last ripple of my release. Only then did he release me, pressing one final kiss to my inner thigh.

I lay there for a moment, imagining him looking at me—completely naked and at his mercy—wondering what he would do next, how he would claim me.

"Turn over," he decided, his voice rough with need.

Gently, he turned me onto my stomach and positioned my legs to the floor, spreading my thighs apart. I was still unable to see anything, feeling only the table against my heated skin and his warm hands on my body. His fingers trailed along my spine as he lined himself up at my entrance.

"I love you, Scarlett," he said, pushing himself in an inch at a time.

When he filled me completely, I rested my cheek against the table and breathed, "I love you too."

He began moving, gentle at first, gripping my shoulders and holding my body against his. But it wasn't long before he found his rhythm, thrusting harder, filling me, stretching me in that exquisite way that still took my breath away.

I would never get used to how incredible his body felt against mine. How perfectly he fit inside me, my walls already clenching around him as I rose toward another release. When we came together, he stilled above me, pressing tender kisses across my shoulder blades, his breathing gradually slowing to match mine.

We cleaned ourselves up, put our clothes back on, and settled by the fireplace, staring at each other in silent joy as the flames painted shadows across his face.

"You know I will buy you anything you want," Jace said softly, orange embers dancing in the reflection of his eyes. "I'll take you anywhere. I will give you anything you desire."

But what I wanted had nothing to do with material possessions. Not the gleaming fixtures in this massive penthouse, not the breathtaking view of the city sprawled below, not even the obscenely expensive red-soled shoes he'd bought to replace the stilettos I'd attacked Marcus with. There was only one thing I needed in my life, one thing I couldn't live without.

"All I want is you."

EPILOGUE

DAKOTA

"Take a seat, my *beloved* fiancée." Axel gestured toward the chair in front of his desk, the corner of his lips quirking into that infuriating half smile that made me want to commit felonies.

Did I sit? Absolutely. Not.

Instead, I leaned against his pristine mahogany desk, both hands palms down, and invaded his precious personal space until I was close enough to count the flecks of amber in his irritatingly perfect blue eyes.

"Call me that again, and I'll snap your dick off, Satan's Spawn." I delivered this with my sweetest smile. The one reserved for photographers and people I fantasized about pushing into traffic.

Axel didn't even flinch. His eyes lit with amusement as he leaned closer, meeting my challenge instead of backing down. "Better get used to the term, Sunshine. It's about to go public."

A traitorous shiver ran down my spine. I'd rather die than admit what his stupid nickname did to me. And I'd rather die than admit that something took flight in my stomach when his eyes wandered down my body with an appreciation.

"Stop staring."

"You'd better get used to that too. We have a lot of selling to do if we're going to convince the world we're a happily engaged couple."

Happily engaged couple. The phrase alone made me want to projectile vomit across his color-coordinated bookshelf.

"I have an idea," I said, tapping my finger against my chin. "You shut your mouth. Sit there. Look pretty—which, let's face it, is your only real talent—and I'll work my social media magic. Got it?"

He laughed, a genuine sound that was unfairly attractive. "That's not going to work, Sunshine."

"Stop. Calling. Me. That." Each word had its own special serving of venom.

"If we don't sell this"—he gestured between us with one finger, the movement somehow both lazy and precise—"we're both screwed. And not just us. Which, might I remind you, that's thanks to YOU." His voice dropped on the last word. "So, sit down. And let's get to work."

"This is doomed," I snarled. "No one in the world will ever believe I am engaged to YOU."

Especially when they all know I'd rather eat glass than touch you. Voluntarily. In public.

His lips curved into a smile that reached his eyes. "We'll have to make them believe." The confidence in his voice wasn't arrogance; it was assurance. As if we could actually pull this off together.

He moved around the desk toward me, clearly expecting me to back up. I didn't. Not one inch.

He towered over me, six-foot-something of tailored suit and barely contained confidence, and reached out slowly. "May I?"

Wait. Was Axel actually asking for my permission to touch me? That was ... unexpectedly gentlemanlike of him. Also unexpectedly was my stupid head that nodded against my will.

His fingers lightly traced down my arm.

Naturally, I recoiled.

Okay, *recoiled* was what I was going with because *shuddered pleasantly* was not in my vocabulary where this demon was concerned.

"You're going to need to work on that too," he said, his voice gentle rather than mocking. When I met his gaze, I found warmth there instead of triumph. "Unless you want me to stop touching you altogether?" The question was genuine, offering me a choice.

"Your touch burns my skin." *In a good way.* The thought came unbidden, unwanted, and definitely unacceptable.

Judging by the look on his face, he knew that was a lie.

"Then get balm," he shot back, matching my tone with a playfulness that was impossible not to respond to. "Because when you and I go out there"—he pointed to the door, his eyes never leaving mine—"we need to sell this. For both our sakes."

The way he said it, like we were partners in this mess rather than adversaries, changed something in the room's atmosphere.

"I'm aware of the terms." I swatted his hand away, ignoring the tingle that remained where his fingers had been. "I'm just making it clear that I'm officially in my own personal hell."

He leaned down until our faces were inches apart. Close enough that I could smell his ridiculously expensive cologne. Close enough that for one insane second, I wondered what would happen if I closed the gap. The thought didn't horrify me as much as it should have.

"Now go get your stuff," he said, eyes gleaming with something that looked suspiciously like anticipation. "Because you're moving in with me."

I stood taller, meeting his gaze directly. "Let's get one thing straight, Axel. I never meant to unleash hell or detonate a bomb in everyone's lives, and while I've agreed to this fake engagement situation to save my family, I'm not letting you call all the shots. We both have blood on our hands, and we both have equal power in this arrangement."

A slow smile spread across his face, one that suggested he wouldn't want it any other way.

"So, yes," I continued, "I might be forced into playing fiancée to the most infuriating man I've ever met, but I won't do it quietly. When I move into your house, I promise to make your life as interesting as you've made mine."

His eyes darkened with something that definitely wasn't anger. "I'm counting on it, Sunshine."

* * *

* * *

Craving more of Jace and Scarlett? Get an exclusive bonus scene you won't find anywhere else by scanning the code below.
Warning: It's a bit spicy.

If you loved the "how-can-they-possibly-survive this?" energy in **POWER**, you'll devour **FATAL CURE**—where a DEA agent hunts the kingpin who destroyed her family… only to discover he's the man she's fallen in love with…

Or, if you're craving more of Jace and the Lockwood brothers, jump into **SECRET VENDETTA** next.

* * *

Also by Kathy Lockheart

Immerse yourself in this **bestselling, unputdownable romance series** where desire and danger collide. Four couples, four **stand-alones interconnected** by a deliciously dark thread of romance, action, mystery, and shocking twists…

⭐ **Deadly Illusion** ⭐ She was able to hide the bruises from everyone…until an MMA fighter came along. Now he'll die to protect her, maybe even kill…

⭐ **Fatal Cure** ⭐ She'll risk everything to annihilate the enemy who decimated her family. But what happens when that dangerous enemy turns out to be the man she's fallen in love with?

. . .

☆ **Lethal Justice** ☆ Chicago's most wanted criminal has fallen for the wrong woman. She's his hostage in a heist, and if he leaves any witnesses, his colleagues will kill them both.

☆ **Grave Deception** ☆ Her new neighbor is a scorching hot police detective—one she has a massive crush on, but she never wanted to get his attention like this: as the apparent victim of an attempted murder.

Equal parts rapturous and intense, this roller-coaster series will leave you begging for more. **Binge these stay-up-all-night romances if you dare...**

☆☆☆☆☆ "An amazing, gut-wrenching...out-of-body experience."
☆☆☆☆☆ "Raw, emotional, and beautifully written."
☆☆☆☆☆ "T*his* is the kind of fairytale that would change our lives."

Duets Featuring the Lockwood Brothers:

☆ **Secret Vendetta** ☆ I've become the obsession of a killer with serious stalker tendencies.

☆ **Crossfire** ☆ In my defense, I didn't know he was sent to kill me when I fell in love with him.

ACKNOWLEDGMENTS

I'd like to thank you, the reader. Your time is limited, and I can't tell you how grateful I am that you chose to spend it in the Lockheart Universe! From the bottom of my heart, THANK YOU.

I want to thank Skye Warren and all the presenters and contributors to Romance Author Mastermind. I attended my first conference in 2024 and I've never experienced anything like it. Everyone there wanted to share with each other and help each other grow. There was a sense of camaraderie and support that was overwhelming and beautiful. It was at this conference that I discovered the next stepping stones of my career, and I can truly say I learned so much as an author. Thank you for sharing everything you learn with others!

I also want to specifically thank Jill Ramsower and Hannah Shield. I cannot express how much I appreciate you going above and beyond to share best practices with me, encourage me, and help educate me. Your support, encouragement, and wisdom have helped me grow as both an author and an entrepreneur. Thank you!

To my friends and family: your love and encouragement are something I feel grateful for every single day of my life. I love you more than any words I could ever write on a page.

Thank you to Susan Staudinger. Your developmental and content editing made this book far better than it ever would have been without you.

To Amy and Kristen, my formal beta readers. Thank you for helping make this story even better.

To Valentine and the entire staff at Valentine PR! This book wouldn't be what it is without you. Thank you!

To my editor Jovana, your attention to detail polished this story and made it the best it could be! To my cover artists, Hang Le and Sherri with Wild Love Designs, for bringing such beauty to this novel!

To all the authors who came before me—your success paves the road for new writers to do what they love. Thank you.

~ *Kathy*

LET'S CONNECT!

The easiest way to connect with me is to go to my website, www.KathyLockheart.com, and find my social media links. I interact with readers, so don't be surprised if you see me reply to your post or invite you to join a reader team!

Xoxo

Kathy

amazon.com/Kathy-Lockheart/e/B08XY5F2XG
bookbub.com/profile/kathy-lockheart
facebook.com/KathyLockheartAuthor
tiktok.com/@kathylockheart_author
instagram.com/kathy_lockheart
x.com/Kathy_Lockheart
pinterest.com/kathylockheart

Printed in Dunstable, United Kingdom

81403177R00241